Wake the Dust

Rita McInnes

Copyright © Rita McInnes 2023
Published: 2023 by The Book Reality Experience

ISBN: 978-1-923020-36-8 - Paperback Edition
ISBN: 978-1-923020-37-5 - E-Book Edition
*****

All rights reserved.

The right of Rita McInnes to be identified as author of this Work has been asserted by her in accordance with sections 77 and 78 of the Copyright, Designs and Patents Act 1988.

This book is a work of fiction and any resemblance to actual persons, living or dead, is purely coincidental.

No part of this publication may be reproduced, stored in retrieval system, copied in any form or by any means, electronic, mechanical, photocopying, recording or otherwise transmitted without written permission from the publisher. You must not circulate this book in any format.

Cover Design by Brittany Wilson | Brittwilsonart.com
From an original concept by the author.

This book contains content that may disturb some readers:
sexual violence, suicide, and injury and death of animals.

*Earth like your father or mother or brother, because you born from earth.
Your country, he call you. That tree, he'll call you in the night.*
Bill Neidjie

*We are bleeding at the roots, because we are cut off from the earth and sun and
stars, and love is a grinning mockery, because, poor blossom, we plucked it from
its stem on the tree of life and expected it to keep on blooming in our civilised vase
on the table.*
DH Lawrence

For my big friend Karen, true sister of my heart,
and my-forever little brother Jim,
who loved and walked the land with me,
Wiradjuri country, home of my kid-heart.
For Wiradjuri country that put the dust in my veins,
and the burn-in-my-belly for this land I call home.
For the first people who walked and sang that land…

Last entry in red notebook

Guess I must be dead if you're reading this … whoever you are holding my words … my last words? That heap of bones and dust beside this red notebook, was me, is me … this me here, writing in the dark. Hard to imagine myself dead.

I'm like that woman trapped in her car in the blizzard. She knew she was going to die alone too, wrote her last words on serviettes. No one is coming for me. Not even the tyrant who left me down here in this dungeon-and-grave of rock to die. Maybe that woman in the car had to write around smudges of chicken grease or stains of tandoori. At least I've got a notebook. When they found her frozen corpse in its ice coffin, still clutching the pen, every serviette was covered with her last desperate words. That could be my epitaph: she died with a pen in her hand.

I'll be bones and dust by the time you find these words. In the end that's all we are, bones and dust. Unless we are remembered and beheld in another's heart. But who will remember me when I'm dead? This rock? I can feel his warm-pulse against my back, holding me. The rock will weep for me when I'm gone. Can watch over my bones crumbling into dust, in a slow blink of rock time.

… keep writing … I don't feel so alone when I write. This act of writing is all I have to keep out the darkness, save myself becoming nothing.

I'm frightened. I don't want to die alone. Was the woman in the blizzard terrified too? I don't know what her last words were. Now I wish I did. What did the others say? Those men trapped in the sinking submarine who wrote poems or notes to their mothers, their wives and children …

Was that a sound? Probably a rat. Or a snake. I'll be a feast for them soon enough. Eew. Don't think about that. Stop it. Write about all the good things. So many things I'll miss when I am dead. I try to remember them back, hold them against my heart to keep out the dark. But remembering hurts like a blunt knife stabbing under my ribs. All my yesterdays are vague shapes, fading fast.

This darkness swallows everything. All that I was. All that I am. Who am I, anyway? Who are we when there is nothing to hold on to? No one to remember you back. What am I? Only an animal howling in the dark? A writing animal. Yes … keep writing … keep writing … What's the point of words on a page? What is there to say when you are nothing but a heap of bones and dust? But words are all I have. Thin line between me and oblivion.

Why write? Is it to be remembered? That I was somebody? Who once loved and laughed and tried to write it all down, even here in the dark? Is this my Ozymandias? Even when I know that time will turn it all to dust. Except the poet makes it live again. Yes! Yes! Words can trace a line through darkness, beyond time, into something larger, more everlasting. Like finding the beauty or meaning in the smallest, most mundane thing. Some mystery of creating that opens me to eternity. Wish I'd read more Blake. He could speak what I'm trying to say. What is beyond my reach. See you soon, Willy Blake. On the other side of ... this contrary, timebound life.

I don't know what to say, words are too small for this. I only have questions and even they are unsayable.

Wait ... There's the sound again ... no ... almost sound ... Just the throbbing of blood in my ears? ...no ...more like ... murmuring ... voices humming together ... Is it the sound of death come for me at last? What is the sound of death? Or is it the sound of deep earth, calling me home? ...it sounds deep underwater, like a whale singing to warm rock, with me in between ... yes, whale-to-rock-singing ... Ha! I'm inside the belly of whale-song ... it's playing the hollow of my heart. A lament? I bow my head and join the humming song ... hum ... hum ... hum ...

BOOK 1

ELLA

What do you seek little bird?
Turn into the wind;
you are the mystery you long for.
Everything is waiting within.

Olivia Parsons

Chapter 1

You awake? this moment asks, opening to you, inviting: *Come on in*. You shake your head and look around, disoriented. Wondering am I the old man or the butterfly? Dreamer or dreamt; or dreaming still? You blink, stare back at the strangeness of normal, and wonder where you've been for the past few hours, weeks, years. *This* place sees you. Sips the fragrance of you. Please don't look away. Your trembling may be something other than the old fear.

The whole beautiful and stupid world crowds into this singular moment. This world you love and reach for, that fuddles and hurts you, that you run from, all at once. So many contrary longings storming the delicate cocoon of your heart. Don't be disheartened by this lonely confusion. Turn into the wind, let it sing through the cracks opening in you, like an Eolian harp. Step into this moment arriving out of everything, blooming with possibility, beckoning.

***

The street was dead. Nothing stirred but brute-hot air, shimmering in radiant heat from the patchwork of bitumen.

Ella dragged her sunglasses up through a road tangle of red curls, unsettling the stubborn fragrance of dust. Sun stabbed her eyes. She rubbed at them, blinking hard against the too-bright outside.

'Sleep again and do not be afraid, said Gandalf,' the voice intoned. It was a slow, deep voice, polished as the timbre of solid antique furniture and faded tapestry cushions. The voice had journeyed with her for hundreds of kilometres across the vast plain's vanishing-line-of-horizon, swelling the veins of her imagination with elves and magicians, forest-dark with magic, tracing exotic storylines into ancient dust as she drove across the stark-bright landscape. But now she'd arrived, the voice seemed bare-rooted, dispossessed.

'Thanks, old buddy,' she said, reaching to thumb off the audio. Instantly she felt that familiar-strange ache of the book closing, shutting her out of its timeless otherworld. Her mind snatched up the last splinter of words: '…you are not going … to Mordor …'

'Well, that's a relief.' She spoke with a stiff smile.

Silence invaded the cabin now that the spell of story had ruptured. So still. She missed Gandalf already. She stared down the flat-line of the main street. Cocked her head to listen. Was that a crow? Friend or spy? Messenger of hope or doom? Gandalf says I'm not going to Mordor. Hope then.

Her gaze ricocheted back and forth along the short street of heat-crumpled shops, seeking signs of life. There. Movement. A red heeler sidled along the shadowed edge of the street, something dark protruding from its mouth. The lone crow perched above on faded guttering watched its skulking path.

Ella groaned, deflating. Abruptly aware of an urgent tension in her bladder, she clenched her pelvic-floor muscles. Pulling her phone from the pack on the passenger seat, she switched it on. Watched, impatient, as the phone booted up.

No service.

'Fuck.' She screwed up her face. How was it possible to have no phone coverage in the middle of town?

Her bladder screamed more loudly, demanding attention. Again she eyed the almost deserted street. The old heeler had flopped in the gutter beside a red dust-covered ute, chewing its mystery object. The only building that looked occupied was an old pub, the gap-toothed Albion.

Ella turned off the engine, opened the door to step out of the cool bubble of her blue Corolla, and gasped as a fist of heat slammed her in the face. The air was dry-hot, hard to breathe. She mince-stepped across the road towards the pub and into the sudden relief of shade on the other side, bitumen burning through the thin soles of her flat sandals.

'Shit,' she said, stumbling on the rough pavement as the sole of her left sandal gaped wide like a too-hot tongue. It slapped the pavement as she walked towards the pub lifting her left foot high.

Shoving hard against the peeling brown paint of the heavy door, she half-tripped into the bar as it gave way with a jolt. Instant body sigh of cool relief as refrigerated air caressed bare skin. She grimaced, held her breath, muscles clenched tighter, eyes darting around the bar. The man behind the bar regarded Ella's face for the briefest moment, then pointed to the small sign above a doorway: Ladies. She waved a splay-fingered thanks and, with a tight-lipped smile, bolted towards the door.

As she stepped back into the bar with an awkward gait to avoid tripping on the broken sandal, body soft with the relief of an empty bladder, her senses took in the familiar fusty odour of pub. Not a single head turned, but she felt eyes slithering over her.

'What can I get you, love?' the big man said as she dropped on to a bar stool, dumping her pack on the stool beside her. She tried to ignore his protruding gut, but the last three buttons of his dark-striped shirt were straining against his belly so hard it looked as if something had to give. Seeing the direction of her gaze, he patted his belly as if it were a small baby that needed burping.

'Been drinking the profits,' he said, grinning.

She blushed and pulled her eyes away.

'What'll it be?'

'Gin and tonic, thanks.'

The barman upended the gin bottle twice into the glass half-full of ice that rested in the palm of his other hand like a cricket ball. Her mouth watered as he tore open a small can of tonic with a hiss. He dropped the glass in front of her like a seasoned cricketer and stuck a straw into the fizz.

Sucking on the straw, she let the cool, bitter drink fill her mouth. Her tongue tingled as she surveyed the bar. The large Johnny Walker mirror behind a line of bottles reflected a scattering of old men, faces weathered by sun and wind, tough story lines etched into scars and wrinkles like so many ancient landscapes. Their eyes had a faraway look, as if they were dreaming of some other time, some other place. One man was staring at her in the mirror; she blinked and looked away.

Another man stood watching as the barman pulled his beer. At a sound from the TV screen in a high corner of the bar, the barman stopped mid-stream with a heavy clunk of tap. All eyes swerved to watch the ball in slow motion, smashing into the stumps. A murmur fluttered through the bar like a sudden gust of wind that snatches hats and skittish papers then drops abruptly.

The barman was back. He introduced himself as Frank.

'Ella.'

'So, what brings you to the back roads this time of year Ella? We don't see many visitors this late in the year. Too hot for tourists.'

'I'm a writer … well, I want to be a writer. I came out here to write.'

'What are you writing?'

She hated that question. How could she know what she was writing until she'd written it? 'Um, probably something about a woman who comes to the desert to write,' she said with a daggy half-smirk.

Frank sauntered off to attend to a customer at the other end of the bar. Next to him, the man from before was still staring at her. She raised her hand in a tentative wave, lifting the corners of her mouth, but his face didn't change. He continued to stare. She dropped her gaze to the fizzing glass but could feel his eyes burning into her. She shivered as the pub scene from some half-forgotten thriller flashed in with Technicolor terror. Get a grip, Ella.

Playing with the ice in her glass, she watched the men in the mirror. It was like waiting inside a Samuel Beckett play, a world in slow motion. A loud roar from the TV made everyone look up. Then the bar fell quiet again, returning to the hypnotic tones of cricket.

Ella pulled the phone from her pack and stared down at it with that same sinking feeling of nasty surprise. Fuck. How was it possible not to have any reception in the middle of town? Fuck. Why hadn't she written down directions to the property? Fuck. No. It's not possible. She switched the phone off, then on again. Still no service.

When Frank came back to stack glasses into a tray, she held up her phone. 'Where can I get reception around here, Frank?'

'Yeah, that ridge around town blocks the signal. Telstra's been promising a new tower for the last ten years. Should get reception up at the cemetery. Highest point in town. Crazy bastards up there need all the help they can get when they pack up their tent.'

She frowned.

'Kick the bucket,' Frank said.

Another voice spoke, deep and resonant with rough edges, like unpolished oak, 'Take a dirt nap …'

Other voices chimed in, but the men didn't look up or move so it was impossible to tell who was speaking. Disembodied voices spoke into cool air.

'Tits-up …'

'Go over the big ridge …'

'Count worms …'

Frank was grinning down at her. She closed her mouth, smiled, frowning.

'Dead, drop dead,' Frank said. 'The boys are a regular encyclopaedia,' he continued. 'They must like you, Ella.'

'Go home in a box …'

'Assume room temperature …'

Her smile broadened. But not a twitch of smile or movement was visible on the men's faces reflected in the mirror. Frank nodded his head, 'I think she's got it now, fellas.'

'Catch the last rattler …'

'Thanks, Bluey.'

Frank wiped a glass with a soggy tea towel. Not looking up, he said, 'Death came to town last week. Old mayor Baker shuffled off. Mayor of Broken Ridge for more than twenty years. Funeral today. Why all the shops are shut. Most of the town is out at the golf club for the wake. We take our funerals seriously out here.'

'Oh, so the main street's not always this deserted?'

'This time of day there's not much action, but you can usually buy a lamb chop from the butcher. Get a newspaper. You'll find everything you need in Broken Ridge. Just got to know who to ask. Need anything, let me know.'

Ella lowered her voice. 'I need directions to Eldorado.'

Frank didn't ask any questions, he just picked up a coaster and drew a small neat map on the back, explaining how to get to the property. He straightened and turned towards a man standing silently at the end of the bar, zoning in on his customer as if he had eyes in the back of his head. Over his shoulder he said, 'Stand on Mrs McGregor's grave. She's closest to heaven.'

Ella sucked the last rattling-slurp from the glass and picked up the mud map. 'Thanks, Frank,' she said, zipping her pack. 'Thanks, everyone,' she said when she reached the door, raising a hand. The men continued to look down at their beers or stare up at the cricket as if she hadn't spoken.

'Bite the dust,' came a lone deep voice as she pulled at the stubborn door. She turned her head but the scene was frozen. She wanted to laugh, but wasn't sure if it was meant to be funny or was some kind of warning.

***

You swallowed that commonplace lie of time and buried your heart under a surly dust of forgetting. Ran the other way, trying to shake off the past. But the past is a shallow grave; time is rooted in an intricate mycelium of memory, threading and reweaving between yesterday and tomorrow, between singular and multiversal.

The present offers itself to you – a bunch of probability, blooming out of the between of what was, what will be and what is becoming, forming each new wave of memory breaking into now. Everything is within you. Lost or confused? Listen to that slow pulse of deep time through your veins. Remember when you are dust and worm, brown fingers painting ochre on to rock. When you are song of eagle and whale, and ant and bee, snout and fin. You are the old song humming in that eucalyptus tree. Breath of story told in wide-eyed circle of firelight under forever night sky. You are made of wonder, belonging to vast star time.

***

Following the bullet-holed signs to the cemetery, she flicked on the audio, trying to recover the fellowship of book that had accompanied her across the plains. 'You do not comfort me, said Pippin.' But it was hard to concentrate as her mind flared and scolded. Words from the audio drifted through the car without landing. What was I thinking? Why did I agree to this? It's the middle of fucking nowhere. I can't stay out here. Panic squeezed her chest, a fist clenching tighter with each running thought; the familiar ache of tension surged in her legs, urging her to run, just get the fuck out of here. She gripped the wheel. This had seemed like such a good idea back in Melbourne and then driving the plain for long days, journeying under the spell of the book. But she felt the enchantment of hope and possibility collapsing in the face of this bare-dust reality.

10

She stopped the car to catch her breath, trying to slow the drumming against the walls of her chest, she felt the screech of her zipped-up inside-skins sliding open. Familiar feelings threatened to break loose, relentless as the sleepless malice of Black Riders circling, ready to ambush the moment she stopped running.

During the past twelve months, cosying up with that lost-in-your-life feeling clinging like the smell of decay in dark places, friends had called, tried to jolly her out of the misery that had bloomed into a dull ache of melancholy. As if she lived down deep in shadow while the rest of the world was in bright daylight. She watched the strangeness of ordinary. For a while she tried to pretend. Until her jaw ached from the fake grin around her sorry heart.

Suddenly everyone was an expert on how to be okay. Telling her what she should do. They messaged her ten tips on happiness, or how screen time could impact mental health. Some took her out drinking, suggested activities, travel, a fuck buddy. One offered to take up that position. They shared their stories of what they did when they had the blues. Oh, *that's* what's wrong with me. Determined to give her a label. Black dog. Depression. Oh, *that's* what I am? They had other names for it. It was as if she had grown a tag on her forehead that flapped in the wind between them so that they couldn't look her in the eye.

When she finally understood that questioning the slow ennui of her existence made them uncomfortable because they didn't want to look at their own small, neat lives, she stopped talking. Withdrew. Wrote instead. It was hard to know when being alone had turned into the knotty enclosure of loneliness then, finally, into the need to escape that grew like secret mould on an orange at the bottom of a fruit basket. She needed to get away. Lose herself. Get lost. Somehow shake off the dark shadow that had become her life. See who she was – really. Without everyone trying to fix her, tell her who she was, what she should do. How she should be.

A car drove alongside and moved slowly past. The driver stared at her. Ella lifted a hand; the woman didn't wave back but frowned and shook her head. With a jolt, Ella realised she had stopped in the middle of the narrow road. Dust drifted in through the open window. She coughed, rushing to close the window, but too late.

A pair of dilapidated boots hung on the sign at the broken-gated entrance to the cemetery. She smiled as she parked the car, 'Hung up your boots, mate?'

The late afternoon buzz of the bush swallowed her thoughts as she settled into the stillness, sighing into eucalypt-warm air.

'Where are you, Mrs McGregor?'

Ella skirted a fresh mound of dark red dirt. Mayor Baker? Small signs of recent human activity spilled out around the mound. Cigarette butts and discarded lolly wrappers. A dollar coin, half-hidden in dust. She picked it up, shoved it into the pocket of her shorts. 'Thanks,' she said, eyes to the open blue sky, thumb up.

Mrs McGregor's grave rested at a crest in the cemetery. It was a large cement slab with an angel on top. The angel, mottled grey, had a black eye where the stone had discoloured, and the left wingtip was broken. She read aloud, 'Mary Ellen McGregor, nee O'Brien. 1921–1999. Always in our hearts. Hiya, Mary, just want to stand on you for a bit. Hope that's okay?'

Stepping on to the cement platform, she held up her phone. Only two bars. She moved around the platform, checking. 'Two's as good as it gets, Mary,' she said, and pressed Jaz's number.

'Hey, Jaz. I've arrived.'

'Hey, Ella. How's the desert? The house-sitting?'

'Hot. Dry. Lonely. Full of flies and weird old men.'

'God, sounds awful …'

'Jaz … hello, hello, Jaz …' She pressed his number again.

'What happened?'

'Dunno. Not a good signal here. Anyway, it's good to hear your voice.'

'Yeah, you too. I'm worried about you. If it doesn't work out, come home. You've been through enough.'

'All good. It's only three-and-a-half months. Then I can head up to Darwin.'

'Yeah, the big outback adventure, I know.' His voice dropped into concern-tone. 'But just don't …'

She cut him off, hated when he did "chook-ma"; their pet name for his clucking around her when she was vulnerable. They'd had umpteen conversations about it. Ella hated anyone fussing over her. It felt like pity.

Mostly he remembered to check his clucking like a mother hen. 'I'm heading out to the property now … Jaz … Jaz?'

She pressed his number again. Nothing. Looking down at the useless phone, she felt a sinking in her belly. Jaz and all her friends in Melbourne seemed so far away, in another world. For the past twelve months the city had felt crowded, that last share house relentlessly noisy and nosey. The city crowded her insides too, as if she had too many organs, too much meat inside. She felt at once too much and not enough. Stuffed with emptiness. She needed space inside and out. Had to escape. But now suddenly she missed everything she had been so desperate to escape only weeks ago. Her eyes itched and burned; she blinked firmly.

Around her long shadows crawled over the graves in the way sleepy children settle into a grandmother's arms to listen to the old stories. A kookaburra laughed up at the cloudless sky, the first blush of pink showing as the sun dipped low against the horizon.

The low hum of an approaching engine broke the spell. Jumping down from Mrs McGregor's tombstone, she stepped lightly towards an acacia tree and stood behind it peeking through the foliage as a dusty white four-wheel-drive slowed and drove alongside her car. It stopped for a moment, continued slowly past, then turned in a wide arc and drove off. She shivered, frowned and squinted, watching the vehicle disappear through the trees.

She drove the corrugated road to Eldorado as slow dusk descended across the land; like journeying into an alien dreamscape. Country was dry, ravaged by years of drought. Spindly trees threw their long shadows in artist's fingers across the land, painting strange impenetrable shapes on the desert canvas like an Ian Fairweather painting. The tough mystery of wild-dry beauty with its muted colours snagged her senses, pulling her gaze to that perfect arc of tree trunk silhouetted against radiant pink to blood-orange sky. The silence and space were like a slow exhalation.

The old Eldorado homestead was a large, rambling weatherboard, verandas wrapping all round. It reminded her of an elderly gentleman still wearing his moth-eaten tuxedo, even though his shoulders were shrunken and his face had grown too small for that wide elegant smile of yesterday. The western side of the veranda was listing like a sinking ship. A skeletal garden surrounded the house, a cemetery of branched corpses and spindly twigs unlikely to revive even if it ever rained again.

Ella opened the car door but before she could step out a wiry kelpie jumped up at her. The dog's pretty black-and-tan face was grinning wildly, pink tongue lolling and darting with excitement.

'Sully!' a woman's voice growled from the veranda. 'Get down.'

The dog dropped and pulled back, tail wagging furiously as it turned and ran-jumped towards the woman with the quick grace of its breed, as if joy for life buzzed under its sleek lines, its body bursting with energy, one ear flopping lopsided. The woman took hold of the dog's collar and waved Ella over.

'Sorry. She goes a bit wild when we have visitors. But I didn't want to tie her up till you got here so you could meet them.' At that moment another dog sauntered towards Ella from the shadows under the house, older, more distinguished, with the markings of border collie.

'That's Harry,' the woman said. 'And I'm Maria.'

'Hi, Maria. Ella,' she said, scratching Harry behind the ears.

'Come in. Hans'll tie the dogs up when he gets off the phone.'

Ella squatted to pat Sully. Sharp-curious green eyes the colour of deep water watched her, taking in the truth of her. Sully lunged and hit her target, Ella's nose, with a wet lick-kiss. A surprised laugh burst out of Ella. The joy of dog contagious.

Maria smiled. 'I think you'll get along just fine.'

***

Ella drifted through the old house after Maria and Hans left for Europe. Opening doors and looking into rooms, looking into the eyes of strangers framed in photographs and paintings hung in hallways, she tried to acquaint herself with the place that would be home for the next few months. She breathed in the unfamiliar odours of the house. But he resisted her. It was definitely a *he*, a belligerent, grumpy old man. And she was an intruder, disturbing the order of things.

Only the library, Hans's study, seemed to welcome her. A giant pine tree stood outside the window, creating a serene soundscape. Hans's collection of books was vast and eclectic. Shelves of books that she had always meant to read one day: Kafka, Nietzsche, Plato, Dostoyevsky and

Chekhov, Borges, Goethe, Proust and Hesse, and so many names she had never heard before. One wall was filled with books in German and French, and a few in Spanish, but many were in English. She wandered around the library touching the books, sensing the life-worlds inside like sleeping creatures waiting to wake and reveal themselves. She picked up books at random, stroking the pages, drinking in the scent of words.

Long hot days arrived, lazy and unhurried. When the writing refused to come, as it did most days, she read. Reading, she sank deep into her happy place, imagination waking into each close-particular world bound inside the book.

Slowly the rest of the house opened to her. Exhaled, and stopped fighting. It wasn't home exactly, but comfortable. Comforting. During the day, at least. The nights were long and offered little comfort. It was hot. Unbearably hot. And it was only November. The wooden walls were too flimsy to keep out the heat and old night demons: memories beat against the too-thin-skin of her heart, threatening to erupt. She jammed them down, rolled over again.

***

A slow lump of time breaks away from the whole. You are trapped inside. Floating in the relentless time-space between this now and then. Futuring spills its milky weight into barren-dark of discordant missed conceptions, save the infidel hope of distant morning.

***

Can't sleep. Can't sleep. She tossed and turned, basting in the hot oil of one thought: can't sleep. Over and over, around and around: can't sleep, can't sleep, sheets tangling around her body like a shroud. Her scalp sweaty, damp hair sticking to her back and neck. She pulled her thick bundle of curls into a bunch and tied it into a knot. But it refused to hold, spilled out over the sweat-damp pillow. She slid a hand under the cool underbelly of pillow and flipped it over. For the briefest moment her cheek lay against cool cotton.

The central air conditioning barely reached the bedroom. But she knew from other nights that if she opened the door and stepped outside, she'd realise the inside of the house was cool. An ancient overhead fan clunk-squeaked on its vertiginous eternal round, stirring warm, rasp-dry air. She lay staring up at the fan's slow gyration. Could write. But she felt too tired to wrangle with a blank page. And what would she write anyway, some Proustian piece about not sleeping?

'Ha!'

She'd spent the last two days reading Proust, translated and annotated by Hans. Losing herself in the slow intimate intrigue of Proust's mind. She rolled over, switched on the light and pulled out the book, *Remembrance of Things Past,* and flicked open a page at random.

She read: 'I woke, not knowing where I was. I did not know who I was. I had only the most basic sense of existence, with insufficient human capability; like a flickering in the depths of an animal's consciousness; an ignorant cave-dweller. Until a memory came, like a ladder lowered from above, so I might climb out of this chasm of non-being. I could never have escaped using my own diminished resources. My sight recovered; I would be astounded to find myself submerged in darkness …'

She sipped the strange comfort of another's words, reaching through the invisible perplex-of-normal that divides people and into shared space, speaking into the heart of her own experience of sleepless nights. How had Proust tracked his inner landscape? Had he sat up in the middle of the night, lost in that same relentless blunt timelessness, to write it down?

Ella walked naked along the hall into the bathroom, stepped into the shower and turned on the cold-water tap, then instantly jumped back, remembering that bore water was hot. Here the water needed to cool down, not heat up. She held her hand under the water to test it, then stepped back under the strong stream, washing away the sticky sleeplessness of a long night.

Dripping, she stood in front of the mirror, tugged at her hair and pulled the wet tangle into a knot. Several strands stuck to her face, tendrils of long dark-wet curls covering her neck and small breasts like strands of seaweed. Bunching the mass of wet hair on top of her head, she opened the top bathroom drawer with the other hand, rummaging for some kind of hair band. At the back of the drawer her fingers touched warm metal. She grinned. 'Ha!'

Holding the scissors up like a salute, she spoke to the face in the mirror, 'To Marcel: dawn of a new era.' She picked up a long stray strand of dark-wet auburn hair but it snagged in the gold chain around her neck. Wincing, she dragged her hair free, pulled it out to its full length and cut it close to her face, aware of the tearing sound as the scissors cut through. She picked up the next strand of wet curls and snipped. And snipped. Each errant curl dropped into a fuzzy cloud of drying hair on the floor.

Cutting felt like freedom: with each cut a crimp of old buried and unnamed shadow fell away. A slip of image: curly-headed Proust teased by that nasty uncle. His after-cut freedom without the puerile curls. Crimps of expectation fell with each snip. Snip. Years of comments about her 'beautiful hair', as if she *was* her hair. She hadn't known how much she hated those red curls until now, exposed by Proust. She held another strand to its full length and snipped even closer to her face.

Finished, she stared down at the halo of curls around her feet. Reaching up behind the door she pulled down a stained sarong from a hook and wrapped it around herself, tying a thick knot at her chest. She retrieved the book from the bedroom then headed along the hall towards the kitchen, rubbing her hand up the cool back of her neck. Free. She made a pot of tea and, tucking the book under one arm, went into Hans's study. Poured the dark-gold tannin into a large cup. Deep in the old leather lounge chair, she breathed in the perfume of book. Picked up Proust and read slowly in a whisper, listening to words that felt like tiny torches lighting undiscovered corridors in her mind. 'It must be my own mind that discovers the truth. But how? What a chasm of uncertainty the mind enters whenever some part of it strays its own borders, when it, as the seeker, is both the dark region through which it must seek, and the equipment used for seeking. To avail it nothing? To seek, and more than that: create. It must face that which does not yet exist; the mind alone (or the imagination?) can give it substance; make it real.'

'Yes, create. I need to create; re-imagine. I need to write.'

Hot fingers of dawn poked through the pine tree and the open curtains of the study. She ran a hand up the back of her neck, shaking her head to feel this new tingle of lightness.

Chapter 2

Time tasted different out here. Not the sleek relentless tolling of urban time, colonised and contained. More variable. One moment there was a sudden salty burst in the mouth, followed by an obstinate trickle that tasted of dust, then a sharp wedge of infinity that left tiny cuts.

Her mind ran over the conversation with Kylie the hairdresser like a curious tongue testing the shape and edges of new tooth after a trip to the dentist. She ran her left hand up the back of her neck. Kylie had snipped her Proustian cut into some kind of shape as she passed on the local gossip. Kylie didn't look old enough to have a son in his last year at high school.

Body-jolt to attention. Slamming on the brake pedal, she clutched the steering wheel, knuckles white. Her father's voice sounded in her head: 'Don't swerve, don't swerve!' Her hands yanked the steering wheel turning the car away from the huge kangaroo frozen in the middle of the road, swerving in slow motion. Thud of kangaroo. The car juddered to a halt, engulfed in a cloud of red dust.

Ella sat gripping the steering wheel, sucking in air. The huge roo staggered to its feet and lurched off towards two smaller kangaroos that stared back at her from the verge. When they had retreated to a nearby scruff of trees, she got out of the car and walked around to the front passenger side to check for damage. Only a slight indent. Headlights okay.

Note to self: concentrate when driving country roads. The roadsides were littered with decomposing kangaroos, an ear or a snout protruding from an organic mass of fur and guts. White bones picked clean, ribcages jutting up out of red dirt. Clouds of black flies covering the fresher bits. Crows pecked at the bloody flesh, hopped back just long enough to let a vehicle pass, then crowded again to the feast.

She drove off slowly. The hard-baked land flicked past, dams cracked and dry. Even some of the oldest eucalypts were dying. She turned on to the narrow gravel road, her Corolla rattling along the track to the house. Once over the judder of the cattle grid, eyes scanning the yard for the dogs, she caught the glint of a line meandering up the windscreen. Was that crack getting bigger? She leant closer, trying to measure it against memory. Yes? Note to self: get windscreen fixed.

Movement distracted her, and with relief she saw Sully and Harry scramble out from under the house and run towards the car. Relief not just because they were her only friends out here. Maria had instructed her to keep the dogs tied up at night or whenever she was away from the property. But she hated tying them up.

'Okay, okay, let me open the door,' she said through the car window. Sully leapt up at the door as she parked under the shade of the old peppercorn tree, and kept leaping, wild with excitement, as Ella stepped out of the car. Harry hung back, tail wagging.

'Yes, I'm glad to see you too, girl,' she said, holding the dog against her body and letting Sully lick her face. 'Oh, yuck, Sully, too much love. Come here, Harry. She's too much, isn't she? Too wild. Good boy,' she crooned, as Harry allowed himself to be patted. Sully continued to jump up and push her nose between them. Ella laughed. 'I know what you want Sully, you greedy bitch. Yes, I went to the butcher.' She pulled a white paper parcel from a cooler bag on the back seat and dumped it on the bonnet.

Sully's jumping frenzy went up a notch as Ella tore the paper, chose the two biggest bones and threw them on a small patch of lippia, the only green spot in the drought-ravaged front yard. 'There you go.'

Sully leapt on to the largest bone while Harry sauntered over to the other. 'You're so cool, Mr Harry. Harry Cool Junior. Don't let her take your bone.'

She bundled up the bag of bones and pulled more cooler bags from the back seat.

***

Ella laid awake, staring into darkness, listening to the obstinate wind. It was a Valkyrie, howling, nagging, tugging. A papery whisper of dry, distressed leaves, bark crackling under sharp probing fingers, whipping up red dust and tossing it back against the hot earth. She hated the wind out here. There was no escape. And the interminable fine dust in everything, everywhere.

She couldn't remember being this lonely. Not even in those last twelve months. There was always something going on in the city, someone to catch up with, or avoid, coffee or movies, drinks and dinners, her phone always busy. But out here, nothing. No internet. No phone except the landline. In Melbourne she'd craved silence; now she hated it. How could anyone think or write in this roaring silence?

She had laughed and teased Robyn, who was always going off on silent retreats. 'What would you want to do that for?' she teased one day after Robyn had given them a blow-by-blow description of her time at a silent retreat: 5am bell, meditate, meditate while eating a grain of rice.

'Just lock yourself in your bedroom and unplug, Rob,' Ella had said, laughing.

Robyn turned on her with fire in her eyes. 'You wouldn't understand, Ella, you're always so busy on your phone, checking Facebook, playing Miss Popular. And you know why? Because it hides your loneliness. Underneath all that busyness, you're really lonely.'

They all stared at Robyn. No one spoke. Finally, she said, 'Sorry, Ella, I didn't just mean you. I mean everyone who's addicted to Facebook or their phone. We don't know how to be alone any more, how to be silent.'

'Oh *daahling*, being alone is highly overrated,' Jaz said in his Dame Edna voice, swiping the air with a limp wrist. They all laughed.

But now, out here alone, that afternoon on the deck of the Salty Dog they called the Dog's Breakfast came back as if it were yesterday. Robyn had been right about the loneliness. It had been hiding there all along. The heat and silence of the landscape was a hothouse for loneliness, and all the other hidden things that she had for so long ignored. Now they burned her insides.

Grief had circled in after her father died. A sharp grief that bit the inside skin of her heart and wouldn't let go. Grief over-ripened into loneliness, became a familiar dull ache deep in the bones, the way acute illness becomes chronic, the wound that won't heal. An implacable pain. At first she kept hoping it would go away. Struggled against it, trying to find ways to heal. But after a while she had given up, stopped fighting, surrendered. She learned to live with it. It stood at the centre like a maypole and she lived around it, made room for it. Stopped talking about it. The loneliness bird settled into her heart, nesting in secret chambers. It was who she was when no one was watching.

Ella brushed away tears, took a deep breath, reached over and stroked Harry's soft head on the pillow beside her. If it weren't for the dogs she couldn't stay out here in the violent, sharp-edged loneliness that had grown into a beast scratching at the window each night. She had gradually allowed Harry and Sully to creep into the house in the evenings, and eventually into the bedroom at night. In the morning she woke with Sully's hot breath in her face and those beautiful green eyes full of mischief watching her, waiting to play.

She had barely written a word since she'd come to Eldorado, except for a few anecdotes about the dogs. Each morning, arriving at the blank screen, her mind had sat empty, heavy and dank as a dishwashing rag.

Ella rested her hand on the pillow above Harry's head as she struggled to push past the mundane irritations of her thoughts, the heat, and lazy mozzies, fat on her blood after feasting through the night, their insistent drone circling her ear.

Laughter burst from her like a sudden shift of light on a cloudy day. A haiku. 'Fat mozzie whining in my ear. Do you think I am deaf?' Ah, Issa! Whose humour and sharp-close wisdom had pierced the shadows of her heart. Quick-pulse of memory, mind loosening back to her poetry-writing phase. She had memorised poems, especially haikus, hoping to change the tempo of her mind. Given up when her own words sat lumpy and mouldering on the page.

She flicked on the bedside light. Harry opened his eyes and watched her. 'It's okay, boy. Go back to sleep.' She spoke in a low voice, stroking his head. She reached across and drew her red notebook from the pile of books on her bedside table. Only the first few pages were marked in a neat scrawl. So much for her promise to keep a journal on this trip. On the first page in large purple letters she had written, *Desert Writing*.

Her eyes grazed the page. She read random lines.

Why do people take things so literally? They ask me, which desert? I don't mean desert as place. But desert as experience. Phenomena. Particular textures of geography, inside and out. Wide-open space, blue forever skies, long horizons, driving that single ribbon of road, disappearing into the horizon that shimmies into sky … that desert. Desert as space. As freedom. That's what I mean by desert.

She smiled, remembering those last days packing up in Melbourne, the anticipated freedom of the desert, and the road. It seemed an eternity away.

Yes, journaling was different to other writing. It was a different way of seeing, like a compass reset to the inside – turning to all the inside things that could slip by unnoticed in the rush of normal. Uncharted territories. Secret beauty hiding in half-forgotten caves. Journaling interrupted the howl of loneliness in some inexplicable way. As if she became *other* at the same time that she encountered the phenomena of herself. Meeting herself, not who she thought she was or should be, but as a mysterious friend who surprised her when she sat down to listen with curiosity rather than disapproval or certainty.

Ella picked up a pen from the bedside table and wrote.

***

Seated on her regular stool at the bar, sipping icy beer, she followed Lil's gaze in the Johnny Walker mirror. Lil had stopped talking abruptly when the four men walked in as if they owned the place. Big men, thick stubble shadowing their big faces under big hats.

Lil groaned under her breath, leant towards her. 'Pig shooters, I reckon. Might want to get out of here soon, sista. Got trouble stamped all over them,' she said quietly, not taking her eyes off the men. She headed down the bar towards them. Ella tracked her from the corner of her eye.

Lil had seemed unfriendly that first time Ella drove into town and found her behind the bar instead of big Frank. But by the time Ella had finished her second Great Northern, trying to quench that insatiable desert thirst, Lil had declared that her friends called her Lil. Gave Ella the rundown on gossip around town. Made her laugh with her round-flat-word stories.

She stopped before the men. Her skin was honey-tan and she had the dark eyes of her ancestors. Long thin legs. Soft-bellied muffin top hanging over her jeans, covered by a loose black T-shirt. When Lil smiled her radiant smile, it was such a contrast to the heavy-clouded face she could show a moment before. But Lil wasn't smiling at the men leaning over the bar.

'Hey, boys, what can I get ya?'

'Schooners of fourex all round.'

Lil picked up four glasses frosted with ice and lined them up in front of the tap. The men watched as she held each glass in turn on an angle, creating a smooth flow of amber liquid, white froth gathering on top until the glass was almost full and the tap clunked off. Then she filled each glass to a good head, tap clunking, beer almost spilling over the edge of the glass. The men stared as if she were performing a sacred ritual. In the mirror Ella could see their Adam's apples swallowing as they waited.

Glasses in hand, they moved to a high table near a window, stretched, scratched and looked around the bar. Ella watched in the mirror as one man ran his eyes down her back and shorts, taking in her tanned legs. He nudged his mates and cocked his head in her direction. They all eyed her up and down.

Before Ella had time to finish her drink, the youngest one swaggered to the bar and bought another round, though their glasses were still half-full. He took three of the beers back to the table and muttered something. There was loud laughter. The particular laughter that every woman recognises but can't describe, knowing it's some smutty joke about her or her sex. He sculled the last of his beer and swaggered back to the bar, pelvis leading the way. He picked up his fresh glass and smirked up to Ella.

'What's a pretty girl like you doing in a place like this?'

Oh, fuck off, she wanted to say. 'Minding my own business.'

Lil busied herself closer along the bar and Ella felt the gaze of the other men on her back.

The man leant against the bar. His body was stocky, powerful. He had blond hair with darker rough stubble masking his lower face: ruggedly handsome, and so ugly. Thick male, animal-hunting smell. She rubbed her nose, drained her glass and stood. 'I'm off. See you, Lil.' She bent to pick up her pack.

'Hey, don't go yet,' the man said, grabbing her by the arm.

'Let go of me!' Ella jerked her arm from his grasp.

'I was just being friendly. I want to buy you a drink.'

'I don't want a drink.'

'Don't be like that.'

The man blocked Ella's way, moving in front of her as she stepped left and right as if they were in a loose dance.

'Hey, mate, let her go,' Lil said, moving closer.

The three men at the table were hollering and clapping. Ella tried to thrust past him. He stood in front of her again. She turned side-on and jabbed him in the ribs with her elbow, trying to push past. He grunted and grabbed her arm. She felt his fingers press into her flesh, a squeeze of pain.

'That hurt, bitch.' He took a deep breath, flicked a look over his shoulder towards his mates, grinned wide. 'A fighter, eh?. I like a fighter.' His face was so close she smelt his sour beer breath. She tried to pull away but his grip was unyielding.

'Let her alone, mate. Just sit down and drink your beer or leave,' Lil said from behind the bar.

'Yeah.' He turned to face Lil but didn't let go of Ella's arm. 'What are you going to do? Call the cops? Nearest cop's a couple of hours away. Reckon it's every man for himself out here.'

The men fell silent. Waiting.

Time strained into a black hole of waiting. Ella gripped by blind panic. Her body frozen and screaming: *Run.*

The voice behind the man was quiet. Commanding. 'Let her go, mate.'

The young pig shooter let Ella's arm drop and she stepped back quickly as he turned to face the voice. The young man was taller than the stranger who had spoken. But there was something in the older man's ice-grey eyes, the jut of his chin, that made the young bully boy back down. The way a weaker dog curls his tail and rolls on his belly when the alpha male snaps.

The newcomer in khaki stepped between Ella and the pig shooter, turning his back to her. 'Reckon you'd better drink up and move along, boys,' he said, and pulled something from his pocket that Ella couldn't see. The trio downed their drinks as one and headed for the door fast, as if their ute was on fire.

Chemicals of relief washed through her. Knees shaky, she grabbed hold of the bar and flopped on to the stool. Lil reached across and patted Ella's arm. 'You okay?'

Ella nodded.

'Get her a drink, Lil,' the stranger said, still watching the door.

'Thanks.' Ella clasped her hands tightly to stop them trembling.

Abruptly the man strode to the door and disappeared outside.

'Arrogant prick,' Lil said, staring hard at the door as it swung shut. She sat a tumbler with a shot of amber liquid on the bar in front of Ella.

'Who is that?' Ella said, sniffing at her drink. Brandy.

'Sarge.' Lil pulled a face, as if she had just smelt something disgusting.

Ella took a sip. Felt the fire burning down through her stomach, warmth penetrating her blood. She blew out a long breath. Blinked, realising Lil was speaking.

'... hates our mob ...'

'Well, I reckon he just saved my butt.' Ella gulped down the rest of the brandy.

'Yeah, loves playing the big man'.

'Did you say Sarge?'

Lil nodded.

'A cop?'

'Was. That's the mystery, but ...' She broke off and busied herself at the sink as Sarge walked back in through the door and approached Ella.

'You okay, girlie?' He didn't wait for an answer. 'Troublemakers that lot. Got a few guns and bellies full of beer. Bored with shooting pigs and think they can run amok in town. Should be the last we see of them. Call me if they come back, Lil.' He touched his fingers to his large Akubra. 'You too,' he said turning to Ella. 'Any trouble, just call.' She couldn't see his eyes now through the wraparound sunglasses.

Before the door had closed behind him, a group of hot and bothered people came in, multiple eyes scanning the bar. Lil pointed towards the toilet signs. They bolted.

'Grey nomads. Stragglers. Most have finished for the year. Might buy a lemonade. Just come in to use the loo. Place is swarming with them in winter,' Lil said, watching them rush through the bar.

'Thanks, Lil. Catch you later,' Ella said to Lil, and picked up her bag, suddenly needing to move.

***

Opening the door on the heat of late morning, she almost choked in surprise. The dark-and-handsome stranger in the Akubra who had hollered 'Hello' was a young Hugh Jackman lookalike, wearing dusty moleskins that wrapped around strong thighs, open shirt revealing a smooth, tanned chest.

As she stepped out on to the veranda in her shorty pyjamas, his face clouded with confusion as he swept the hat off to reveal thick, dark wavy hair. But not before his shooting gaze had taken her in. Her nipples instantly hardened, burning against the flimsy cotton. She folded her arms across her chest, feeling unexpectedly vulnerable.

'I came to see Maria or Hans,' he said, frowning.

'I'm Ella.' Smiling, she extended her hand, keeping the other crossed over her chest.

'Liam,' he said, 'Liam MacDonald, your neighbour.' He jabbed the air with his thumb to the left, then rubbed a palm down his moleskins before reaching out to shake her hand firmly. Her body quivered with the momentum. The name sounded familiar. Oh, yes, Kylie the hairdresser was right. He's hot.

'Maria and Hans are away overseas. I'm house-sitting.'

'Ah, yeah. Forgot.'

'Do you want to come in for a cup of tea or something?' A rising heat burned slowly up her chest and neck. The air between them felt hot and sticky. Liam MacDonald grinned down at her with perfect white teeth. Her body was bombarding her with some primal instinct of desire, or was it an instinct of loneliness? She leant against the wall, slightly breathless.

But then, like a surprise sun shower out of clear blue sky, his smile dropped. 'I came to tell Maria her dogs were in the top paddock yesterday. Back of our property. She'd better keep them locked up or someone'll shoot them. I don't want it to be me. That's what I came to say. But you're not Maria.'

'Nope, not Maria … I'm not sure what I should do,' Ella said, flustered. 'God, I don't want them shot. I've been taking them for walks … uh … but maybe I should … um …' her words trailed off, directionless.

'Just make sure they stay on this property and don't go wandering off, otherwise one of the farmers'll shoot them. They won't warn you or let you know if they find them at their sheep. People have lost enough stock in this drought. They'll shoot to protect them.'

So many words. Her mind flummoxed, trying to take it in.

'You'll work it out. You look like a smart woman.'

Woman. He didn't call me girl, or lady, or love … woman, bravo. Where did you go to school, she wanted to ask, but instead said, 'Uh-huh, okay.

I'll work it out.' Her mind raced, trying to think of something else to say to keep him talking.

'Got to go. Good to meet you, Ella.' He was down the front steps in a couple of long strides. Holding open the door of his maroon Toyota ute, he called back, 'Hey, want to come to the pub Friday night?' He was grinning again.

'Yeah. Great. Thanks.'

'Pick you up about five.' He waved and leapt up into the ute. Drove off without looking back, red dust rising under the tyres.

Chapter 3

This furtive wishing for something that's hard to name blisters like a slow burn under the skin. Wanting something more substantial, significant, more lasting than this little life that grows heavy and slack around your neck. It has a thousand secret names and hiding faces. Some might call it love. But this longing is too complicated and wriggling to fit inside just one small word. It reeks of that most unsayable ingredient of human wishing – plaything of gods and poets – immortality! Could it be that all your heroic wishings for something everlasting are also the sharp fangs of your loneliness?

***

The Albion was a different beast on a Friday night compared with the slow monotony of the daytime bar. Liam held the door open as Ella stepped inside, and instantly her mind recoiled from the memory of the pig shooters. She rubbed the tender spot on her arm, gazing around the busy bar, taking in the sights, smells and sounds of the Friday night reverie.

'See you've met your neighbours,' Frank said over the din as she walked up to the bar, flanked by Liam and his twin brother Tom. While Liam was tall and dark, Tom was taller and fairer, sandy-haired with dark brown eyes that were so dark they appeared to be black. Tom was the designated driver. Quieter than Liam, who had talked all the way into town.

They sat at the bar, Ella between them. Liam didn't stay long; he soon began to wander around the bar, talking, flirting. Tom was quiet. It was an effort making conversation with him after the initial getting-to-know-you questions and answers. How she came to be housesitting in Broken Ridge over summer. She told him Hans and Maria's son Jacob, a doctor from her workplace, had suggested it. 'An offer too good to refuse. Timing was perfect,' she said. Had to get out of Melbourne because the walls of my life started closing in after the court case, suffocating: *that* she didn't say. She took a deep gulp of beer, letting her eyes scan the bar, landing on Liam in a far corner.

Ella dragged her attention back to Tom. 'Have you always lived out here?'

'Whole life, except boarding school and uni. Armidale.' He lifted his glass to his lips, then replaced it neatly on the coaster. 'Have you always wanted to write?'

Ella picked at her fingernails. Suddenly craving a cigarette, though she hadn't had one since she left Melbourne. She didn't want to tell a near stranger that she had begun to suspect she was a fraud. More attached to the romantic view of being a writer than the tough reality of arriving at the blank page every day. A failed writer. This was not the conversation she wanted to have on a Friday night at the pub.

She shrugged. 'Hey, tell me about the opals out here. Jacob said this was opal country.'

Hooked, Tom began to give her the history of opal mining in the area. She only half-listened as her eyes followed Liam. When Tom's voice drifted off, she saw that he was also watching his brother, an unreadable mix of emotions passing across his face. He turned and smiled at her; their eyes met, communicating something beyond words, not yet comprehensible. Ella picked up her beer and took a big swallow, and both looked to where Frank was talking loudly to a group of big men further along the bar. One man raised a hand in greeting to Tom and sidestepped his way through the throng towards them.

'Hey, Tom,' the large man said, extending his hand.

'G'day Bob,' Tom said, shaking hands. 'This is Ella. Our new neighbour for the next few weeks.' Bob shook Ella's hand vigorously. It was large and warm. Everything about Bob was big. Big voice, big laugh, huge white moustache. She liked him instantly.

'Welcome to Broken Ridge, Ella. Picked the hottest months for your visit.'

She nodded and grinned. 'Yeah, I'm into extreme sport.'

Tom grew animated as he and Bob talked farming, weather, stock sales, drought. Others joined them and she was introduced to a string of friendly men. The conversation ebbed and flowed around her, and all the while her eyes tracked Liam as he moved from one rowdy table to another.

The night loosened with booze and cooler air, and the pub grew louder. Liam was standing beside a young robust woman, jillaroo probably, and Ella watched as she rubbed one long tanned leg against his thigh, then slid her hand over his crotch. Liam looked over the woman's shoulder and locked eyes with Ella. Grinned. The young woman, keeping her hand on his crotch, twisted to see what was distracting Liam, and mirrored his grin. She raised her glass to Ella in a mock toast, swayed and gulped half of her beer.

The conversation around Ella had moved on to different types of aircraft, especially Bob's latest purchase. She gave Tom a quick smile, shouldered her pack, picked up her beer and headed towards the back of the pub. She swung through the bottle shop to buy a packet of rollies. It was quieter outside, with just a few stray punters talking and smoking. A fat gibbous moon hung over a big old peppercorn tree at the back of the block, softening the evening with silver light. She breathed in the night air with its whiff of cigarette smoke and stale butts.

Her body and mind felt relaxed from the wash of alcohol. It was good to be away from the farm and that brawny bully of loneliness. But even here in the midst of the crowded pub the loneliness was a thick skin around her heart. She wandered over to the peppercorn tree, sat on a metal bench in its shadow and slowly rolled a fat cigarette. The particular satisfaction of rolling a cigarette was possibly better than smoking it. She licked her lips the way her father always had so that the cigarette paper didn't stick to them, lit it and took a good drag. Spat off the tiny bits of tobacco stuck to her lips.

'Mind if I join you?'

She jumped. Couldn't make out the face in the darkness. 'Tom?'

'Liam.'

A thrill of heat ran up her spine and back down, settling between her legs. She held out the pack of rollies. Liam took it and dropped on to the bench beside her.

'Thanks.' They were silent as he rolled a cigarette. She held out the lighter when he was finished. He didn't take it immediately, but his fingers, warm and strong, lingered around hers. That momentary warmth of his touch penetrated dark-cold hollows, waking an ache like hunger.

Liam lit his cigarette. His face glowed in the flare of light, making hard, angular shadows. He grinned at her before the light went out, as if he knew she was watching him. Expected it. She grinned back, then looked away towards the silhouettes huddled in small clusters at the back of the pub dotted with the red glow of cigarettes.

They smoked in silence, surveying the crowd around the back door. Without a word, or changing his position, Liam's free hand slid up her leg. She held her breath, heart hard-drumming. He leaned down, putting an ear to her chest.

'Excited,' he said. A statement. He turned his head to nuzzle and kiss her neck. Suddenly his hands were everywhere, stroking, tugging her tank top down to uncover her lacey red bra, yanking the lace to expose one hard nipple to the night air. He teased, sucked and nibbled. A soft moan escaped her lips and she let the cigarette fall to the ground.

His hand moved inside her shorts, probing the thin cotton, expert fingers finding crevices, rubbing and sliding. She moaned, arching her back. His lips came up, kissing her hard on the mouth. Her body throbbed against the thrust of his hand pressing into her. He unbuttoned her shorts, tugged and grunted. She lifted her bottom, letting him drag the fabric constraints down her legs for her to kick free. His fingers probed inside her, his body rubbing hard against her leg.

The sound of unzipping.

'Have you got a condom?' she whispered, not wanting to break the rhythm. Wanting him inside her. Urgent now.

In reply he grunted, pushing his fingers deeper. She tried to pull away. Did she have a condom in her pack? Be too old anyway. He resisted when she pushed his hand away, groaned. She felt warm air, cooling wetness where his hand had been. An ache of emptiness spilled through her, wanting him inside her. He kissed her neck, nuzzling. You're good. Really good. For a moment she tried to calculate. Risk. But the brain-fog of beer and thick longing mixed with loneliness made it hard to reckon. The ache between her legs throbbed louder than reason.

'Let me in, babe.' His words were a muffled moan around a mouthful of breast.

Urgent fingers, hers, reached out, pulling his face up to her lips. Teeth knocking, tongues tasting the inside secret pink of mouth, sparking a burning rush down her spine into shivering flesh.

'Fuck me. I want you to fuck me.' Her voice was hard, rasping, demanding. She spread her legs. In an instant he was on her, inside her. Two animals thrusting together in ancient primal rhythm. Rushing into that gap beyond reason, filling the ache of wanting.

It was over before she came. Now she remembered why she had stopped fucking men. Too quick. Impersonal. But right now, that's what she wanted.

Liam collapsed on to her chest. She was pinned underneath. Undies and shorts twisted around one ankle. Instantly she was aware of the hard iron seat pressing into the bare flesh of her backside. But the other ache was gone. Now it had a different hue, a sour taste of something she couldn't name. Some old, troubled part of her that had been buried for a time, was back. Some beast. Devoid of beauty. A deep need wrapped up in regret.

***

Friday nights became a thing. The main event of her week. In the days and nights between she was restless, agitated, obsessing about Liam. As if having sex had allowed him to breach some invisible skin around her heart and he had taken possession, hijacking her thoughts and imaginings, even her dreams. They had sex under the peppercorn tree the following week. She had taken her own condoms. But it hadn't happened since, not at the pub anyway. He practically ignored her the moment they arrived, and she was left with Tom. Her famished gaze stalked him around the bar as he flirted with the gorgeous toned and tanned jillaroos.

It wasn't her bright heart of friendship he'd taken possession of. It was a shadow-heart. A dark hunger. He squeezed it like an overripe avocado. The bruise of wanting in his absence was replaced by a moment of relief each time he penetrated her. And was just as suddenly gone. A glimpse of possibility smouldered inside that moment, smoking her mind like a drug. She was an addict. A love addict. No, not love. She knew it wasn't love. She was caught in a web of longing disguised as love or lust that had bewitched her through Liam's form. Wanting what she couldn't have. The impossibility of it made it far more desirable. It was as if she were standing

32

outside herself, watching in at the peculiar arising of monsters from the deep, drumming their foreboding … doom … doom … doom …

Gandalf said you're not going to Mordor. There are greater dangers than Mordor, my precious. Oh, stop it. Then aloud, in the sharp whisper of a disapproving school ma'am, 'You're an idiot, Ella, like a sex-crazed adolescent.'

Her bedroom reeked of sex. Liam had shown up in the middle of the night when she was already asleep. The first time it happened he'd called out to her from the back door, banging loudly, dogs barking. Half-asleep, she had unlocked the back door to let him in. He was drunk. After that she left the back door unlocked just in case. The dogs disappeared now each time he crept loudly into the bedroom.

Last night she was woken by him kissing her on the back of the neck, stroking her butt. 'You got the sweetest arse, babe. And sweet wet cunt.' He rolled her over and kissed her hard on the mouth. He stank of beer and cigarettes.

Her blood raced, heart a wild drummer. Yes-yes-yes. Fuck-me-fuck-me-fuck-me drum. He was rough. She wanted it hard and rough. It was like scratching an itch that you can't quite reach, so you scratch harder and harder until you tear skin but the itch keeps itching. When she woke in the morning he was always gone.

You're playing with fire. The words didn't land but floated off like a puff of smoke. Ella rolled over to the empty side of the bed. Nuzzled into the pillow, breathing in his scent. She slid her hand down her after-sex-animal-body tingling skin. Rested her fingers into her sticky vulva. It was sore, pungent with sex. She smiled, remembering, and rubbed hard into her stubborn knot of longing.

***

He was drunk when he crashed into her bed that night. She was sleep-heavy from the bottle of red wine she had finished trying to drown her restless agitation. Her vibrator lay on the sheet beside her. He picked it up and turned it on. Toyed with it. Pressed it against her clitoris. Stroked her slippery vulva, teasing. Sucking. His hands were everywhere. Knowing, urgent hands. He flipped her over on to her belly. Unbuckled. Unzipped. He kept the vibrator stroking her vulva; she moaned each time it passed her clitoris, engorged with sudden pleasure. Still sleepy, her body surrendered. He held the vibrator to her anus, circling. Her body moved to the rhythm and pleasure of his hand rubbing, sliding. A sudden burst of pain as he thrust hard into her anus. She tried to move but he had her pinned flat against the bed. He rammed hard, grunting. Pain stabbed her inside. She was instantly awake, all pleasure gone.

'Liam, stop.' She tried to move but his full weight pinned her. 'Stop it, you're hurting me!' she screamed at him.

'Come on, you like it rough. You love it; I know you do.'

She struggled against him. He grunted loudly, thrusting into her, bang-slap of flesh against her buttocks. The pain was like a tearing bruise inside her. Struggling made it worse. She lay still. The pressure changed as he shifted position. Sensing a break, in one quick-fluid wrench of movement she rolled out from under him. Turning, her arm came up and flew for his face. A split-second glimpse of his eyes, glassy. The same eyes she had seen a hundred times in A&E. Drugs. The back of her forearm struck his face. Teeth gritted against pain of impact. Fury of words through clenched teeth.

'Fuck you! Stop when I tell you!'

The words were barely out and her arm still finishing its juddering arc against the flesh of his cheek when his fist struck the side of her face. The force flung her off the bed. Lying still, curling into herself, she groaned softly.

'Don't ever hit a guy in the face unless you want to get hit back. Stupid bitch.' He was standing over her, looking down. Eyes strange, unfamiliar, not seeing. 'Animal instinct, babe. No stopping it.' Did he even know who she was? He rubbed the knuckles of his hand. Opened his palm, spat, reached down and took hold of his penis. Started rubbing. Harder and faster, his eyes staring at the wall straight ahead. He looked wild, dazed. Moaned as warm wetness sprayed across her face and hair. Salty tang on her lips.

'Animal instinct.' *Zi-iii-p.*

Her body lay unmoving and limp as his footsteps receded along the hall. The front door slammed. Voices and laughter. Someone was with him. Tom? The engine revved and the vehicle sped off, a squealing-judder across the ramp at the front gate.

Ella hid out at the farm. Calculated that she had nearly enough supplies until the swelling and bruising went down. Long-life milk, frozen meat, plenty of eggs from the chooks. The few precious greens from Maria's veggie patch that wilted in the fierce heat, recovered in the evening when she sprayed a trickle of bore water over them. Surviving, not thriving. They needed rain. Everything needed rain. There was plenty of frozen bread. Enough beer if she rationed herself. She might have to raid Hans's secret stash of red wine in his study. Replace it before she left. Rollies could last if she rolled racehorses, as her Dad used to call them. Maybe she'd give up. She only smoked at night when she was drinking anyway. Wasn't it time?

As the days dragged on, she felt herself sliding into a familiar black hole. In an effort to stop the fall, she prowled Hans's library for something to hold on to. Homer, Goethe, Nietzsche, Kafka, Proust. No, she was done with Proust. She picked up books, opened them, scanned pages searching for words that could grab and hold her. Something visceral, direct. She picked up a battered book. Dog-eared and faded as if it had been read often, pages touched by many fingers or the same fingers many times. Tarjei Vesaas. She stroked the rough texture of the book and opened the first page.

'Siss. A young, white forehead boring through the darkness. An eleven-year-old girl. Siss.'

Book open, she walked to the lounge, bumping her toe as she went.

'Shit,' she said through gritted teeth, dropping on to the leather lounge, not taking her eyes off the page.

All afternoon she read, lost inside time, the words reaching tender places in her heart. She read the last line and closed the book. Stared out to the cypress standing close against the window. Shook her head. She had never read anything like it, it was as if her thirsty heart had been drenched in rain. Tears wet on her face, she went to the bookshelf. Still holding *The Ice Palace* against her chest, she found several more works by Vesaas and gathered them into a small pile. Back on the lounge, she cleared a space for the newcomers among the open books and empty cups on the coffee table. Gingerly, she touched her fingertips to the puffy-pain around her cheek and eye, rubbed the ache in her forehead. Picked up a book and read.

For the next few days she read and reread every book by Vesaas she could find in the library. She became immersed in the worlds inside each book, the characters nestling into her heart, closer than family. The reading pushed back unwanted realities that crowded to come inside.

Between reading sessions she walked. It became a rhythm that carried her through the heavy days and slow nights. She walked head down, barely aware of the ground beneath her feet, body as light as air. The feeling of each book inside her was brighter than daylight. She was aware of an ache behind her eyes and nose, engorged with tears that wouldn't cry. But she was far on the other side of crying. Disconnected, yet saturated in sorrow – some from Vesaas's characters who reflected her own heartache, baring familiar longing. She walked with sorrow and all its infolding textures and shades, glad there was no one there to interrupt this feeling. Hugged it to her like the taste of asafoetida, strange and particular – almost a dislike but wanting it anyway. No, *needing* it. Her body, or some unknown part of her, needed to be with this sorrow. Savoured it hungrily.

Ella lifted her head to see Harry trotting along beside her like a faithful butler. Sully was racing out ahead and circling back, wide and graceful in full flight. She squatted and Harry came over and leant against her.

'You're a good friend, Harry.' She nuzzled into the soft thick coat of his neck, smelt the dog and dust smell of animal comfort.

Chapter 4

No wonder you're confused. Part-animal and part-dreamer, laced with metaphoric. Biological and mythological. Time-bound in your biology and free to roam in timeless wonder in your imaginings. What a mystery you are, creator and created. How can you know what to wish for?

Yet the quieter wonder in all this, the one you have forgotten, is that you are not alone. You belong, a participant in this wild choir of everything. A breath in the wind of those far-off mountains of Peru, a tiny flicker inside a great burning, a droplet of water carried in the arms of the river rushing, always returning towards that ocean of possibility, atom and dust, mitochondria …

Look to the tree. He is calling to you, bending his loveliness like an invitation into the old song. Reach towards the light of beauty humming in everything and inside your own stuttering heart. It vanishes the moment you close your fingers to grasp or try to hold it, gone.

***

It was Tom who finally showed up to break her long spell of isolation. Ella's eyes narrowed as she pulled open the heavy front door and stood behind the thin shield of flyscreen.

'I dropped in to see if you need anything in town. Haven't heard from you for a while.'

Has he come to check up on me? See the damage his brother caused? Was Tom there that night? How could she trust a guy who waited outside while his brother did that to a woman?

'I just want to be left alone,' she said. 'To write,' she added.

'I'm heading into town to pick up a part for the truck. Do you want to come for a ride? Anything I can get you?'

Tears pricked her eyes. Why is he being so fucking nice after what his brother had done? She pushed against the screen door and stepped out, nothing between them. Heard Tom's sharp intake of breath as she moved into the hard light. Stared down at the dust coating the floorboards.

'What has …?' His words faded even as he spoke, losing momentum. As if in asking the question he instantly sensed the truth of the dark yellowing bruise across her cheek, and her puffy eye. 'God, Ella … was this?'

She shifted from one leg to the other, watching Tom's mind working across his face. Storm clouds, lightning bolt of recognition, dark rain of anger and other complex emotions she couldn't read.

'Want to come in for a cuppa?'

There was pity in his eyes. She hated pity. He must see her as pathetic. She felt pathetic. But to see it reflected – that was something else. The old fire in her belly sparked, kindled into life. She pulled back her shoulders, stared directly up into his eyes, eyebrows high, head back, chin jutting. Ready for a fight.

'Yeah, thanks.'

All the fight drained out of her. He sounded sad, defeated. A long pause hung between them, and neither of them moved. Almost a whisper, 'I'm sorry if …' again his words fell away, fragile as dry leaves carried off by a hot wind.

Tom became a regular visitor. They never spoke about Liam. She hadn't seen him since that dreadful night. Apart from her fading bruise, it was as if Liam had barely existed. Or those Friday nights at the pub.

Getting to know Tom was slow, meandering in gentle streams of conversation, winding through quiet lagoons into deep eddies. So unlike Liam's straight-to-the-point, hand-under-skirt approach. Tom was curious, introspective, almost shy. Usually he was the listener. But he loved poetry and grew animated talking about it.

'Favourite poet?'

'Hmm, that's a hard one.' Tom stroked his chin. 'I guess I'd have to say the old guys. Keats, Wordsworth .. Coleridge.'

Ella nodded.

'Oh, and Olivia Parsons.'

Ella shook her head. 'Never heard of her.'

'No. No one has. She was my mother's favourite poet.'

The next night Tom arrived with a small leatherbound book. He passed it to her as they sat on the back veranda. She read the title: *Olivia Parsons, Lost Letters and Poems.* Opening the book, she stroked the fine paper, the writing too small to read in the dim light. The silence felt alive between them.

'I used to read to my mother in the evenings.' Tom said and fell silent for a slow beat of time.

'Mmm.' She willed him to keep talking.

He stared out into deep-blue night blinking with stars. 'My mother was an invalid the last few years of her life. In constant pain.' His words came haltingly, the way an unused pipe stutters when water finally starts to flow again.

Ella sipped her beer. Stared at the side of his face. His eyes glistened.

'I read those poems to Mum. It seemed to help her pain. It was our thing. Just the two of us.' He pinched his eyes between thumb and middle finger into the bridge of his nose, wicking away moisture. He blew air through his lips. Paused for a long breath. His voice measured. 'I learnt some by heart.'

'Go on, then.'

'Hmm. It's been a long time.' He cleared his throat and gulped a mouthful of beer. Smiled and nodded. He recited several lines of poetry, faltering only occasionally.

'Who will remember me when I am dead? Who will mourn my bones, burnt white under dust…' His voice was resonant, the timbre of the land and dry wind in trees taking shape as words in his mouth.

'…. Red dust wakes in our blood, remembering the wild thing we sing for….' He shook his head slowly as if to call up wisps of line from a threadbare or vanishing past, to taste the forgotten rhythm of words. He gazed out into the night. 'Each star burning with its own time-lost story, ancestor songs, shimmy …'

He looked up, blinked, waking from a trance. 'I never could remember what came after shimmy.' He half-laughed and took a slow draught of beer.

'Thanks,' Ella said quietly.

'It's about finding something larger to hold on to in dark nights.'

She nodded, watched him lean back and close his eyes, and knew the moment was over.

Out of the silence his voice erupted, 'If I were a tree, oh what a tree I would be….' He waited a long moment, then shook his head slowly. 'It's all I can remember. Should remember that one, Mum and I recited it together so many times.'

He looked the other way and she couldn't see his face. They sat in the deepening breath of silence.

When he stood to leave an hour later, she handed him the book, still warm from her holding it between her palms like a prayer, and he said, 'I thought you might like to borrow it.'

'I'd love to. If that's okay. Thanks'

He smiled, nodded, and was gone.

In the kitchen she flicked on the fluorescent light, dropping into a chair at the table. Opened the small book. The inscription inside the front cover read: 'To our darling Margaret, I found this little book and knew it was for you. May these words bring you solace and delight. Warmest wishes, Maudie and Jack.'

Ella flicked through the book, words snagging her gaze. She read aloud to the night, invoking the poet and the presence of Tom and his invalid mother.

'I am the blind man afraid of the dark, that dreads the coming of the night…'

Letting her eyes graze over the pages. 'Rain singing on tin roof, like a jazz quartet, filling my dancing shoes with tears … My body full of crying …'

She studied several pages more closely, searching for Tom's unfinished lines. 'Gotcha!'

'… shimmy in, to wake the dust in these sorry veins. "Bright Star steadfast as thou art" hold my trembling heart, forever at thy breast, or else let me "swoon, gentle into easeful death." '

'Hmm, Keats. Who else were you reading, Olivia?'

She tore scraps of paper from a paper bag at the end of the table, marking the place so she could copy down the lines.

In the morning she opened the little book and copied the lines of poetry into the back of her red journal. She couldn't remember when she had started to copy lines of poetry or beautiful words that seemed to possess her, change her in some secret way that she couldn't explain. Perhaps it had started after her father died. Somehow copying made them stick, as if the words formed by her fingers into shape and texture allowed her body to remember, sink into her. The living breath of poets change her through their words.

She flicked through pages, scanning for Tom's tree poem. Other lines caught her attention. She read aloud, 'All the world's a fly.' What an odd title. 'Such a tiny thing, yet your buzzing murders everything… Now you come to sit upon my page, rubbing your wicked wings with glee. Like a shot, I slam it shut, but you, little villain, fly free.'

She smiled, wondering if Olivia had read Issa's mosquito haiku.

Reading, she found herself moved between the mundane, things such as flies and beetles or daily routines of the household, to mystical musings as Olivia reached for something that was hard to name. It poked Ella's own unsayable questions.

She whispered as she wrote, letting words soak in, trickle down into the soft bones of her heart, and deeper still.

'In my imaginings,
I can dream myself anything.
I can dream myself legs
that run and dance
and ache for love.
I can dream myself into far-off lands,
with mountains and rivers
forests of trees and wild birdsong.
I dream myself a star,
watching down upon this wretched heart
watching back in wonder.'

Ella flicked through pages, threaded with Olivia's constant battle with pain. As she read and copied lines, her own shadow of hiding pain like sticky grief and other nameless emotions that had hardened around her heart, stirred and raised their heads, sniffed, and turned towards the light. She shoved it all back down and jumped up, shaking her head to dislodge that familiar thing sliding into view.

Two nights later when Tom showed up again they sat on the back veranda, glasses of red wine in hand. Ella held up the book that she'd been poring over for the past two days.

'What do you think?'

'Yeah, really interesting. Surprising.'

He nodded, studying her face.

'In some poems it's like she's speaking to me. Seeing into me, somehow.'

'Yep.' He nodded vigorously then turned away.

'What a story, though.'

'Yeah, quite something.'

'I'd like to read more of her poetry. Find out more about her.'

'Apparently all her writings were destroyed in the housefire that killed her. Did you read the intro?

'Yeah. It's got me curious. Nothing like a good mystery to start an itch in the brain.' She grinned across at him. The red wine mellowing her body in its delicious spell.

Later, after their slow conversation had circled wide, occasionally dipping or diving like the flight of an eagle across the plain, Tom returned to his favourite topic. 'Poetry starts with wondering, even when it's wrapped in pain. Lured towards beauty, to arrive into deeper wonder.'

She nodded, leaning forward to listen more closely.

'Beauty's a thirst of the heart. But we mistake outer appearance for the truth of beauty.' He stared at the stars glistening back as if they were listening. 'We reduce the mystery of beauty into what we can possess, capture or manufacture. Like plucking the poor blossom from a tree, cut off from its heart-roots it never blooms. We lose it, then spend a lifetime chasing its shadow. We can never possess beauty, only glimpse it in a line of poetry, smell of rain in dust, or a beloved face.'

'Who said that?'

'Me. Just now. With a bit of inspiration from Lawrence.'

Her skin tingled with the truth of his words. Yes, her heart said. Yes. Yes, the stars said yes. The night said yes. 'You're a poet!'

'Took some electives in literature at Uni.' He fell silent. 'Perhaps it is beauty that will save us in the end.'

She raised her eyebrows, nodding, held the glass to her lips and took a sip.

'Dostoevsky.'

Each morning she tried to remember the taste and texture of their nightly conversations, to write the questions stirring. It was like trying to grab on to a dream as it slipped back into a dark pool of dreaming. The slow late-night exchanges with Tom, swapping books and reading to each other, roused something in her in the way a beautiful line of poetry speaks into mysteries that cannot be named. Old-deep relentless questions, abandoned or forgotten, rose like thirsty ghosts. Who am I? What do I really want? How should I live my life? Newer questions, the Liam questions: How can I be the same person who wanted Liam like a rutting she-goat, then enter these wide-open moments in deep wonder with Tom? And darker, brooding questions that she pushed down.

Her mind rolled back over last night's conversation. She closed her eyes to concentrate, hands resting on the laptop keyboard.

'The Mexicans tell of three deaths,' Tom had said. 'The first is when we realise that we're not immortal. We're going to die and so are the people we love. The second is our physical death.' He'd paused, frowning. 'Ah, yes, the third is when the last person calls our name for the last time. Forgotten, we cease to exist. That's the final death.'

Something quavered inside her, pushing up like a tiny shoot through a crack in concrete. A jumble of thoughts and words trembling into a question between life and death. She needed to understand, sensed the urgency to know. She wrote to track the question, give it form in words. Words bumbled and bumped together on the page. 'To be forgotten is death. And to live, yes to live. But how should we live? Fully alive? What is reality? What is truth?'

A more urgent thought stirred unbidden, flopped into her mind with a thud. Better to be hated than forgotten. She sensed a shifting of plates deep in the geography of her ruminations raging against Liam. She had flip-flopped between dumb emptiness and fury since it had happened. But this new question, triggered by Tom's three Mexican deaths, struck like an arrow into the heart of the space between her numbness and rage. Her mind hit a wall even as she pressed in hard towards understanding, banged her head against not knowing. Ella knew from experience that she couldn't push, needed to be patient and live quietly into the question. Let it bend and shape her until understanding arose at some far-off hour when she had forgotten to worry at it.

Yes, better to forget Liam rather than rage and hate, which only bound her to him. Let him die that final death. A sudden twist came treacherous in her heart, a different voice. What about justice? Retribution? And her mind was off again, racing.

***

They saddled up and rode out early. Sun hugged the dark horizon, slowly unfurling gold across the land beneath an ever-cloudless sky. The ride was Tom's idea in response to her complaining about the heat and drought, flies and mozzies, 'the ugliness of the land'.

Tom had replied, 'If you really love nature, you can find beauty everywhere.' Then, after a pause, 'Van Gogh.'

'Yeah, but he wasn't in the outback in the middle of a drought.'

That's when he'd suggested the ride to camp out overnight. Promised to show her the beauty of country. 'Seeing with eyes of the heart, not the ordinary eyes that are always searching for what they want. Poetry of the land,' he said, as if he'd rehearsed it.

They rode side-by-side, mainly in silence, with the dogs criss-crossing patterns across the land around them. Ella settled easily into the gentle rhythm of the small grey mare, Zelda, short for Esmerelda, an easy creature who cantered along in the shadow of Tom's giant horse. Tom was a different man riding the land: at home in himself. She watched him take in country the way he tasted the lines of a poem on his tongue. His eyes and breath plucked and sang the land in a melody she couldn't hear. Now and then he told stories about the places and trees they passed or pointed out a roo watching them through the gum trees. Silhouette of ears swivelling like small radars. Tom's face was open, all hard lines gone.

Ella tried to take in the land the way he did, reimagine it through his gaze on beloved country. And slowly, as slow as waiting, the land revealed itself, uncovering layer upon layer of protective skins. Her view shifted imperceptibly as her senses opened to the treasures around her: the lacy tracks of tiny creatures, the intimate world of spiders and insects, the brisk, drenched-green mint smell of eucalypt, a quick soft rustle of snake or lizard.

In late afternoon they set up camp, lit the fire and rolled out their swags. Tom cooked. She offered to help but he had it all under control. He had his own rhythm out here on country.

After they'd eaten some kind of bean stew that tasted of salt and a cacophony of herbs and spices, mopped up with soft-hot damper, they sat drinking sweet billy tea, watching the fire. The land and vast night sky hung with an infinity of stars, so close it crowded her heart. Senses crackled with the grandeur of it, making her feel at once small and filled with possibility. This beauty was too large to be spoken in words. Harry, Sully and Tom's kelpie, Penny, were collapsed near the fire, dozing or staring into the flames. Ella soaked up the lopsided pearl moon rising large from the horizon, spreading gauzy-bright light over the land beyond the circle of fire that held them.

'She's beautiful tonight,' Ella said.

'He is.'

She glanced at Tom. When he didn't speak, she said, 'He?'

'The local Aborigines call him brother moon.'

She tried it on. Brother. Felt the shape of moon shift into *him*.

Tom spoke softly, his eyes on the fire. 'A friend told the story when I was a kid – how the sun and moon travel under mother earth in a great round to return to their home in the east. Each wandering across father sky. Sister sun through the day. And brother moon crossing at night.'

As she listened, the desert night wrapped around her like grandmotherly love. There was space for everything, all was welcome; no need to hide anything in this vast, star-freckled universe.

Her words burst out of nowhere, like a shooting star. 'Don't you get lonely living out here?'

Tom was poking a stick deep into the red coals in the heart of the fire. The angles of his face were accentuated in the flickering shadows of firelight. He was silent for so long that she wondered if he'd heard her.

At last, he spoke. 'I never get lonely out here with birds and trees. The loneliest I ever felt was at boarding school surrounded by hundreds of boys.' Still staring into the fire, he continued, 'Cities are the loneliest places on earth. You can't see the stars.'

He lifted his face to the night sky. Ella followed his gaze, drinking in the immense creature of star-crowded night. He was right, but she had no words to explain why it was too large and wondrous for human loneliness.

'We confuse loneliness and solitude. People don't know how to be alone with themselves,' Tom said quietly.

Close-remembered loneliness sniffed at the edge of this warm circle. But she didn't want to speak her loneliness here, that would be like spitting at the stars.

'No, I don't feel alone out here,' he said. 'Land is alive, like family, and I'm part of it. It's where I belong.'

Ella nodded, held her hands out toward the warmth. 'It's not the same, I know, but I've felt something like that when I write.' She had never tried to describe those rare glimpses that kept her wanting to write. She closed her eyes, took a deep breath in. 'It's like entering a living stream that dissolves me. I'm connected to the family of everything, and everything is in me, all possibility. And for a moment I remember I'm part of something larger, vast, that I can't yet know, discovering it as it arrives on to the page, barely held in words.'

She opened her eyes and tilted her head back so that she could see only the night sky. 'Then it's gone. Leaving an imprint that turns to longing, like hunger.' She felt the precipice of words where understanding hung over an abyss of unknowing, an impasse beyond which she had never been.

They sat in shared stillness for long minutes without edges.

Tom's voice seemed to melt into the night. 'Words can barely hold that mystery of deep belonging. Sometimes in a poem …' He began reciting: 'But oft in lonely rooms, and mid the din.. these wild secluded scenes… return… Sweet sensations in the blood, with tranquil restoration.'

His eyes met hers, bright with firelight. He took a deep breath in, and continued, staring into some far-off place. His voice deeper, unfaltering. 'For I have learned to look on nature and have felt a presence that disturbs me with joy. A sense sublime of something more interfused. Whose dwelling is the light of setting suns .. and living air. A motion of spirit that impels and rolls through everything. Anchor and guardian of my heart.'

Ella held her breath and waited.

He turned towards the fire. 'Sorry Will. Reckon I completely butchered that.'

'Hm?'

'Wordsworth.'

'Works for me.'

He didn't look up. His voice lower now. 'At boarding school I started memorising poems. Recited them at night when I couldn't sleep. Homesick.'

'Hiraeth?'

His eyes met hers. Questioning.

'Hiraeth. It's a Welsh word meaning nostalgia or homesickness. A longing for a place, real or sometimes imagined.'

He nodded and reached down to pat Penny's head.

'Hmm,' she exhaled. 'Yeah. Poetry speaks into that loneliness of longing. Maybe all poets are lonely and that's why they write.'

'Maybe.' Penny rolled over and he scratched her belly. 'And dogs. You're never alone when you've got a dog.' Harry raised an eyebrow and regarded them through slitted eyes. Sully slept on, her back leg twitching as she chased a dream rabbit.

***

'Were you just talking to that tree?'

Tom jumped back from the giant eucalypt, pulling his palms from the huge rough expanse of trunk and shoving them into his pocket. A magpie called to his brother across morning air that was filling with warm light, insects humming.

'You *were* talking to it, weren't you?'

'He's my friend.'

'Yeah, guess it does look Entish,' Ella said with a laugh.

There was an echo of mirth in his voice, 'A fool sees not the same tree that a wise man sees,' he said, still with his back to her.

'I guess I'm the fool then?'

'That's not what I meant.' His posture became more upright, 'The tree which moves some to tears of joy is in the eyes of others only a green thing which stands in the way.'

'Stop throwing cliches at me.'

'So, Blake's a cliche, is he?' Teasing.

'Just stop avoiding my question.'

'Well …' Tom toed the ground with one dusty boot. 'Mostly I find people strange and difficult. I'd rather talk to a tree any day. They're more hardy friends.' She heard the grin in his voice.

'Thanks a lot.'

'Present company excepted, of course.' He still didn't look at her. 'Compared to the rest of the natural world, the human voice is ugly. A monotonous drone.'

'Is it that bad?'

'Haven't you been walking in the bush, taking in the sounds and smells, the beauty and serenity of it?' He turned now and met her eyes. 'Immersed in the place. Then you hear human voices and it breaks the spell. Even if you can't hear what they're saying. As if humans suck up all the space, invade everything with their great need.'

Thoughts catapulted through her mind, leaping to defend the species. What about singing? How about a baby gurgling? Lovers whispering on dark nights? But she also knew there was truth in what he said.

'We don't listen,' he said. We are so full of our own small importance that we have to spread it, voice it. We don't need to find our *voices* … as people go on about. We need to find our silence. Our stillness. Learn to listen.'

As if the music in a child's game had stopped, they stood still. Hot air hung with the buzzing hum of the bush; the tang of eucalypt pinched their nostrils, refreshing their senses. Sticky flies, hungry for moisture, crowded eyes, nose, ears and mouth. Ella broke the spell, flicking her hand across the dark irritation. The flies scattered, returned a breath later, her hand still waving.

Tom reached out and again pressed his palm against the tree. When he spoke, his voice sounded different. 'Tree says: I'm here, I'm alive.' He paused, eyes sweeping wide, 'Land, wind, dirt, alive. All talking …'

A crow cawed loudly. They both looked up into the wide grey-green canopy of eucalypt. It was sitting in one of the higher branches of the old tree.

'And crow, talking.' Tom half-laughed, a puff of chuckle.

'Ca-a-a,' the crow replied.

'All different voices.' He closed his eyes in a long blink, still with his hand on the bark. 'We need to listen.'

Ella tasted the salt-truth of it. Fell quiet as a thin membrane of small-self stretched out to listen and call back, joining that wild chorus of things. She stepped towards the huge eucalypt and self-consciously pressed her ear against the rough trunk.

'Listen from inside,' Tom said close behind, making a thumping sound. 'You are part of it …' he drew in a long breath, 'all.'

You are part of it. His words echoed around the cavity inside her. She closed her eyes, pressed the length of her torso against the great trunk, palms flat, fingers splayed, cheek to warm bark. Inhaled the complex layers of eucalyptus scent, rupturing deep receptors in her brain, skin memories too close to recognise. Sensed the strength and warmth of the ancient tree. Life moving through it. And listened through some other possibility. Was that a tiny pulse against her palms? Against her chest, where their hearts met? A different pulse to her own familiar beat. Without warning, something shifted. That small thing of this-is-me separate from other, a tight sense of certainty, buckled and surrendered into largeness, becoming tree. She opened her eyes and the feeling vanished.

Newly aware of Tom close beside her, she felt exposed and pulled away. *Tree hugger.* A childhood friend's cruel words and laughter rang in her head, though she couldn't remember the scene. Only the shame of it in her small-kid body.

They packed up and for a while rode without talking.

'A friend of mine,' Tom said eventually, 'a good friend, once told me that the trees are our ancestors. And the trees sang humans into existence because they were lonely.' He leant down and patted his horse's mane, unsettling a soft cloud of dust. 'I never forgot it. Each tree has a particular character, like an old friend or grandmother.'

***

The water in the spring was milky-soft aquamarine, artesian. Almost too hot to swim in, reddening the skin on contact.

'We don't know if it's natural, or one of the early bores that someone abandoned. But it's been here for a while. My grandfather brought some of the big rocks in and planted the trees,' Tom said, pointing to the white cedars scattered with deciduous exotics that created a rambling garden around the spring. Off to one side, down an incline, was a stand of desert oaks like craggy sentries.

'It's hard to tell because we've been riding all morning, but we're back close to the boundary of our properties. Eldorado homestead's closer than home, only about three clicks that way. Rough old track though.'

'It's beautiful.' Ella felt at once expanded and tiny, as if she were a speck of dust in an eternity of desert. She helped Tom gather kindling and watched as he put the billy on for an early lunch before the ride home. 'So beautiful.' But the words seemed insufficient to hold or express this experience of opening her heart, letting all the world sing in, as if in belonging. Beauty, yes. Beauty as poetry, as Tom said. She picked up a long, crooked stick and drew in the dirt, her mind quiet, allowing herself to be present.

'Dadirri.'

'What?' She looked up from her stick drawing.

'Dadirri.' He was standing over the fire, watching her.

'Never heard of it. What does it mean?'

'That's hard. It's an Aboriginal word. A friend showed me.' Tom leaned down and shuffled the billy closer to the fire.

Same friend? A girlfriend maybe? Tom manoeuvred the billy with a fat stick. She knew to wait. Let him take his time. The fire hissed as a trickle of water spilled from the billy. Tom lifted his eyes to meet hers. She nodded slightly, willing him to go on.

He took a deep breath, like a diver about to leap. 'It's an experience of stillness … deep listening, to the land … but also … maybe … your own heart. Like they are connected. The land and … as if there is an inner spring that flows between us, you and the land, me and the land.'

Her skin prickled. Her body knew there was something here, some profound thirst within her responded to those words as if they were drops of moisture. And she was so, so thirsty.

'It's about our relationship with the land. Indigenous people are born into it. It's in everyone. But most have forgotten it.' A quiver of emotion crossed his face in an expression that had become familiar to Ella – a soft sorrow, close and distant at once. He turned and walked towards his horse, pulled the lunch bag from his saddle pack.

She rested her forearms on her knees, waited. The silence grew louder. She listened, wanting Tom to keep talking. Didn't know if she could find it on her own. 'It's strong here,' she said.

Tom nodded, bending over the fire.

'How do you spell it?'

He straightened. 'D-a-d-i, double-r-i. An Aboriginal friend used to talk about it when I was a kid. It sounded more like Dadidi. I thought it was just her word. Something she made up like the stories. Years later I read an article. It's a thing.'

The friend again.

He continued, 'You can't really understand it in words or concepts; it's a feeling, an experience of body, of land. An experience of belonging. Belonging with the land.' His eyes fixed on the far horizon. 'Like you are part of a song and you join in with your own particular harmony. Like poetry.' He brought his attention back to lunch preparations, unrolling a plastic wrap. 'It's hard to put into words.'

'Like speaking tree?'

He grinned and shrugged his shoulders. 'I guess.'

After lunch they lay in the shade on a tartan blanket, each with their hat over their head, listening to the quiet hum of the land. It seeped in through Ella's skin, trickled down into her veins and curled in, possessed her. She sensed a familiar fragrance tinged with sweet sadness. It mingled with the land, clung to her nostrils, an old memory waiting.

Her father felt close. Yes, it was his land too. She remembered the way he'd walked the land, held it open for her, showing her small miracles when she was a child. His love of the land was the familiar fragrance that Tom evoked in the way he loved and tracked the earth, like a tender, sad song that hung in her chest, making her breath thick and slow.

She sat up with a jolt. Must have fallen asleep. A pleasant dream of walking the farm with her father. Sully was flopped in the shade of a tree down near the spring, crunching loudly on a dry bone. Harry, with his head on crossed paws beside Penny, watched Sully. Sharp teeth cracked against the grey-white knuckle of bone, dirt around her snout. Ella shook her head.

'Why can't you be more like Harry or Penny?' she said. Harry shuffled forward for a pat. 'Always into mischief, isn't she, boy?' She stroked

Harry's head, and his tail soft-clapped against the red dirt, raising a small cloud of dust.

'Come on, better get going,' Tom said, looking at his watch.

Ella felt groggy from her dream. 'Funny that you wear a watch. I thought you'd use desert time.'

'Need to get moving before that sun bakes us alive.'

Chapter 5

You sit in the same room every day. Everything is familiar. Unexpectedly, the light changes. A brightness pierces the gap in the curtain, illuminating the room with new wonder. Your gaze shifts. You look around the room through this close stranger's eyes. What was invisible has become visible. A fine layer of dust on everything reveals fingerprints and other markings. There is remembering under dust. Nothing has changed and everything is different.

Voices of the land stir, old songs roll over to sniff the possibility – *a listening heart?* Emu song and rock song, moon and sky and eagle, deep voice of grandfather tree, all waiting to tell. One blood, one song-beat humming in breath and teeth, under bones. Your body remembers this, your first language, your mother-tongue. Your infant fingers reaching out to touch and taste, then laughing, grinning back. Awake to every voice and flutter murmuring in the old song of earth and homecoming.

***

Next morning Ella wrote in a frenzy. It was as if the presence of the land was still alive in her. Not just in the ache of her muscles from the ride but deeper down. The way a striking line of poetry lands in the filament of your heart. Then on some bleak, far-off night, as the heart muscle contracts against fear or closes around unsayable pain, the strings across the mouth of your heart strain tight. And the melody of that line, of that place, plays through you again, a quivering beacon of hope.

Bright rememberings opened up, a river of words poured through her. *Rememory.* Where had she heard that word before? Her memory felt alive, reweaving fresh memories as she wrote. Her brain drilled down into old foundations, let in light, turned each discovery over and washed it in imagination and sensuous detail. She was listening. Deep listening to something she couldn't quite name. It was as if all her words, all her writing, was an attempt to know that thing – a song she couldn't quite remember:

the sound of her father's voice as he called the dog or the scent of lavender in her grandmother's garden as they picked strawberries hiding under green foliage. She cried and laughed and wrote it all down.

Hours later she walked the land around Eldorado homestead. The trees were animated in the hot wind, whispering ancient songs. A gnarled and stunted tree bent like a grumpy old man, arthritic-bulbous and thick-skinned. A moon-white trunk, in graceful arc-and-twist against blue-blue sky. Salmon belly-pink bark, smooth and shiny-scaled, covered in tiny jagged lines of ants marching to the top. She had a kid's skin-and-bone memory of tree. Climbing, hugging, inhaling, hiding in trees that held her close, the playmate that every farm kid knows. She stroked the copper-green skin of a eucalypt. It was warm, alive. Why can't I love people like trees? Harry nuzzled her leg. She scratched his head. Or dogs?

'Or birds?' She looked up as a galah emerged from a carbuncle on the tree and swaggered along a sturdy branch. His little pale grey suit and bright pink chest were unkempt, like he'd had a rough night.

'You look like you're just getting home from a B-and-S ball, mate,' she grinned up at the galah. Another small tousled head popped out and looked around. 'Ah, been on the nest?' Ella chuckled at the galah, who was watching his sweetheart scramble from the nest.

Turning for home, she called, 'Come on, boy. Sully, here, girl.' Sully appeared from behind low scrub, covered in dirt, carrying a filthy black bone. 'You're disgusting, Sully. Come on. Too hot out here.' She jog-walked towards the homestead, Harry beside her, Sully trotting behind, carrying her stinking prize, grinning drool.

Ella veered off the track to the mailbox. Pulled up the flap on the drum and saw an envelope with her name on it. Inside was a page covered on both sides with neat handwriting. Must be from Tom. She smiled as she read, *The actual lines from Wordsworth, not my bungled recital.* She read aloud as she walked. Turned the page.

'And a bit of Hesse from the borrowed book': written in Tom's neat hand.

'Trees are sanctuaries. Whoever knows how to speak to them...' she stumbled on a pothole in the gravelled track. Slowed her pace and continued reading, 'whoever knows how to listen to them, can learn the truth ... the ancient law of life ...'

She stopped in the middle of the road, Harry on his haunches, watching her. She squatted, eye-to-eye with Harry and stroked his head, 'You already know the truth, don't you, boy?'

Out of nowhere Sully barrelled between them, knocking Ella onto her backside. Sully nuzzled Ella so hard against her chest that she rolled back and lay on the ground as the dog licked her face excitedly. The scrap of paper was snatched up in a gust of wind.

'Get off, Sully,' she said laughing, trying to push the dog away. Harry looked on, slapping his tail hard. 'You're the sage, Mr Harry. Can't you be more like him, Sully, you mad thing?' She hugged the dog against her chest as she sat up. 'Augh, you stink. What've you been rolling in?' She pushed the dog away and jumped up to chase the skittish scrap of paper. Sully barked, joined in this new chasing game. Finally Ella stomped on the paper and shoved it into her pocket.

Each morning she wrote. The land crowded on to the page like a neglected child, this near arid-tough landscape, along with *rememories* of her childhood home, her father. The land ran through her hard and fast; her fingers raced to take it all down. Dadirri, yes-yes, she invited.

Beloved, by Toni Morrison. Yes, that's where she had read that word *rememory*. She thought of it as living, twisting sinews of memory coming alive and writhing under the skin, old memories breaking open until they thrummed in her veins. What had the psychologist called it? Body memory. Her mind sprang back to her most recent psychologist, Dr Dunne, Dr Portia Dunne. The court case, and months leading up to it. That night.

A frozen chunk of time broke away, shuddered into close full view, dragging the whole heartache open. The stone wall of forgetting cracked, ruptured those hard-to-reach places that sat on the other side of logic and thought, beyond words. Her animal body awoke. That animal body of desire and belonging and humming mitochondria, now the crouching animal of survival. Her breath shallowed, eyes narrowed into dark tunnels of watchfulness, heart drummed its wild beat, signalling alarm, muscles contracting, ready. As cracks opened inside the icy thing that had held back remembering, she fell and fell, fell awake.

Marion, senior nurse on night duty, had come in while Ella was waiting for the intern. A textbook nurse with no common sense, Ella's nemesis. They circled each other when they worked together, like two dogs with a bone between them. Ella tried to keep out of Marion's way, which was easy because Marion usually locked herself in the nurse's station, pretending to be busy. Except when she came out to micro-manage Ella.

After checking the baby's obs, Marion looked at the small, dark-eyed mother with the awkward English, and said loudly as if the woman was deaf, 'Take the baby home, give it some Panadol and keep the fluids up.'

It's a *him*, Ella wanted to say. Instead she said, 'I've called for the intern,' and put a hand on the woman's shoulder to keep her in the chair.

'No need for that. The intern has more important things to do than look at floppy babies who need to be home in bed under a cool face-washer.'

'There's something not quite right here, I'm sure of it. It won't hurt to check him over.'

'Ella, I'd like a word outside, please.'

They stepped outside the cubicle and talked in a loud whisper.

'We don't have time to waste on every anxious mother whose baby has a raised temp. The intern is run off his feet. You always overreact to mothers with floppy babies. And don't forget, I'm the one in charge here.'

'Malcolm's already on his way,' Ella replied, her voice taut with restrained fury.

After Malcolm left, Ella read the label slowly to the woman. 'Bring him back if he gets any worse, and come and find me, okay?'

'Okay.' The woman smiled up at Ella, her lips trembling. She grabbed Ella's hand between her own small, clammy warm ones, and kissed it. Ella smiled back awkwardly. I'm only doing my job, she wanted to say, but stayed silent, letting the woman hold her hand.

Later that night Sam found her in the dispensary.

'That woman came back with the baby. The migrant mother. She was upset, asking for you. I couldn't find you.'

'What happened?'

'Marion heard her and came out. Gave bub the once over and sent her home again. She was practically yelling at her. Talked at her like she was an idiot.'

'Shit. Shit. Shit.' Ella turned in circles, scanning around the small room as if the answer hung on a shelf. A buzzer sounded and Ella followed the sound.

An hour later the small, dark-eyed mother had run in, looking around wildly.

That particularly greasy membrane-of-memory stirred, writhed under her skin, ready to strike. Her throat contracted, mouth dry, she felt the I-can't-breathe-feeling grab her chest.

'Stop it, Ella. Stop it. Don't go there,' she whispered into the hot air.

She slammed the laptop shut and jumped up. Pulled on her cleanest dirty socks and runners. Grabbed a cap and water bottle and leapt down the steps two at a time, calling the dogs. Harry and Sully wriggled out from under the house, tails wagging. She ran and ran until sweat poured out of her and her body trembled, letting the crazy heat burn away the clotted memories that threatened to break loose.

*****

Ella picked up the urgent, ringing phone and put it to her ear.

'You'd better batten down the hatches,' Tom said, 'there's a dust storm coming.'

'Oh. What do I need to do?'

'Close every door and window in the place and put anything you can find along the gaps. Dust gets into everything.'

'Okay. Thanks.'

'And it's coming fast. You can see it coming in from the west. Lock the dogs in the laundry, they go wild in these storms. Ours started going berserk about an hour ago. Got to go and check the stock. See ya.'

'See ya.'

Ella stepped on to the veranda, bare feet pressing into the smooth-grit of dust covering the boards, and looked towards the west. It was as if a dark-fisted genie had been loosed from its bottle and was spilling across the horizon. Dread boiled up from her belly. She looked around the yard and whistled. 'Here Sully, Harry, here, boy.' There was no sign of them.

She went inside and pulled on her boots, clomped down the front steps, and bent to peer under the house. 'Here, Harry,' she called, 'Sully, where are you?' She thought she could see a stirring in the dark shadows at the back. Crawling under the house, she called softly, screwing up her face as cobwebs snagged her and she snatched them off. Then she heard the familiar soft-slap of tail and smelt cool dust. As her eyes adjusted, she saw Harry in the far corner.

'What's the matter, boy?' As she drew closer, she smelt blood. She reached out to touch Harry's front paw. He growled softly, withdrawing his paw protectively. 'You in pain, boy?' Her eyes darted left and right. 'Where's Sully?' Harry licked his paw and whimpered. 'Shit, shit, shit.' She'd been so lost in her writing that she hadn't checked the dogs since early morning when she let them outside. She peered around the dim underbelly of the house. Nothing stirred.

Where's Sully? Liam's words flashed in. On that first morning, what had he said? 'Someone'll shoot them. Keep them locked up.' Why hadn't she kept them locked up? 'Sully,' she whispered. Harry whimpered.

Turning quickly, she bumped her head. 'Fuck!' Scowling, she crawled back out, stood up and dashed the cobwebs off her face and out of her hair. She ran around the house, through the row of oleander bushes to the sheds, calling until her voice grew hoarse. The sullen dark shape on the horizon prowled closer.

'Where are you, Sully?' An image of Sully's grin flicked behind her eyes. 'Do something, Ella. *Do* something.' She spoke loudly, feeling strength return with a burst of determination. A flash came of Sully at the spring, chewing those bones she had found. 'The spring. Yes.'

Heart drumming wildly, bare legs in heavy boots pounding the earth. Breath in hard gasps. Behind her the bruise-fisted storm knuckled down the late afternoon. She stumbled on the corrugated track. Almost out of breath, she climbed through the fence with a quick backward squint, knowing the storm was almost upon her. She pushed herself through a heavy blanket of exhaustion and heaved her body the last two hundred metres.

At the hot spring she doubled over gasping, resting a hand against the rough warm bark of a craggy gum tree. She gagged. The air was fierce with fine dust. She licked her lips and tried to swallow but her throat was too dry.

'Sully! Sully, here, girl.' She ran calling, words falling into red-dust-air, as feeble as a child's slap against the wrath of a drunken brute. Her eyes darted and blinked, searching through the now swirling storm-dark. 'Sully, here girl! Come *on*.'

There was no response, only the burning howl of wind. She'd been so certain Sully would be here with her big stupid grin, tail wagging, old bone in her mouth. She had imagined herself finding the dog and giving her what for before they raced home together, relieved and safe. She wanted to cry. She looked behind. The full force of the storm was bearing down fast.

She called again, 'Sully! Sully! Here, girl!'

The storm struck. Everything was dust, writhing-biting dust. Rushing to a small cedar tree for protection she saw, through thick claret-stained air, a dark shape protruding from behind the tree. She moved towards it. The storm howled against her, stabbing at her eyes. Dust, like needles, pricked her skin. It was Sully's limp body, dark patches covering matted fur on the chest and front legs. She bent and touched the tacky fur. Blood. A deep wound where the bullet had penetrated the upper belly. '*No, no-o-o!*' she wailed into the wind as it howled back.

Kneeling, she tried to lift the lifeless bulk, but it flopped through her hands. Head down, she grunted and shoved her arms under the dog and lifted it against her chest. It was still warm, but cooling. She collapsed under the weight of it. Fell, and fell into that other body memory, the weight of death in her arms.

Her body remembered with exquisite precision the breathless shock of that small lifeless baby cradled in her arms, his perfect pale face, eyes closed. She had held the baby close, wanting to protect him. The memory imprinted like a dark stain under her skin. And then another memory was there, like a familiar smell without a name. Older, buried deeper in her bones, it had waited, swelling, the way a tumour invades dark crevices, feeding on living tissue. You don't know it's there until it's too late.

Ella howled, an animal sound that met the wind and red dust, burning in her ears against throbbing blood. She laid her head against Sully's hide and gave herself up. Sobs jerked her body like a plastic bag tossed on a frenetic wind.

Finally she stirred, gently laid Sully back down, and made for the house. She ran headlong into the dark broiling storm that beat against the purple-bruised blur of sky-and-land, strangling the remaining day. She ran until her lungs were on fire, then walked, then ran, between sobs. Her breath came in hard gasps of dust-thick air. Gagging, she pulled her T-shirt up over her mouth and nose and slowed her pace. It was impossible to keep running into the storm along the rough, pitted road. She could barely see more than an arm's length ahead. All she could think about was getting home to Harry.

The storm ripped at her clothes and belted into her face, stinging from the fine-spiked needles of dust-wind. She raised her free arm to shield her eyes from the biting dust that felt like sandpaper inside her eyelids. It was hard, so hard to breathe. The dark above grew darker and darker; the air was a red-to-pink bloom and the sun a hazy bloodshot eye.

The worst of it was over by the time she stumbled through the gate into the yard. She staggered up the front steps and through the door. Only then did she realise that all the doors and windows were still open. Now her tears burst like breaking pipes, spilling down her face, stinging tracks across her cheeks.

Sobbing, she climbed under the house and crawled to Harry. He was whimpering quietly. She put her arms around him, buried her face in his pelt and sobbed. Harry howled a kind of strange mourning song. 'Sorry, Harry, sorry,' she kept muttering, 'Sorry. Sully, sorry.'

It was dark when she woke. It took a few moments to remember where she was and why. Sadness returned sharply to poke her bones, dig its teeth into her heart. She groaned. Harry licked her face and she hugged his dirty hide.

'Come on, Harry. One thing at a time,' she said. 'Come on, boy.' She tugged at his collar, trying to coax him out from under the house so that she could take a good look at his leg. But Harry gave a soft growl and pulled against her hand. 'You stubborn old mutt. Come on, Harry, please. Sully is dead. Dead. I can't let you die too.' Tears leaked down her face. She swallowed a sob. *'Please*, Harry, come on, *please.'* But Harry laid his head on the ground and closed his eyes. 'Oh, suit yourself then, stupid old mutt. It's your fault for going off like that anyway.'

She turned and banged her head. 'Fuck, fuck, fuck! I hate this fucking place!' Crawling out into the soft darkness of night, she stumbled towards the dog kennels and the drum of dog biscuits. The image of Sully's body alone under the tree sprang up. She died alone. Poor Sully. She brushed the tears away with the back of her arm.

Fumbling to find Harry's bowl, she filled it with water from the silhouette of tap, grabbed a handful of dog biscuits from the drum and shoved them into the pocket of her shorts. Awkwardly, she crawled back under the house with the supplies and sat the water bowl in front of Harry. He didn't stir. She rolled on to her side and stretched out her leg to free the dog biscuits and put them close to Harry's nose. He didn't move or open his eyes.

Ella patted his big soft head and bent to kiss it. 'Don't die, Harry, please don't die. I'll come and see you first thing in the morning. Sorry Harry. You stupid mutt. Don't die Harry, please don't die.' She turned and bumped her head again, growled through clenched teeth.

Once on the veranda she registered the clear night sky. It was hard to believe that only a few hours ago the sky had been a ferocious yowie unleashed. Now it was infinitely quiet. She pulled off her boots at the door and felt fine dust under her bare feet in the hallway. She flicked the light switch. Nothing. She flicked it several more times, willing it to bring light. Stumbling along the dark hall, she stubbed her little toe. 'Aa-agh!' she screamed to the ceiling, 'Gimme a break, stop picking on me!'

In the kitchen she stood momentarily frozen in the doorway as a chaos of thoughts flooded her brain, a scramble she couldn't unravel. Forcing her legs to move, she staggered to the table, sat down and laid her head on her arms. She wanted to cry, to run away. She sat resting her head on her arms with a blank inside her as if she'd blown a fuse, had a blackout in her brain.

A sound came to her. Movement. The front door creaked. She held her breath and waited. Someone was there in the darkness coming up the hallway. She listened with her whole being, every sense straining as the sound came towards her. Then she heard soft clicking beneath panting breath and rushed towards Harry.

He was limping and panting hard. She patted his head and guided him into the kitchen. He flopped on to the floor. 'Hold on, I'll make you a bed,' she said, and groped along the hallway wall towards the linen press. In the dark she pulled at the neatly folded linen, grabbed whatever came free easily and bundled it into her arms.

She made a lumpy bed on the floor next to Harry and tried to move him on to it. 'Good boy, come on, Harry, help me, you stubborn old thing.' But after a lot of grunting and shoving she gave up and left Harry where he was.

A wave of weariness hit her like a rubbery fist. She sank to the floor and rolled on to the mess of bed she'd just made for Harry, wrapped her arms around him and fell asleep before she took her next breath.

Chapter 6

Hard banging woke her. Bright daylight streamed through the glass doors, smacked her in the eyes. She blinked. Confused and groggy, hot, tacky with sweat. No, blood, dried blood. She looked around in panic. There was no sign of the dog, only a smear where he'd lain next to her. 'Harry, Harry?' Suddenly she became aware of eyes looking down at her through the glass doors.

Tom lifted a hand slowly in an open palm wave. He was frowning. She staggered to her feet, walked towards the door on unsteady legs.

'Ella, what happened?' Tom rushed in, concern creasing his face. He helped her towards a chair at the table that was covered in fine red dust. 'Sit here. I'll get you a drink.' He came back quickly with a glass of water.

She held it in both hands like a mug of hot soup and gulped. Gasping when she had finished, she held out the glass. He took it and refilled it. God, had she ever been so thirsty? As she drank in large gulps, she watched him foraging in cupboards. He pulled out a white plastic jug, filled it with water and sat it on the table.

'I'll make you a cup of tea,' he said, putting a hand on her shoulder. She felt the warmth through her T-shirt. But it was too-quick gone, leaving a sudden cooling emptiness.

'Harry,' she whispered, trying to stand, but half-falling as her legs wobbled. How could her body be so weak? How could it betray her like this? The hand was back, this time two hands pressing her down into the chair.

'Just sit there till I get you something to eat. How long since you've eaten?'

She pushed her mind back over the past few days to find some semblance of food. She ran through the dark storm and Sully's lifeless body. A sick, hollow feeling oozed in with remembering. But there was no food to be seen amongst her tangled memories.

'Breakfast yesterday,' she said, 'no, maybe that was the day before.' Her voice was a whisper, her throat dry and raw. Tom poured her another glass of water. She drank in a trance, staring out into the bright day.

'Thought so. I'll cook you breakfast.'

No power, she didn't say, sipping the water.

'Power was only off for a couple of hours, so stuff in the freezer should be okay. Do you know how to start the generator?' Her mind flashed to Hans showing her the generator, instructing her in his strongly accented English how to start it. But she hadn't even thought of the generator last night. 'I'll find some bacon and make you a big breakfast,' he continued, looking in the fridge. He plucked out a carton of eggs.

Shit, the chooks. Fuck. She hadn't checked them since the storm. Well before the storm. She'd do it after breakfast. Staring out into the glaring heat of day, she sipped water, her mind blank.

Ella's stomach growled loudly at the smells Tom was conjuring at the stove. By the time he placed in front of her a plate loaded with bacon and eggs, and toast covered in melting butter, she knew she was famished.

Tom poured himself a mug of tea and watched her eat greedily. She made soft grunting noises as she gobbled and chewed, sighing her way through the plate of food. Only when she had scoffed two eggs and four rashers of bacon and was slowly nibbling the second piece of toast did she lean back in her chair and sip at her tea. Sugary, milky tea that tasted good, so good, the best cup of tea she had ever tasted, and she hadn't taken sugar in her tea since she was a kid. She smiled at Tom. He rubbed a hand across his mouth and she mirrored the gesture, removing crumbs of buttery toast.

'What happened here last night? What's with the blood?' Tom paused and looked out the glass doors, where heat pressed in like a wild animal caged and barely contained. 'When I saw you lying there, blood all over your clothes, I thought you were … I thought it was your blood.'

'Oh god, Tom.' She instinctively reached across and put her hand on his arm. Quickly pulled it away. 'It's Harry's blood. He was shot.' Tears sprang to her eyes and she brushed them away and looked outside.

'Damn. That's the way of things out here. Law of the land. If a dog's out chasing sheep, they eventually kill. Farmers shoot to protect stock.'

Rage burned her throat and she clenched her jaw. Patriarchal rules protecting the ones in power, she wanted to spit out. But the guy had just cooked her breakfast, so she looked out the window and shook her head. Why does it have to be so tough, so brutal? Everything's so hard out here, wild like the land? But her thoughts of blame and frustration, like a loaded shotgun, rounded back on her, took aim and fired. She'd been warned. It was her fault Sully was dead. Harry injured. Yes, this was all her fault. She wasn't sure if she had spoken, the words sounded so loud. She sipped her tea and stared out the window.

'Where's Harry now?'

'Probably under the house. He came in last night and slept in here but he must have gone back down during the night.' Dread stabbed her like a blunt knife. She wanted to leap up, find Harry, but knew she couldn't bear to find him flat and lifeless like Sully.

'And where's the other dog, the young kelpie?'

'Dead.' She glared up at Tom, ready to tell him to stick his fucking rules up his fucking arse. But she saw the tears in his eyes and the violence washed out of her, leaving her as wilted as a wildflower picked and left out in the sun.

'I'm sorry this happened Ella. I hate this place sometimes,' Tom said, shaking his head.

She stared at him, at the strange blow of recognition that echoed her feelings. 'Then why do you live out here if you hate it so much?'

Tom met her gaze, his black eyes shining, drilling in. 'Because it's my home. This dirt is in my blood.' He paused. Tapped his hands on his knees. 'We'd better find Harry. Are you feeling strong enough?' There was a hard edge to his voice now. As if she had tripped an invisible wire that set off the tough side of Tom MacDonald, switching off the sweet man who had just cooked her breakfast.

When they didn't find Harry under the house, she was sure he'd be at the spring with Sully. She pushed out the other thought scratching to come in: that Harry had gone off somewhere to die.

Tom's ute was a diesel Toyota, the same as Liam's, but white. The cab smelled of grease, dust and hard work. Her mind jumped back to the trips into the pub with Liam and Tom, riding between them. The pinching pain was there again, the body memory of Liam like cold metal around her heart. She caught sight of her face in the side mirror as they bounced along the track. Almost cried out. Her face was covered in red dust, streaked where the tears had run. She spat on the tips of her fingers and tried to wipe off the fine red mask without Tom noticing.

'Yeah, I didn't know whether I should mention your face or not.' He kept his eyes on the road, but she sensed the smile behind the words.

'I look like a madwoman.' She pulled down the mirror behind the visor, rubbing at her face furiously. Tom slid her an amused sideways glance but said nothing.

She quickly gave up; rubbing her face with spit just made mud, like streaked cake make-up. Her face felt as if it had been dragged along bitumen where the wind had scored it. She watched the blushing land bumping past. Everything had taken on a reddish glow, almost as if it had snowed red-pink but finer. How wild and terrible the sky had been yesterday afternoon when she'd run home in the storm. It was so quiet now, peaceful, the way a violent drunk falls asleep after the horrors he has inflicted on the innocents around him.

Tom pulled up at the fence near the spring in a cloud of dust. He held the fence apart while she climbed through. They walked the last two hundred metres in silence. Something in Tom's mood frightened her. He was a MacDonald too. But that line of thinking was ripped away at the sight of Harry lying motionless next to Sully.

'Oh Harry, please don't be dead.' She ran to the two bodies. As she came closer, she saw that crows had picked out Sully's eyes, leaving hollow cavities. A thick mat of flies covered the dried blood on Sully's carcass and buzzed around Harry's injured foot.

'I'll get a shovel,' Tom said, and jogged back towards the ute.

She lay her head against Harry's chest. He was still breathing. He looked so peaceful. She thought of him limping all the way here to be with his mate, and fat tears rolled down her stinging cheeks on to his filthy coat.

Tom strode towards her with a shovel over his shoulder like a soldier carrying a loaded gun.

'Harry's still alive, we have to get him to the vet.' She tried picking the dog up, but he was too heavy for her.

'Vet won't be out for another week. Best put him out of his misery, poor old fella,' Tom said, bending to stroke Harry's head. 'I'll get the gun,' he said, standing.

'*No!* I can't let him die, I can't. I won't.' She tried to lift him again.

Tom shook his head. 'Here, let me help if you're so determined.' He scooped Harry up in his arms and grunted as he walked back towards the vehicle, stumbling occasionally on the pebbled ground. He called over his shoulder, 'There's a blue tarp in the back of the ute – you can cover the dog up till we can come back to bury her.'

She overtook Tom and held the fence apart for him to get through with Harry, then grabbed the tarp and ran back to Sully. She tucked it over her like a warm blanket over a small child and dumped four large rocks on each corner. The ute was running when she climbed in, Harry lying on a blanket between them.

'I don't think he's going to make it. It'd be kinder to put him down,' Tom said, staring straight ahead.

'*No!*' she wailed, as if something had come unhinged and taken possession of her voice. 'No, I won't. If you won't help me, just take me home and I'll go and find a vet on my own.'

'No vet for hours. Harry'd be dead before you got there. No point.'

Ella felt the frustration of powerlessness burning in her chest. 'I can't let him die.' She half-choked on the words, swallowed. 'I won't.'

Tom reached across and patted her arm. 'Well, there is Queenie,' he said.

'Queenie?'

'An Aboriginal woman. Nungkari.'

Ella frowned.

'Healer. Some say she's mad as a cut snake. But one time when Mum was sick we took her down there. Ted didn't know. I was only a kid …' Tom trailed off, shaking his head. 'She might be able to help. Lives down in one of the camps near the creek.'

'Anything's worth a try,' she whispered. 'Thanks, Tom.'

As they parked under the speckled shade of a huge eucalypt, five or six dogs of different colours and sizes rushed up to meet them, snapping and barking at the car.

'Wait here,' Tom said, 'she doesn't like strangers. She may not see us.'

Ella kept her hand on Harry as the dogs followed Tom towards the house, jumping up at him, barking, but not snarling. The door opened and a young woman, a girl maybe, looked out from the shadows. Tom stood at the door, talking. He turned towards Ella and waved, then disappeared inside. She stroked Harry's ears while she watched the house. It looked deserted; not even the dogs stirred now.

At last the door opened and Tom and the young woman emerged. Her eyes met Ella's as Tom strode towards the ute. Ella wound down the window. Hot air and sticky black flies rushed in, crawling over her face and into her eyes, landing on Harry's mangled paw.

'Yep, she'll look at Harry,' Tom said, opening the door. He stood aside while she jumped down. The biggest dog sauntered over and sniffed her crotch. She shooed him off but the dog persisted. Tom growled and hissed between his teeth, 'Get out of it!' The dog backed away then trotted towards the shade where the other dogs were collapsed in a crowd of fur and tails.

Tom gathered Harry's flaccid body awkwardly into his arms. Harry opened an eye and closed it again as if too tired to care that someone was carrying him into a strange camp surrounded by other dogs.

'You wait here,' Tom said to her, hugging Harry against his chest. The dog's legs flopped out in front.

'No, I'm coming in.' Her tone made the camp dogs raise their heads to stare at her.

'She doesn't trust strangers. It'll be worse if you make a scene. Trust me. Wait here.'

Ella felt a surge of limp-fisted rage. That tight familiar feeling of being held down, trapped by rules and other people telling her what to do. Rules she didn't understand. She climbed back into the vehicle, felt the cool relief of the air-conditioned cabin, swatted a pesky fly.

The feeling of powerlessness was a toxic chemical that she knew could erode her insides, eat into her sense of purpose and confidence. Eat away reason, even her sense of identity. As the feeling bit hard, her mind tore back into those last twelve months at work, memories quivering on the brink, spilling over.

After the baby had died, waiting for the court case was like being trapped in a slowly sinking ship. Cold water rising around the ankles, rising and rising. The conflict worsened with Marion, the unit manager who had been on duty that night, with subtle bullying that no one else witnessed directly, though the other nurses knew what went on. She rostered Ella on every weekend. Lates followed by an early shift, especially on a Sunday morning. Allocated the toughest patients. Badgered about case notes. Checked and micromanaged all her work. They both knew it was Marion who was responsible for that baby's death. Before the court case Ella still believed in justice, that Marion would get what she deserved. Understood that rules existed to protect the innocent. She laughed out loud. Her laugh filled the cabin, and with a jolt she remembered where she was.

Ella focused on Queenie's front door. It seemed like decades before Tom emerged, his arms empty. He strode towards the vehicle, eyes on the ground. The dogs didn't stir.

'What did she say? Will he live? When can I see Harry?'

Tom ignored her questions and stared straight ahead as he drove. His mood was as impenetrable as granite. Ella gave up and stared out the dusty window into the bright-hot day, watching sparse scrub and scraggly trees flash past. The silence blistered between them like the soft spot in a boot after a long walk, and she felt watery resentment fermenting. What is his fucking problem? I haven't done anything wrong, so why is he stonewalling me? You're just like your brother, Tom MacDonald.

As they reached the turnoff, Tom slowed to turn left towards the spring.

'Just let me out here,' she said, voice tight.

'But we need to bury Sully,' Tom said.

'I'll do it myself.' She reached for the door handle. 'I want to get out now.' A swirl of red dust choked into the cabin as she opened the door. Tom stamped on the brake. She leapt from the vehicle while it was still moving, landing with a thump on the packed red dirt. The ute stopped and she slammed the door shut. 'Thanks, Tom.' She stomped off across the dry paddock towards the house, not responding when Tom beeped the horn as he turned and drove away.

The main door of the house stood open, the flyscreen door the only thin skin between the interior and the cruel heat of day. Inside the hallway she groaned. There was red dust everywhere. It'd have to wait. She clomped through the house in her boots, flicked on the kettle and closed her eyes at the blood on the floor mixed with crumpled linen and red dust. Fuck. One thing at a time.

The back door slapped shut behind her and she strode across the yard to fetch a shovel from the roasting-hot shed. The warm wood of the handle felt smooth and comforting in her palms. On the way back to the house she detoured to check the chooks. The corpse of an old black hen was lying against the fence, covered in ants, eyes gone.

'Fuck. This fucking place.' Inside the coop the other chooks were gasping, the water dish empty. 'Fuck, fuck, fuck!' Dropping the shovel, she turned on the tap above the water bowl and let it run over. The chooks flared out of the coop as the water gushed, bent and raised their beaks again and again, drinking in life.

Ella manoeuvred the dead bird on to the shovel, carried it out of the pen and laid it in the shade of a large oleander. She dug in close to the trunk, but the ground was like concrete. Sweat poured down her face as she worked, grunting. She made do with a shallow grave. Knew that if Sully was here she'd dig it up in no time. But Sully wasn't here. Would never be here again. What am I going to tell Hans and Maria, or Jacob? Don't want to bother them with all this while they're away. No. Let them enjoy their holiday. Besides, they are working dogs, not pets. But a memory flashed in – waving Hans and Maria off the morning after she arrived. Hans hugging Harry. Harry's face when they drove away. Hans loved the old dog. Please don't die, Harry, please, please …

Inside she filled her largest water bottle and made a pot of tea. The greasy frying pan from breakfast had become a frenzy of feasting ants. She dropped it into the sink on top of all the other dirty dishes, set the water running and watched the ants scatter towards survival.

She sat at the kitchen table sipping milky tea from a delicate china cup, the only clean thing left in the cupboard other than a plastic wine glass. For a moment she thought about taking her car but knew the track to the spring was too rough for her little Corolla. There was a farm bike in the shed but she hadn't ridden a motorbike for years and didn't even know if it would start. The farm ute was an old Land Cruiser, a manual. It was so hot, but maybe a walk would clear her frustrated fury. She needed open space to get away from her stuffy thoughts.

Holding the shovel over her shoulder like a rice farmer, she set off down the track. The sun was high overhead. She felt the empty space where Sully and Harry usually trotted beside her, but no tears came. Her anger was building a wall where those soft tears had leached out of her. She was damming it up as she always did. Safer that way. Her thoughts pinged back to the MacDonald brothers like a too-tight elastic band. 'Stop it, Ella,' she scolded aloud, and dragged her attention to the landscape. Plugged herself into the day. 'Here and now, here and now, it's all there is, baby.' Far up in the blue-bright sky, an eagle circled. 'Here and now,' she called out, cackling at her own rough wisdom.

As she relaxed into the rhythm of walking, her mind drifted back to the court case. The unfairness. Those sad, dark eyes of the small mother, standing hunched and alone in the dock. She had looked like a tiny bird. Stumbled over thickly accented words as she gave evidence, quivering as she wept. There was no comfort for the mother. And Marion. So direct and clear. Certain she had done what was necessary. Invincible stone heart.

By the time Ella arrived at the spring, her T-shirt was dark with sweat. The day felt airless, waiting, like the silent waiting before the first handful of dirt is thrown in on the coffin, when all the talking is done. She had gone to the baby's funeral. A graveside service. It was raining. The little mother dressed in black, her large husband standing beside her in a suit, awkward. His attention was everywhere but on that small white coffin being lowered into the wet earth. He found Ella's eyes, frowned and looked away.

As the coffin disappeared, she remembered the weight of the small lifeless body in her arms. The woman wailed, her heart tearing open. Ella had sobbed and put a hand over her mouth to stem the despair. She had no right to take up the grieving space. It belonged to the family. Who was she to these people, this infant whom she had held only in death? She touched the mother's arm when the service was over. The woman didn't look up. Blind with grief.

Ella let the shovel slip to the ground as she climbed through the fence, her shoulder aching from the weight of it. The rocks still anchored the blue tarp and the lump beneath it. When she tried digging into the ground nearby in several places the shovel bounced off the surface. Everywhere she tried was like stone. Now she wished she hadn't sent Tom away in such a hurry. She sat down and opened her pack, fishing for her water bottle. Gasped. There was no water bottle. 'Shit, shit, shit. Wake up, Ella!' She pictured it sitting near the sink, felt her thirst come alive, clawing inside her throat. Alarm rising in her. Not just the thirst. But that she had forgotten to bring water. 'You idiot. Wake up, Ella.' Her voice a growl against still air.

Kneeling at the spring, she scooped hot water into her hands. It tasted of rotten eggs but she gulped it down anyway, burning her throat. She beat her fist against the ground. 'Ow!' she yelled as the side of her hand hit a sharp rock and started to bleed. 'Fuck, fuck, fuck! What am I doing in this fucking hellhole?' she yelled at the crows sitting in the tree above Sully. She picked up the rock and threw it at them. They scattered, landed again a moment later.

Tears of frustration spilt down her cheeks and she knuckled them away with filthy hands that made her eyes sting. She wrenched off her clothes and lowered herself into the spring. Hot water burned her skin, every cut and scratch on her body stung. It felt good. The pain felt good. Better than feeling hopeless. She floated light as a leaf, letting the hot artesian water burn into her.

Ella flinched reflexively as a shadow struck her face. At first she thought it was something that had fallen into the water. She looked up and saw a blurry figure. Wondered for a moment if the figure was real or imagined, and rubbed her eyes with her fists. But the figure only grew clearer, silhouetted. She was instantly aware of her nakedness.

'Tom?'

'Hello, girlie,' said a deep gravel of voice. 'Bit hot for a swim in that, isn't it?'

She swam to the other side so the sun wasn't behind the figure, circling towards her abandoned clothes. She wanted to lift her arm to shade her eyes from the sun so she could see the man's features, but held them down hugging her breasts, aware of the soft milk-clarity of the water.

'I thought this was private property,' she said, trying to sound brave.

'Yes, my property.'

Who is he? Tom had said the spring was on their property.

The man continued, interrupting her thoughts. 'Mad dogs and Englishmen go out in the midday sun.' He paused as if enjoying his captive audience, 'Shouldn't be out in this heat. Can give you sunstroke.'

'Yes, I'm heading back now, thanks.'

'You want a lift home?'

'Um …' It was tempting; she'd been dreading the walk home since she'd realised she'd forgotten her water bottle. But she didn't trust this guy. The way he'd snuck up on her. The way he called her girlie and she couldn't even see his face properly. 'Um …'

'Those boys worry about you over there on your own.'

'Boys?'

'Liam and Tom.'

'Oh, you're Mr MacDonald?'

'Ted, everyone calls me Ted,' he said, touching his hat.

'Um, yeah, a lift might be good but … um.'

'Okay, I'll go and bring the Rover around while you get dressed. Back in a blink.' And with that the silhouette strode off over the rise and disappeared.

She dragged herself out of the water, heavy as lead. All she could think about was lying down in the shade. She knew she had to get out of this heat and get some water into her body. She pulled on her crackling hot clothes and within moments her skin was dry.

Ella heard the vehicle before it appeared around a rocky mound. She hauled herself up into the cool cabin. Ted talked about the drought, the dryness of the land, as he drove. She stole a few glances at the side of his face. Noticed a lump in his cheek, wanted to stare at it. But next time she looked it was gone. He was sucking something. That explained what sounded like a soft speech impediment. She could see he had once been handsome. But now the face was cracked and beaten by the weather, rugged like the land and bitten by dry wind with the bright-veined nose and cheeks of a heavy drinker.

He handed her a round tin and she opened it. Inside were small, round, dark lollies. She was thirsty and took one. Aniseed. She screwed up her face, sucking hard on the round brittle lolly. Replacing the lid, she shoved it into the console overflowing with dusty paraphernalia. Her mouth filled with saliva around the sweet-burnt taste.

They drove along the worst of the bumpy track on the MacDonald property. Once on the side of the homestead, the road levelled.

'You need to be careful out here in this heat, girlie,' Ted said. 'Place kills people.'

I'm not a fucking idiot. Don't treat me like an idiot. And I'm not your girlie. She sucked hard on the lolly. Lips pressed together to stop words erupting that she might regret. But another thought charged in fast behind.

She *had* acted like an idiot. Wandering out into the heat at midday, forgetting her water bottle. Spending so much time in the sun without a hat. She put a hand to her face; it was burning. Sunburn. She knew the heat out here could kill.

'People come out here from the city and think they can wander around like it's a picnic. This place will kill you if you're not prepared.'

The warning sounded like a threat. I get it. I get it. I know. Okay. 'Yes, thanks, Mr MacDonald,' she said quietly. They passed the MacDonald homestead, the sign over the gate naming it Melville. An enormous eucalypt stood over the back yard. Green lawns all around. Her eyes drank the green. The garden was beautiful. The house rambling and elegant. She saw a figure in the window. Liam? Tom?

'It's beautiful, Mr MacDonald.'

'Yes. It is.'

Ella watched the garden for as long as she could. She was so thirsty for green. Thirsty for beauty. As they turned out the gate towards Eldorado, she asked, 'Are you a gardener?'

'Nope, not me.'

'But your garden is … unexpected out here. In the drought.'

'My wife loved that garden. We've still got the same gardener.' She heard the clack of lolly as it shifted against his teeth. 'Old as Methuselah, tough as old boots. Outlive the lot of us, I reckon. Tom gives him a hand. Bit of a greenie, our Tom. Always different, that one.' His voice held a tinge of regret. About his wife? Or Tom being different or a greenie?

When Eldorado came into view Ted said, 'I've told Tom to stay away from that black witch.'

She felt the punch-shock of his words. Blood rushed to her face, enraged by his racist, sexist, brutish words. 'You mean Queenie?' she said, through clenching teeth.

'Yes, that black bitch.' He paused, drew in breath, 'You city folk come out here and think you know how it is …'

She sucked hard at the burnt sweet of aniseed.

'You've got no idea. No idea,' he said as the vehicle rolled up in front of the house and stopped.

'Thanks, Mr MacDonald.' She didn't look at him.

'Ted, call me Ted.' He smiled, showing stained and crooked teeth.

You're a Ted alright. She said 'Ted' as if it was a glob of slime in her mouth. Didn't smile.

'I've told Tom not to go back to the black camp. Suggest you stay away from that place too if you know what's good for you.'

Is he threatening me? 'Tom's a big boy, Mr MacDonald. I'm sure he'll make up his own mind.' She jumped out of the cabin, slammed the door and marched up the front steps. Kept her eyes straight ahead, shoulders erect as the car drove away. Once inside, her body sagged.

Ella trudged along the hallway, leaving footprints in the red dust floor. A wall of heat struck her in the face as she entered the kitchen; the curtains were wide open, letting in the full blast of sun. The room was in chaos: dried blood and a tangle of linen on the floor, fine pink dust covering everything, greasy frypan and dirty dishes in the sink, ants everywhere. It was hard to believe it was still the same day that Tom had cooked her breakfast.

She stood at the sink, gulping water from the plastic wine glass. Her body still felt like lead. All she wanted was to lie down but she needed to bury Sully before dark, hated thinking of her body lying out there another night all alone. She pulled off her boots and walked around every room, assessing the storm damage. Only the lounge room and Hans's study, which had been closed up, had escaped the dust, mostly.

She showered, trying to wash off Ted's hateful words, muttering to herself about not speaking up against racism and misogyny. The argument grew loud in her mind. She let Ted have it, the imagined argument filling her thoughts as water ran over her burning body.

'Stop it, Ella,' she said aloud, lifting her eyes to the stained ceiling. Note to self: don't talk to anyone who isn't here.

Why didn't she speak up to pricks like that? Bullies like Marion? She was voiceless when she faced them. Then she gave them what for afterwards, told them what she thought, in her head. Memories romped in of other times she hadn't spoken up, times she'd kept the peace instead of expressing her point of view.

'You're a coward, Ella,' she said to the bathroom mirror as she dried herself.

One of her writing teachers had told the class that people wrote because they'd been silent or invisible, unable to speak up. When she'd heard it, she thought it was just more writer's poppycock. But now, staring into the mirror, she wondered if it were true.

Naked, she headed down the hallway, eyeing the old-fashioned heavy black telephone as she walked past. She wished she could call Jaz, or Corey, but they'd be at work. Everyone would be at work. Maria had asked her not to call mobiles from the landline unless it was an emergency. But her friends only had mobiles. 'Fucking place. Hate this fucking place.' She went into the coolish chaos of the bedroom, rifled through the piles of clothes on the floor and found the cleanest items. Note to self: do some washing.

I'll just lie down for a minute. Just for one minute. Her body sank into the bed and it felt so good.

Chapter 7

Eyes tearing open. Body rigid. Skin damp with sweat. Heart pounding. The whole world drumming in her ears.

Ella strained to listen. Yes, someone calling her name. It sounded far away, but not a dream. As she bolted towards the back door, the banging grew louder. She pulled back the curtain to reveal Tom standing behind the glass, a worried frown beneath the rim of his hat.

'We'll have to stop meeting like this,' she said, opening the door.

'I was worried about you. I've been banging on the door for ages.'

'I must've fallen asleep.' Behind Tom the sun was falling into the darkening line of horizon. 'Want to come in for a cuppa, or a drink?'

'Ted said he saw you at the spring. Did you bury the dog?'

She shook her head. 'Ground was like rock.'

'I knew you'd never find the right place to dig. But you're so stubborn.' He said it without smile or accusation, just stating a fact.

'Sometimes,' she said.

'I came to help.'

The image of Sully's corpse lying under the tree flashed behind her eyes. 'I'll get my boots.'

'Okay, meet you around the front.'

As the car bounced over the rough track, she stole a side glance at Tom. He was like his father and yet so different. 'Sorry if I was a bit short today. It's been a rough day.' She wished she could talk to him about feeling shut out and powerless, his awful father cursing Queenie, but she didn't want to pick at the uneasy peace between them in case it unravelled. Now that she'd met his father she understood why Tom was remote sometimes. Who wouldn't be, growing up in the same house with a horrible man who calls a woman a black bitch?

'I won't be able to go back to Queenie's,' Tom said, interrupting her hijacker mind.

Her eyebrows jolted up in sting-of-surprise disbelief. She waited as a scrabble of words churned in her mind, rushing towards her mouth ready to burst out. But she kept her lips squeezed tight, waiting for the right words to speak. Don't let that old bastard tell you what to do, he's a racist, sexist pig. Oh really, um how is your relationship with your dad, anything you want to tell me? Well, fuck you … turns out you're just like your brother … and so how am I meant to get Harry back? She was so busy rummaging through the rag-and-bone mess of her thoughts that she missed what Tom was saying.

'… understand, Ella.'

'What? I missed that,' she said, almost yelling above the grinding engine.

'I said, you don't understand.'

Blood rushed to her face. What is it with these fucking MacDonald men that they think I don't understand? That I'm some stupid city chick who doesn't *get* anything? Breathe Ella, breathe. 'What don't I understand?' she said in a tight voice.

'About my father. About Queenie. About this place.'

'Care to enlighten me?' She heard the mocking tone in her voice.

'We don't talk about it. No one talks about it.'

'Maybe it's time you did.' Maybe you all need fucking therapy. At least one of you needs locking up. Her mind snapped to attention at the sight of the spring through the fence. She could see a mass of crows in the distance, crowding over the flapping blue tarp.

The moment the Toyota stopped she flung open the door, jumped down and clambered through the fence, shorts snagging on barbed wire. She tore herself free and ran to chase the crows away. They croaked and cawed and flew off before she reached them.

'Oh, Sully.' She stared down at the dog's face, covered with ants, teeth exposed in a leering grin, flies buzzing in a thick black cloud. Some of the fur had been pecked away from her head, leaving an open wound. She put her hands over her face, 'Oh, Sully, I'm so sorry,' breath ragged around indistinct wet words. She jumped when Tom put a hand on her shoulder.

Tears rolled down her face. Tears in Tom's eyes too. Wiping her nose with the back of her hand, she said, 'I feel so bad I let this happen. Now look what the crows and ants have done. I *hate* this awful place.'

Tom held her against his chest. She smelt dust and work in the tough fabric of his shirt, her breath coming in the gasping sobs of little girl lost. She leant into him, hardly caring who he was or what he was, just needing the comfort of a warm body.

'It's getting dark, we need to get the dog buried while there's still light,' he said gently, but with a firmness that made her step back. She fisted away tears and snot. Tom pressed a large, folded checked hanky into her hand. She wiped her eyes and blew her nose, offered it back.

'It's yours for keeps,' he said with a half-grin. She regarded the snotty damp material in her hand, exhaled a laughing breath and shoved it in her pocket.

'Okay.'

Ella followed Tom down towards a small huddle of trees a short distance from the spring. He stopped under a desert oak and started to dig. Circling behind, she noticed a small headstone beneath a neighbouring tree. Leaning to peer at it in the dimming light, she read aloud, 'Margaret (nee Ellis) MacDonald …' She couldn't read the dates, 'loved wife of Ted, beloved mother of Liam and Thomas.'

'It's the only place where the ground isn't hard as rock.' He spoke without looking up. 'Can you drag the dog down here on the tarp?'

'This is your mother's grave?' Half-question, half-statement.

'We don't have time for that. We need to hurry before the light's gone.'

She grunted and shoved, trying to drag Sully on to the tarp. It was covered in sticky, stinging ants.

Tom appeared at her side. 'Here, let me,' he said nudging her gently. 'Dead weight is always heavier than you think.'

She nodded and watched as he dragged the corpse on to the tarp, jumping back abruptly to brush ants from his hands and arms. 'I need to get the torch. You keep digging. I'll drag the tarp down.'

It was difficult to see under the desert oaks whispering to the wind. It was a shivering kind of whisper, like a mother hushing her babies to sleep after a long day. Squinting, she dug into the hole Tom had started. The shovel scraped and jarred as it hit something hard. Maybe a tree root? She tried again, slicing in at a different angle. The shovel scraped again. On hands and knees, she picked up a sharp rock and scratched at the dirt, revealing the outline of a long, pale object. 'Shit,' she cursed through gritted teeth, pulling hard. It didn't budge. She scratched away some more earth and pulled again, grunting loudly with the effort.

Tom appeared, dragging the tarp behind him. The flickering light from his headtorch bounced wildly in front of him. 'Ants everywhere,' he said, dropping the edge of the tarp, brushing his arms and hands furiously.

His torchlight shone into the hole. 'It's getting too dark. We need to hurry.'

'But there's something buried here. I can't get it out of the way,' she said, still trying to tug it free.

He took the shovel and started digging. It scraped and jarred. 'Damn,' he said, bending lower. She squatted and watched as Tom dug and scraped into the tough ground, shrunk to a sharp circle of light from the headtorch. To the west the last light was gone, only a hint of colour outlined the land.

Finally, he straightened, the object in his hands. They both understood what it was in the same moment, stared at each other, eyes wide.

'I think it's human,' Tom said in a hushed whisper, as if the ghost of the bone might be listening.

Her skin shivered. 'What do we do now?'

'Well, we can just ignore it. Looks like it's been here a long time.'

'But shouldn't we … report it or something?'

'There's no reason to think there's anything suspicious. Just an unmarked grave. Lots of them around here. Old miners who've fallen down holes, literally drunk themselves into the grave. But I don't know how this came to be here, so close to my mother's grave.'

'It's not a man's,' she said with certainty.

'No, too small for a man.'

'What should we do?'

'We need to sleep on it. It's been a big day. We can't make a decision right now. We'll cover it up. Better take the dog up to the house and bury her there. Don't want to dig up any more bones. We can decide what to do in the morning.'

'Good plan.' Her body felt heavy with exhaustion and she desperately wanted a cold beer. She swallowed and licked her lips.

Tom laid the bone back in the shallow grave. Together they threw dirt over it.

'Grab the other end,' Tom said, picking up one corner of the tarp, wincing and turning his nose away in disgust at the stench.

Gagging, they staggered to the ute and dropped the tarp in the back with a thud, jumped away, stamping their feet by crazed torchlight, arms flailing, trying to dislodge the ants.

***

Eyes open. Heart drumming wildly in her throat, a scream in her ears. The dream. Again. What's the time? 3.10am. Ella sat up and blinked at the night-lit shapes in the room around her, trying to remember herself back into her body from the cloying disorientation of the dream. She sensed the precipice close. Familiar panic rose from her belly where that yellow-eyed wolf lived, ready to pounce.

Tears stung her eyes. She knuckled them dry. This wasn't good crying that flushed out the detritus of a bad relationship, or let you hold open those sweet-ache memories wrapped in the pain of losing someone you love. It was the pathetic, poor-me-crying of a drunk locked outside, can't find her keys because they're hidden in her closed fist.

I'll take the dogs for a run. Use my headtorch. Yes. She swung her legs out from under the sheet, stood up. The memory of Sully's dead weight in her arms rushed in with the speed and force of a boot to the gut. She gagged, sank back on to the bed, rolled over and surrendered to the tears.

Each night the dream ended with that same lurid image. It had started when she was eleven, almost-twelve, when her mother left the farm and moved with Ella to Melbourne. She'd wake up screaming each night, sobbing inconsolably. Her rattled mother would come in to console her and she'd describe each dream, always ending with her father's bloody face. Ella begged to ring him in the middle of the night, but her mother would say, 'Wait till morning; just look at the photo of him on the bedside table.' After the first few months her mother grew impatient. Annoyed when Ella called out in the night. Told her to stop being silly and go back to sleep. It was just a dream. How could she have known it was a premonition? And after … after he … died, the dream came back, now with the gun in his hand. Her mother had sent her to a psychiatrist.

When the baby died, the dream returned. Her father's bloodied face staring at her, calling out silent anguished words that she could never understand or never remember. He was carrying a baby, holding it out to her, calling to her. She screamed. And the screaming woke her.

Now as the days came and went in a blur she realised how everything had revolved around the dogs: waking and sleeping, running, talking to them, feeding them. They had been the centre of her world out here. Without them there was nothing to hold back the gargoyles of loneliness and other prowling monsters. She felt trapped, bored and restless. She paced and wandered through the house when it was too hot outside to move. Meant to clean and do the washing; somehow it never seemed to get done. Tried to read, but her eyes slid across the page without understanding or remembering what she was reading, as if she had an oil slick over her mind that words couldn't penetrate. Writing: an impossibility. She felt numb-and-dumb as petrified wood on the outside, husk-hollow on the inside. She was tired, so tired, but afraid to sleep.

Something had changed with Tom. How could he listen to his stupid prick of a father, racist misogynist old Ted? Turned out Tom was just like his brother after all. Those first few days after they had buried Sully beneath the elm tree in the back yard, under the floodlight, they had both made an effort to relax with each other. But tension stifled the air between them, the silence growing rank as the unspeakables crowded larger: Tom's father, Queenie, and of course Liam. Tom hadn't dropped in for at least a week. She missed him but refused to be the one to make the call. She'd done nothing wrong. She reached for her journal.

***

Caught in the maelstrom between your longing for that deeper hidden thing that you can never name and the hot throb of animal instinct urging you to run, *escape*, you lurch and buck like a sinking ship inside a storm. Arms outstretched, you reach for something to grab on to, to save yourself. Wrists bound to the crosstree of the topmast by habits of your past, ears unplugged, you struggle against the sirens calling you into deeper waters, to drown in forgetting. The tug-o-war inside your being-becoming stretches your heart open to the wind, widening. Something dark and wet is crowning now, wanting to be born. Will it be the slouching beast or some immortal ideal, a poem, dancing star, a god perhaps, or some new question (turning primeval mystery that time forgot) ripe with possibility, of both in one, waking to sniff the air?

***

On her trips to town she scoured the library shelves for something to read that would let her escape her relentless mind. The books crowding Hans's shelves – Kafka and Dostoevsky, Proust didn't cut it as light relief but couldn't penetrate the thickening wall of meaninglessness either. Lil had suggested crime fiction or true crime. Ella was willing to try anything. She wandered along the shelves, touching books, trying to remember the names of the authors Lil had recommended.

'Can I help you?'

Ella jumped. Turned. A woman she'd never seen before stood a metre away holding several books beneath large breasts that bounced out like friendly puppies swathed in vivid fabric dotted in psychedelic fruits. A blue pear hugged her generous cleavage, a multicoloured apple sat on her shoulder. The name badge proclaimed 'Alicia'.

'Oh, hi. My friend recommended a few crime-fiction authors, but I can't remember them. Except Patricia Cornwell,' Ella said, glancing down at the two books she was holding.

'Do you like crime fiction?'

'Mmm. Never been my thing, but I need something to … well, I really need the unputdownable shelf.'

'Well, in that case maybe I can help. This is my first week.' Alicia smiled broadly, the thrill of books bright in her eyes. 'What do you love to read?'

Ella felt a squirm of embarrassment at her usual reading matter, prior to Hans's library. '*Lord of the Rings, Harry Potter* … fantasy. But I thought I'd try some more … mature reading. I'm a writer.'

'Oh, how wonderful. A writer.' The last word she enunciated as if remembering some faraway dream, and her eyes shone. Her attention shifted back to her customer. 'Now, Harry Potter for grown-ups, let's see. Let's see.'

By the time Ella left the library, she had two bags bulging with books. Compelling reading of all kinds.

Lil was right, crime fiction certainly held her attention. Snagged curiosity and conjured dread. She could disappear into another world even if it led into blind terror. Her imagination, engorged, grew into a feral thing, erupting with every creak of the old house, but at least it was an escape from her own demons. Until she shut the book.

When she fantasised about leaving, the image of an injured Harry arrested her mind – Harry limping, Harry losing his best mate – and she knew she had to stay. Wait for Harry to recover. Besides, what would she tell Jacob? He had treated her like family after she agreed to house-sit for his parents. She started counting the days and weeks until Maria and Hans returned. Less than six weeks. Yes, she could do it. For Harry.

Each night the old dream gatecrashed her sleep.

She stayed up late trying to anesthetise herself. Drank red wine, smoked rollies on the back veranda, maudlin with memories that lined up like ducks in a circus alley, until everything began to blur into a fugue of red wine and she could breathe again.

Tonight, an empty bottle of shiraz lay on the floorboards near her feet. The night sky, deep-freckled with stars, was so beautiful it made her heart ache. Slow tears rolled down her face.

'I can't do this. I can't go through this again,' she declared to the deep night. 'Make it stop, *please* make it stop.' Her voice was a howl clamped inside words. 'Just let me die, please let me die. I can't go through this again. *Please.*'

She drained the last of the wine from her glass and stubbed out the ragged rollie into the already full ashtray. Resting her head back against the couch, her thoughts drifted, body exhausted from the sleepless nights.

She felt her father, sweet memory, kid-skin close. Then other rememories slithered in from that last night when she'd left him there alone. She tried to remember what Aunt Rose had said, the words that always refused to come. Other gagged memories, cusping. She opened her eyes, seeking solace from the stars.

'Please stop. Please. Help me, Dad, help me.'

She pushed herself to remember the good things: his beautiful sun-brown face, weathered and worn by the earth, as if the land lived in his skin and lit his eyes. She found his smile amid her bric-a-brac mind, their long walks, their favourite places on the farm, planting trees together.

The wide silence of night hung close and large the way a father's strong arms carry their small sleepy child in from the car after a long day at the river. Sleep hung close. Held gently in that thin-strange space between waking and dreaming, she drifted into memory.

Rugged up against the cold, she had gone down the hallway and into her father's bedroom to say goodbye. Sat on the edge of his bed with a body sigh. The only time she felt truly at peace was when she was with her dad, where she belonged. It was strange seeing him in bed. She'd never known him to be sick until the past few weeks, and for the past two days he hadn't been out of bed.

'I'll be back Sunday night, Dad. Then I'll look after you. Get you better.'

He'd smiled and squeezed her hand, his blue eyes shining at her.

'I'd better go, I need to get back for this lecture,' she lied. It was a simple, soft lie to make it easier to escape back to Melbourne for the party, though she knew he'd want her to go anyway, have fun, rather than stay to nurse him. 'Aunt Rose'll be here tonight. She's leaving Melbourne early to beat the Friday night rush. She'll stay for the weekend and I'll be back Sunday night, okay?'

He patted her hand again. 'You go, love. I just need to rest.'

She hugged him. Buried her face against his neck and breathed in the scent of him. A safe, warm smell that made her body relax, like coming home. But his cosy smell was buried beneath the close, sour-sweet odour of sickness. The feel of his bony shoulders beneath the striped blue pyjamas shocked her. How had he become so thin? He hugged her in return but had little strength in his arms to hold her.

'I'll be back soon, Dad.'

She moved to leave but her father held her hand and said, 'Let me look at you, Ella. Let me look into your eyes.'

His blue eyes glistened. She felt a strange pang in leaving. Maybe she should stay. But Rose would arrive in a few hours. Reassuring herself, she smiled, reaching out to touch his cheek with the back of her fingers. 'You're a funny old thing. I'm only going for a couple of days. I know Melbourne seems like the end of the earth to you, but it's barely three hours away. I'll be back soon. Then I'll stay with you till you're better. I promise.'

'I love you, Ella, my beautiful girl. You're the best thing in my life.'

'And you're *my* best thing, Dad. I'm coming back to take care of you. I'll stay with you.'

He patted her hand. 'You'd better get going or you'll be driving in the dark.'

'There's soup in the fridge if you're hungry.'

'Go, love.' He dropped her hand.

She stood and kissed him on the forehead.

He smiled. 'I love you,' he whispered, eyes shining.

She turned, brushing away tears. Felt the pull to stay. But it was an old pull she had always felt since her parents' separation. She hated leaving him out here alone. But he never seemed to mind. Did he? He loved this place. She turned back at the door.

'Dad, maybe I should stay till Rose comes?' But her father was already asleep.

The party was in full swing when she checked her phone and saw three missed calls from Aunt Rose. Panic rose in her throat as she went outside to the relative quiet of the front yard.

She pressed Rose's number and paced, waiting.

'Ella, thank god. I've been calling and calling you.'

'What's up?'

'Ella, is there someone there with you? Someone to sit with?'

'I'm fine, Rose. My friends are inside. What is it?'

'Your father passed away. He was gone before I got here.'

She felt the world grow cold and sudden-dark. All light gone. Nothing to hold on to.

'Ella … Ella … Are you there?'

'No. *No*! It's not possible … I just saw him. *No*! It can't be.'

'You need to go and find your friends.'

'He died alone … I should never have left him. I knew I shouldn't have left him. I *knew*.' Her words tumbled out, aimless words, flooding into the phone. She sank on to damp grass, sobs erupting.

'You couldn't have known. I got here later than … The traffic was horrendous. But there was nothing we … Ella? Ella? Ella, can you hear me?'

Words. Meaningless noise.

She sobbed violently, the phone limp in her hand. She put a hand over her mouth to slow her breath, trying to stop panic taking over completely.

Her mind kept going over and over the same words: I should have been there. I should have been there …

'Ella … can you hear me?'

'I'm here.'

'Go and find your friends. Is there someone who can stay with you and take you home? Maybe you should call your mother.'

Ella became vaguely aware of a couple making out on a garden seat tucked under some bushes across the yard.

'You shouldn't be alone.'

'I'm coming out there now.'

'It's too late to come tonight. Have you been drinking?'

'I've had a few.' She knew it was more than a few. She'd been drinking hard since she arrived at the party, trying to forget the memory of her father's bony frame, the strange smell in his room, in his clothes, his eyes glistening and telling her he loved her as if he were saying goodbye. He *was* saying goodbye. Another sob erupted.

'You can't drive out tonight. Promise me you won't. There were roos everywhere. It's too dangerous. Find your friends and go home and have some sleep and come first thing in the morning. Promise me.'

'Okay, okay. I won't drive tonight … But I want to see him … where he is. Don't move him before I come. Please.'

'Ella …' the phone fell silent, the sentence unfinished. When Rose spoke again her voice was thick and wet. 'I had to call the police. They've been to look at the … look at him. They're taking care of it.'

Police? Her head was spinning. Nothing made sense. He was in bed sleeping when she left. She had to get back to see him before they took him away.

'He … he's …' Rose's voice choked and Ella held her breath, waiting.

Dead. Dead. Dead. The word, unspoken, hung in the air between them, between everything, like a veil, a wall between yesterday … no, today. It was still today, when she had hugged her father, and tomorrow, where he was dead … is dead … dead.

'Don't let them move anything till I get there. Promise me. And I'll promise not to come till the morning. I'll be there early.'

There was a long silence, then, 'Okay. Go and find a friend so you've got someone with you. And I'll see you in the morning. Love you, Ella.'

'Love you too, bye.'

She'd looked up at the sky and felt a vast silence, larger than the hum and jangle of the party spilling on to the street. Dad, oh Dad, I'm so sorry I left you there alone. I'm sorry, Dad. Sobs rose up out of her belly like bloated, slippery bubbles bursting into the air. She clamped a hand over her mouth. God, I need a drink.

She walked inside along the wide hallway, barely noticing couples locked in airless kisses against the wall, and went straight to the fridge. Ignoring the swaying figures in the kitchen, she plucked out the first cold thing her hand touched, headed back down the hallway, grabbed her backpack from behind the door and stepped out into the cold night. She tore off the top of the can and gulped down the fizzing liquid.

Alternating between sobbing and drinking, she stumbled along the side of the road, drained the can and threw it into the bushes in someone's front yard. Out on the busier road she hailed a taxi.

'Number 72 Gardener Avenue,' she told the driver as she slipped into the back seat. Her voice sounded strange. The taxi driver eyed her suspiciously in the rear-view mirror. She leaned her head against the seat and closed her eyes as the cab began to move. Everything started spinning. She bent forward, held her head in her hands and groaned.

'Hey, don't throw up in my cab. Hey, you hear me?' The taxi driver pulled over to the curb and stopped the car.

She raised her head, her face wet with tears. The driver turned on the light, making her blink, and said, 'Crying's okay though,' then more softly, 'You okay, love?'

She shook her head but didn't speak. Pressed her head down into her hands again as the taxi pulled out on to the road once more. All she could think about was her father out there alone. Alone. He died alone. The weeping started again. She wanted to howl.

She was bent over sobbing when the car door opened. She looked up into the huge floral belly of the man. The taxi driver had come around and opened the door. She hadn't noticed it stop.

'Come on, love, I'll help you inside.' The big man reached down and helped her out of the car. She let him. Stood like a lost child as he reached into the taxi, grabbed her small pack and handed it to her. She turned and let herself be guided up the front path.

'My father died,' she blurted out at the bottom step. Repeated the impossible truth, 'My father just died.' She collapsed into the arms of the big man, against his large belly, sobbing into his shoulder. The man patted her back and she felt small, so small.

There was a dark, slippery spot on his floral shirt when she raised her head. She tried to wipe it away.

'Sorry,' she said, barely controlling her shuddering breath.

'That's okay. Got a daughter about your age. She's always crying on my shirts and messing them up. Washes out. Sorry to hear about your dad.'

'Thanks,' she said, stepping back. 'Sorry ...' her voice trailed off. She didn't know what she was sorry for. She felt sorry for everything.

The big man put his arm around her gently, turned and guided her up the steps to the front door.

'Can you find your key, love?'

Usually she hated men using those pet names. But it felt nice when he said it. Warm, real. She fumbled in her pack and found her key. Put it in the lock and opened the door.

'You be alright now? Someone here to look after you?'

'I'll be okay, thanks. I'm okay.'

'You should have someone with you. Can you call a friend?' His voice held genuine concern.

'I'm good. Mum'll be home soon,' she lied. 'I'm fine, really. Thanks' The man was almost at his taxi when he turned and waved, opened the car door and was gone.

***

Ella woke with a start. Her whole body instantly pitched for listening. Was that a motor driving off? Heart thudding loudly, she held her breath, listening to the click-and-groan of the old house settling in for the night. She shivered. Her bladder shrieked and strained. She stood shakily. The house was in darkness except for the soft light above the stove. Shadows shuddered and shifted as she staggered into the kitchen. A loud creak. She stopped, held her breath again.

Moving quietly, without drawing breath, she slid the butcher's knife from the block, the handle heavy and smooth in her hand. It was the knife she had watched Tom sharpen to cut raw steaks. The fast-soft, slap-grating rhythm of the blade against stone was mesmerising. Then he'd put the blade to his forearm and run it up against the hairs, leaving a smooth path. Sliced into the deep-red flesh of fillet steak like it was butter.

Another creak. A floorboard? She shuddered. Holding the curved knife out in front, she pulled back her shoulders and went through the house turning on every light, opening every door. Checking each room.

'There's no one here. It's because the dogs are gone.' The sound of her voice was strange in her ears; it seemed to echo through the big house. Blinking out images that leapt up from her imagination ripened by the thrillers she'd been reading, she tried to talk herself out of the dread that huddled in her watery belly. But it was as hopeless as telling herself not to drink, not to smoke, not to cry, not to scream out in the nightmare.

She retraced her steps, the large knife dangling limply by her side, and stood in the doorway of each room once more, scanning. Her bladder could no longer be ignored, and she waddle-hopped to the bathroom, put the knife on the floor in front of the toilet and tugged frantically at the tight button on her shorts, sat just in time.

A loud creak. She clenched muscles mid-flow to stop her urine. Listened intently. 'It's nothing, Ella,' she whispered, just the house settling in for the night, cooling after the long, hard heat of day. She released her pelvic floor muscles, expelling air as her bladder emptied.

The knife. She couldn't take her eyes off it. She leant down, grunting as she grabbed the handle. Held the blade to the inside of her wrist, heart racing. She stared at the pale delicate skin inside her wrist, the intimate geography of blue veins pulsing life through her body, beating her heart. She lifted and turned the blade, pressing it against the thick, soft pad of her thumb. A line of blood appeared, bright red under the hard fluorescent light. A moment later she felt the stab of pain, as if her body needed time to process the hurt.

The blood oozed over her thumb and dripped on to the pale tiles in small splats. Holding the knife underneath her thumb, she let her blood drip on to the blade. She laid the flat of the blade against the soft inside flesh of her wrist and dragged it upward, leaving a vivid streak of blood. All her attention was on the blade, the blood. She stared at the streak of blood as if her life depended on it, as if there was some message in it that she couldn't understand.

She turned the blade and felt its fine sharp edge touching, tickling the delicate thin skin that protected her. Pain throbbed in her thumb. She sucked at it, tasting the sweet-metallic tang of her only beating life. Flung the knife to the floor. It clattered against the cold tiles, slid until it hit the wall.

Ella stood up shakily, pulled up her undies. A thick sob erupted as if it belonged to someone else, someone far away that she didn't know or couldn't remember. She washed her hands; a pink line of blood disappeared down the drain. A stranger stared back at her from the mirror. The unprotected anguish on that face made her heart ache, like watching a movie with a sad ending. She shook her head and the reflection blurred and bumped. She started laughing. 'Who are you, you crazy bitch?'

Chapter 8

'Hi, Ella.' Bruce rushed out the door of the butchery, rubbing his hands on a stained blue-and-white striped apron. 'Haven't seen you for weeks. I've been saving the best bones for those dogs of yours.'

'Hey Bruce. Yeah, the dogs … um … they were shot.'

'Fuck me. Who shot them?'

'Don't know. Some farmer, I guess. Harry's okay, probably lose a leg. But alive. Sully …' Tears pricked her eyes, her throat caught. She fired the word. 'Gone.'

'Gee, I'm sorry. I know how much you loved those dogs. Best entertainment I had all week, your dog stories. Can I get you something for the barbie? On the house.'

'No, thanks. Not much appetite lately.'

'Wait there, I'll get you a nice little fillet steak for your dinner. Have to keep your strength up.'

Before she could object, Bruce was back through the glass door, a tinkle of bell following. She waited in the shade of the awning, watching as he picked up a small steak and slipped it into a bag. His random act of kindness pierced through her defences: she felt something buckle and snap, and tears sprang out. She brushed them away with the back of her hand before Bruce returned.

'There you go. You look after yourself. I know how it is to lose someone you love.' He held her hand in both of his for a long moment as she took the small parcel. His large warm hands enveloped hers like a thick, soft coat on a freezing day. Warm-skin-of-kindness melting everything. Tears leaked down her face.

'That's it, you have a good cry. Good cry and a nice bit of steak – just what the doctor ordered.'

'Thanks, Bruce.' She laughed, trying to hold back the sob that was pushing upwards.

'See ya, Ella. Don't be a stranger.' Bruce opened the door into the shop, where a cushiony lady customer was waiting, watching them. She heard his big voice, muffled by the closing tinkle of door, 'What can I get for you today, Mrs G?'

Ella bolted towards the car, parked in half-hearted shade at the back of the main street. Once she'd slammed the door, shutting out the world, the sob erupted. She held her head in her hands and surrendered.

Finally she became aware of the stifling heat inside the car and the small parcel of steak lying in her lap. She plucked a freezer bag from the scrummage of mess on the passenger side floor and slipped the package in beside the melting freezer block. After rubbing her forearm down her face then blowing her nose on a used tissue, she stepped out of the car. A small huddle of young people sat smoking in the deeper shade at the back of the supermarket. One waved and Ella raised her hand. The young woman came towards her, taking one last drag before dropping the cigarette butt to the ground.

'Hey, sista.' The young woman's dark eyes regarded her. Ella frown-smiled. She looked familiar.

'You coming to see that Harry? He's missing you.'

She had a quick flash of Queenie's camp: the girl at the door.

'Oh, hi.' Ella's voice was spongy from crying. The small, ageless girl-woman stood before her, smiling as brightly and broadly as a clear desert morning. Ella thought of Lil. 'How is he? How's Harry?'

'He's good. Queenie's looking after him. He's doing good. You coming to see him?'

'I'd like that,' Ella said, wanting to explain how Tom had deserted her and she wasn't sure if she could find her way out to the camp again without him. 'Yes, I'll come soon.'

'Okay. See ya later then.'

'See ya.' Ella smiled as the girl turned away to join her friends, who were talking loudly and laughing. She walked around to the passenger door and pulled out more freezer bags. When she turned again the small huddle of faces was watching her, the girl at the centre talking; they ducked their heads abruptly.

Groceries, then call Jaz, then the pub. Mentally she ran through her plan as she passed the group, which ignored her as she headed for the small supermarket, keeping her eyes on the magpie pecking at something hidden inside a paper bag.

At the cemetery she listened to the three messages from Jaz on her phone, pressed call and waited, eyes wandering around the dust-bitten cemetery. She was about to hang up when a breathless voice answered.

'Hello, you …' He was breathing hard.

'You sound like you're having a heart attack.'

'Damn near am. Had to grab my phone and get out of the ward before bitch-face sprang me. Can't talk long. Just wanted to hear your voice.'

'Me too. It's been awful.' A sudden burst of sobbing made it hard to talk.

'What is it? What's wrong?'

'They shot the dogs.'

'Shit. Who shot the dogs?'

'I don't know. Some farmer. Maybe … MacDonald … Tom's brother … or father … I don't know.'

'Fucking arseholes.'

'Law of the land and all that, they keep telling me.'

'God, are you okay?'

'Not really. The dream is back. The old dream.'

'Oh, no. The one with your dad?'

'Yeah. I can't sleep.'

'You have to get out of there. You can't stay now.'

'One of the dogs is still alive, just, Harry. I've got to look after Harry. I can't desert him now that his mate's gone.'

'Ella, come home. You can't stay out there alone.'

'I can't come back, Jaz. Not yet, besides, I know the dream'll just follow me.'

'But at least you can get some help back here. What about that therapist, that last one when, you know, after the baby died? The court case?'

'I don't want to talk about it. Go over it all again.'

'But she helped, didn't she? You said she helped.'

'Yeah, I guess. I don't know. Once Harry's back I'll be okay.'

'Ring her. Promise me you'll ring her. Don't go back down that black hole. Remember we talked about doing it different next time.'

'Okay, okay. Don't do chook-ma, Jaz.'

'I'm worried about you.'

'I'm worried about me too.'

'Call her.' There was a loud noise and voices in the background. 'I have to go. Promise me you'll call her.'

'Okay, I promise.'

'Bye.' The phone went dead.

Ella slumped down on Mrs McGregor's cement platform and looked up at the headstone. 'I forgot to tell him about the bone we found. I wanted to tell someone. Someone normal. Not one of the ...' her voice trailed off. But Tom isn't just a brute like his father or his brother. He's also kind and gentle. So why is he avoiding me?

'I don't understand men, Mary,' she said to the headstone. 'Except queers, they're okay.'

***

During the night when the dream woke her screaming, she crawled out of bed and switched on every light in the house, opened every door. She played music full volume, Aretha filling the silence.

Her mind rolled back over the past few weeks, then folded in through time, pooling into the sessions she'd had with the most recent therapist. Psychologist Dr Dunne, Portia Dunne. 'Psycho-P' she had called her when talking to her friends. Yes, those sessions had helped her climb out of the black hole that had opened up and swallowed her after the baby died.

Looking ahead now there was only blackness, no way out. She had promised Jaz. But she didn't want to go over it all again. Relive the past, wake up her ghosts. Aren't they already awake? Yep, wide awake. Did Psycho-P really help or would I have recovered anyway?

In her bedroom, the overhead light glaring down, she caught sight of her reflection in the mirror. She smiled and waved at the sad stranger staring back. She moved towards herself, the unfamiliar reflection calling like a spell.

'Who are you?' she said to the reflection. 'What do you want? What do you really want?' There was no reply. That question fell into thick, warm air, like a deflating red balloon at the end of a child's party after the enchantment has broken.

She stepped over the piles of dirty clothes scattered around the floor and knelt in front of her large backpack, eased a wad of dog-eared papers from the top pocket and sat back on her heels, rifling through them.

'Gotcha.' The card for Dr Portia Dunne, Psychologist. She placed it on the bedside table and thought about Jaz. She missed him, her bestie. And her other Melbourne friends, Corey, Jenna and Mel.

She opened the door to Hans's library. Drew in a deep breath, taking in the fragrance of books and leather, and a bit of dog. Vesaas was lying face down on the coffee table where she had left him. She flopped on to the lounge and picked up *The Boat in the Evening*. Flicked through pages, stopping at a random page.

'Be drawn towards the slime? Don't think. Don't think. Climb away from the slime.'

How strange that the same writing spoke to her now, saying something different than when she'd read it weeks ago, before the dust storm. As if Vesaas understood her depression and despair, wrote into it. Used words like a sword to cut into the heart of things, allowing her to enter the tangle of her own despair and look it in the eyes.

'His own riddles walled him in … his own sorrow is there too. Sorrow that neither he nor anyone else can explain … He is not uttering any cries, yet it is I who am crying.'

She held the book against her chest, breathing in words like salty nourishment.

At first light she pulled on her runners and pushed open the front door. The air was cool and free of the relentless heat that she knew would hit the world like a hard fist once the sun boiled over the horizon. Her belly was full from the porridge she'd eaten at 4am when all other tactics of distraction had failed.

She burst into a run and felt tears prick her eyes, wishing the dogs were running beside her. Sully grinning up at her, rushing ahead, Harry trotting along beside, the loyal butler.

'Harry,' she whispered into the hot wind.

A flock of raucous galahs crowded an enormous eucalypt. 'Morning,' she called up as she trotted past, but they were too busy squabbling to notice her.

She jogged past sorrow, through the thick fug of loneliness, beyond thought, until she found the rhythm in her legs, endorphins kicking in. She swam along in a delicious sea of sweat and grunt, free from thoughts and feelings. There was only running.

Once through the fence she walked the last two hundred metres to the spring and pressed her palms against a white cedar to catch her breath. The sun was well over the horizon and burned her back. She scrambled up on to a boulder that gave her a view from above the trees, searching for any sign of dust. Nothing. The land around was still under the bright morning rolling in. She headed back down, stripped off her clothes and entered the aquamarine water.

Hot sulphur water burned her skin, penetrated her emptiness, drenching her with a warm flood of hope. It felt so good, almost too hot. She felt lightheaded. Dog paddling lazily, she scanned around the spring. Her gaze snagged involuntarily on the tree where she had found Sully's lifeless body. A livid image of the dog's eyes eaten away by crows, face crawling with ants and flies, made her flinch. She shook her head to dislodge the cruel memories. Moving to the side of the pool she rested her arms on the rocky edge, elbows making a bow, head on fists. So beautiful. Peaceful. She kicked her legs gently, staring into the shadows beneath the trees that sheltered the graves, the dirt disturbed where they had dug. She thought of the bone lying there and shivered.

Ella dragged herself out of the water, her body heavy and relaxed, pulled on a T-shirt and shoved her wet feet into her shoes. It was only about twenty metres down the gentle slope to the trees. She knelt and scooped away handfuls of loose warm earth until the long grey-white bone lay exposed. Lifting it from the dirt she brushed it off and peered at it closely. The radius. Held it against her own forearm. It was longer; it belonged to someone taller and finer-boned than Ella.

'Who are you? What happened to you? Why are you here?' She laid the bone gently back in the warm earth and covered it again before going across to the small headstone. Tom had been young when his mother died. Ted his only parent. Old MacDonald's ugly words echoed inside her head. No wonder Tom's got problems.

Back at the house she took off her sweaty clothes and stood under the shower. Her stomach growled. How can I be hungry again already?

Dressed in her cleanest clothes she headed barefoot to the kitchen, the grit of fine dust shifting under her feet. Her body felt good, clean, alive.

The stove clock read 9.56am. No wonder she was hungry. Breakfast was nearly six hours ago. She broke eggs, cut thick slices of stale frozen bread for toast and made a large pot of tea. She thought of Tom as she moved about the kitchen. She had left two messages for him in the past week, asking him to call. Why is he ignoring me? Does Liam listen to my messages? Instantly she felt exposed. They all knew about her. She had never been to their home. Never been invited. Hadn't seen Liam since that night. Didn't want to see him. Or Ted. And Tom is their brother, son. Blood's thicker than water.

***

Ella recognised the weariness around the doctor's eyes and other telltale signs of burnout. People didn't understand burnout, they thought it was caused by hearing too many sad or bad stories or witnessing too much suffering. But it wasn't the stories or the suffering that were the problem. It was the powerlessness mutating into hopelessness to do anything about the suffering being witnessed day in and day out. And sometimes, often, that powerlessness was created by administration and red tape, tying people's hands behind their backs, making it harder and harder to respond effectively. Always being watched and checked. Like the prying eyes of predatory senior nurses such as Marion, trying to tell people what to do, treating them like idiots. The system forcing people to witness and hold the suffering but taking away more and more power to do something about it.

She looked into his tired eyes. His voice, an exasperated grind. 'Didn't anyone warn you about the outback?' He was lecturing her about the heat, the comment she had made. 'This heat is nothing. Wait till we get a couple of weeks over 45. Then you'll know what hot is.'

I was only making polite fucking conversation, you dick, she didn't say. A surge of rage pounded her temples, reacting to his smugness, as if he was the expert on the desert, king of the outback. I have my own experience of desert, you drongo. Drongo? I haven't heard that for years. It's all inside your head, Ella. Who knows what junk and old words you'll find in there-here? The doctor's loud, grating voice interrupted her thoughts. He was staring at her, waiting.

'Sorry, I didn't hear the question.'

'I said what did you come for today?' That peevish sigh inside his words again.

'I need a script for antidepressants.'

'Oh, so you already know what you need, do you?'

Fuck you, you patronising old prick. She bit her lip, stared down at her hands and picked at ragged fingernails.

'And why do you think you need antidepressants?'

'Because I'm depressed.' She didn't look up.

'And who decided that?'

'I've been on them before.'

'Do you have your previous script?'

'No. I didn't bring it out here with me.'

He moaned. Or did she imagine it? She didn't want to look up. The silence stretched out like a lazy lizard in the sun, as if he had all the time in the world. Ella focused on the dead beetle on its back near the leg of the desk. Her skin itched. She needed to move. She looked up. He had a pained expression on his face. I didn't know someone was going to shoot the dogs and the nightmares would come back. Didn't know I was going to have sex with a brute. End up feeling like this again. She pressed her lips together.

'Why do people come out here without their medication?' Yes, he was definitely sighing now. And shaking his head. 'What were you on?'

'Fluoxetine.' Her voice sounded tight with the tension between wanting to get up and walk out and needing to play the game to get the meds. She knew about medication. Knew she didn't want to take it. But she was desperate, her mind slippery as a trout flicking beneath the dark mirror, sliding away beyond her control. All the signs were there: the close-forgotten-memory of losing her grip had returned since the dogs were shot. And now this fuckwit is looking down his nose at me, shaking his head like I'm a fifteen-year-old in the headmaster's office.

She put her index finger to her teeth, biting the ragged nail. It tore. The sting made her wince. There was blood where the nail bed was exposed, so vulnerable and pink. He was watching her closely, as if she were an insect he planned to dissect.

'Ella,' he said, his voice quiet, almost gentle. She felt drawn in and leant forward. 'Maybe this isn't the place to be if you're mentally unwell. Perhaps you need to return home to find appropriate support.'

Was that a question? Everyone's so sure they know what I need to do. But there's nothing back there for me. How could she explain her complicated jungle of feelings to this smug twat? She didn't understand them herself. This feeling of homelessness, that she didn't belong. It had been there since she could remember, whenever she was still. But the last twelve months in Melbourne had been much worse. Being an outsider with friends and family was worse than being alone. At least out here she *was* an outsider. And how could she go back after all the fanfare of leaving on her 'big desert adventure'? Return a loser. Failed adventurer. Return to what? To be trapped in a life that doesn't fit? At least when she was travelling there was the possibility of finding that missing thing that had no name. Better to die trying than surrender to normal and be eaten alive by boredom and loneliness.

'Ella?'

She straightened her shoulders, looked him in the eye with a defiance she didn't feel. 'I can't go back.' Her voice betrayed a hairline crack. She swallowed hard against the pressure of complicated emotions that wanted out.

But he had heard it. She saw the flicker in his gaze. Softening.

'Well, there's no support for you out here. No mental health services. You're asking me for help.'

'No, I'm asking you for medication. I can take care of myself.'

He looked out the window and his body seemed to sag around his heart. She stared at the side of his face and saw laughter lines etched deep. His face looked so set it was hard to imagine this man laughing. He turned slowly and their eyes met.

'I don't think you can get the help you need out here. I believe it would be remiss of me to prescribe antidepressants without further assessment and support, and those services aren't available out here. I think you should find somewhere to go that has good mental health services.'

'Thank you for your concern, doctor, but I can take care of myself. I know what I'm dealing with and what I need to do. I just need some pharmacotherapy to get me going.'

'Do you have a medical background?'

'I'm a registered nurse.' She felt the relief of solid ground under her feet. Yes, she could convince him with her professional background. 'I'm aware of medications and ...'

'Knowing about medication and what causes depression doesn't mean you can treat yourself. I think you need help. I am reluctant to give you medication without assessment and follow-up, and ongoing support.'

She felt the old desperation strangling her innards. Play nice Ella, play the game. She pulled out her last card, the trump.

'I have a psychologist in Melbourne I can contact. She treated me last time and said to call her if I had any concerns.' She saw his body relax as she told him about Dr Dunne, who specialised in post-traumatic stress.

'Excellent,' he said, picking up a pen and scribbling on the prescription pad on top of a pile of notes. Without looking up, he said, 'I want you to make another appointment for a follow-up with me in six weeks so we can see how you're doing.' He tore the script from the pad and handed it to her. She reached out her hand and her fingers closed around it, but he didn't release it. 'Okay, Ella?'

She nodded, pulling at the slip of paper, but he continued to hold it.

'And you will contact the psychologist to make an appointment and come back in six weeks?'

She knew she'd be gone by then. Just agree, Ella, get the meds. His eyes were locked on hers. 'Yes, I'll contact the psychologist. And yes, I'll make another appointment.' He released the paper and she folded it carefully, a smear of blood from her fingernail across the white page.

'There's one other thing.' The words pushed out. She heard herself speak what had barely registered, sensed the gut-truth of the words arriving, 'I think I might be pregnant.'

Chapter 9

Ella stood in the hallway staring down at the phone, but there was no blinking red light telling her that Tom had returned her calls. She pressed the button anyway. 'You have no new messages,' came the bright American female voice.

She picked up the phone and dialled the number on the card. Listened, then left a message, 'Hello, Dr Dunne. I don't know if you remember me … Um … I went out to the desert … you helped me … um … when the baby died … well, you said to ring…' and hung up.

Fuck, Ella. Get it together. What sort of message was that? For a long moment she thought about not ringing back to leave her name and number. She could tell Jaz and the prickly doctor that she *had* called the psychologist. It wouldn't be a lie. Did she really want to open that can of worms? No, maybe she'd leave it. An image of the doctor's face was bright and close in her mind's eye. Finger wagging, yet somehow kind. Genuinely concerned? She felt like a stupid teenager when she told him that she was pregnant. One fucking night. That first night with Liam. It must have been. They'd had vigorous sex, rough. Maybe a condom had broken. She had tried to ignore the signs. Sore breasts and hunger-nausea. The exhaustion. But it hadn't registered fully until she had spoken the words aloud to the doctor. As if speaking it made it true, truth as sharp as a knife, slashing hope through the belly of her dreams. Her body already knew it was true. Stupid Ella. So stupid.

She stared down at the phone as if waiting for it to speak. A memory flashed in, a slight murmuration of complex patterning. She needed to listen closely to the humming, to make sense of it. If you get a message twice, you'd better listen. She couldn't remember who had told her that. Was it that curvy storyteller she had dated for a while? Yes. In stories, if a message is given twice, it's important. So, you'd better listen. Failure to do so is *always* catastrophic. She picked up the phone and dialled the number again. Left her name and number and asked Dr Dunne to call her.

Shame arrived slowly, circling.

Shame had a particular physiology that wrapped people up in a stinking wet blanket, dragging them down. It was an ugly feeling, one to avoid at any cost. It wrapped around her now, seeped into tender places under the skin, into hollows and cracks, soaking into any comfort and turning it into rank wasteland.

How could I let this happen? She thought of the women she had known, friends and patients, who had unwanted pregnancies. She had judged them, shaming them in her head. For god's sake, don't you know about contraception? She wanted to spell it out for them, *con-tra-cep-tion*. Not to mention STIs and sexual health. She had worked in the sexual health unit for two years. Yeah, okay, she understood how younger women, teenagers, didn't take precautions and fell accidentally pregnant. But not at her age. She knew better. You're an idiot, Ella.

Next morning she was still sleeping when the phone rang. The bedside clock registered 9.08am. Scrambling, she banged her shoulder against the doorframe in her rush to pick up the phone.

'Hello?' she said, rubbing her shoulder.

'Ella? Ella Burns?'

'Yes.'

'It's Dr Portia Dunne. You left me a message?'

'Sorry about that garbled message … I'm not sure if you remember me?'

'Yes, of course I do, Ella. I had concerns about you going out to the desert alone after such a significant trauma, and so soon after the court case. Especially with your previous history.'

God, she sounds like a psychologist. Ella waited. She felt her resistance like a wall of water falling and crashing against her, sucking her away from this. But underneath the sucking away, behind the wall, was that familiar feeling of little girl lost, wanting someone to reach through the flood, take her hand and show her the way home.

'Ella, are you still there?'

'Yes, I'm here. Sorry, I got distracted.'

'Is something the matter? Has something happened?'

'Yes. Everything's back, worse than ever. The dreams are back. I can't stop crying. Can't stop shaking. I'm scared.' Her breath caught in her throat as she swallowed the sobbing that was thrusting up with her words. '…

and they shot the dogs and Sully died and we had to bury her and Harry's probably going to lose his leg ...' It all came tumbling out in a rush of words and sobs.

'Ella ...' Portia's voice was strong and clear, a line to cling to. 'I want you to slow down. You don't need to tell me everything. I want you to look around and tell me what you can see, okay, Ella? Do you remember this is what we do when you're overwhelmed and lost? Come back to here and now through the senses, in the detail ... describe what you can see in front of you. Ella?'

'Lots of eyes watching me.'

'Ella?' Portia's voice was spiced with alarm.

Ella's cackling laugh erupted into the hot air. 'I suppose that sounds crazy. I meant the photos on the wall.'

'Oh.' There was relief in her voice. 'And what else can you see?'

'Um, there's a black-and-white tiled floor and it's covered in dust, with some of my footprints making patterns in it.'

'Good. And what else Ella? What else can you see?'

'There's a hallstand with a mirror in a dark, sort of golden wood, it looks smooth.'

'Can you touch it?'

'Yes.' She reached over and touched the smooth wood.

'I want you to run your open palm over it and describe how it feels.'

'It feels smooth and warm.'

'Anything else?'

'Sort of hard and creamy. '

'Good, Ella, that's good. And what can you hear?'

'Silence. Nothing but fucking silence ... oops, sorry, Port ... Dr Dunne.' She had thought of her as Portia after their first few sessions. But Portia Dunne was ultra-professional, and people called her Dr Dunne. She wasn't cold exactly, but there was nothing out of place. Perfect, yes. Perfect hair, dark, straight, tied back. Perfect make-up. Tall and elegant. Straight back. Long neck and strong jaw. Classic outfits – plain pastel cotton shirts, nicely cut, slacks or skirt black, maybe navy. And matching jacket. That was her uniform. Conservative with a modern cut. Dr Portia Dunne was considered the best in her field: trauma. Post-traumatic stress disorder.

Dr Dunne had been called as an expert witness in the hearing, the case notes subpoenaed. Had Portia known all along she'd be called? Back then Ella had felt betrayed, abandoned, exposed when the barrister read out excerpts from the case notes and asked Dr Dunne questions about what she had written. When Portia gave evidence, she didn't look at Ella once. Ella was relieved that she had never told Portia the one dirty little secret that made her culpable.

She didn't see Portia after the court case. Just sent her a message cancelling the next appointment because she was going to the desert, even though it was months before she'd finally left Melbourne.

'It's fine to call me Portia …' There was a long pause. When Ella didn't respond, Portia said, 'And beyond the silence can you hear anything, any sounds in the silence?'

Ella listened intently. Yes, there were noises, the distant hum of a plane, or maybe a truck. Was that the air conditioner on the roof? And the ubiquitous crow off in the distance. She described it to Portia.

'Good, Ella. Can you feel your feet on the floor?'

Ella brought her attention to the soles of her feet. 'Uh-huh. Gritty.'

'Excellent. Tell me what you're noticing in your body now, do you feel more present in your body?'

'Yes. I feel like I'm back. I can breathe again … I didn't know I wasn't breathing … I don't think I've been here for weeks, maybe since the storm.'

'Your survival brain has been activated. You've likely been dissociative. Remember the language we use?'

'Sort of … not really.'

'Activation is the word we use when you feel stuck in fight-flight-freeze, survival mode, feeling lost and overwhelmed. Not present. Your nervous system is reacting as if it is caught in a life-and-death struggle, even though there is no current threat. Ringing a bell?'

'Yeah, sort of.' Of course, Ella knew it intellectually. Had studied PTSD in her nurse's training. But this was different. Portia had given her a way to use that knowledge when her own PTSD was activated. But now it felt like a blur, except when Portia held her with her voice and oriented her attention, drawing her through the activation. It was like tossing a line to someone trapped in a dark cave.

'The main thing is to recognise it as activation, a survival reaction from the past. Unless you're in immediate physical danger of course, for then you do need your survival brain activated.' Portia paused.

So many words. It was difficult to listen. Ella screwed her eyes closed, trying to concentrate.

'Our job, your job, is to give your body-brain the message that there is no current threat by bringing the attention into the here and now, through the senses. That is the way back to your sense of safety, through the body-brain. Making sense?'

'I think so. It's starting to come back.'

'The main thing is that you're back now. But it sounds like the dog incident triggered past trauma, activated your survival brain.'

'Yes, a huge dust storm and the dogs were shot.'

They talked for a while about what had happened. Portia interrupted her each time she lost her words in sobs, lost her train of thought, asking Ella to look around and listen, touch something or attend to the soles of her feet, giving her a way to hold the overwhelming pain. Not trying to change it or retreat from it, but letting it be what it was. Like someone holding her hand on a long dark night. The good crying came, washing away some of the ache in her chest.

They arranged a follow-up Skype session in the library for three days' time. Portia was disbelieving when Ella told her she had no wi-fi at the property, only some archaic internet connection that was too slow for Zoom or Skype or anything else. No need to mention the pregnancy.

***

Ella sat for a moment, letting her teeth and tiny bones settle into place after the rattling drive along potholed roads. She had found Queenie's place without Tom, only getting lost once. Dogs were circling the car, sniffing. She watched in the skewed mirror as one dog cocked its leg and pissed on the back tyre. When it was finished another dog, smaller, sniffed and cocked its leg in turn.

A tapping on the passenger window drew her attention. The girl-woman with a mop of dark hair hanging over one side of her face beamed at her through the window.

'Hey, sista.'

The largest dog sauntered up and sniffed Ella's crotch as she got out of the car.

'Git!' said girl-woman in a high-pitched snarl. The dog strolled back to the shade to where the smaller dog had retreated and flopped down in a small cloud of dust. She beckoned and Ella followed her into the flat-roofed dwelling. Inside, it was dark and cool. The musty sweet-pungent tang of close humanity infused the air. Once her eyes adjusted, she saw the pile of fur and wagging tail on the floor and rushed to Harry.

'Harry, *so* good to see you … Harry … how are you, old boy?' Harry wagged his tail with delight as she hugged and patted him. She smiled up at girl-woman leaning against the wall beside her. 'He looks so well.' Suddenly she felt shy, unsure. 'I don't even know your name. I'm Ella.'

'Possum,' said Possum, grinning. 'He's a good fella. Yeah, Harry's good. All betta soon.'

Ella picked up the dog's bandaged leg. Harry didn't pull back. Very gently she felt for the paw. The bandages pressed against her own fingers and she winced.

'Foot gone. Three-legged Harry now.' Possum bent down and scrummaged fingers through the fur on the top of his head. Harry slapped his tail on the floor.

Ella stroked Harry's flank and stood up. 'Where's Queenie? I'd like to thank her.' Possum pointed with a tilt of her head. Ella turned and, with a soft gasp, saw there was a large woman seated on a sagging lounge against the far wall. In the dim light she couldn't see if the woman's eyes were open or closed, but she felt watched. No, not watched, *seen*. As if those eyes could see into her and knew her soul whether they were open or closed.

Possum nudged her forward towards the woman and Ella dropped beside her on to the lounge. She felt immersed in deep quiet, as if she'd entered a cathedral on a hot day and felt the balm of cool silence. The air held a presence to rest into. A lone crow cawed outside, but instead of breaking the silence it seemed part of it. She felt serenity soaking through her skin, bones. Then she sensed some impulse or urgency beneath the silence.

At last Ella spoke, 'Thanks for helping Harry … um … Mrs Queenie.' She was still not sure if Queenie's eyes were open or closed. It was an ageless face, honey-coffee skin, smooth, without lines. White wisps of hair curled around her temples. She sat motionless, her head resting against the high back of the lounge.

Ella glanced at Possum.

'Name's Queenie,' Possum said, and laughed. 'No Mrs. She hear you. She seeing you. See inside you.' Possum put a hand on her chest and patted her heart.

Yes. It made Ella shy and relaxed at the same time. In the long silence she watched Queenie's face. If the desert had a face, this was it. Like a quiet morning through soft light, before the hard brute of sun thrust hot violence over the land. She felt an opening inside her as if Queenie embodied some timeless mystery of country. Tracking and unfolding hidden paths to secret places and songlines that must be approached quietly in bare feet, ready to drop to your knees in surprise, eyes wide as a child full of curiosity and wonder. Queenie was like a deep gorge in the desert with cool fathomless water. *Dadirri, Dadirri,* the air sang.

Ella stopped trying to think of what to say to fill the silence. She sank into the wide-open space between everything and rested. Felt her body relax, leant her head back against the lounge, eyelids heavy, almost closed. She heard the creaks and pops of the building around her as the sun burned down outside, a crow in the distance, the smell of earth, skin and close bodies, and she rested into her senses.

It was Possum who spoke first, breaking the spell. 'Want a cuppa?'

Ella jumped and Possum laughed like a leaf dancing in clear twilight.

She grinned back and nodded. When Possum left to make tea in the kitchen, she turned to Queenie. 'Can I pay you something for helping Harry? Or do something for you?' But Queenie didn't stir.

They drank tea, strong and milky-sweet, in silence. Dunked gingernuts into the tea and sucked the softened biscuits in slurpy camaraderie.

When she stood to leave, Ella felt a powerful urge to bend and kiss Queenie's cheek. She hesitated and looked at Possum, who gave an almost imperceptible nod, and Ella bent to kiss her. Just as her lips touched Queenie's soft cheek, a hand shot out and grabbed Ella's wrist. The hand gripping hers was covered in sorry cuts, raised scars criss-crossing up her forearm. Queenie's black eyes were wide, as if some horror lay inside them.

'Find my Biddy,' Queenie said in a rough whisper, though the voice seemed to come from somewhere other than the old woman's throat. And a second time, 'Find my Biddy.'

Just as abruptly, Queenie dropped Ella's hand and closed her eyes. Ella stood for a long moment to see if Queenie would say anything else, but she appeared to be asleep. Ella sensed rather than saw her mouth moving, and a soft chanting filled the air in a veil of sound, infolding.

Half an hour later, Ella parked at the back of the pub in the shade of the old peppercorn tree.

'How's my favourite new girl in town?' Frank said and grinned as she came in through the back door. Ella raised her eyebrows and Frank laughed. 'Okay, *only* new girl in town. Too hot for grey nomads and visitors out here now.'

'Hot. Dusty. Thirsty,' she said, plonking down on a barstool.

'What'll it be, love?'

'Beer, thanks. Great Northern.'

Sipping her beer she watched a couple of old men alternating between reading newspapers and staring out the window as Frank moved leisurely to and fro around the bar. It was too early for the afternoon 'rush'.

'Hey Frank, what's a Biddy?'

Frank jerked his head up and stared as if he were looking for something in her face, then his eyes dropped and he scrubbed at a spot on the counter. 'Some things are better left buried in the past, Ella. Let sleeping dogs lie. That's my advice.'

Ella studied her drink and felt the blood surge to her face. All these fucking men telling me to mind my own business. Yes, well, her sleeping dog was dead. Shot by the same men who told her not to ask any questions. The other dog missing a foot. That's what you get for not asking questions. Fuck you too, Frank, she didn't say.

Frank's voice softened. 'People out here don't like someone snooping around. It makes them nervous. Lot of people come out here to hide. Best stick to your writing, love.'

'Thanks for the free advice.' Her voice was sharper than she'd intended. She opened her mouth to speak again, but the words evaporated fast, like beads of sweat under hot sun. Instead she gulped down the last few mouthfuls of her beer, grabbed her pack, and walked out.

'See ya,' Frank said behind her.

She held her hand in the air but didn't look back.

***

Ella sat up in bed, a gossamer of dream still clinging to her imagination. She flicked on the bedside light and picked up her notebook and pen.

Date – unknown. Maybe Thursday or Wednesday. Eldorado. The desert.

A different dream. Not the old nightmare.

I'm swimming in clear water. It's deep and warm. The water turns to dust and I'm swimming in fine dust. For the longest time I'm swimming inside tunnels, like great veins flowing with red dust. Then a crack opens up in deep earth and I'm sucked down, falling and falling.

I see a young woman. She has half a face. But when she comes closer, I see one side of her face is black. So black it's like nothing. She's carrying a baby wrapped in a white blanket. She's speaking but I can't hear her or understand her words. The baby starts barking and barking, like a warning.

The barking wakes me. I thought the dogs were here. Sully wanting to play. Then I remember.

Chapter 10

It happens in a blink. You look aside, distracted for a moment, and inside that sharp smudge of unwatched time-space a tiny thing enters: a scent, the sound of brakes screeching, a snap, a virus, a phone ringing in late night, an invisible lump growing. When you look up, your life has changed utterly. Your ordinary days, that once offered comfort in their certainty, are now deranged and out of time. The world shifts on its axis. The trajectory of your life has turned irrevocably.

***

Ella parked the car in the speckled shade of a lone eucalypt. A sign hung lopsided on a stake: Le Gerche Reserve. She read what she could of the scratched and rusted information below, and again checked the map she'd found in the library after the difficult session with Portia, who had prescribed engaging in some 'pleasurable activity'. It was hard to believe that was only yesterday and her dream about the baby barking happened only this morning. Time warped and bent out here as if the desert had different laws for time.

The day felt slightly cooler than it had for weeks. She felt the serenity of the place settling around her. She could report back to Portia that she had indeed done as prescribed at their last session.

According to the map, there was a meandering walk of less than an hour through the main section of plantings. The forest of Australian natives had been planted by a woman named Audrey le Gerche around a natural spring that created its own microclimate. Most of the trees had survived the drought.

Ella inhaled deeply as she came to the section of native pines. The scent infused her senses, immediately activating a sticky membrane of memory. Faster than breath, her body throbbed into rememory. In an instant she was back there, breathing hard, gagging and shivering, though her skin burned as the memory gushed in like a stream of boiling water. Now became then, then-now.

The old question pushed its way up into her awareness the way a tiny flower pushes through concrete. A fierce impossibility poking its head in through the scent of pines. It was a question that had plagued her since her father's death. What had Aunt Rose said? What were her words?

The morning after the call from Rose at the party, she'd gone out to her father's farm. She was running hard through icy morning air, heart banging a wild beat, soles pounding gummy mud, carrying her doggedly towards the place. Their place. She'd known that's where he must have done it. Through stinging tears, she ran half-blind on instinct, legs carrying her to the place she'd been with him a thousand times.

The grove of native pines had been planted on a sandy ridge when she was a toddler. She couldn't remember planting them, but she'd seen the photos. Her mother laughing, holding little Ella chewing on something, dirt smudged across her cheek. The picnic, the sausage sizzle. It was all there frozen into the faded photo. They looked so happy, brimming with life and love.

She had slowed, head bowed, moving like a sleepwalker through the silent, familiar grove, touching rough bark, damp and cool, inhaling the scent of pine. Her heart had quieted, breath evened out. Another smell, making her nostrils twitch. A dark stain in the air, an odour that twisted her stomach. Stepping into the clearing, the silence shattered inside her head, splitting open like a scream at the sight of her father's old dog, Macca.

'No.' Her voice was a whisper. Her body doubled over, retching watery bile. She reached out to touch the ground, pressing hands into wet earth until she felt it solid, something to hold on to. 'They shouldn't have left you here like this,' she said to the old dog as she came close, looking down at intestines spilling on to loamy soil.

Turning sharply, she ran back towards the shed. Pushed her body, running, sliding in mud. Breath hard and icy in her lungs. She clung to the pain of breathing. Grabbing a shovel from the corrugated wall she loaded it on to the quad and switched on the engine. Roaring out of the shed, sliding in clay ridges of mud along the track, she saw Rose rush from the house, calling and waving as she flew past. Gave it full throttle.

In the clearing she dug into the wet sandy loam. It felt good to work the unused muscles in her back and shoulders. Keeping her mind on the job, she dug, refusing to let her eyes wander.

When the hole was a metre deep, she stopped digging, stood. 'Nearly done, boy,' she said in a rough whisper, noticing the blue collar tight around the dog's neck. Macca, gentle as a lamb, had always refused to wear a collar. Had almost bitten her father when he'd tried to put the collar on him as a pup. He used to sleep inside at night. Every other working dog she remembered had been chained outside.

The collar, bright blue with thick silver studs on it, made her laugh aloud against the morning. 'Macca, you look ridiculous in that.' But her laughter choked on an image of her father putting on this collar. New questions crowded in hard and fast. Did he put it on after or before? Before or after? After or before? Her mind raced after the question, around and around. Before or after? Before or after?

Shaking her head violently to dislodge the questions hiding ugly truths, she threw the shovel on to the ground and squatted to lift Macca's limp corpse, grunting with the effort. Too heavy. She pushed at the dog with the shovel, then with her boot. But Macca flopped back. She gagged, spitting bile on to the ground as the stink of entrails filled her nostrils. Pulling her T-shirt up over her mouth and nose, she grabbed hold of the blue collar, held her breath and dragged him towards the hole. As he fell in, she stood quickly to gulp clean air.

Macca looked peaceful in his shallow grave, cradled by the loamy soil. She focused again on the collar. Had her father left her a sign, a final joke? Did he mean for her to find Macca and see the collar? Before or after? If he had put the collar on before he shot him, Macca would have been … what? Had Macca known what he was planning? How long had her father known?

'Stop it, Ella, *stop*!' she screamed into the cold grey sky. Her mind crashed back to earth and into body-hung-limp against the shovel.

Having covered the dog with dirt, she wandered through the clearing, searching the ground until she found two straight sticks. She pushed each stick into the sandy dirt, making a lopsided X that seemed to sag under the weight of sorrow. With a handful of sand she dirt-washed her hands as her father had taught her. This simple act woke other kid memories they'd shared, so many unhurried, wild things about working the land that he'd shown her. Memories hung in the air like lost children. There was a nameless empty space in her mind where her father had rested, until now.

The words crashed in, unbidden. At first she hadn't understood what Rose was saying. They were sipping steaming mugs of tea in the kitchen after she'd made the longest drive through dawn to get to the farm. Rose's words had slipped over her brain, water over grease, wouldn't stick. Nothing made sense; it was like watching someone talking behind layers of glass.

For a while Rose just stared out the window. Slowly she had turned back to Ella, reached out to hold her hand as if she were a three-year-old, lost. Repeated the strange words slowly and clearly.

'He died by his own hand.' When Ella kept frowning back, Rose whispered, swallowing on her words. 'Ella … he shot himself.'

The world went black, nothing to hold on to, only falling and falling.

Ella was shivering uncontrollably when she got back to the car at the edge of the reserve. She sat on a weathered wooden seat near the entrance sign, rested her head in her hands, elbows staked on knees. She was boiling inside and shivering on the outside.

'What would Portia say? Be here now? Bring your attention into the present,' she spoke loudly into the landscape. Forcing herself to focus on her body, she closed her eyes. Inside was frozen, cold *and* burning, panic rising in her chest. She tried to pull her attention to her feet, feel her feet on the ground, but everything inside was screaming – *run*. Her mind coiled and bucked against itself, trapped.

Ella opened her eyes and felt immediate relief. She gazed around the clearing, trying to focus on something. Her faithful car. The dirty splash of grease along the driver's side, dust caked to it. The different bird calls and soft hum of insects. She leant down, picked up a stick and drew her name in red dirt.

Portia's voice was there, inside her head, guiding her.

'Focus on here and now, not your body when you're overwhelmed. Sensory detail: look, listen, touch.' Yes, that's right; it was like the words in the chorus of a song coming back. She stroked the warm wood of the bench beside her, smooth and rough, traced the fading letters gouged into it. Portia's words circled in her mind, calling her to return. She wriggled her toes inside her shoes; they felt sweaty and hot. She felt the wave of painful emotion-memory ease back into that dark hole somewhere deep inside. She let out a slow -wide-open-breath. How quickly her panic dissolved when she could direct her attention in the ways Portia had shown her. Even if the imprint was always there under her skin, like removing a too-tight ring from the finger.

She blinked. God, what just happened back there? A flashback? Yes. But how could I have forgotten that morning in the clearing? Her curious mind pressed back into the memory and she felt the sucking edge of overwhelm. But the punch had gone out of it. She shook herself and stood up. Don't go there … don't go there alone. She touched her face, warm and damp with unchecked tears. I have to talk to Portia. I need to talk to her. Yes, as soon as I get home, I'll call her.

Ella pulled her water bottle from her pack and gulped. Resting the water bottle on the wooden bench, she fished in her pack for her purse. The letter was still in its usual place, worn at the edges from years of folding and unfolding. She opened it and smoothed it against her leg. Stared down at the neat cursive writing of her father's hand.

To my beautiful girl Ella,
I love you more than all the world. Always remember that.
Doc says I've got the cancer in some nasty places and reckons I need treatment and that means hospitals and money and all that. With no guarantees. And what would I do with old Macca if I was away, or the farm. Doc says it's aggressive. You know how they use those funny words.
This is the best plan I could come up with. Save all the fuss. Leave on my own terms. And take old Macca with me. Even brought him a new collar for the trip. (Smiley face)
I am always with you Ella. Call if you need me. I'll be there. I live in your heart and you in mine. Always my beloved girl Ella.
I love you, Dad.

She stemmed her tears, blotted them carefully from the page.

It was years since she had read the letter. At first she read it two or three times a day, slept with it under her pillow, afraid she'd forget the shape of his face, the smell of him. It was all she had to hold on to. God, she missed her dad. She had tried to hold on to the property, her only true home, though not really home without him. Her mother had wanted to sell. No one listened to what eighteen-nearly-nineteen-year-old Ella wanted. Maybe it would have been different if she had been a guy. A son to run the farm.

She lifted the page to her lips and kissed it.

'I love you, Dad,' she whispered, then folded the letter and placed it back in the small zippered section of her purse.

Ella drove slowly down the track out of the reserve and turned on to the narrow bitumen road. Her stomach growled and she realised she hadn't eaten all day. She could grab something at the cafe on the way through town. Driving out on to the wide plain, she thought of that morning with Rose in the kitchen. Rose had found a letter too, telling her to call the cops, not to go looking for him. But Ella knew where he would have done it.

A sudden movement just up ahead on the edge of the road ripped her eyes from reverie. Her body jolted upright, hands sudden-knuckle-white clenching the steering wheel. Her foot lifted instinctively and slammed on the brakes before her mind fully registered what she was seeing.

Time stretched into slow motion as the wedge-tailed eagle lifted from the roadkill. There was grace and ease in the power of its wings stretching wider, lifting slowly into the air, but unbearably slowly, magnifying wing and feather. Larger dark-brown feathers along the outside, and underneath, tiny white feathers, delicate and soft-edged. The eagle was rising like a dark desert angel, hurrying without haste. Black shining eyes stared back at her as the small car hurtled towards the great bird. Foot pressed hard to the brake pedal, she felt herself rising above the scene, watching the certainty of collision from high above, a slow arc towards the inevitable.

Thud.

She juddered forward, the seatbelt straining to hold her, her head jarring on impact. Her eyes were locked on the eagle's trajectory as it rolled across the bonnet and crashed into the windscreen. Glass shattered into the car. Hot wind and eagle and feathers and claws, gashing. The eagle struggled, flapping frantically. She covered her face. Stillness. Then struggle. Flapping, clawing. Stillness again.

Ella touched the sharp pain down her left cheek. Wet. Blood, bright and hot on her hand. She unbuckled her seatbelt, pushed open the door and fell out of the now stationary car. She laid on the hot ground and closed her eyes, sun burning into her face and neck, listening to the eagle thrashing. Another sound, a hissing. She moaned and raised herself on to hands and knees. Standing slowly, she stared in at the eagle for a long moment. It was caught in the gaping hole where the windscreen had been, shattered glass everywhere. The eagle moved its head to look at her. Black sharp eyes shining. Accusing? Pleading?

'Do something, Ella,' she said. Her voice sounded strange, disconnected. '*Do* something.' She reached in and laid a hand on its exposed wing. It struggled weakly, then stilled, watching her.

'I'm sorry. So sorry,' she whispered, tears spilling, stinging the open wound where the eagle's talons had scratched her face. Louder, to the sky, to the spinifex, '*Do* something!'

She went to the boot and rummaged among the jumble of stuff, finally pulling an old towel from the pile, pale pink and stained, hard in places where it had been used to mop up some forgotten spill.

Ella reached in through the passenger door with the towel. The black eyes followed her movements. As her hands shifted towards it, the bird raised its head momentarily then flopped back. Gently she laid the towel over its head. Her father had shown her how to quiet an injured bird by covering its head.

'Sorry, sorry,' she whispered over and over as she tried to free its wing. 'Sorry, sorry.' Muttering her prayer, she knelt and leant into the car, pulling the wings in close to the warm body of the great bird, stroking feathers. The mantra changed. Crooning softly as a mother does to her distressed child. 'It's okay, it's okay …' Stroking feathers. Half-lifting, half-dragging, she cradled the bird, grunting as the full weight of its body fell from the car. The eagle struggled briefly, then laid still across her lap. She shuffled around to position its head into the small, close shade of the car and removed the towel. The black eyes watched, unblinking. Leaning back against the car, legs outstretched, she stroked its feathers.

Ella sat quietly holding the creature as it died, the horizon shimmering wide into the distance. It was different down low. Like a serpent close to earth, a belly-eye view of the world. Everything close and large. She felt small. So small.

Looking down into the eagle's eye, she sensed something pouring into this crumpled moment. An opening into vast memory of the land between life and death. Creatures and humans walking, crawling, flying, jumping. Animals and humans and trees and rivers all moving across the land.

Different rhythms beating into harmony, living between birth and death. Between what has been and what is arriving. The simple unbroken melody filling each moment, arising and dying.

She sensed the great heart of the bird opening into the infinite rhythm of life. Knew it had forgiven her. Never blamed her. That had been her small mind imposing itself on to animal. This other knowing stirred in her belly, under her ribs. Wanting to free itself and call to that wild unknown, beyond words, beyond time.

One hand resting on warm feathers, she felt sinew and muscle and blood slowing, the heart growing quieter. Releasing. Resting into death. There was no particular moment. Death came in a soft blur between measured time. Between breaths and heartbeats. Stillness descending. The world grew quiet. Her heart and mind and breath grew quiet as if death, what was beyond death, filled everything. It was like a welcome. A coming home. Resting into some familiar place she'd forgotten because she'd been away so long, wandering the world looking for something that was already there, inside her small, warm-beating heart. A remembering older than death, larger than life, held in a moment, and everything pouring into that one particular moment between breaths.

When she sensed the lifeblood in the eagle had stilled, she put her hands over her heart as if cradling the soul of that great bird closely for as long as possible, inviting it into her. Her head fell back against the car and she let the tears come. Slow tears that carried a river of living and dying and more than she had words to say or would ever be able to say.

She tried to swallow but her throat felt as dry as the landscape and refused to obey. She coughed instead. Moved her tongue, thick-rough and surly, around her mouth, seeking moisture. How long had she been sitting there holding the eagle? She dragged herself to her feet. Stood, touching dirty fingers to the side of her face, tacky with dried blood: sharp sting of pain. Fumbling through her pack, she pulled out the water bottle and unscrewed it awkwardly, fingers thick and stiff, covered in tiny scratches. She gulped the warm water. Stopped abruptly and looked around. Nothing. Only the thin straight ribbon of road. A few wretched, shadeless trees in the distance. Three-sixty degrees of emptiness.

'Nothing,' she said in a whisper.

Kneeling to peer under the car, she saw a dark pool, something dripping slowly from the engine. Sliding into the driver's seat, she turned the ignition. Tick-tick-tick.

'Fuck-fuck-fuck.'

Ella held up the water bottle. Four fingers of water left. She stepped out of the car and turned slowly, full circle, one hand up to shield her from the sun searing the land, scanning for any sign of human habitation. Nothing and nothing. Nothing.

She opened the back door, scrabbled through the mess on the floor and seat. 'Fuck, Ella.' She searched the boot once more, pulled out bags and boxes. 'No hat. Why didn't you bring a hat? You idiot.'

In a burst of energy, she rushed around to the passenger side of the car, stepped around the eagle, and thrust her hand in under the seat. Bingo. The emergency umbrella for Melbourne's irascible weather. She opened it to expose long silver prongs where the synthetic fabric had torn, leaving protruding, crooked fingers. Pink fabric stretched out into red bubbles that were no longer round but flattened on the broken side, like pink pancakes. At least it was some sort of shade.

How much traffic was there on this road? She hadn't seen another car all morning. It didn't go anywhere except to the reserve. She stared out across the shimmering mirage towards the endless horizon. Red gibbers littered the ground. A few low, straggling gums broke the flat moonscape. Nothing stirred; there was no sign of life in any direction. Baking sun high in the sky, glaring. How long had she been driving when she hit the eagle? Hard to calculate. Her mind felt sluggish, disoriented. Surely it can't be that far back to town. She held the afflicted umbrella overhead, its creepy fingers pointing in all directions, and set off towards town at a steady pace.

Holding the water bottle above her mouth, she let the last few precious drops wet her tongue. She looked back, eyes sweeping the shimmering mirage of ocean along the horizon, the car now a blue dot, barely visible.

Burning air drilled into the moisture of her body, drawing life to the surface, sucking it from her. Land so thirsty it could drink all of you, leave nothing but bleached bones for the wind to sing. She stumbled, caught herself as a wave of nausea ballooned up from her belly, spinning the world. She walked crookedly to the side of the road and sat on the ground in the speckled half-shade of a small mulga tree.

Ella sat bolt upright, realising she'd fallen asleep. Holding her breath, she listened. Was that the sound of a motor? Staggering to her feet, she stepped towards the road. Dust. Yes, a long, low, barely-there cloud of dust was rising into the wide blue air. It was coming this way.

What if it's a rapist or murderer? 'What the fuck? You're going to die out here if you don't get help,' she told the crow flying way in the distance. She waved the broken umbrella in a slow pink arc.

The vehicle pulled up in the middle of the road, a soft cloud of dust rising on either side of the narrow line of bitumen. She pulled open the passenger door and looked up into the brown-lined face of a man wearing an Akubra and wraparound sunglasses.

'Bit hot for a walk to the park, isn't it?'

She tried to smile but her lips were stiff and thick, stuck to her teeth.

'Hit an eagle. Car won't start. I need a lift into town.' Each word felt impossible, sticking thickly to her tongue.

'Jump in. I'll take you back. Better get out of this heat or you'll be cactus.'

She climbed in with a grunt, body relaxing as cool air wrapped around her hot skin.

'Where's your car? Locked?'

'Not far from the park. Broken windscreen.'

The vehicle grunted forward in a slow arc as he turned it around.

'Better get you home outa the sun.'

'Thanks.' Her voice sounded weak against the thrum of motor. 'I'm staying at …'

'Eldorado. We met.'

The large hat and dark glasses made it difficult to see his features. Her mind was sluggish, unco-operative. Fried.

'Um, sorry I …'

'Bit of trouble at the pub?'

Her mind flinched at the memory of the bullying man's hard grip on her arm. The stocky pig shooter, stink of animal in his skin. Abruptly the smell of Liam that other night; animal smells lining up, tangled threads of memory.

'Sarge?'

'That's me.'

She leant her head against the headrest. Kept her head still but slid her eyes across to watch him. Strong face and jaw. Erect and relaxed. His body said: confident. Maybe arrogant. What had Lil said about him? She couldn't remember.

She jumped when his hand touched her arm. Must have dozed. She looked down. He was holding a small bottle of water against her arm.

'Better get some of that into you.'

She took it and gulped down as much water as fast as she could, spilling some down the front of her T-shirt.

'Hey, steady. You'll make yourself sick. Sip slowly. You're probably dehydrated.' Ella sipped more slowly. 'Better drop you at the clinic. Get checked over by Nurse Jack. That face needs attention.'

Sarge picked up the radio and made a call. 'Jack, you at the clinic?'

Affirmative. 'I'm on my way with a young lady who had a fight with an eagle. Could be dehydrated,' he said, keeping his eyes on the road. About twenty minutes out. See you then.' Her mind drifted between sleep and waking as Sarge talked to the voice on the radio.

The clinic doubled as a doctor's surgery in an old rambling homestead that had served as a hospital in Broken Ridge's opal mining halcyon days. But now there was only the one visiting doctor who came to clinic fortnightly with the Flying Doctor Service. The rest of the time it was staffed by the nurse. She thought about the grumpy-kind doctor she'd seen only a few days ago. Or was it longer? Maybe a week? Longer?

As the vehicle pulled up outside the clinic she said, voice straining over the sound of motor, 'I'm okay. Just want to get home, thanks.'

Sarge ignored her. He killed the engine and came around to her side of the vehicle, opened the door and held out a hand to help her down. Poking out of his sleeve was the shape of a creature, an eye in a faded tattoo. She grabbed the fabric on his arm as she jumped down from the vehicle.

It was cool inside and she sank on to a chair in the waiting room while Sarge went looking for Nurse Jack.

Chapter 11

Ella left a message and put down the phone. Stood staring out the front door without seeing. Turned slowly, walked down the dust-covered hallway into the kitchen and switched on the kettle, then went to the old couch and dropped heavily on to it, lying down while she waited for the kettle to boil.

The ringing startled her. Jolted awake, she sat upright. Ran for the phone.

'Hello?'

'Ella, is everything alright?'

'Um, yeah, I suppose … not really.'

'What's happened?'

'I had a flashback. It was about what happened after my father … shot himself … the dog … I hit an eagle … it died in my arms.' The words flew out in a stumbling rush.

'Ella,' Portia pronounced her name clearly and slowly, 'Ella, can you hear me?'

She felt herself falling awake.

'Ella, you're activated. Possibly dissociative.' Portia's voice was firm and gentle; she clung to the sound and rhythm of it. 'Your body is re-experiencing the trauma … Ella, I want you to look around. Describe what you can see.'

Slowly, Portia talked her through the experience. Brought her back to ground through her senses. She took a deep breath in, releasing it slowly. Her body felt like lead, so heavy she had to sit, lie. She let herself sink to the floor.

'Good, Ella. Just rest into your body…' There was a long silence, 'Are you still there, Ella?'

'Uh-huh.' It was difficult to speak. As if all energy had leaked out of her body.

Portia said, 'The exhaustion is normal. Powerful chemicals were released during activation. Now your body needs rest.' When she didn't answer, Portia continued, more quietly. 'Ella, I think you need someone to stay with you tonight. I know you wouldn't have called unless you felt … well … not okay…'

Portia kept talking, but it was difficult to concentrate or make any meaning. Words were lumps of sound bumping past, couldn't land. She heard Portia's last words, 'You need support.' When Ella didn't speak, she continued, 'Is there someone you could call? That neighbour you spoke of? I can't think of his name.'

'Tom?'

'Yes, Tom.'

'He's been away …' She couldn't be bothered explaining that they'd had a fight and she didn't know if she could trust him now. Or even if he would come.

'He sounds like a good friend. It's important that you're not alone. Could he stay with you tonight? Ella?'

'Uh-huh. I hear you.' It all felt too difficult. She just wanted to rest. Have a cup of tea. How long had she slept? She sat up, stared out the window at the blushing sky. The sun was performing its evening roll-over trick with the horizon, turning the sky rose and raspberry against palest blue.

'It's best you're not alone for the next twenty-four hours. Especially without the dogs.' The long silence brewed again, but this time there was no rest in the silence; a hard wall was building between them. 'Ella, will you promise me you'll call him and ask him to come over?'

'Okay.' It came out as a sigh of surrender, petulant. She just wanted to get off the phone. Rest.

Portia started talking again. 'Good. Now I just want to establish some containment for this flashback. Give the brain the message that we are taking care of business so it doesn't keep activating this memory. Okay?'

She didn't answer.

'Are you still there, Ella?'

'Uh-huh.'

'Okay, yes. Difficult to concentrate. Rest now. Call Tom.'

'Okay. I just need to rest.'

'I'll call you in the morning,' Portia said, and the phone went silent.

It's now or never. She knelt up and dialled Tom's number. It rang for a long time and she was about to hang up when a voice answered.

'Tom?'

'Ted.'

'Oh … um Mr MacDonald … is Tom there, please?'

'Just got back.'

She crawled up on to the wooden seat of the hallstand. Listened to the mutter of distant voices on the line.

'Hi, Ella. Is everything okay?'

'Sort of … not really.'

'What's happened? I've been away, worried about you.'

Is that why he hadn't called? He really was away? The lie I told Portia was true?

'Well … I've been having flashbacks and nightmares and Portia, my psych, asked me to call someone. She doesn't want me to be on my own … but don't worry … I just …' Her voice trailed off.

'I'll come over. Give me an hour. Have you had dinner?'

'No.'

'I'll bring some steaks for dinner. And beer. Okay? I'll be there.'

'Thanks.' Tears sprang to her eyes. He was her friend. She took a deep breath. 'Thanks.'

'Okay, See ya soon.'

***

Ella recounted the story of her bingle with the eagle while she chopped tomatoes and cucumber and Tom cooked the steaks on the barbie. It was good to slip into the old rhythm.

'You left your car?' He sounded angry.

'Well, I …' Her words trailed off. Confused. She hadn't been concentrating, just letting the story tell itself.

'Thought you said you're a country girl? Surely you know not to leave your vehicle.'

'Rural Victoria's a bit different to this country. And … I was probably still activated ….' How could she explain to Tom that strange lost in another time-and-place feeling when she was activated. Yeah, Portia called it activation, sometimes dissociation. As if a single word could describe the unshakable disorientation of that unwanted experience.

'I don't know what you mean.' Tom was holding the large tongs out in front, waiting.

'I had a … flashback I suppose, at the park. And the shock of the eagle … I can't explain it. I wasn't thinking straight.' She had felt fully present as she held the dying eagle. But not in a practical, decision-making way. It was as if a different part of her was awake. Her practical self far away.

'Out here it's lethal to leave your vehicle.' He turned back to the sizzling steaks. Shoulders tight.

Arguments flew around in her head, defending herself, crowding the air between them. She bit her lip.

'Ready,' Tom said, holding two plates loaded with steaks.

They sat on the back veranda, stomachs full, sipping a cleansing ale. She glanced sideways at Tom again. He seemed distant. But also different, quieter, or something she couldn't quite put her finger on: more contained, inside himself. But maybe it was because she felt so fragmented, frazzled from the past few days. She didn't want to break the peace, but the words burst out before she could stop them.

'I thought you weren't talking to me.'

'Why?'

'Because you didn't return my calls.'

'I didn't get your calls. I've been away. Needed to do some work on the fence at the western bore head, check on stock out there. What's left of them. Thought I'd ride out and camp for a few days. Brian met me out there. Was good to be away for a bit. But the drought …' His words drifted off.

She was in too much of a hurry to get things off her chest to wait or ask about the effects of drought. What was there to say that hadn't already been said a thousand times? The endless dry was like a bad taste that never left.

'I said some things that I didn't mean, and I wanted to …' She couldn't remember what had been said out loud and what was in her head. Tom was in the wrong for defending his father, the misogynist racist pig. But she had missed him more than she wanted to admit. Why was it so hard to apologise? Because I'm right and he's wrong. Why should I apologise? I was only reacting to his pathetic compliance with Ted.

Tom gazed into the deep night sky, as if his thoughts were somewhere out there among the stars. She gulped down a large draught of beer. Wanted to tell him she had missed him, wanted to slap him to make him look at her and talk to her. Wanted to get back that lovely thing that had grown between them in the weeks sitting here on the veranda. But the shadow of his brother was always there, and now his racist father, like a high rock wall between them. She watched the stars flicker against their deep indigo backdrop. Pressed bare feet on to the still-warm floorboards, wriggling her toes to interrupt her racing mind.

'Ella … I…'

The phone rang, splitting the air like a fire alarm, and they both jumped. Ella didn't move, but Tom stood. 'Will I get it?'

'No, leave it.'

'It might be important.'

Ella rose slowly and went to the phone. 'Hello.' She listened, rubbing at the deep frown between her eyebrows. 'I'm really sorry to hear that, Jacob. No, don't worry about things here, everything's fine.' She nodded. 'Okay. No, don't worry. I'll be here. Okay, take care. Okay, bye.' She put down the receiver. A thick coil of emotions tangled her mind.

Tom looked up as she stepped on to the veranda.

'That was Jacob.'

Tom raised his eyebrows.

'Friend from work. Maria and Hans's son.' She took in a long breath. 'Hans collapsed. He's in hospital in Vienna. Sounds like heart or maybe a stroke.' She sat with a thump into the chair. Picked up her rollies. 'They're doing tests. Jacob's flying out in the morning. He asked me to stay on for a few weeks. I said yes … I couldn't tell him about Sully and Harry.' She didn't mention the familiar feeling growing in her belly that she wanted to run, get the hell out of here. Now she was even more trapped. But she had just promised Jacob.

'That's dreadful. When did it happen? Is he okay?' Tom's face was pinched with concern, his brow creased.

With a jolt Ella saw the gaping hole where compassion had once resided in her own heart. But she felt numb. Empty. As if there was no care there, not even for herself. 'I barely spoke to Hans…' she said, somehow trying to excuse her lack of feeling. 'But reading his library has been …' She didn't have words to describe the curious intimacy she felt with Hans's mind, through his library and books that had enfolded her on sleepless nights. She told Tom what Jacob had said. Flicking on the lighter, she sucked hard on a cigarette.

'Do you want a cup of tea?'

Tom, so practical. 'Yeah, thanks.' She stood to follow him into the kitchen.

'I'll get it. You stay there. Enjoy the view.'

God, she needed to get away from here. But now she had promised Jacob she'd stay. It could be months before Hans was well enough to travel. Her head was spinning. She gulped down the last of the warming beer.

Tom returned, carrying a tray with teapot and cups, and they sat talking about Hans and Maria. Tom called them outsiders. They didn't belong to either of the two white camps in Broken Ridge, farmers or miners. The couple were liked well enough but had no particular friends. A bit of a mystery. The land they owned wasn't enough to make a decent living. It was a long strip that ran up into a rocky ridge. Some people reckoned Hans was mining.

'Hey, who or what is Biddy?' Her question burst into the night like a flare.

Startled, Tom turned his head to look at her, his eyes wide and glistening. Silence stretched out into the infinity of night. She felt small in the expanse of waiting.

'Who told you about Biddy?'

'No one told me. That's the point. I don't even know what or who Biddy is.'

'Where did you hear about her?'

'Okay, so it's a she. Good. Queenie said something.'

'What did she say?'

'How come you get to ask the questions? It was my question. Can't anyone in this fucking place talk straight?'

'There are things in the past that people want to forget. There's no point digging them up. What good can it do?' Ella sensed rather than heard the sadness in him.

Leaning forward, she rested her elbows on her knees and dropped her head into her hands. The deep scratches down her cheek stung as her palm pressed against them. God, how she wanted to get out of this place. Everyone was hiding something. Too many secrets and lies. She was on her own again. The only one asking questions, trying to find the meaning in things, refusing to take things at face value. Why doesn't anyone else care about the truth? They just bury it … but wasn't that exactly what she had done with her own truth, buried it? Tried to keep it buried. Good luck with that. She grunted aloud, half-laughed.

Tom frowned at her. She shifted, gazing out to the stars. Yes. She was happy poking her nose into other people's past lives, digging up their bones while her own bones remained locked in the cellar. But she didn't want to think about her own bones and skeletons right now.

'Ella?'

'What? Sorry, I was distracted.'

'Why do you want to know about Biddy?'

Ella paused. Sat back and crossed her arms. 'Something strange happened when I went to see Queenie.' Her mind bolted back to the days when Tom didn't return her calls, all the unsaid things that had gone around and around, fuelling a full head of rage. The way he had abandoned her, refusing to return to Queenie's. Listened to his stupid father. She felt a deep tsunami of fury heaving under her diaphragm. But he had been away. He was here now, wasn't he? Had just cooked for her, again. She clenched her jaw to stop the rush of accusations pushing up.

She took a deep breath in and described what had happened at Queenie's. ' "Find my Biddy" – those were her exact words.'

Tom didn't respond. She continued, 'There's something about Queenie … I don't know what it is … I feel like she knows me somehow … I can't explain it. Like she's … I don't know how to describe the feeling.'

Tom poured more tea and handed it to her.

'Yes, she's one of the old people, a true elder,' Tom said so quietly she had to lean towards him to hear. 'I think she lives in the Dreaming, at least since Biddy left. For years she went around asking people to find her Biddy. Walked up to strangers and grabbed them, "Find my Biddy", she'd say.'

'Biddy left? When?'

'Just leave it.' There was a sharp finality in his voice.

They didn't speak again as she made up a spare bed. Tom had already agreed to stay the night. But he was 'gone'. Shut down. Unavailable. Ella went to bed, so tired.

***

'Ella, Ella!' Tom was shaking her. Body shuddering. Breath coming in short gasps. Tom wrapped his arms around her, rocking her. She leaned into his shoulder and breathed in the comfort and warmth of him.

He stroked the back of her head, speaking softly. 'It's okay … it was only a dream … shoosh … you're safe now…'

When her breathing finally calmed, she pulled back from his embrace and looked up at him in the half-light from the hallway. She wanted to say something but her mind was blank. No thoughts, no words.

He held her shoulders, watching her face carefully, 'Are you okay now?'

She let out a long breath. 'Yeah.' Her voice trembled. Words arrived, bumpy. 'I'm okay … the old nightmare. Dad's bloody face … gun in his hands.' Tears rolled down her face, plopped on to her leg.

'Do you want to talk about it?'

She shook her head, lips clamped together.

'Get some sleep. I'm just in the next room. I'll leave the door open.'

'Stay with me, please.'

He opened his mouth to speak. Closed it again. Nodded, chin up, as if in surrender.

'Please, just sleep there beside me. I don't want to be alone.'

Tom laid down on his back.

'Thanks.'

Ella could see the glint of his eyes staring up at the ceiling, hands behind his head. She smelt the slight musky odour of his body, his armpits close, and something stirred in her. Soft-animal hunger, rousing between her legs. Liam was there too, lurking in the shadows of the room.

Tom rolled away, his back to her.

She laid awake listening to his steady breathing. He'd barely spoken since her questions about Biddy. A shaft of light from the hallway made angular shapes on the ceiling. Sleep was far off, but at least she wouldn't have the nightmare again if she didn't sleep.

When she closed her eyes, Sully's green eyes were there. And Harry, the last time she had seen him. Who shot them? Was it Liam? Ted? Think about something else. She turned and watched Tom breathing. Not that. Think about something else. How can I find out what happened to Biddy? She owed Queenie. There was something about her. She felt pulled towards Queenie in a way she didn't understand. The mystery of her words, *Find-my-Biddy*, like a mantra in her head. Everyone telling her to leave it alone only made her more curious. Her mind ran around and around in circles, chasing the tale.

She watched Tom's back. Her heart flopped like a fish on land, confusion spilling over into the night. Two brothers, so different. But Tom didn't seem interested in her as more than a friend. How much did he know about what had happened with Liam? Tom's a good friend, and then the next thought, an unbidden force that wouldn't be denied: I want more than a friend. Why? Relationships always end in shit. Friends are forever. And I sure as hell need a friend right now. But she did want more from Tom, and now that she had admitted it the greasy thing was hard to poke back inside its black box.

She laid still, watching the contour of his back, a familiar-strange geography, so different to Liam's, and so alike. She listened to his breathing and wondered what was happening inside his head. What or who filled Tom's dreaming? Her fingers spidered across the sheet towards his back. Splayed fingers lying still, almost touching skin, while her mind twisted and turned itself into tighter and tighter knots. The impulse to touch his warm skin grew large, more intense, aflame. She rolled over and faced the wall, hoping to dislodge her burning thoughts. But the two old enemies raged inside her.

I want to sleep with him.

You are sleeping with him.

Ha-ha. You know what I mean. I want to fuck him. Feel him inside me.

It'll fuck up a good friendship. Always does. Besides, you already fucked the brother. He mightn't like seconds.

But I need him. I need skin. I need him to hold me. I want him.

You're still drunk. He's staying as a friend. Don't fuck it up.

But he's right here in my bed. It might be the only chance I get. I can blame the alcohol if it blows up.

Yeah, in the same bed where Liam gave it to you up the arse. Remember?! Stop lying to yourself. If it blows up, girlie, the friendship is over. That simple, babe.

Don't babe and girlie me. I'm no one's babe. Fuck off, what would you know anyway? You want me to be a nun. I have appetites, you know.

Go fuck someone in town.

Like who? The old guys in the pub? Bruce the butcher? Frank?

There must be some nice young men in the area.

Oh, fuck off, you sound like grandma twinkle.

Who's that?

How the fuck should I know. I just made it up.

You're always making things up. You crazy bitch.

Fuck you. Leave me alone.

She took several deep slow breaths, and rolled over again, facing Tom. She inched her hand across the sheet towards him, holding her breath to listen to his breathing. In slow motion she lifted her hand and held it a few centimetres from his shoulder, felt the warmth from his body. She held her breath again. What are you doing, you crazy bitch? That voice crashed inside her head so loudly, so abruptly, that she jumped. She waited. Slowly exhaling, she pressed her palm gently on to his skin. It was warm and smooth. She felt his breath. Was that a slight shift in the rhythm of his breathing as she pressed her hand more firmly? She listened without moving a muscle. It seemed regular. She moved closer, drawn to the warmth of his body, though the night was hot. 'I missed you,' she whispered.

She let her hand slide back down to the sheet and rolled on to her back. Somehow it was lonelier having someone in your bed whom you couldn't touch or wouldn't touch you back. Warm skin to curl into, skin on skin, those soft animal noises of content. This was different wanting to the hard and fast way she had wanted Liam. This was slow, tender wanting. She slid her hand over her breast, squeezing her nipple hard. Ran her hand down the soft contour of her stomach, reached under thin cotton of her pyjama shorts. Felt her slippery labia, aching-moist. She rubbed her clitoris firmly and proficiently, until she felt the sweet release of desire spilling into a muffled gasp.

***

Voices woke her. She sat up and peered through a crack in the curtains. Who's that talking to Tom on the veranda? Indistinct words.

'MacDonald lads … keeping the girls …' Muffled. Tom's voice was too low to hear. He looked angry. She pulled the curtain a breath wider, angled her vision to see who was speaking. It was Sarge. He looked small next to Tom. Wiry. There was something about him. Controlled? Powerful? Commanding? Yes, commanding.

Rummaging around on the floor to find something to wear, she pulled on shorts and a T-shirt, and raced to the toilet. When she opened the door from the bathroom, drying her hands on her shorts, Tom was walking down the hallway towards the kitchen and almost ran into her. He barely looked at her; his face was set in an angry mask. She followed him into the kitchen.

'What is it?'

'That prick. Mind in the gutter.' He flicked on the kettle and started pulling out cups and teapot, preparing tea. The kitchen was spotless.

'You've cleaned up,' she said, stating the obvious. 'Thanks, Tom. I really appreciate everything you've done for me.'

His rigid shoulders softened a little. 'I thought you were going to sleep all day. Then *he* showed up.' Tom jabbed his thumb towards the front door.

'Guess I must have crashed after the nightmare. Haven't had a lot of sleep lately.' She watched him as she talked, trying to assess whether he was angry at her, if he had felt her hand on his skin in the night, heard her. But there wasn't even a hint; he seemed more concerned with Sarge.

'You don't think much of him?' She mimicked Tom, jabbing her thumb towards the front door.

'Yeah, don't like some of his attitudes. But reckon the SES would fall apart without him.'

'What did he want?'

'He wanted to let you know that Tony has your car at the servo. He towed it in late yesterday. Could take a few weeks. Needs a new radiator

132

and of course the windscreen. Has to order parts from Adelaide or Brisbane.'

'Shit. I can't stay out here without a vehicle.'

'Isn't there an old Land Cruiser? Hans drives it.'

'It's a monster and a manual. I've never driven a manual.'

'I'll teach you. You need a vehicle.' Tom latched on to the task of driving lessons as if it were a relief from whatever was burning him. 'I'll make you some breakfast and we can have a driving lesson. Then I need to get home and do some work.' He busied himself at the stove.

'Full MacDonald breakfast?' he said over his shoulder, then glanced at the kitchen clock, which read 12.07. 'Lunch?'

Chapter 12

'Fuck you, Tom MacDonald,' she growled as she paced the kitchen. The argument ran through her mind, re-ran. Then the argument against herself. Loud. Filling her mind.

You shouldn't have said anything, Ella. Blood is thicker than water.

Well, he didn't have to call me an ungrateful brat.

You have been a brat.

If he hadn't gone off and left me and refused to go back to Queenie's because of his shit-for-brains father, none of this would have happened. The rage surged, foaming as it crashed against words and memory. She hadn't meant for it all to come pouring out like that when they were locked in the cabin of the stiff-geared beast of a cruiser. He was only trying to help.

'*Stop!*' she screamed at the window and the silent glare of sun.

A moment later. But he's just like his father. Complicit in silence. Why doesn't he stand up to the old prick? And suddenly Liam was there, vivid body memory throbbing her imagination. The smell of him, the feel of him. Before that last horrible night. She spread a hand over her belly, trying to calculate dates.

The doctor had given her the numbers for clinics in Adelaide. Or maybe she should fly back to Melbourne. She knew what she wanted. She stood at the window, staring out into the back garden. Filtered late afternoon light danced through the faded foliage of the tired-looking elm tree. A mound of dirt marked where Sully lay.

Now that she'd promised Jacob she'd stay, and her car might not be ready for weeks, she'd have to fly out for a termination. Then come back to this hellhole. But at least she could bring Harry home when she came back. He'd be fine at Queenie's while she was away. She'd given Possum plenty of cash for dog food. What about the chooks? Maria had left the number of someone on her list if she needed help. A good neighbour. Not the MacDonalds.

Ella paced, itchy-scratchy under the skin, fired by ricocheting thoughts, looping mind-to-body, lasso pulling tighter into a noose. She dragged the gold chain at her neck from side to side with her index finger.

***

Ensnared by the world with its raucous-thirsty ghosts, you stop listening. Close the ear of your heart to that other, quieter knowing, knowing that remembers the secret name of things, senses the scent-and-rhythm in everything before words, including your own mystery. You stagger through the day-bright world, a sleepwalker in your own dreaming, lurch from one event to the next. Mind buzzes like a frenetic fly, hostage in a bottle. You hide-and-seek yourself. Forget what it is you are looking for. That imperative you said you'd remember, swore never to forget, slides into murky waters in your deep unchartered mind, a quiet splash. Will you wake?

***

Ella stopped pacing, spoke into the hot air, 'I've got to get out of here.'

The gears in the Land Cruiser grated as the vehicle shuddered into slow motion, then stalled. 'Fuck, you old shit of a thing!' She turned the key again and jiggled the gears. Tom had made it look so easy. This time the old vehicle stuttered, lurched, gained momentum. She reached inside her small pack, half-covered by a towel, to double-check she had brought her water bottle.

Ella parked the vehicle at the fence, climbed through on to the MacDonald property and walked the last two hundred metres to the spring. After the swim she sat on her towel, bathers wet and cooling in the twilight, and watched the sun sinking slowly and turning the sky crimson and vermillion. She scanned the landscape, averting her eyes from the tree where she had found Sully's stiff body. The land softened into long twilight, unbuttoning the tough corset of a scorching day. Slipping free, the hot land seemed to breathe out like a sigh, fingers of light caressing warm earth-skin to rest into the cooling air.

Her body felt clean, refreshed after the hot spring. She gulped mouthfuls of warm water from the water bottle. Her mind wandered, faltered past the pregnancy, what she had to do, catapulted back to Tom, the fight.

Shaking her head, she stood and walked down the slope to the graves. She rubbed at the words on Tom's mother's headstone. Why was his mother buried here? It seemed far from the homestead. She surveyed the disturbed dirt of the other grave.

'Who are you?' She kicked a dry clod. 'And why are you buried here?'

She turned with a jerk, like someone suddenly remembering they'd left a pot burning on the stove, and ran back up to the ute. She pulled the shovel from its brace and headed back down the rocky slope. Hesitating for a moment, she scanned the horizon for dust, but the world was still: nothing stirred, only the long shadows of evening crawling towards home and rest for the night.

Ella scraped loose dirt off the now familiar bone. Laid it aside on a nearby rock. She dug and pulled and picked through the tough red-dry-dirt until several smaller bones came free. She laid them with the longer bone.

The twilight was fading. Shivering as if a cold wind had passed through her, she cast her eyes around. Held her breath. Fuck, Ella, stop freaking yourself out. She gathered up the scattering of bones, placed them gently back into the warm dirt and covered them. She stepped carefully in the near dark, heading back to the spring. Bundling up her towel and water bottle she shoved them into her pack and made her way back to the old Land Cruiser. It was only as she was driving off that she realised she had left the shovel. But no way was she going back now.

Next morning the same feeling was there, stronger. A very particular restlessness. As if she'd lost or forgotten something important. Like a water bottle in the desert. There was something missing, but she couldn't remember what.

'Gotta get out of here.' Could she drive into town in the Land Cruiser? Thank god it was Wednesday, Lil would be at the pub. The only person in the whole town who might tell her the truth about Biddy.

***

'Ran off with a miner. Maybe twenty years ago,' Lil said in her flat, matter-of-fact voice as Ella sipped a gin and tonic.

Lil headed to the opposite end of the bar to tend to a customer. That same man was there, staring at her. She waved to him but he didn't respond. When Lil came back she whispered, 'That guy always stares at me. Who is he?'

Lil bent over laughing, as if she had just heard the funniest joke of her life. She had tears in her eyes and was breathless when she finally stopped laughing.

'What? What's so funny?'

Lil grinned. 'Come and meet Henry.'

Ella frowned; she wanted to avoid meeting this guy who looked kind of creepy for the way he always stared at her. It was okay for Lil, she was on the other side of the bar. But Lil grabbed her by the arm and pulled her along. When they stood in front of the guy, who still hadn't looked away, Lil said, 'Hey, Henry, this is Ella. Reckons you giving her the evil eye, mate.'

Henry grinned widely then laughed like a chugging train. 'She must be blind,' Henry said, and Lil snorted and laughed loudly.

Ella put out her hand to Henry, but he didn't respond. She looked into his eyes and realised they didn't move. They were glassy, unresponsive.

'He's blind as a bat, girl. You a bit paranoid sitting up there thinking blind Henry doing a line for you, eh, sista? You're a funny one.' Henry and Lil laughed.

Smiling, she went back to her seat and had almost finished her drink by the time Lil returned. Each time Lil looked at her she burst out laughing. 'Best joke I heard in weeks, you thinking blind Henry watching you, girl.'

The joke was well over for Ella. She wanted to change the subject. 'So, what else do you know about Biddy leaving?'

'Some folks reckon she pregnant. Maybe why she run off with old Herman.'

'The shearer's name was Herman?'

'Herman the German. A miner. Just did odd jobs to make ends meet, like a lot of them old miners. Then run off with Biddy. Stranger things have happened.'

Lil went down the bar to an old man with most of his teeth missing, stood grinning and chatting as she pulled him a beer, then returned to Ella.

'But what's Queenie got to do with Biddy?'

'Queenie's Biddy's mother.'

'Oh. So Possum is Biddy's sister?'

'More like cousin. Queenie's not her mother. Like surrogate. Auntie. Happens a lot with our mob. Everyone takes care of them kids. Biddy lived at MacDonald's, worked in the big house.' Lil turned away to pull a wire tray from beneath the bar. 'Possum's my cousin too. Mother's mob.'

So many loose ends. 'So do you know where she went?'

'Nah. No one knew where she went. Black Queen went missing same time. They reckon Biddy stole it or was in on it. Don't reckon Biddy had it in her myself.'

'What's the Black Queen? Something to do with Queenie?'

'Nah,' Lil chuckled in her easy way: laughter always close. 'Nope, nonthin' to do with Queenie. Queenie never seen an opal in her life, I reckon. Unless she tripped over it or threw it at them pack of mongrels run wild out her place.'

'So the Black Queen is an opal?'

'They say it's a fabulous opal. Priceless. Belonged to Mrs Mac by all accounts. Dunno much about it. Just the gossip after Biddy left. I wasn't living out here them days. Only reason I remember that whole thing, Mum was all excited. Couldn't stop talking about it. Queenie gone out to MacDonald's with a gun, aimed at old Mac's head, gonna splatter his brain all over the desert. Can you imagine?' Lil shook her head.

'What happened?'

'Can't remember, but word was Queenie blamed Mr Mac for Biddy leaving.'

'But why did Queenie think Ted MacDonald … had something to do with her running off with Herman? I don't get it.'

'Well …' Lil leaned more closely across the bar, scanned to see if anyone was in earshot, and whispered, 'Some reckon old Mac playing hide-the-sausage with Biddy. Mrs Mac always too sick to be doing the jiggy-jig with that old coot MacDonald.' Lil pulled back, eyebrows raised, nodding, watching Ella's face closely. 'Maybe just gossip, but where there's smoke there's fire, I always say.'

'I don't know what to make of all this.'

Lil made a clicking with her tongue, not looking at Ella now. 'Happens a lot with them young black girls working on those properties, no one to look after them. Lovely young girls. Drunk old men thinking it's their right to go poking around.' Lil didn't seem to care who was listening now. Her face was hard, eyes glassy, as if remembering something painful. A man standing along the bar coughed loudly. Lil blinked and went to serve him, took the empty glass he was holding out to her.

The truth and the stories about what happened, or what could have happened, were all tangled up together like Chinese whispers. The story changing over the years. Memory was such a fragile, changeable thing. She knew that as well as anyone.

When Lil came back, she picked up the same thread, as if she had been wanting to spin it for a while. 'Same with them silly cowgirls.'

Ella cocked her head, inviting Lil to continue.

Lil continued, 'Them jillaroos. Come out green as. All tanned legs and waving their tits around. Act shocked when things go wrong.'

Ella felt the tight ache of a frown pucker between her eyebrows.

'Yeah, I know, not PC. Shouldn't be about what a girl's wearing an all that. I'm with you in theory. In the city. Out here it's like walking through a prison naked. Men are starved for it out here. It's a man's world, this desert country. Like it or not.'

'What happens to the jillaroos?' This conversation was cutting too close to the bone and Ella felt her breathing quicken.

'Well, something goes wrong. Starts out being a bit of fun. Then goes bad. Booze and drugs. Someone ends up getting hurt.'

'Sounds like you're saying a woman can expect to get raped out here? That all men are rapists?'

'I'm not saying nothing, just what I seen and heard. Those girls come in here pouring their heart out, captive audience me, this side of the bar. Crying in their beer. Bullied, harassed. Some stations okay. But some treat them girls like cattle.'

'Awful.'

Lil nodded. 'Like them guys come in an' hassled you that day. Pig shooters. If they think they can get away with it, they will.'

***

'Hey, girl, how you doing?' Lil called out the following week as Ella walked into the bar after a strained session with Portia. When she had told Portia about the bone, Portia called it 'her new obsession'. She had suggested that Ella was 'too isolated … hard for a person to keep a grip on reality. The mind can play tricks.' Portia didn't say the words, 'Ella, you're crazy', but near enough. She sure felt crazy. She remembered blind Henry and Lil's laughter the last time she was in the bar. Maybe she was paranoid.

'Hey, Lil,' she said, trying to smile.

'You okay, you look a little peaky or something' Lil raised her eyebrows like two question marks, then frowned, her eyes dropping to Ella's belly.

Ella looked away, felt the heat of Lil's crow-sharp gaze, and waved to blind Henry.

'None-a my business, I reckon. But here if you need a hand, girl …' She said it in a soft, matter-of-fact way, as if she had guessed what was hiding beneath Ella's sundress. All her shorts had become uncomfortably tight.

Ella nodded but didn't meet her eyes.

'What can I get you?'

'Northern Light, thanks, Lil.'

When she returned with a frothing beer that made Ella's dry mouth water Lil said excitedly, 'Hey, I forgot to tell you; thought of it after you asking bout Herman an' all that.' She set down the glass, froth trickling slowly down one side. 'Bushy Bill reckons he met Herman somewhere out west.'

'How much further west can you get than this?' Ella said, gulping a cold mouthful of beer.

'Yeah, right. Lotta desert out there.' Lil laughed. 'Maybe south somewhere.'

'Anything else?'

'Na, dunno. Not much. No one believes Bushy Bill stories. He's a bullshit artist. Ask him yourself, I reckon.'

'How would I find him?'

'Be in at six most nights.'

The large clock on the pub wall showed 5.20pm. She could wait until six. No reason to rush home now the dogs weren't depending on her. Only the chooks to check and lock in. She'd still be home before dark.

'How will I know Bushy Bill?' she asked when Lil came back carrying a stack of glasses.

'You'll know when you see him.'

At 6pm exactly, a man with the blackest, bushiest eyebrows she had ever seen walked into the bar. Lil grinned up at her from the line-up of beers she was pouring and nodded, raising her eyebrows.

Bushy Bill was a tall, laconic man with a downturned mouth that somehow balanced his huge eyebrows. She waited until he was settled, with a beer in front of him. Picking up her drink, she walked over and pulled up the stool next to him.

'Mind if I join you?' she said. Bill grunted but didn't look at her. This was going to be tough.

The conversation was slow. Bill never met her eye. When he finished his beer she offered to buy him another. Ordered one for herself. Frank served her quickly and was gone. Lil had knocked off at six and disappeared.

Bill didn't say thanks but at least he started responding to her questions. She launched her real question, crossed her fingers. 'Lil told me you met Herman the German after he left Broken Ridge?'

Nothing. No reply. Bill didn't even seem to have heard her question. She pushed on, 'Only a few years ago?' Bill picked up his beer and drank deeply, staring straight ahead. 'Out west somewhere, Lil said you saw him?'

'Andamooka.'

She didn't understand what he had said, 'Sorry … what was that?'

'Anda-mooka,' he said it more distinctly.

'Is that a town out west?'

'South Australia. Mining town. Opals.'

'Oh. I see. And Herman was there?'

'Same as you're sitting there. In the Andamooka pub. Large as life. I'd know those eyes anywhere. Changed his name.' Bill took another long draught of beer.

'He was living out there?'

'Mining. Once it's in yer blood, yer always looking for that bit of colour.'

'Any luck?'

'Reckon he must've. He had a little shop an all. Happy as a pig in mud.'

'Married?'

'Don't reckon. At the pub eating a counter meal. Like I'm about to do now. Reckon if you got a missus at home cooking, you won't be eating grub at the pub.' With that Bill signalled Frank and Frank nodded.

'Did –' she felt hot breath in her ear and froze.

'How's my favourite house-sitter?'

Ella pulled her head away, shrugged the arm off her shoulder.

'How's the best rump in town,' the voice said, patting her bottom.

Between gritted teeth she whispered, 'Don't. Touch. Me.'

Liam stepped back, feigning surprise, hands in the air to gesture surrender and innocence. 'I want to buy you a drink.'

'I've got a drink, thanks.' She held up her beer. Bushy Bill was staring up at the television in the corner, seemingly oblivious.

Liam stepped around her and leant on the bar. His thigh pressed against her body. She drew back.

'I have to go now. Thanks, Bill.' Bushy Bill barely moved, just gave an almost nod. She grabbed her pack from the floor, flung it over her shoulder and stomped out of the pub, not looking back.

It was almost dark when she drove over the cattle grid into the front yard. Why hadn't she come straight home instead of trying to call Jaz? He hadn't answered again. She left a third, or was it fourth, message for him to call the landline. Then called Corey, who didn't pick up. Then several other friends. But everyone was either busy or could only talk briefly, promising to call again soon. It felt worse than if she hadn't tried to call them. But she needed a friend after meeting Liam at the pub. Now it was dark. The house looked sad, lonely. She shivered, though the temperature had barely dropped below forty. She pulled freezer bags from the car and staggered into the house, flicking on lights as she went. She shoved the cold stuff in the fridge and headed out the back, the door slamming behind her. Cursed as she tripped on a pipe. Should have brought a torch.

It was quiet when she got to the chook yard. Already in their coop for the night. She toed the brick away from the rickety gate, pushed it shut. There was something stopping it. Grunting, she tried again. In the dim light from the back porch she could just make out a dark lump, spongy as she pushed the gate against it. She reached down and felt soft feathers, sticky, warm. Blood? 'Fuck. No. Fuck.'

She went back to the house, retrieved a torch and pressed it on. Her legs felt heavy. Remembered Maria's warning about foxes. Okay if the dogs were around. Nothing to keep the foxes away now.

She shone the torch on to the headless carcass jamming the gate. Scattered around the yard were three other hens, all with bloody stumps instead of heads. Where was the other one? She leaned into the coop, shone the torch around. The terrified chook was staring back at her, wide-eyed.

'You poor girl.' She placed the torch on the ground, crawled in and tried to grab her, fingers closing on her wing. But the chook squawked and skipped away from her grasp. 'It's okay, girl. Must have been awful seeing your sisters slaughtered like that. I'm not going to hurt you. How did you escape? Clever girl. Come on,' she crooned. But the chook backed further into the corner. She felt her knees sticky with chook poo. What was she going to do with it anyway? Keep it locked up in the kitchen? Would have been better off dead. She made one last lunge, but it squawked and flapped away.

She crawled out backwards, dragging the torch, then rubbed her knees. 'Eew.' There was chook shit everywhere. Nudging the dead bird out of the way with her foot, she pulled the gate closed behind her. She'd have to deal with the massacre in the morning.

Inside, she pulled a not-yet-cold can of beer from the fridge and walked to the phone. There was no red blink telling her there was a message. She pressed it anyway. The American voice said, 'You have no new messages. Thank you.'

She wished Jaz would call. 'Hey Jaz, call the landline. Remember those old things connected to the wall in some houses? Here's the number again …' was the last message she had left.

On television she watched the dreadful fires in NSW, crying as images seared her imagination. Exhausted ash-smudged firies eating icy poles, waving from the fire truck. An orphaned baby koala drinking water from a firie's water bottle, then curled up asleep cuddling a teddy bear. A little joey caught and incinerated in the fence. He looked like a child's abandoned toy, eyes closed, lifeless, hanging from a line of wire. The bulging terrified eyes of a white horse, fleeing for its life. Blackened and burning trees, walls of flame and clouds of smoke rising from the planet like a nuclear explosion.

The phone rang. Finally, he's remembered to call the landline.

'Hey, Jaz.'

Silence.

'Hello? Jaz? Is that you?'

She listened.

'I can't hear you. Hello?'

She listened, holding her breath. Tiny hairs on the back of her neck crackled, alert, ready for danger.

'Who is this? What do you want?'

She banged down the phone, went to the front door and turned on the porch light. The earth was still. She listened, but all she could hear was the occasional birdcall, a dog barking in the far distant night. Was someone watching her? Trying to scare her? Stop it, Ella. Stop.

She slammed the heavy front door.

Half an hour later the phone rang again. She stood in the hallway, watching it as it rang. Don't answer it. Might be Jaz. It's just a phone. No one can hurt you from the end of a phone. She picked it up and put it to her ear.

'Hello.' Her voice sounded little girl lost.

'Hey, hon.' Her body sagged with relief at the sound of Jaz's voice. 'You sound so far away, like you're on another planet,' Jaz said.

'I thought it might have been … I've been getting some weird calls, a heavy breather.'

'Jesus, Ella. You have to get out of that crazy place.'

'Well, did I tell you I had a bingle with an eagle?'

'No. What, you're flying now?'

She heard the grin in his voice and laughed. 'In my car. Low-flying eagle. Looks like the car won't be fixed for weeks. So, I can't leave even if I want to. But I thought I'd escape to Adelaide for a week. There's some cheap flights. Well, relatively – no flights are cheap out here.' She didn't tell him she was going for a termination. Wasn't ready to go into all that yet. 'Can you get some time off to meet me?'

'Don't know how much leave I've got. I'll check it out. No promises, okay?'

'For my birthday.'

'Of course. Why don't you come home? We could have a party.'

She couldn't face all her friends in Melbourne. Even if she didn't have the scratches and scabs down her face and feel fat, not to mention pregnant, she didn't want to celebrate. But she didn't want to be alone either.

'Ella? Are you still there?'

'I can't face a party.'

'Never thought I'd hear you say that, hon. What *is* that desert doing to you?'

She tried to laugh, but it came out as a strangled grunt.

'I'll see what I can do. I'm sure I can organise a few days off.'

They talked about the gossip at work. Friends. Corey working day and night to get enough cash to go on an extended trip to Europe and America.

It wasn't until after she put down the phone that the idea of Andamooka clicked in. She scoured the shelves in Hans's study, igniting a sudden-sharp pang of Hans in a hospital bed on the other side of the world. She found an old road atlas buried under a pile of maps. Opening it, she found the right map and stabbed her index finger on the tiny dot of Andamooka, in the middle of nowhere. About six hours' drive from Adelaide. Could work. She'd have to break it to Jaz gently, work on a convincing line. She'd promise him wineries and Adelaide hotspots, not desert, dust and old miners.

Chapter 13

Jaz walked past Ella at the airport. She ran up behind him and tapped him on the shoulder.

'Hey you,' she said, as he turned. They hugged. He stepped back, studying her. 'I didn't recognise you without your locks! You didn't tell me.' They hugged again.

They dropped Jaz's gear at the hotel and hit the town. She'd been so looking forward to seeing him, but it was hard to feel light-hearted. The termination had gone without a hitch. It was what she wanted; she never questioned that. Rationally and technically, it had been a breeze. She just hadn't expected the emotional reaction. The crying. The innate sense of loss, as if her body was grieving for what might have been.

As they walked to the bar around the corner, Jaz flicked away his lopsided mess of blond-streaked fringe, and gave her a side glance. 'I miss your hair. Weird seeing you without your Rapunzels.'

She smiled back, grabbing his hand, 'A new woman. That's me.' She swung their hands between them. 'So good to see you. I missed you.' She stopped and hugged him. With Jaz it was easy to drop into the refuge of friendship, like slipping into your favourite tattered Uggies. The familiarity of their friendship asked for nothing; they were comfortable with silence, or loud noisy gossip and joking. Nothing required explanation or justification. It had been like that since the beginning.

'What's the matter? I thought this was supposed to be a reunion party, not a funeral,' Jaz said, watching her over first drinks after he had given her a blow-by-blow description of his latest beau. He'd fallen hard. 'He was a proper tart. Broke my heart. Should've seen it coming.' Jaz had laughed at himself, but the pain was alive on his face.

Ella wanted to tell Jaz why she'd come to Adelaide but shame was like a glob in her throat, stopping her words.

'What's going on?'

'I feel stupid. That's why I didn't tell you.'

'I reckon I've got first dibs on stupid, hon.'

'Yeah, well, I've been doing a pretty good job of stupid lately. Just had a termination. Two days ago.'

'Shit. How'd it go?'

'Yeah … actually, I feel really sad. Cried all yesterday and read trashy novels in the hotel. I'll get over it.'

'Did you want it?'

'No. But I still feel sad.'

'Who's the guy? What did he say?'

'A guy in Broken Ridge. Doesn't know. Doesn't care.'

'But I thought you were into women. Given up on men? Can't say I blame you.'

He was there. I was lonely. Barely-there thoughts unfurled like tiny fronds in a shadowy understorey. I needed someone to break the spell of loneliness. She felt Jaz's eyes on her and stared down at her glass. Took a mouthful of gin and tonic. Swallowed hard against the sharp biting-sour of shame-tangled memory at the back of her throat. 'Oh, that was so yesterday, *dahling*.' Her laugh was flat, unconvincing.

'So, who is he? Are you seeing him? Fuck buddy? What?'

'Turns out he's an arsehole. My neighbour. Hot-hot.' She flicked her fingers in a gesture of too-hot-to-touch. 'I was stupid. Really stupid.'

'Well, like I said, I got stupid written across my forehead. We can start a stupid club!' He grinned at her, then his voice changed. 'You alright, though?'

'I'll be okay. Road trip'll be fun. So good to be out of that dump. Wish I didn't have to go back.'

'Why do you have to go back?'

'To get my car, for one thing. Make sure Harry's okay. And I promised Jacob I'd stay on for a bit. Hans had a stroke and they don't know when they'll be back.'

'That's not your problem. I thought you were heading up to Darwin for work. Was waiting for you to get settled up there so I can come visit.'

'Yeah. I'll work it out when I get back. Let's not talk about that now.'

She felt the trapped feeling rise in her belly, dread at the thought of going back to Eldorado. But she had no heart for adventure either. Starting a new life in Darwin seemed like a dark mountain from where she stood.

They talked details of the road trip. Pick up the hire car the day after tomorrow and drive six hours to Roxby Downs, where they had accommodation for three nights. They could drive out to Andamooka from there, only a half-hour away.

***

Jaz had opted for a morning in his room, with his games. As much as she loved Jaz, it was a relief to be alone, sink into the serenity of driving across the land. The landscape flattened out as she drove towards Andamooka, became a wide plain all the way to horizon. Not a tree in sight. No sign of human habitation, except the ribbon of road that wound through red dunes covered in tufted grass the colour of dirty olive leaves, scattered through with bright green-lime, low shrubs. Gibbers shining. Finally, a vehicle. The woman gave her a one-fingered wave, as if saying, I'm here too. You are not alone.

Driving into Andamooka was like entering an alien planet. Mounds of dirt rose on all sides, showing colours from palest sand to pink and red, dark brown, and everything in between. The houses were squat, some makeshift as if thrown together from found materials, mismatched and ramshackle. Some stone buildings resembled puzzle paving; oddly beautiful patterns created out of chaos. Round windows revealed white lace curtains. A wrought-iron door to a tin shack of rusted corrugated iron. There were small scrubby trees around some houses, but most were surrounded by bare red dirt with found objects lying around, like mini-junkyards. One innovative gardener had built a retaining wall out of discarded tyres, with cactuses erupting out the top alongside other tough-stunted plants. Survival of the fittest. She pulled up in the sparse shade of a small eucalypt. The place looked deserted.

Ella walked across the road to a low, lime-washed building, where the blurb on a faded metal board announced 'The Cottages'. A museum of early miners. Wandering through the small rooms, she snapped images with her phone to show Jaz what he had missed. But how was she going to find Herman?

She left the cooler interior of the squat dwelling and stood for a moment, shading her eyes from the sudden light. So, what now? There were a couple of shops down the road, service station, pub, post office.

She hadn't really thought this through, didn't know what name Herman used out here, or if he wanted to be found.

Ella headed along the dusty gravel road towards the shops, scanning abandoned dwellings and hand-painted signs as she tried to work out her story. Her imagination played out various stories, all dead ends. Unconvincing. Didn't Bushy Bill say Herman owned a small opal shop? Maybe that's the way to start?

A dust-covered vehicle passed her, turned into a lane and parked. She watched as the driver emerged and entered a large, stumpy building. On impulse she followed her inside and into a large, high-ceilinged hall. Heavy red velvet curtains hung over a stage at the front. At the other end was a temporary screening of hessian fence.

The woman who had just entered was scooping change from a box underneath a sign that read 'Book exchange $3'. Above a blue-and-white-striped awning on the far wall was a sign, 'Andamooka Yacht Club'. Ella smiled at the bush humour. A long window beneath the awning showed a heavily bearded man wearing a cap, talking to someone out of sight. She walked over to the doorway and entered a small cafe with a cosy feel, colourful tablecloths and wooden chairs, throw cushions along one corner, smell of coffee strong in the air. The man behind the counter chatted over the noise of the coffee machine to the customer, but she couldn't follow their conversation. She put in her order and wandered back into the large outer hall, peering at old photos along the wall. Miners standing in front of mullock heaps, alongside blowers and other large equipment. Pictures of opals everywhere.

The coffee was good, really good. She sat at a low table in the main hall, still unsure how to go about looking for Herman. She took out a notebook. When there was no one else around she chatted through the opening to the man behind the counter. Big Al. Born in Istanbul. Married an Australian.

'Any opal shops here?'

'Yeah, Pete and Margo at the post office sell Andamooka opals.'

'Ah. Anywhere else? Those other small shops look deserted?' Bushy Bill's news of Herman was a few years old. Maybe Herman had left town. Maybe he was dead. Must check the cemetery. But what name?

Al gave her directions to the old cemetery, along with the legendary account of its origin. It became the first cemetery when an old miner died there on his way home from the pub, drunk. Fell over in the heat and never got up. Someone found him a few days later, decomposing. The small crowd of miners had stood around in the midday sun, wondering what to do with the bloating corpse, and quickly decided to bury him on the spot rather than try to move the body. They dug a hole and rolled him in. Someone said a few prayers, then they all went off to the pub to wash out the dust of death and toast the new Andamooka cemetery.

She wandered between unmarked graves. Some were no more than a slab of cement, unadorned. Others were a simple arrangement of rocks. Dirt with a cross made of stones, a collection of gibbers. A few headstones were more ornate. 'Friends from Andamooka' donated one headstone, but the name had faded. Several names were still visible. Hungarian, Croatian maybe. No Herman.

When she got back to the Andamooka Yacht Club, she ordered another coffee and a bacon-and-egg roll, and sat on a stool asking questions as Al busied himself at the hotplate.

'Some of the old miners sell a few opals locally,' Al said, wiping his face with the dishcloth, 'but only by appointment these days. Not busy enough.' He wiped counters and stacked dirty dishes between flipping egg and bacon and toasting the roll. 'Most miners just want to mine. Not that interested in the business side of things.'

'Are you a miner?'

'Would love to be. Wife thinks it's a mug's game. No better than gambling. Except hard work.'

'Actually Al, I'm more interested in miners than opals. I'm doing some writing and I'm interested in migrants who came out to the outback. Especially opal miners.' It sounded so dodgy. 'For a book I'm writing.'

'Oh, yeah, what's the book?'

'Um … like a murder mystery. And some guy … well, he steals an opal. I don't want to give away the plot line. You might find yourself in it, Al.'

'Fine by me. Always wanted to be a celebrity.' He grinned, showing even white teeth hiding in his black beard.

'Well, you make great coffee. So anyway, do you know any old miners who might speak to me? For my research?'

'There are a few Americans. One big family came out in the early days. Six kids, maybe seven. I reckon Ray or Freddie would be good for a chat.'

'I was thinking more European.'

'I dunno, mate. Lots of guys around here you could talk to. Stan, Russo, Bullet. Maybe Bert. Some of them are cagey when you meet them. But friendly once you get them going, especially after a few beers. Never talk about what they find though. Worried someone might rat on them.'

She nodded, waiting for him to continue.

'Might want to talk to Bert. He keeps himself to himself, but had a little shop. Don't think he opens it these days. Old rail carriage. Could try. Up the hill there.' Al pointed towards the front door, sweeping his hand in a vague direction. 'Best way to find anyone in this town is the pub about six. Thirsty work, opal mining.'

'Okay, thanks, Al.' She ate her food and walked up the dusty road to the carriage marked with a faded sign that read, 'The Opal Carriage'. She called out, but there was no answer. A dog barked nearby.

***

Jaz groaned loudly when they pulled up outside the pub. It was a low, flat-roof building, all greys and browns. Someone in a creative rush had assembled a stone wall out the front and cemented in around it. It looked as if it would hold its own against a Mack truck. A few heavy tables were lined up outside under a tin roof, covered in dust.

'Really?! You brought me all the way out here for this?' he said, screwing up his nose. He was dressed to kill in kick-arse Melbourne gear. She was in denim shorts and tank top, with flat sandals. She had told Jaz what an amazing place Andamooka was. Full of characters and stories about the wild days. Jaz had reluctantly agreed to come. She had bribed him with the offer of buying his drinks all night, and dinner, and she would be designated driver. As she parked the car she wondered if maybe it would have been easier if she'd come alone.

'It's called adventure, Queen Dag,' she said, using her old name for him. 'Adventure. Never know what's coming next.' She grinned at him.

'You're good at that. Always a surprise.' He smiled, eyes laughing, shaking his head.

Inside, the pub was dark, with a low ceiling. An air conditioner belched noisily but effectively. The floor was large, once pastel-coloured lino tiles, stained and worn down to the dirt-brown underlay. A small TV high in one corner was calling horse races, a couple of men sitting around nearby, heads tilted. Other men, old and craggy, were scattered along the bar. No one looked up when they walked in.

They ordered drinks. Light beer for Ella, scotch and dry for Jaz.

'Make it a double,' he said as she ordered. 'I need something to lift my spirits.'

They sat at the bar, eyed the men.

'What does this guy look like?' Jaz said in a loud whisper.

'I don't know.'

Jaz frowned. 'So, we're in a pub in the middle of nowhere, looking for a guy. But you don't know his name or what he looks like. Jeez, that makes sense.' He took a large gulp from his glass and shook his head.

'Yeah, tricky, eh?.' She nodded.

Jaz got drunk. Started chatting to anyone who would listen. After they finished their counter meal, he challenged a couple of guys to a game of pool. Dragged her into the game. They were losing badly.

'Anyone sell opals around here?' she asked, after she had sunk one of their balls and they had whooped and hollered.

The younger of the two said, 'Yeah, a couple of the old guys sell opals. Pete at the post office sells some. He polishes and sets them.'

She had seen Pete's opals and had tried to quiz him about Herman. But Pete had kept the conversation close to his own business.

'Anyone else got a display?' The conversation meandered and stumbled. She felt an almost prickle at the back of her neck. A man sitting alone at the far end of the bar was watching her. He had the bluest, sharpest eyes she had ever seen. Herman. She was sure of it.

When the game finished, she opted out, leaving Jaz to negotiate another round with the friendly strangers. She walked slowly towards Herman, trying not to stare at him. Stood next to him and ordered Jaz another drink and a bowl of hot chips.

Ella sat to wait on the stool next to the man, back against the bar, watching the pool game. Jaz pranced up and down, wriggling his butt for the local guys, who didn't seem to notice. Acting like Priscilla, Queen of the Desert.

'You looking for opals?' the man with blue eyes said, interrupting her thoughts.

She nodded, met his gaze. His eyes were penetrating, bright and curious.

'I might have some to sell. You staying around here?' His accent was thick. Unmistakably German.

'Roxby Downs. Couldn't get any accommodation out here.'

'Place's not the same since the opals dried up.'

'Are you a miner?'

'Yep.'

'Been here long?'

'About twenty years. More opal back then.'

'Not so good now?'

'Not like the old days.'

'Hard work?'

'You got to move a lot a dirt to strike colour. Too hard for these young fellas. Do more drinking than mining, I reckon.'

'Young people these days, eh?!' She smiled at him.

His eyes smiled back, though his lips barely moved. He gave a nod.

A million questions crowded in. She bit them back, letting the smile linger between her and the bright-eyed man, aiming to soften into camaraderie.

'Could show you some stones tomorrow,' the man said, breaking the silence.

'Great, thanks.'

'Hot chips.' The barman plonked the bowl in front of her.

'That was quick.' He didn't respond.

'See you tomorrow, then,' she said, picking up the bowl and Jaz's drink. She swivelled on her stool, ready to stand, then placed the chips back on the bar and held out her hand to the man beside her, 'Ella.'

'Bert.' He smiled at her and shook her hand firmly. She felt the calloused hardness of his warm hand.

'How will I find you tomorrow?'

'What time you likely to be here?'

'Maybe ten? That work?'

'See you at the Yacht Club at ten for coffee.'

'Perfect. Thanks. My shout.'

He nodded and angled his glass towards her like a nod.

***

Al grinned at her the next day like she was a local. She ordered coffees, extra strong for Bert.

Bert was chatty. He regaled her with stories from the wild days of Andamooka when it was a thriving mining town, full of larger-than-life characters. He talked about mining. Making the cut. Scratching down into dirt covering an ancient seabed to find opal.

'What about the women, Bert?'

'What do you mean?'

'Well, I always hear stories about men in the outback, mining towns. Outback characters. But women's stories aren't often told or remembered. That's the problem with history. It's a record of those in power, the educated, who could write it down. Mostly white men. Women's voices are silent or lost. And Indigenous voices.'

Bert nodded, took a large sip of coffee.

'Did you ever marry, Bert?'

'Na, not old Bertie. Married to the pretty rock.'

'And where were you before you came to Andamooka? Did you come straight from Germany to here?' She felt her heart racing, coming close to the possibility of learning the truth, teetering on a precipice. One false move and she could slip.

Bert was quiet for a while, stared at his coffee. 'Place further north. Had a claim out there. Once those opals get in your blood, can't stop. Never went back…' His voice trailed off.

'And why did you…' She stopped abruptly. *Wrong.* The question clanged. She was pushing too hard. She felt it and she knew Bert-or-Herman felt it from his look, his eyes narrowing. Her mind swerved and bucked, trying to come up with the next right question. Not too close but drawing him towards what had happened when he left Broken Ridge.

Bert stood. 'Enough questions. I'll take you to look at some stones.'

One end of an old train carriage had been converted into a small shop. But it was obvious that Bert rarely opened it; the glass cases were almost

154

empty. He flicked on lights inside the cabinets and the stones lit up. Eyes shining, he plucked different opals from the cabinet, moving them to catch the light. Watching him handle the opals was like looking at someone in love.

Bert talked on and on about opals. It was hard to steer him back to his past; the conversation slipped away whenever she came too close with her questions. After she'd spent ten minutes studying the opals and making ooh-ah noises, Bert started packing away the stones. Their rendezvous was coming to an end. Just do it, Ella. Nothing to lose now. As he put the last opals back in their cabinets, she said, 'Bert, I'm looking for an Aboriginal woman from Broken Ridge called Biddy.'

His hand froze. He stared at her, eyes piercing. 'Who are you? What do you want?' He wasn't hostile, just wary. 'I don't like being tricked. Thought you wanted to buy some stones.'

'Sorry, Bert. I am interested in opals. I think they're beautiful.'

'You tricked me into this so that you could ask your questions.' He rested the last of the opals back in the cabinet, closed and locked it, without speaking further or looking at her.

'I didn't know how else to talk to you. I wasn't sure who to ask … I thought you might know something.' She had a sinking feeling, but could understand why he was pissed off, felt deceived. From their brief conversations, she sensed that Bert was a good bloke. An honest gentleman in the true sense of the word. 'I'm sorry, Bert. I didn't think it through. I just want to know what happened to Biddy.'

Bert was silent for a long time. He leant against the bench and studied his dirty fingernails. When he finally spoke, his voice was quiet. 'Shoulda been honest with me. Hate liars and cheaters.'

'I was stupid, Bert. But I thought you might not talk to me.'

'True enough.'

'And I wasn't sure you were Herman. You are Herman?'

He nodded.

A dog barked outside. The old miner stared out the low window of the carriage to the dusty track outside. His face frozen. But she knew his mind was working. She waited. Deep lines of laughter and sorrow were etched into his face, toughened from hours under the sun. This face belonged to the desert. Those eyes saw eagle and ant, and blue fire shining in rock.

Abruptly Bert turned to her, eyes glistening. 'Come around back. 'About time I told someone. I did nothing wrong. Got nothing to hide. Come through; I'll make coffee.' His voice was matter-of-fact.

The back of the carriage was a one-room affair. Neat. Compact. Comfortable. He gestured to the only lounge chair in the space. The faded fabric was torn and roughly patched on one arm.

'Not really set up for visitors.' His face barely changed, but his eyes smiled at her. He didn't speak while he made coffee on a Bialetti over a small gas flame. The black-black coffee came in a small cup; she savoured a mouthful and felt the rush of caffeine.

Bert sat on the wooden straight-back chair at the small table. Took a sip of coffee. 'Now. No more lies.'

She started slowly, faltering, 'It started with Queenie …' She told him what Lil had said, and Bushy Bill. 'I want to know what happened the night you left Broken Ridge.'

'I'll tell you what I know. But don't reckon it's much help finding the young woman, Biddy, you said?'

She nodded.

Bert looked into his coffee. The cup was like a doll's cup in his large hands. He took a final sip, upended it, placed it back on its miniature saucer, and turned to her. 'Hardly knew the girl. 'Cept she brought us morning smoko and lunch to the shed at shearing time. I did a few jobs there for old Mac. Make ends meet.'

His eyes wandered, reaching for memories that went twenty years back, covered in the dust of neglect. The words arrived slowly, as if the memories were in fragments that he had to piece together as he spoke.

'Mr Mac, he come to me in the night. Woke me, eyes wild.' Bert spoke in a deep, hard-edged accent mixed up with the twang of the outback, coating his words with an exotic-familiar vernacular. 'Said he'd give me the Black Queen if I left before morning and never come back.'

He stared down at the floor. Ella waited.

'Had a wad of money. Counted off a thousand. I said, "All of it." He didn't argue. Nearly two thousand.' Bert paused and looked around as if searching for something. 'Made him sign the back page of my Bible. Left and never went back. Luckiest day of my life. First time I had money. I was careful. Took my time. Looked around and then came out here. Couldn't give up them opals. They get in your blood.'

'Didn't you wonder why he was willing to give you so much money to disappear?'

' 'Course I did. But I was broke. I mean broke, where you don't know where your next meal is coming from. Man doesn't ask too many questions when he's starving. Most people don't know that unless they been there.'

'Did he say anything else?'

'Nope.'

She watched his blue-blue eyes full of sky.

'Been a long time now. Years I was always watching over me shoulder, thinking someone would walk in one day and cuff me, drag me off. Even though I done nothing wrong.'

'No one's ever come asking about it?'

'Old fella remembered me once.'

'Bushy Bill?'

'That's him. Reckon he knew my eyes and the accent. I had a beard in those days at Broken Ridge, easier than shaving. Shaved it off when I left with the Black Queen in me pocket. But you can't change the eyes or the accent. Reckon it doesn't matter now. Not my secret anyhow. I done nothing wrong. Never told anyone, though.'

'Did Bushy Bill say anything?'

'Said rumour was Herman run off with an Aboriginal girl. Stole the Black Queen. Best opal in the district, probably best in the country. And she's mine.'

'So you had nothing to do with Biddy?'

'Barely knew her. Like I say, only time I spoke to her was bringing down smoko to the shearing shed. Saw her round the big house when I done odd jobs.'

'Did you sell the opal to get this place?'

'Couldn't part with her. She brought me luck. Want to see her?'

'Sure.'

'Better turn round now. Don't want you seeing me secret stash. Not that I reckon you going to rob me.'

She twisted around in the armchair, eyes to the back wall. She heard clanking and banging noises, metal creaking. Then she felt a gentle nudge.

Bert held the flat case open with both hands, like a holy man with a sacred offering. He moved it slightly to catch the light, and the large, dark green-blue opal came alive. A fleck of vibrant red danced as he moved it. He smiled down on it with a look of awe.

'Oh … it's beautiful,' Ella gasped. 'I've never seen anything like it.' She couldn't take her eyes off it; it was as if a universe lived inside the stone. She peered in, bound in its spell.

'Ain't she a beauty? Better than sex, this girl. And she's mine. Luckiest day of me life when he gave it to me. I just hightailed it out of there. Never looked back. She's my lucky girl.' He lifted the opal and kissed it.

'She's beautiful, Bert, truly beautiful. So, if …'

'Better turn around again while I put her away.' She faced the wall again until he gave her the word to turn back. He was leaning back in his chair, watching her.

'So, if Biddy didn't run off with you, where is she?'

'Like I say, hardly knew the kid. She was always with them MacDonald twins.'

'She disappeared the same night you did, Bert. And her mother went kind of crazy. Blamed Ted MacDonald. Tried to shoot him.'

'I don't know what happened when I left, but I didn't steal the Black Queen and I didn't do anything wrong.' Bert rifled through a pile of papers on a dusty sideboard and extracted a yellowing piece of paper that was almost falling apart. He opened it carefully, handed it to her. 'Here it is.'

The writing was awkward, chaotic and hard to read. She read aloud, 'I Ted MacDonald of Melville, Broken Ridge Australia (something indecipherable) freely give the opal called the Black Queen opal to Herman the German, of my own free will. It now belongs to him.' It was signed and dated.

'Yes, I know you've done nothing wrong, Bert, but I think something happened that's been covered up. Some injustice.'

'Best let sleeping dogs lie, I reckon, miss. First law of the outback. Mind your own business. More than twenty years ago now. Nothing you can do.'

'I think something bad happened that night Biddy went missing. I want her to get the justice she deserves, for Queenie.'

'Want to be careful, miss. That MacDonald got a bad temper. Back then anyhow. Reckon he got a few of the dark women duffed too. But no one talks about that.'

'Do you know something else?'

'Just gossip missy, I reckon. Just gossip around Melville station.'

'What, Bert? What was the gossip?'

'Some said that little dark girl – not too dark though, fair-skinned, pretty smile – the one I's supposed to run off with … funny they reckon I run off with her. Hardly knew her.'

'And the gossip?'

'Some reckon those two boys were her little 'uns, from him, you know, Ted.'

'What, Biddy was the mother of the twins? The MacDonald twins?' Bert's words struck an invisible switch, making the hairs on the back of her neck stand up. Her mind went haywire, leaping with rapid synaptic connections, jamming with new information. Think about it later.

'What else was the gossip, Bert?'

'Well, they said the missus, Mrs Ted, always sick in bed … said she couldn't have babies, something went wrong … women's business. Mr Ted always taking after the young black women, just girls. Sent 'em away when their bellies blew up.'

Bert shook his head slowly, watching the floor. 'Who knows what's true? One of them kids got blackfella eyes as I remember. Didn't see much of them after they away at school. But real black eyes. Only gossip. That place full of gossip.'

'Yes, Tom's eyes are very dark,' she murmured, staring out the small dirty window on to the dusty road.

'Kids always with the black girl, too, when Mr Ted not around. Mrs Ted never left the house. That dark girl look after them bubs. Nice kids. She was just a kid herself.'

Ella's mind raced. Liam and Tom, Biddy's sons to Ted MacDonald, was it possible? No wonder Ted MacDonald had told her to keep away from Queenie, that she was crazy, told crazy stories. Was it all to keep people off the scent of what he'd done to Biddy?

'What, what was that, Bert? Sorry …'

'I said, she loved them boys, like her sons. Maybe that's why the gossip started. Who can say? Probably never know.'

Bert stood to make more coffee. She declined, her heart was already racing against her ribcage. He chatted as he moved around the tiny kitchenette, a giant in a doll's house, his movements efficient, skilled. She probed and poked, hoping for more clues. But Bert had nothing more.

When she stood to leave, he said, 'Better let it go, miss. Bad stuff buried out there. Go and find a fella and settle down. Nice girl like you.'

She tried hard not to roll her eyes. 'Marry a cowboy, you reckon, Bert?'

'I was thinking one o' them MacDonald boys. What I remember, good-looking lads. Be about your age?'

'Yes, nice-looking boys, Bert. Did they know that Biddy was their biological mother?'

'Dunno. Don't reckon. If she was their mother, Mr Mac wouldn't've wanted anyone to know. Not the way he was about blacks. Something cruel in him; you don't want to cross him. Do his block. Specially on the grog, as I recall.'

***

Settled at the bar of the Roxby Downs pub with cold beverages, Ella recounted her meeting with Bert. By the time their meals had arrived Ella had filled him in.

'Some story,' Jaz said, 'but what has all this got to do with the Aboriginal woman Bitty?'

She nodded, swallowing a mouthful of steak. '*Biddy*. Yes, that's exactly what I want to know. If she didn't leave with Herman aka Bert, where did she disappear to? And why didn't she ever contact Queenie?'

'I wish someone'd pay me to leave. Not big on opals, though. Nan says they're bad luck.'

'The opal, the Black Queen is its official title, is fabulous.'

'What, so opals have names, like they have a life, and pay tax?'

She laughed, cut a small piece of steak and put it to her mouth. It was tender, salty. 'Herman said the gossip was that the twins, Liam and Tom, are her kids, fathered by Ted MacDonald.'

'Right. Is that important?'

She had a memory flash of riding with Tom, how he'd talked about his 'good friend'. The way he'd said it, like remembering someone beloved, gone. It must have been Biddy he was referring to. He hadn't wanted to talk about her, even name her. She had abandoned him. At least that's what he believed. Yes, there had been both pain and sorrow when he mentioned 'the friend' who had told the stories.

'Don't stop now, it's just getting interesting,' Jaz said, shoving chips into his mouth.

'I don't think Tom knows Biddy is his biological mother, if she is. He does have black eyes. Blackfella eyes, Herman called them.'

'So, he's Indigenous. He'll be happy about that.'

'I don't know.'

'Oh, everyone wants to be Indigenous these days. Find a bit of black blood in their ancestry.'

'I don't think that's PC, Jaz.'

'Since when've I been PC, hon?' His attention shifted her abruptly. She followed his gaze. A tall man had just walked through the door. A cowboy, complete with big hat, boots, moleskins and a red-and-white checked shirt. The man looked towards Jaz and an indefinable something passed between them.

'Now *that* is interesting.' And that was the end of the conversation about Biddy and the MacDonald twins.

Chapter 14

'Hey, I forgot to tell you the news about your nemesis, Maid Marion.'

Instantly Ella's stomach tightened, her thoughts dragged back into those months of apprehension waiting for the court case.

'She's facing another tribunal. Bullying. That's the word anyway. Maybe they'll get her this time.' Jaz was excited, his words spilled fast into the cool-stale air of the airport.

'Add negligence to that, and racism, stupidity … bad make-up,' Ella said, watching an aircraft land, but inside sinking into marshes of memory. 'I should have gone over her head, I should have made it more official, should've …' She raked her fingers through her hair. The aircraft was taxiing towards the landing.

'Should've what? You know what would've happened. They would've had your guts.'

'That poor mother needed someone to speak for her.'

'But no one could prove anything. You saw the coroner's report. Besides, you had to save your own bacon, girl. Don't forget that. They could have done you for interfering with evidence before the coroner arrived.'

'It doesn't make it right, Jaz.' She didn't want to think about the court hearing.

'They could have hung you out to dry, Ella. You had nothing left.' Jaz reached across and put his hand on hers. 'Anyway, maybe the bad karma has finally caught up with the bitch.'

'If I'd been there … If I'd been there when the mother came back that night, the baby might've lived.' The same old loop of blame and recrimination chased her dogged mind, around and around.

'Don't do this to yourself again, Ella. You're not responsible. You can't save every baby.'

But she knew she was responsible. Knew that if she hadn't slipped out to the car park for a cigarette, needing to calm herself after the run-in with

Marion, she would have been there when the mother came back the second time. She'd never told anyone, not even Jaz or Portia, that she'd gone out for that cigarette. Stood shivering in the carpark sucking nicotine into her lungs while that woman's baby was dying. Yes, she knew she was responsible. Shame burnt under her skin like a blood tattoo that flared in darkest night when she was alone and her mind filled with the dirty secret she carried, hiding in the deep shadow of who she was.

Like an unwelcome guest in the night, her newest dirty secret lined up, insistent. What Liam had done to her that night. She hadn't told anyone. Who was she going to tell? Jaz? Police? Psychologist? She had known she was playing with fire. Had felt something hard and cruel in Liam after that first time. If she reported it, who would believe her? She knew how victims of sexual assault were treated by the legal system. Especially if they'd had consensual sex with the perpetrator previously. She knew how victims were interrogated in court, as if the woman's accusation was the crime. Yes, it was usually a 'she'. The victim's dirty laundry aired to show what a slut she was. With no right to say no, because she had said yes too many times. As if there was a quota of yeses that unbalanced, undermined and silenced her no. For all the public campaigns to change it, she knew this was how victims of sexual assault were still treated. And she didn't trust the system, the police, the lawyers. It was all bullshit, one big fat lie; the court case had showed her that.

She felt Jaz's eyes on her, and for one panicky moment felt a lurching urge to tell rising up inside her. Which secret? It didn't matter. It was the telling of shame that mattered. She felt words forming, thick and gelatinous at the back of her throat, pushing against the panic of being exposed, vulnerable, even with her best friend. Was she ready to talk?

Jaz shifted on the red pleather seat, cocked his head. His flight was being called. Jetstar to Melbourne.

Walking back to her hotel room after dropping off the rental car, Ella tried to block out the memories of the small mother and her wide, frightened eyes. But it was like trying to herd black cats. Her mind winced back to that winter night. The tendons and membranes that held the memory packed down tight began to loosen, unravel. Snatches of conversation, images, spilled into her mind. She saw Marion in vivid detail, the way she tied back her bottle-blonde hair, the slight lisp, sharp nose, and heavy matt makeup. She always looked colourless, beige. Marion was beige, blancmange. Does anyone make blancmange any more? Her grandma used to make it.

The hotel room had been serviced. She closed the curtains against the glare and laid down, closed her eyes.

***

The small woman had rushed into Emergency again an hour before the end of night shift. She was carrying the bundle of white blanket, her face pale, set in a stone-mask of anguish. Ella grabbed the bundle from the woman without a word.

Inside the cubicle she laid the motionless infant on the trolley, buzzing for help as she grabbed equipment. Her heart drummed at her temples as her body snapped into emergency autopilot, giving sharp commands to other nurses coming in, moving the mother aside.

'There's a pulse, but it's weak,' Ella said, as people in pale blue poured into the tight space.

The small crowd clustered around the trolley, poking and probing the infant, working frantically to bring life back into his small heart and lungs. But his tiny heart was weak from its long struggle between life and death that had raged through the night. They kept trying, one more time, hoping for a miracle.

The fluttering-stuttering heart finally gave up the fight. It was the intern, Malcolm, who put a warm hand on Ella's arm and said, 'He's gone. Let him rest now.' The room fell silent.

Marion was staring down at the baby on the trolley, her face pale under the fluorescent light. Her lips were pulled tight, and Ella didn't know if it was a grimace or a crazed smile. Marion raised her face, eyes shining, and saw Ella watching. Her face changed in an instant. She lifted her chin, sniffed, and walked out.

The small mother was standing frozen near the door, a hand over her mouth. Her eyes didn't move or blink as staff exited around her. The light buzzed overhead, accentuating the deep shadows beneath her eyes. Had she been there all the time? Or slipped in afterward? Had she witnessed everything? Before-or-after? Before-or-after rolled through her head like a familiar lost mantra.

164

Alone in the cubicle, Ella had walked over to the woman and put a hand on her shoulder. The woman looked up, startled. She began muttering something Ella couldn't understand. In her heavy accent it sounded like a prayer, stuck on repeat. And then through the rhythm, the words became clear, 'Bad-mother, bad-mother …'

Ella shook her head. 'This is not your fault,' she said, in a round, clear pronunciation of her words.

The small woman's dark eyes were shifting wildly. 'Bad-mother, bad-mother …'

Ella stood directly in front of the woman, stooped to her line of sight, and repeated, 'It's not your fault.'

The woman shook her head and pointed at herself, 'Me, fall asleep,' she wailed in her thick accent, and began to sob. Through the ragged breaths, she kept repeating the words, 'Me fall asleep … fall asleep …' Ella held the woman against her chest and her own tears spilled on to her head.

A loud yelling in the corridor made Ella look up. She couldn't tell how long they had stood clutching each other. The little mother was quieter now, but her arms were still locked around Ella's waist.

Ella removed herself gently from the woman's grasp and led her to a chair. The mother seemed to sink into herself, eyes wide but unseeing. Ella went to the baby, unplugged tubes and removed the Resus equipment from the trolley. Picking up a silver bowl, she walked slowly to the sink and turned on the tap. A blast of water sprayed the front of her uniform. She fiddled with the tap until the water flowed warmly over her hand, filled the bowl, then pulled a clean white cloth from the metal cabinet. Walking slowly, as for a solemn ritual, she went to the trolley where the infant lay, and rested the bowl of warm water on a towel close to his head.

The room sank into the silence of an underwater cave. Everything outside was quiet and dark, as if this cubicle was all that existed. A bright shaft of fluorescent light pierced through into this world that only Ella and the small mother occupied, with the infant on the trolley between them.

The woman's eyes stared unblinking, fixed on that small, lifeless face, her hand covering her mouth.

Ella squeezed warm water from the cloth. Cradling the infant's head in her left hand, she pressed the cloth gently on to his face with smooth strokes, as if she were cleaning the most fragile glass. She dipped the edge of the cloth into the bowl again, squeezing it between her fingers. Ran the cloth over one closed eye and then the other, clearing away the crusted tears on his long dark lashes. Still cradling his head, she dipped the edge of the cloth and washed away thick hardened clots around tiny pale nostrils, squeezing his nose gently between the cloth, the way a mother holds a tissue for her small child to blow their nose.

Mind blank, as if death had filled her head with emptiness, she sponged dried spittle from each side of his mouth and perfect lips. Her whole being was present to wash this small pale face. There was nothing else in the world. She wanted to bend and kiss the bud of his lips that would never smile again, never taste a ripe peach or laugh at a butterfly. Her fingers moved slowly, her tears falling on to the baby's closed eyes.

She forgot where she was, forgot the woman, forgot herself. There was only her hand washing this infant's pale face.

When his face was clean it reminded her of an old grainy photo she'd seen of a waxy porcelain doll. She bent and kissed his cool cheek, a primal reflex of love for the child of a stranger, more urgent than her clinical mind or training. The silence inside her was so profound she heard her breath against his cheek. For an instant she wondered if his eyes would flicker open and he would smile at her. In that moment, he seemed more alive, more real than any other human.

Straightening, she became aware of the mother staring at her. The woman's hand had dropped to her chest, fingers wide. The other hand was clutching the white blanket. Their eyes fixed as strangers' do across a bloody war zone when everything seems too terrible to speak. Eyes connecting, beyond exhaustion, beyond unspeakable grief, beyond difference and separation, contacting some mystery inside each. Seeing into another human heart without flinching, even when it hits your lungs like icy air. They looked at each other as sisters who know what it is to lose someone you love more than life itself.

Ella blinked. Tears rolled down the side of her face and on to the pillow. All her chronic unanswered questions about death had opened up after that night. Like cracks in the foundation of an old house, invisible at first, until everything starts to shake and tremble in the slightest zephyr.

The vortex of uncertainty she'd felt after her father died had pulled her to write, trying to probe the tsunami of questions and hold on to herself at the same time. But her questions had only led to frustration and confusion, that longing she couldn't name. She'd given up. Taken up drinking and fucking instead. Easier. But the woman and her baby had ruptured sutures that held things in place. The questions had spilled out again as if they'd been lurking in a dark corner, waiting to rush in at the first opening.

As her eyes had met with the little mother's across such unbearable suffering, the pain had somehow become more endurable because someone else knew. But knew what? What did that woman know that Ella couldn't articulate? The need to know – to find words that could help her hold and dive deeper into understanding that encounter with death and suffering – festered into a longing that compelled her to write. Tangled up in her own powerlessness, she kept trying, battling the insufficiency of words that were too small to hold or express the feelings she had experienced that night.

The itch that couldn't be scratched made her feel crazy, like a bag lady wandering through the park, constantly scratching. Yes, that's how it felt, this hunger to write, like an itchy-scratchy bag lady. All her questions in crumpled plastic bags, small treasures, broken and meaningless stuff that had become ridiculously precious, crammed into bulging bags, carried but never used; useless stuff, useless questions.

Chapter 15

Ella stood in the hallway listening to the messages on the machine.

Her car was ready.

Jacob updating her on Hans, and thanking her for taking care of things.

Aunt Rose. Two messages. She'd forgotten to call Aunt Rose before she went away. 'Happy birthday, darling.' And the second message, 'I hope this is the right number. Your mobile always seems to be out of range. Ella, I'm worried about you. Call me please, love. Just to let me know you're okay.'

Corey. 'Hey, Ella, it's me, sorry I didn't get back to you before you left for that place. Would have loved to come, but life is hell on a stick at the moment. I'm working three jobs trying to get cashed up. It's only six weeks till the big trip. So excited … You and Jaz will have a ball. Talk soon. Happy birthd–' The message stopped mid-sentence.

Portia. 'Ella. Please call and let me know everything is okay.'

A second message from Portia: 'Ella call me …' She sounded pissed off, or worried? Had she told Portia she didn't want any more sessions after the last one? She couldn't remember. The weeks before the trip to Andamooka were a blur. It had been so good to get away, and now she was back in this hellhole. It was the last place she wanted to be.

She missed the rest of Portia's message and played it again. 'I need to know you're okay. I have a duty of care …' Oh, stop all the fussing. I know you're just covering your arse. She played the message again. 'I know last session was difficult … and well … We don't always make the best decisions for ourselves when we're distressed or overwhelmed … I'm concerned about you, Ella. Please return my call.'

Ella slumped down on to the wooden seat of the hallstand and played the messages again. Didn't want to ring any of them. When it came to the first message with the long silence, she leant down close to the machine and listened. Could she hear someone breathing, or was that just the buzz of the recorder? Maybe it was Tom or Portia. 10.45 pm Tues. Late. She listened again to the second message. Nothing but long silence. She played it a second time. This time she thought she could hear a sound like a motor running. 2am Tuesday. The middle of the night. None of her friends would call that late. Not even Jaz. Besides, the message would have been recorded while she was with Jaz.

She pressed the 'Delete all messages' button. Just ignore it. Might be something to do with Maria and Hans?

She tried to remember when the calls had started. Should have written it down. She didn't want to get into some conspiracy theory with Tom or Portia. Portia already doubted her sanity, and Tom … who knew what Tom thought of her? Probably thinks I'm a crazy bitch, too. Who could blame him? She didn't want to talk to him anyway, and stir up the hornet's nest that had settled into a background hum while she was away. No, best just ignore the weird phone calls. What could anyone do about it anyway?

'Ella, thank goodness you're okay.' Portia sounded breathless, as if she'd been running.

Why did everyone think she wasn't okay just because she went on a little trip for a few days? 'I just wanted to get away for a few days. You suggested it would be a good idea, remember. But everyone is acting like I went AWOL.'

'I was concerned about you. I had no way to contact you. I tried your mobile several times but it went directly to message bank. I couldn't leave a message.'

'Well, I'm back now.'

'Being out there alone is a concern. You've had some challenging experiences lately, on top of your previous traumas. Your mental health … I think you're at risk.'

Risk of what? She tried to think of a joke, but humour was huddled in the naughty corner and didn't look up. 'I don't believe I'm at risk. I feel heaps better since I've been away. A road trip was just the ticket.'

'Perhaps we can work out a way to check in if you disappear again.'

'I'm not going to disappear.' She wanted to argue that she hadn't disappeared this time; it was all a commotion people had created around nothing.

'I called your mother but she didn't know where you were. I had her name as emergency contact on your file.'

'She's the last person to know where I am.'

'Who is the best contact?'

'Jaz, probably.'

'Could I have her contact details?'

'His.' She reeled off the number. It was easier than arguing.

'What about the friend next door, could I get his number too?'

'I don't know why all the fuss.' But she gave Portia Tom's number.

They arranged an appointment in three days, though Ella wanted to say no. She needed some time to work out how to tell Portia that she didn't want any more sessions, and what she was going to tell the grumpy-arse doctor.

***

'Cheers, Jaz. Thanks, my friend.' Ella raised her beer as she swayed to the music. Hanging out with Jaz, laughing at his stupid jokes and commentaries, had broken the spell no, the curse, of this place. It would be good to see Harry tomorrow, bring him home. She had plenty of fresh bones. Bruce had given her his best when she dropped in to get steak for dinner on her way home. She grinned, thinking of Harry. Took a deep draught of beer.

What was she going to tell Queenie, or Tom, about what Herman had told her? She'd think about it in the morning. First, she needed to pick up her car. Better call Jacob. Her mind wandered through a vague plan for tomorrow. She felt the cool caress of freedom in the possibility of escape now that her car was ready. She padded around the house, turning on every light, and letting the house fill with music. Dancing, she opened doors and windows to the gauzy veil of night, letting in cooler air. She plucked another can of Great Northern from the fridge, pulled the ring-top with a mouth-watering hiss and drank deeply.

Flicking through the vinyl she pulled out Credence, *Green River*. For an instant Hans flashed up. His collection of music was incongruent with the fierce and eclectic intellect of his library. He didn't seem like an old rocker. She tried to imagine Hans and Maria gyrating around the lounge room. Grinned. Flicked up the music to full volume and danced. It felt so good to dance. She sang loudly into the song, remembering occasional lines.

A sweet-warm breath of memory brought the presence of her father close: those hot nights dancing on the back veranda at the farm. She smiled and let the music wash through her, eking out grief, rinsing away the stains of secret buried shame. Her muscles unwound as music pulsed with the rhythm of her blood.

Ella turned over the record, then pulled off her T-shirt to let night air kiss her damp skin. She took another swig, savouring the hop-tang of beer, and surrendered to the dance with its flood of rememories.

She sang loudly, swaying into trance, her body all music.

Her breath froze. Was that a sound? She kept her eyes closed trying to listen over the music. Skin prickled. She opened her eyes, blinking against the sudden glare. A man leaned in the doorway watching her, his face shadowed by the door frame. She gasped, crossed her arms across her chest over the thin cotton bra, wet with perspiration. Rage burned under her skin, mingled with terror as close as the scream in her throat. No one to hear you scream. Reaching behind her, she flicked down the sound. Then stood facing him, muscles tensing, ready.

'What do you want? How dare you just wander in here without knocking?'

'Oh, I knocked and knocked, and called, but you didn't answer.'

'You could have...' but she knew it was true, the music had been deafening. 'I'd like you to leave now please, Liam.' Please! Ella? Fuck the please. Tell him to fuck off.

'Aw, don't be like that.' His tone was faux-offended, words slurring. Drunk. 'Thought the place was being burgled. Tom said you were away. Saw all the lights on 'n thought something was up and came to check.'

All the wind went out of her argument.

'Nice moves,' he said, grinning.

'I want you to leave.'

'Don't be like that. I've missed you.'

'Fuck off!' She started screaming, 'Get out. Get out!'

'Okay, okay, I'm leaving.' He held up his hands in mock surrender, backing into the hallway. 'Now I know you're okay, just having a party, I'll send Tom over. He's been pacing the floor since you went away. We've all fallen for you, Ella.'

She followed him out to the front door.

On the veranda he turned and looked her up and down, smirking. 'Look after yourself, Ella. Don't you go getting into any more trouble.' He stumbled down the front steps and out to his ute. Ella stood in the doorway and watched until he had driven away.

What trouble did he mean? What had Tom been telling him? Did they sit around discussing her each night? Or was he referring to that night? Fuck you, Liam MacDonald. Fuck you, Tom. And Ted MacDonald. You can all fuck off. I don't need any of you. She threw the near-empty can after him and the last of the warm beer sprayed out across the veranda as the can flew into the night. She slammed the heavy front door, shutting out the night. Turned the lock.

Now the fear was back.

***

'How was Andamooka?'

Ella faced Sarge in the front yard in mid-morning heat. He stood close, under the shade of his wide-brimmed hat. He had driven her car out from the mechanic's. A random act of kindness? But without her consent. Hatless, she felt the sun burning into her skull. His gaze was so piercing that she felt herself shrink back. 'Yeah, good.' Staring down at the ground, her skin prickled, each tiny hair on her arms and neck erect as if listening for the imperceptible rustle of snake in the grass. How does he know I've been to Andamooka?

'What did you find out there, girlie? Any opals? Old miners, maybe?' He was still staring.

'Um … I went to meet a friend.' How the fuck did he know? Bushy Bill? Lil? Frank? How was he watching her? She hadn't told anyone in town. Did he know about the termination too? She shivered.

'Funny place for a holiday when you're house-sitting at Broken Ridge. Most people go for city or beach, not more desert.' He leant forward, so close she felt his breath on her face. 'You'd better watch what you dig up. People out here don't like busybodies.'

She watched his eyes the way you watch a snake about to strike. Every cell in her body was screaming, *Run*. Paralysed, she couldn't look away.

He took a step back and shoved his hands in his pockets. 'Guess you'll be leaving town now your car's fixed. Best be on your way. Nothing for you here.'

He strode towards the cattle grid as noise and dust announced a rapidly approaching vehicle on the house track. She stood unmoving, her eyes following the vehicle as it drew closer, then slowed almost to a stop on the other side of the ramp. Sarge stopped and clamped his eyes on Ella. He spoke as if on stage, taking command of the space across the yard, filling the hot air. 'There's something rotten in that car of yours.' He pinched his nose for effect and made a gagging sound.

The vehicle scream-clunked over the grid and stopped. Sarge opened the door and stepped up into the cabin. Her stomach lurched when she recognised the driver. Ted MacDonald. In a burst of adrenaline, she ran up the steps and through the flyscreen door, letting it slam behind her, then banged the heavy front door closed. She watched them through a crack in the curtain. They sat for a long time, seemed to be arguing, but she couldn't see them clearly, and she didn't want to move the curtain wider and possibly give herself away. Finally, the vehicle reversed back over the grid and drove off. But instead of going towards town or Melville, it turned towards the spring.

Is Sarge protecting Ted? Is that what this is all about? How did he know I went to Andamooka?

Ella slumped on to the box seat in the hallway, taking deep, gulping breaths until her heart stopped racing. She went back to the front door and checked outside. Everything was quiet. She locked the door, walked to the other end of the hallway, stopped. Her mind was adrift in a frenzy of white noise. She walked into the kitchen and stopped again, staring at nothing.

'Get a grip, Ella,' she said aloud, shaking her head. 'Focus.' She put the kettle on.

Sipping tea at the kitchen table, she let her thoughts have free rein.

Maybe I should just get the fuck out of here.

What about Maria and Hans? You gave Jacob your word. They're relying on you. And what about Harry?

Go get Harry.

He can protect you.

Hardly, he's got three legs.

At least he can bark if anyone comes ... Like Liam walking in unannounced. Sleazy Ted, Sarge. She shivered.

Harry can stay at Queenie's, plenty of dogs out there to play with.

And where will you go?

I don't fucking know.

Darwin? Go home?

What home? I don't belong back there.

Fuck-fuck-fuckety-fuck fuck.

She drained her tea and took the cup to the sink. Almost dropped it when the phone rang and she ran to pick up the receiver.

'Tom?' she said. Silence. Held her breath trying to listen for some clue. Then banged down the phone. She strode to the front door and opened it. Stared unseeing into the front yard. The phone rang again. She turned and watched it ringing. The answering machine kicked in, recording endless silence, terminated by the bright voice, 'Thank you for calling.'

Ella stared out through the screen door. Abruptly, she flung it open so forcefully that it smacked against the weatherboards, and marched down to her car. She walked around the car looking inside, opening doors, sniffing. Gagging. Pinching her nose between thumb and forefinger, she went to the boot, her heart drumming. Hard to breathe. She yanked the boot open and put her arm across her nose and mouth.

She reached in and shifted the shovel. It was Hans's shovel, the one she'd left at the spring, the long wooden handle snapped in two. Pulling back the blue tarp, a strangled sob erupted from her throat and tears stung her eyes.

'*Harry*. Oh, no, *Harry*.'

BOOK 2
TOM

My heart was dusty, parched for want of the rain of deep feeling; my mind arid and dry, for there is a dust which settles on the heart.

Richard Jefferies

Chapter 1

'Hey, Lil.'

'Tom. What can I getcha?'

'Schooner of lemonade, thanks.'

Lil scooped ice and soft-squirted lemonade into the glass, plonked it on the bar. He held out a twenty-dollar note. When she dropped the change on the counter, he picked up the ten, pressed it neatly into his wallet, and left the coins in a small pile.

'Did Ella come and say goodbye to you, Lil?'

She pulled the corners of her mouth down, frowning. 'That girl gone and left town without saying goodbye?' she said in a sing-song voice, each word ending with a flat twang. She shrugged, but the deep furrow in her brow remained. 'Didn't know she was thinking a leaving.' She scooped up the coins.

'I don't know what to think.' He took a gulp of lemonade, then a second. It buzz-quenched against his tongue. Lil raised her eyebrows. 'I had a call from some psychologist in Melbourne. She was seeing Ella. I s'pose Ella was seeing her.'

Lil shrugged one shoulder and stuck out her chin in a nod of surprise and acceptance rolled into one. Her black eyes stayed on him, sharp as a crow's.

'She's worried about Ella.' He breathed out like a sigh. 'Thinks she's in trouble ...'

'What sort of trouble?'

'Mental health.'

'No shit ... What do you reckon?'

'Dunno. I thought she'd done a runner, headed for Darwin. She sure had a rough time here. Dogs shot, 'n I reckon that dust storm spooked her. Maybe other stuff.' He lifted the glass and took another mouthful. 'Did you see her after the trip to Adelaide?'

'Didn't know she went to Adelaide.'

'When she got back, she left a short letter in our mailbox saying she was leaving. Heading to Darwin.'

'What's the problem then?'

'This psych … Portia, reckons she was…' he paused as a lean old miner came to stand further down the bar. Lil went to pull him a beer, and Tom drained the last of his lemonade. Fiddled with a coaster.

Lil came back and leant across the bar. 'Sounds like she's done a runner to me. Just some pesky psychologist thinks she knows everything. City folk love a bit of drama.'

'She thinks Ella's suicidal.'

'Might be other reasons a girl needs to leave town.'

'Do you know something?'

'None-a my business, mate. Have to ask Ella. She'll pop up somewheres, I reckon.'

'But there was something she said, the psych, made me wonder if she's right. Ella apparently left the same message on her mother's phone a few days ago too. But I know Ella doesn't talk to her mother.' He twisted on to one elbow propped on the bar, stared up at the white figures moving against green on the television. 'Something's out of whack. As if she doesn't want to be found.'

'Maybe she doesn't.'

'Do you know something, Lil?'

Lil wobbled her head. Shrugged one shoulder. 'Reckon she'll call when she's ready.' She picked up his glass and held it up, eyebrows raised.

He shook his head, picked up his hat. 'If you think of anything, let me know. I don't know what to think.'

'She be fine. Probably out there somewhere having a whale of a time.'

'See ya.'

He sat in the vehicle, staring out the window. Lil was probably right. Ella had done a runner. Had enough of the place. She had no reason to stay at Eldorado now the dogs were gone. An extra dog wouldn't be noticed at Queenie's. Had Ella gone back to Queenie's before she left?

He re-ran the conversation with Portia.

'I think Ella's in trouble. She missed her last appointment. I know she would have contacted me to let me know.' Portia had spoken with authority.

'She could be irresponsible at times.'

'It's not just that. It's an instinct.'

Tom heard the worry in her voice.

'That's not very scientific, I know,' Portia said. 'It's like one of those puzzles where something is out of place, or something's missing. You're looking straight at it but can't see it because it's not what you expect.'

'But she left a note in the mailbox to say she was heading north,' Tom said. 'Plenty of black spots out there where she wouldn't be able to make contact. Maybe she decided to leave while she was away on that trip to Adelaide.'

'There's something else.'

He waited. There was a long pause. He could hear his father banging around in the kitchen. Ted was hopeless in the kitchen, usually left it up to Tom to cook. The woman who'd cooked for them for years had died of cancer last year, and there'd been no one to replace her. What was the old man doing? It sounded like he was breaking plates.

'Are you still there, Tom?'

'Yes, I'm here. What's the something else? I need to get going. There's some kind of catastrophe happening in the kitchen. Dunno if you can hear it?'

'Oh, is that what it is. I can hear a lot of banging.'

'Yeah, that's my father. Louder than words. So, was there something else?'

'Of course, I'm not at liberty to speak about Ella's case, but … I do believe she is … at risk.'

'Risk?'

'Of harming herself.'

'What, you reckon she's gone off to top herself?'

'Her mental health was unstable. And she … was struggling with things from her past that increase the risk. She had no support out there.'

'Ouch.'

'I meant not her usual support, family and friends. Access to services. I know you were a friend to her. But she was alone out there.' Portia paused. When he didn't speak, she continued. 'I advised her to return home where she could receive appropriate support. Not that Ella takes people's advice. I know she's extremely independent …'

Stubborn, Tom mouthed silently. It was hard to get a word in, or concentrate on what Portia was saying.

'I think she's in trouble. She seemed obsessed with an Aboriginal woman who disappeared twenty years ago. She was confused, talking about human bones … possible cognitive distortion … it could indicate some kind of … break. Hard to assess over the phone.'

'Yes, she did have an obsession with Biddy.'

'Biddy?'

'The young Aboriginal woman who went missing.' *Missing.* Funny he'd never thought of Biddy as missing, except for him missing her. Was leaving the same as missing?

' … don't know what to think. I know you've got to go. But…'

He listened. The kitchen was worryingly quiet now.

'I lack the capacity to follow up from here. I believe someone needs to check that she's safe. Travelling to Darwin, as the message said. Her phone is continually out of range. I've left several messages. The police aren't interested in following up. I didn't know who else to ask. I'm asking for your help, Tom.' He heard the discomfort in her voice.

'Can't make any promises. But I'll see what I can do. I've really got to go.'

'Call me if you find anything, please.'

'Okay. Will do. See ya.' He hung up and went into the kitchen. Ted was sitting at the table, eating from a huge packet of salt-and-vinegar chips, torn open and spilling on to the table. A can of lemonade in one hand, he was leaning over an old copy of *The Land*, his face close to the page.

'I think you need new glasses, Ted,' Tom said, heading for the fridge.

'Poppycock.' Ted didn't look up from the newspaper.

***

The old Eldorado homestead looked lonely, abandoned. The garden was lifeless, scattered with shrubs and trees that were wizened caricatures of the originals. A row of unrecognisable exotics, once planted optimistically along the western fence-line, waited for rain, but were unlikely to recover. It was such a contrast to the garden at Melville. It had become an unspoken pact between father and sons that they would use precious water for the garden. It was the only way to keep the memory of their mother alive. In a landscape of red dust, only the garden suggested hope: the possibility of life beyond the drought.

Tom stepped out of the vehicle into the eerie sound-scent of *missing* and empty space. Wanting to hear something but already knowing it's gone. He stood and listened for a long moment. Only the sound of a skittish wind wriggling unruly green tendrils of leaves through the gnarled peppercorn.

He walked around to the back of the house, scanning the yard but with no idea what he was looking for. Nothing seemed out of place. He tried to open the back door. Locked. Strange to lock doors out here. He'd just thought it was a city thing. But maybe she was already scared. He'd never asked. And couldn't remember why she had shown him where the key was hidden. It was there, nested inside an old gardening glove in a basket of odds and ends.

The kitchen was clean. Forensically clean. He opened the fridge. Empty. Wiped clean. The small freezer compartment was almost empty. As he looked around the room, a flood of memories soaked in, brimming with Ella. The presence of her absence was like invisible dust on everything. Ella gone. The empty space where she had been was filling slowly with a fuzzy shadow-ache of regret.

He stared around the room. It was too clean. He thought about the mess he'd cleaned up after the dust storm. He'd thrown out the linen, knowing those stains of blood and dust would never come out. And Ella had left it there. Or was that the state of her mind, this stuff the psychologist was talking about? Maybe she was unstable. He had just assumed that was who she was, messy and chaotic. But maybe she was … at risk? Of suicide? Such a loud word, like a stab in the chest with a blunt knife. He blinked hard. Shook his head. Splashed water from the kitchen tap on to his face and over his head, then straightened and let the drops run down the back of his neck.

Ella's bedroom was tidy, the bed made, a pastel bedspread pulled up, smoothed out. He slowly turned in a full circle, eyes flicking around the shadowy room. The blind was pulled down. It was airless and hot. Memories crowded in. He turned sharply and walked back out into the hallway. The other doors were closed. Nothing to see here.

Tom pulled the back door shut behind him, locked it, replaced the key. He wandered along the veranda to where they had sat together in the evenings, and dropped into the familiar chair with its view of the large elm tree. His eyes fell on the mound of recently turned dirt where they had buried Sully. Memories tugged and grabbed like small, insistent children. He blinked and peered into the shadow of the tree, then bolted from his chair.

The second mound had two sticks lying across one end, making a rough cross. Turning quickly, he strode along the side of the house to his vehicle and pulled a shovel from the back brace.

He dug until he hit something soft, fleshy. The stink made him gag. The soil was dark, damp with whatever was buried there. He wiped an arm across his face, brushing off sweat and pesky flies. Dug resolutely to uncover the dark spongy mass, protruding from a dark plastic bag.

At last, he rested the shovel against a tree, rubbed sweaty hands on his jeans and stared down into the shallow grave. Lifting his hat from his head, he wiped his forearm along his brow, thick cotton wicking moisture, flies scattering. Grabbing the shovel again he nudged the stinking object, grunting as he turned it over. The stink of decay erupted even louder and flies crowded in for the prize. He stared down, then in a flash he realised what was missing. A leg. There were only three legs. Harry. But why here? Last he'd heard, Harry was alive and well at Queenie's.

***

'Yeah, Poss told me.'

Tom frowned.

'My cuz, Possum. She's me cousin. She said you were out there with Ella and brought Harry, that three-legged dog, for Queenie to fix.'

'And Ella said he'd recovered. Sans leg.'

Lil pulled a face.

'Sans – without. Without his leg. Shakespeare.'

'He's not my cup a tea. Give me a good murder mystery any day. Or a bit of true crime.'

Horses erupted loudly across the screen of the television in the top far corner, in a cacophony of sound and galloping legs. An old man stood underneath, flat beer in his hand, eyes glued.

'I don't know how Harry ended up out at Eldorado.'

'Smell a rat.'

Even looking at Lil's face, it was hard to know if she'd meant it as a question or a statement, or maybe a joke. He nodded. 'Yeah, something's up. But what?'

'Betta ask Queenie. Might know something about Harry.'

'I guess.' Lil was stacking glasses into a tray. Long dark fingers, beautiful hands. 'Do you know if Possum's around town? She might know something.'

'Hard to find that one. Comes and goes. Hanging out with bad eggs. S'posed to be looking after Auntie. Ol' Queenie.' She jerk-nodded her head as if to indicate something.

'Okay, yeah, I guess I'll have to go out to Queenie's. She doesn't like visitors much.'

'Nah. Especially not some rich white-arse like you.' There was a laugh of kid-giving-cheek in her words. Her eyes danced, though her face barely registered mirth.

Smiling, he said, 'Only arse I got Lil, white or otherwise.'

She grinned back. 'I'll come with you. ' 'Bout time I saw Auntie. Frank's in at four. Come back then, eh.'

'Thanks, Lil. I appreciate it.'

***

Lil banged on the door. Three large dogs strolled across the yard and the largest sniffed her crotch. 'Git!' she yelled. The dog drew back. 'Hey, cuz, you in there? Auntie … Queenie? It's Lil.' They waited. Finally, the door opened a crack, Possum's dark eyes peeking around the edge. She stepped into the late afternoon sunlight, grinning, and hugged Lil.

'What you doin'-t-yerself girl?' Lil said, holding Possum's chin as she stepped back from the hug. Possum's dark mop, slashed with blonde, fell away to reveal a darkened swelling around her left eye. 'You in trouble, girl?'

Jerking free of Lil's strong fingers, Possum shrugged one shoulder and turned to the dogs, which had circled closer again. 'Git!' she said in a nasally snarl. The dogs loped off to the giant eucalypt and dropped into its soft-dust shade.

Lil stepped past Possum, who followed her inside. Tom closed the door behind him. He blinked, eyes adjusting to the cool darkness. A flickering

TV muttered on the far side of the room, throwing off staccato light. Queenie nested into a corner of the sagging lounge, head resting back, eyes shining, watching them.

Possum pointed to a chair and Tom sat facing the old woman. Lil perched on one side of Queenie, Possum on the other.

'Queenie, do you know what happened to Ella's dog, Harry?' His voice sounded loud, out of place in the flickering quiet. He peered at Queenie, but she didn't stir. It was hard to know if she'd heard his question.

It was Possum who answered. ''E gone. Run off.'

Tom shook his head. 'No … Harry's dead.'

Possum's hand shot to her mouth with a soft-sharp intake of breath. 'Harry,' she whispered, hand fluttering in front of her mouth, eyes filling with tears.

'Looks like someone did this to Harry. He's buried out at Eldorado next to the other dog. And now Ella's missing. We think she's in some kind of trouble.'

He sensed the old woman flinch. Lil picked up Queenie's hand, and the old woman's fingers curled gently around hers.

No one spoke for minutes. Then, abruptly, Queenie gripped Lil's hand. Without moving her head, the old woman whispered loudly, 'Find my Biddy.' Her eyes sprang open and she leant forward to whisper in Lil's ear. Lil leant in to hear, her eyes locked on Tom's. Just as suddenly, the old woman dropped back against the lounge and closed her eyes, her hand open, fingers limp.

'What did she say?' Tom asked, as he turned the ute in a wide arc around the yard, the huddle of dogs watching but not moving.

'You heard her, "Find my Biddy".'

'Yeah, but what did she whisper in your ear?' Lil brushed the back of her hand across her eyes.

'It broke Queenie. Biddy going.'

'Yeah. Don't reckon she's ever been the same. Not the only one.' He blinked hard. 'So, what did she say?'

'Hard to say. Maybe, "crow-tell"? "Crow talk"? "Rock see, seeing …" something like that. "Rock weeping", maybe?'

'Crow tell … talk. Rock weeping …' He mouthed the words again silently. 'What does it mean?'

'I dunno.'

'You think it's important?' He spoke loudly over the growl and bump of the Toyota on the rough track.

'Dunno. Might be just her muddled head.'

They were silent for the rest of the drive. When he pulled up in front of Lil's house, they sat for a long minute, staring straight ahead.

'Check out the sour-faced old bitch next door watching us,' she said, pointing to the twitching curtain at the neighbour's house. 'Always talking bout going to church and Bible class. "I'll pray for you", she says, like I'm some kind of wicked creature needs saving.' Lil's voice grew louder, faster, building momentum. 'Look what the holy cow did.' She pointed to the shared fence. 'She poison everything I plant there, shrivels up from the top down. Uses Round-up wand like a gun. Can't prove it, of course.'

Lil's garden was a wild thing. Scrubby plants burst out all over the ground; others grew out of unidentified rusting objects, except along the near fence-line, which was littered with the shrivelled corpses of plants.

The neighbour's garden sat behind a perfect white picket fence, bearing a neat sign that read, "Bore water in use," prominently displayed. The prosperous bright green lawn was trimmed to within an inch of its life, edged with neat rows of thirsty exotic greenery. He thought about the garden at home. Working with old Daniel to replace alien species with drought-tolerant plants had taken years of devotion and defeat, experimenting to find plants and grasses that adapted to the tough climate.

Lil snorted. 'Thinks she still living in that garden of Eden, not in this hell-hot place.'

The picket-fenced garden was like an exhibit for aggressive colonisation, an invasion that ignored the extreme climate and attempted to impose a foreign pastoral ideal from a distant past. The out-of-place lawn reeked of early settler ignorance and conquering arrogance, a declaration of war on the land. He'd learnt, as had many before him, that this land always won. Learning to listen to the spirit of the land, and adapt to it, was wisdom learnt with blood, sweat, and yes, tears of futility. But this drought was testing that wisdom and his faith in the land.

'Holy cunt,' Lil burst out, 'that's what she is, a holy cunt.' She laughed, as if enjoying her new title for the nosy neighbour. 'This'll give the sour old bitch something to talk about. She be looking so hard her eyes going to pop.' Still looking out the window, she said, 'Want to kiss me and really fuck with her head?' She turned her head to see his reaction. 'Ya look like I asked you to eat a rat. Am I that bad?'

'No, Lil. You're an attractive woman. I was just a bit surprised by your line of questioning,' he said, raising his eyebrows and pulling his chin into his neck with a half-shrug, grinning.

'Maybe another time.' Lil laughed easily, the sound of sunlight on water. She picked up her bag, a large faded tapestry creature lying between them, and smiled widely at him, 'Nah. You're not a lush like that brother a yours, are ya? Nothing like him.' It wasn't a question. She opened the door and stepped out with a grunt. Giving the middle finger to the white lace twitch of curtain, she mouthed, 'Holy cunt.' With a grin for Tom, she slammed the door and strode towards her house.

Chapter 2

'I did find something. But I don't know what it means.' Tom lay back on his bed as he spoke to Portia. The house was quiet, settling into the night. Ted was inebriated in his study, dozing in his chair opposite a small, murmuring television. Liam was in the lounge room, probably passed out by now too.

He told her about the discovery of Harry's carcass and the trip to Queenie's with Lil, and was hit with a barrage of questions.

'Biddy was Queenie's daughter,' he explained. 'She left town about twenty years ago with a miner. Word was, she was pregnant.' He paused and drew breath, explaining that Biddy had worked at their house, been their carer. Like a mother, he didn't say. Memories tumbled in: how the family had loved Biddy, how bereft he'd been when she left. As Portia talked, his mind drifted to Lil, Queenie's jumbled mind, the rock and crow. And something else. Something Lil was hiding about Ella. What had she said? *Might be other reasons a girl needs to get out of town.*

'Pardon, what was that? … No, I don't know what happened when she got back. I didn't see her after the trip to Adelaide.' There was no reason to discuss the fight he'd had with Ella. He pinched the skin between his eyes; his head was beginning to ache.

More questions. This woman was relentless. Like a dog with a bone. Not a good analogy.

'Yes, we were friends.' He just wanted to shut her up. 'Look, we had a fight. We hadn't spoken for a while before she went to Adelaide. I didn't know she was going… It really is none of your business,' he said, clenching his jaw. 'I need to get going.' She was still talking when he disconnected.

Tom laid on his bed with the light off, staring out through the flyscreen of the window and into the gauzy night. That woman's concern for Ella kept poking into his thoughts. Finding Harry's body had been a jolt. It could have been some kind of accident. But then why didn't Queenie know about it? Maybe Ella never intended to stay when she got back from

Adelaide. But that didn't explain Harry buried in the back yard. Or why Ella wasn't answering any calls.

Rolling off the bed, he stepped through the French doors and on to the veranda. The boards were rough and still warm under his bare feet. Around him the air buzzed with insects and bugs. Across the lawn and through the boughs of the huge eucalypt, the moon was fattening towards full.

He headed to the kitchen and switched on the kettle. His thoughts settled into a quiet herd as he moved through the slow ritual of making tea. A large message on the whiteboard beside the phone grabbed his attention.

Ted Call Bob, the message read. There was a sudden break in his docile flock of thoughts. One thought bolted. He lassoed the stray and brought it to ground before he knew what it was. Bob's aircraft! Yes!

Bob could fly over to check for any sign of Ella's vehicle. It was a needle in a haystack for sure. And if they found nothing, then she probably was sailing up to Darwin with the wind in her hair, playing Credence or Aretha, singing her heart out.

***

In predawn darkness, he pulled up close to the shed. The soft growl of the tiny aircraft crowded the still morning air. The aircraft was small. Bob large. He had to squeeze himself into the cockpit.

Tom never tired of flying over the desert and its mysterious patterns and vibrant colours. With a soft, inward jolt, he comprehended anew what Aboriginal artists created in their dot paintings, and wondered how they had been able to perceive the country with an eagle-eye view. The land rolled out like a canvas before the artful sun. He sensed Bob's eyes on him and looked across. Bob nodded slowly, his eyes moist. Tom nodded back. The mystery of beauty beyond words crackled between them as they flew across the edgeless gold-dawn, the ancient spirit of land awakening below.

An hour or so later they had flown almost full circle in a wide radius around Broken Ridge, and seen nothing out of the ordinary. He stared down into the scattering of scrappy trees and tough spinifex. The wide plain spilled out forever, all dawn softness gone. Futility and heat pressed at the window, the way a bothersome cat rubs against your leg. The tiny cabin of the aircraft was heating up, even though the aircon was full blast. Bob looked sweaty and uncomfortable.

Tom squinted down into the trees. The aircraft dropped suddenly, and Bob pointed down to the right as he circled. Tom peered down towards where he pointed, pulling his sunglasses onto his head. Yes, there, a sharp light, metallic reflection. A mirror? Bob circled in. Tom's heart jumped into a gallop as they flew closer. There was a brief flash of metal through a denser patch of trees. And flashes of sharper light – sun reflected on metal or glass.

He kept his eye on it until he was sure, and nodded at Bob. It certainly looked like Ella's vehicle. The metal was shiny blue, the colour of Ella's car.

Tom detoured through town on his way home. Maybe he could catch Lil. He was sure she was hiding something about Ella. The air in the bar was liquid cool as he stepped inside. Big Frank nodded as he strode towards the bar.

'Bit early for you, Tom?'

Tom smiled, 'Lemonade, thanks, Frank. No Lil today?'

'Be in in about an hour.'

When Frank dropped the large fizzing glass in front of him, Tom said, 'Did Ella say anything to you about leaving?'

Frank shook his head slowly, bottom lip protruding, showing the inside pink.

'Looks like we located her abandoned vehicle. Northwest.'

'Odd,' Frank said, frowning. 'Lil said she'd done a runner. Can't say's I blame her. She had a rough trot with them dogs being shot. Heading for Darwin, according to Lil.' He shrugged one shoulder. 'It's all I know.'

'Yeah, but she didn't tell anyone till after she left.'

'Maybe she didn't want to say goodbye.' Frank's bottom lip came out again, deep pink and blue-veined, and he dropped his head to one side in a who-knows gesture.

Tom sipped lemonade.

'Thought you two were best buddies?'

Tom shrugged.

'Who can understand women, eh, mate?!' Frank raised his eyebrows in an outback salute to the cliche. He turned towards the television as the animated cricket commentator announced a six. They both watched the replay, the red ball sailing into the crowd to be caught by a grinning kid with a green cap who held it high over his head.

'You reckon she broke down,' Frank said, 'hitched a ride from there?'

'Maybe. But the vehicle's a good forty or fifty kilometres off the highway. Maybe further.'

'Stolen?'

'I guess so.' Tom shook his head and stared down at the fizzing liquid in the glass.

'Don't know any car thieves round here likely to fix a car to steal it,' Frank said, and went to the end of the bar where a man stood holding an empty glass.

No, it didn't make sense. And it looked like the vehicle had been deliberately hidden. It was only the flash of sunlight on the mirror that allowed them to detect it. He gulped down the last of the lemonade, dropped his hat on his head and waved to Frank as he headed for the door.

He needed to think this through. Maybe he'd call that neurotic psychologist when he got home. Irritating and pushy as she was, her mind was like a steel trap. She might have a new angle. But until he could drive out to the vehicle to check that it was Ella's, he wouldn't know for sure. To do that he needed to find the right maps.

Tom sat in the air-conditioned cabin of the Toyota, letting his thoughts gather into a coherent thread. A vehicle flashed across his line of vision, SES logo on the driver's side door, Sarge at the wheel. Tom put the ute into gear and followed him to the SES shed.

'Hey, Sarge,' he said, jumping down from the cabin.

'Hi, Tom.' Sarge dragged open the enormous shed door. He dropped the long bolt smoothly into its hole in the cement, stepped towards Tom and shook his hand.

'I was flying with Bob this morning and we spotted Ella's abandoned vehicle, about two hours' north.'

'Right.' Sarge stared down, fussing at a bundle of keys.

'But I think there's something wrong. I think she's a missing person. Reckon we need to get a search party.'

'Probably done a runner, mate. Ted said you got a message to that effect.' Sarge was still fiddling with the enormous mess of keys, trying one after another in the door marked 'Office'.

'Yeah, but it doesn't –'

The radio in the SES vehicle crackled and a thick voice spoke loudly, 'Sarge, you there?' Sarge went to the vehicle, reached in and answered, 'Yeah Alex, whatcha got?' Crackle, mumble, crackle.

Tom couldn't pick up what the voice was saying.

'Yeah, shit. That's bad. Real bad.' Crackle, crackle, mumble. 'Fucking tourists.' Crackle. Mumble. 'You're breaking up, mate. Should be there under an hour. Yeah, better call the flying doc, word them up, sounds bad. South team's rounded up. Boys'll meet us there.' Mumble, crackle. The winch….Okay. I'll bring the truck…. Yeah, might need to tow it out.'

Sarge came back to the shed, found the right key and opened the office door. He went to a large cupboard and started pulling out equipment.

'Need a hand?' Tom said, following behind.

'Bad accident on the highway. Down south. Bloody tourist in a caravan doing a U-turn in the middle of the road on a rise. Hit by a semi with a load of sheep. It's a bloodbath.'

'Shit.'

'Here, hold this while I get the blowtorch. Guy's trapped.' He handed Tom a heavy mess of ropes and other gear and grunted as he shoved things about inside the cupboard.

Tom tried again. 'About Ella –'

Sarge straightened and fixed his eyes on Tom's, his voice sharp. 'Look, mate, you got to let her go.'

Tom flinched. Shook his head. 'No, this is … there's something …'

'Maybe it's not her car.' Sarge bent back to the cupboard and cursed loudly as he dislodged a tangle of rope. 'And if it is, maybe her car broke down. She left it for dead and hitched a ride. Someone stole the car and abandoned it.'

'But … if –'

'Look, I don't have time for this. A guy is burning up out there. Give me a hand or piss off. If that girl hasn't turned up in a week, call the police.' His voice was low, his head inside the cupboard, dragging out equipment.

'Yep. Okay. How can I help?'

'Throw those in the back of the truck. Got a full team meeting me there. Might need more able bodies later.' He gave a low growl of irritation. 'Who put this away? Look at this fucking mess.'

When the SES truck was loaded and Sarge had locked the shed, he hoisted himself into the cabin and stared down at Tom, who was standing to one side. Sarge's eyes were sharp as a knife. 'You need a new squeeze, mate, not a search party. Best let her go.'

Tom's gaze followed the truck's taillights. Maybe Ella *had* done a runner. Maybe there was a simple explanation about the dog in the back yard. Maybe the dog tried to get home and was hit by a car and Ella found him, brought him home to bury him. It was too much for her and she did a runner? But why did she call her mother and not that best friend? The psych kept going on about it. And what was she going to tell Maria or Jacob? The dogs were dead. Nothing left to save? Maybe Ella wasn't the person he thought she was. Maybe she didn't care.

'I need a drink,' he said to the big blue sky. His head was a mess of scrambled thoughts, like the gizzards of the SES cupboard.

'Hey, you,' Lil said as he dropped on to a barstool.

'Hey, you, too.'

'What can I getcha?'

'Great Northern, thanks.'

They didn't speak as Lil set the beer in front of him and he paid, leaving the change on the counter. Lil scooped up the coins, drizzled them into a jar beside the till, and turned away to serve another customer.

He drank deeply, then shook his head almost imperceptibly as he put the glass back on the counter, like a man in a beer ad. It tasted so good.

Lil came back and stood in front of him, her hands resting on the counter. She was staring at him. Frowning. But her eyes were glazed, as if she were seeing right through him.

He waited.

When she spoke, her voice sounded faraway. 'Just remembered a dream, eh.' Her nose wrinkled. ' 'Bout Ella. Like I'm Ella, and not Ella. It was dark, scary dark. Not good dark like desert night. But like all them stars've gone out. Like I'm in a cave. Rock all round. Nothing but rock, whispering and singing strange-like …'

Lil stared somewhere off past his shoulder, still with her eyes half-glazed. Stayed quiet for a long breath.

'Old songs. My mob songs. An' I'm running and running. Someone's behind me. I'm scared. Can't breathe. Can't call out.' A slight tremor passed through her. 'One o' *them* dreams.' She brushed a hand across her face as if she were brushing away cobwebs.

Now she did focus on Tom; blinked, her eyes sharpening. She pointed a finger at him. 'And you were there. An' I woke up.'

The skin on Tom's scalp tingled. 'Was I chasing Ella?'

'Nah. You were just there. Like you were waiting for her.' Her eyes lost focus again. 'Maybe you were looking for her.' She blinked. Nodded. 'Reckon that's it.'

'Well, I *have* been out looking for her. What do you reckon it means?'

Lil shook her head and gave a soft shrug.

'Think we found her car. Went flying with Big Bob. In the middle of nowhere. Reckon it must be hers. Right colour. I'll head out tomorrow to check.'

'Stolen?'

'Maybe. But if it broke down on the highway when she left … if she did head north to Darwin … car thieves around here aren't going to fix it to steal it, and if they did steal it, why would they go way off the road to dump it?'

'Nah. That mob too lazy to fix a car to steal it an' then dump it.' She grunted softly as she bent low to slide a full rack of steaming glasses into a cavity behind the bar. 'Nah, doesn't make sense.'

'Tried to rustle up a search party, but there's been a bad accident down south. SES team's heading down there now.'

'Shit. Tourist I s'pose.'

Tom nodded. 'Caravan.' When Lil said nothing, he continued, 'Sarge reckons I'm broken-hearted and need to accept Ella left town to get away.' Lil stayed quiet. He picked up his glass, drained it in one gulp and replaced it on the counter. Spreading his fingers over the top of his caramel-coloured Akubra on the barstool beside him, he lifted it in a smooth arc and dropped it on to his head, pinched the hat rim in a farewell salute to Lil, and headed out on to the street. Not sure where he was heading. He needed fresh air to think.

He wandered along the almost deserted street, hugging the shade. Thoughts stuck in his mind like spiky thistles. There was something he needed to understand but couldn't. When he looked up, he was standing outside the butcher's. He peered through the window. Bruce was chatting to someone hidden from view on the other side of the counter. His round face was smiling and bright; it reminded him of a Renaissance painting of cherubs. Tom pushed open the glass door. A bell tinkled.

'There you go, Frannie. Say hello to your ma. I threw in a few bacon hocks for gran's soup. An' you tell your bullying brother from me, if he don't knock it off and leave you and the other little 'uns alone, I'll come round there and give him a right bollocking. See ya.'

The small girl smiled shyly up at Bruce, holding the white bag high. She scurried out of the shop like a frightened animal, head down.

'G'day, Bruce. How's it going?'

'Can't complain, mate. Can't complain. Living the dream.' Bruce bent and waved out the window at the girl, who was pressed against the glass, snub-nosed. She held a small filthy hand up, almost smiling. When she hurried away, he turned to Tom, 'What can I getcha today, Tom?'

Tom checked the glass cabinet. 'Give us a couple of kilos of that lean mince.'

Bruce pulled a bag from the roll and placed his hand inside, swift and elegant as a performer doing a magic trick. Through the plastic he divided a large portion of red minced meat, talking at the same time.

'How's that pretty neighbour of yours?'

'Ella?'

'Course, Ella. You don't think I'm talking about old Mrs Jamieson, do ya?' He grinned, half-laughed.

'Ella's gone.'

Bruce jerked his head back, frowning. He dropped the bag of mince on to the scales: 1.9957 kilos. He swung the weighty bag in a loop inside his forearms, performing his routine in fluid movements, then tied a loose knot. 'Don't make sense.' His frown deepened. 'She was in the other day to get bones for that three-legged dog. Excited he was coming home. No mention of leaving.'

'When was that?'

'Couldn't say exactly. Few days ago. She was picking up the dog was shot and needed a bag a bones.' He rested his hand on the plastic bag as he talked, as if it were a small animal. 'Anything else I can get ya?'

'Some of your pork sausages, couple of kilos.'

Bruce pulled out the bag for his next performance. Tom stared, unseeing, his mind skittish with the new information.

'Did she say anything else?'

'Nope. She was in a bit of a hurry as I recall. Just back from Adelaide.' Bruce grabbed a large handful of sausages. His hands were enormous, there was a faded tattoo on one hand at the base of his thumb, a fading name, blurred at the edges. He tugged the line of sausages. 'Mmm … There *was* something else? What was it?' He grinned across at Tom. 'Memory's as soggy as a wet sock. Reckon I better lay off the late-night port wine and brandy.'

Tom smiled back. Waiting.

Bruce leant into the glass cabinet to finish his ministrations. 'She was all excited about something. What was it?' He froze for a moment. 'Reckon the shop was busy an' I didn't take much notice.' He held up a neat string of sausages. Pulling a knife from the leather pouch over his blue-striped apron, he slit the tiny twist of gut, and the small herd of sausages fell free into his bagged hand. He dropped the soft bag on to the counter scale: 2.0021 kilos. Bruce lifted the bag, performed his trick of spin-and-twist, tied a knot and dropped it on to the counter beside the other bundle of meat.

Tom waited.

Bruce kept one hand on the counter as he stared out the window.

'Something about … she found a clue to some mystery she was chasing?' He met Tom's eye. Shook his head. 'That's all I can remember, mate.' He exhaled loudly. 'She's a bit of a riddle, our Ella.'

Tom drove over the shudder of the cattle grid into the yard at Eldorado. Everything was still. Nothing stirred as he walked the broken footpath to the back veranda. He found the discarded gardening glove and fished out the key.

Inside, silence and dust had settled more deeply. He stepped into the darkened laundry and opened the chest freezer. Sitting on top was a huge bag of frozen dog bones. He shifted the wide mesh divider to look further into the freezer, not sure what he was looking for. As he stared down at the crowd of icy plastic bags, his eyes fell on one oddly shaped protruding packet. He leant in and dragged it out. Held it up to the dim light of the curtained window. It was long and thin, like a bone. Understanding bolted in with stuttering surprise.

He laid the bag aside on the nearby washing machine and dug into the freezer, searching for any other odd-shaped packets in the same dark clingwrap. Pushing and shoving miscellaneous parcels aside, he scanned the frozen throng for another odd shape. And finally, there it was. Jammed deep on the far side, as if it had been hidden. He tugged it free and held it in both hands. It was the size and shape of a small child's plastic ball. The ice burned his fingers and he dropped it on to the washing machine beside the other packet. He dug around in the frozen assembly for a few more minutes but found nothing else unusual.

Tom picked up the two parcels and carried them to the kitchen table, where there was better light. He stood back looking at them for a long moment, then began unwinding the plastic, occasionally rubbing his hands on his jeans to relieve the burning cold.

When he'd finished unwrapping, the bone that he and Ella had dug up at the spring lay exposed. Beside it sat a human skull. Silence pressed in, whispering ancient mystery of death and life. He picked the skull up and turned it over, staring closely at the crack across the top of the bony dome. Dropped it again as it burned-cold into his fingers.

He inspected the crack. It would have taken a heavy blow to crack the skull like that. When did Ella go back to the grave? What else did she discover? Had she uncovered something dangerous? Maybe she *was* in trouble. But not the kind of trouble Portia was talking about. He turned the skull on the table so that the empty sockets were facing him. Bent down to eye level.

'Who are you? And what happened to you?' As if it might speak back.

Leaving the bones on the table, he wandered through the house randomly opening doors and looking into rooms. Nothing seemed amiss. In Ella's bedroom the air was stuffy, the light dimmed by closed curtains. He went around the room opening drawers and cupboards. Everything was empty. There wasn't even a lolly wrapper to show that Ella had ever been here. He knelt and looked under the bed. Only the usual dust and fluff gathering in vacant spaces.

He slumped on to the bed. A memory came of Ella asking him to stay the night, her burning hand on his skin in the darkness. The scorch of wanting. Her wanting, hot and clear in the searing skin of her palm against his bare back. The feel of her so close. How easy it would have been to turn. To reach across the divide, towards that hot desire, sheathed in gorgeous flesh. He could smell her she-animal smell, her arousal filling the air and his own body's response throbbing.

The old shadow pressed in. Older and tougher than hot desire. Thick skin around the heart. His brother's name tattooed in burning shame. He blinked, staring at the floor. Ella's sweet breath seemed to fill the silence in the airless room, so close he shivered.

But he hadn't reached for her that night. Things might have been different if he had. He blinked his eyes tightly to clear the mist of remembering. Dragged thumb and forefinger inward across closed eyes, pinching into the bridge of his nose. Opening his eyes, his gaze snagged on something on the floor, something shiny at the edge of the mat. He stood and bent down to lift the mat. A gold chain. Ella's? Did she wear a gold chain? His mind stretched back. Yes. Yes, she had that habit of rolling it across her lips with her forefinger sometimes, when she was … what? He tried to remember the look that went with that gesture of dragging the chain across her lips. He shook his head. Who knew what Ella had thought or felt? He moved into the light and held the chain to examine it. Broken. As if torn from her neck.

Chapter 3

Back at Melville, he parked under the old white cedar tree beside the shed and sat for a moment herding his thoughts together into one coherent, urgent thought. Finding Ella.

Liam was in the kitchen, his hair wet, a dark towel tied around his waist. Tom walked in soft-socked as his twin opened the fridge.

'Hey,' Tom called and threw the package of meat at him. Liam turned, instinct-quick to catch it against his chest. He raised it triumphantly, tossed it into the fridge, and came out holding up two cans of beer. Tom nodded.

'Cheers. Cheers.' Call and response, the archaic male ritual and click-of-cans.

He looked at the clock: 5.22pm.

'Could've used a hand at the shed this afternoon.' There was no accusation in Liam's voice; it was just matter-of-fact.

'Yeah, got waylaid. All done?' Tom drank half his can in one swig.

'Nah. Near enough. Brian'll finish off tomorrow. He'll swing out to pick up the cable in the morning.'

'What's on for tomorrow?'

'Should check the western bore. Haven't been out there since you fixed it weeks ago. Want to come?'

'I need a hand with something. Could check the bore afterwards?'

Liam took a long draught of beer. 'What?'

'Go out to Ella's car. Check it's hers and see if we can find any tracks. Reckon she might be in some kind of trouble.'

A sharp silence jabbed the air between them, full of unspoken memories and questions. Tension shimmied, stumbled along the blade.

'Mate, you got to let her go. She left. Done a runner. Probably in Darwin shagging her tits off by now.'

Tom jumped up, his fists clenched, chair crashing to the floor. Liam grinned up and turned his cheek slowly, never taking his eyes off his brother: inviting the blow. Tom turned and strode to the door, yanked it open.

Words like poison flew through the air, scorching the inside of his ears.. 'Never could hold on to your women.'

Liam's laughter was the last thing he heard as the door slammed behind him with a loud crack.

He drove, rage-blind.

He blinked, waking. Shook his head. Slowing the vehicle when he realised he was nearly at the spring, and parked under a mulga tree. Wrapping his arms around the steering wheel, he buried his head against the dusty smell of his khaki shirt sleeves, wanting to forget. Too late. The memory, folded and stored in fine tissue, pristine, exiled for years, sprang open and unfurled. That bright spring day in Armidale. Suni's lovely face. She was his first love. His final year at uni. He'd skipped morning lectures, something he rarely did. Had been into town to buy her favourite food and wine for a picnic, red roses. Planned to drive her to their favourite spot at the waterfall. He wanted to talk about their future. Maybe marriage. The day was perfect.

Holding the roses behind his back, he knocked on the door of her bedsit at the end of the hall. He knocked again, below the sign that read, 'Tutor'. Suni called out, 'Who is it?' He didn't answer, just waited. Listened. Thought he heard voices. Knocked again. 'Who is it?' she called again. He waited. Clenched the long-stemmed roses, palms sweaty. Finally, she opened the door a crack, holding a dressing gown around her, hair messy. The expression on her face changed from one of irritation into *that look*. You never forget a look like that.

Tom pushed the door open. Liam was lying in her bed, the bedclothes pulled back. Naked. Grinning. Tom threw the flowers at him. Liam laughed. Suni started crying, grabbed his arm as he turned to leave, called behind him that she was sorry. But all he could hear was Liam laughing.

Through the dirty windscreen, the fierce blue forever sky was softening into twilight. Dragged his thumb and middle finger together across his eyes to the bridge of his nose. Blinked away the tears that had been waiting so long. He closed his eyes and Ella was there inside the flickering wet blackness. Regret, close as a black crow pecking the eyes of his heart.

At last, he looked up again to see the sun oozing behind a horizon of liquid amber gold, saturated with red, magenta and plum, like some exotic ripe fruit squashed against the fading sky. Halos of light radiated out of the blue-pink-indigo bruise of sunset. He got out of the car as Penny jumped down from the back and stood against his leg. He reached down and scratched the top of her head, her bright eyes searching his. She trotted beside as he strode up the slight incline towards the spring and scanned the nearly three-hundred-and-sixty-degree view. Penny dropped on to her haunches beside him and for a moment they stayed in a motionless salute to land and sky, the first pale stars revealing themselves in land's oldest melody of day opening into night.

Tom stripped off his shirt as he walked towards the spring. He pulled off his boots, peeled off jeans and undies, and lowered himself into water that was almost too hot to bear, until the body adjusted. His skin pinked. He let the ancient water penetrate, burn through him, cleansing. Penny dropped to her belly, head on paws, keeping her eyes on him. He floated on his back and stared up at the trembling stars. Gradually his mind grew quiet as he watched the moon rise large and orange-butter-round, almost full.

Ten minutes later, his body relaxed by the heat and minerals, he slowly pulled himself out of the spring and sat on the rough edge, legs dangling in the water. The night air felt cool after the heat of the artesian water. He stood, brushed the pebbles from his backside, pulled on his clothes and boots, and set off along the rocky path towards the graves. In front of his mother's grave he gave in to a soft stretch of timeless. Penny sat beside him, distracted by the silhouette of a crow perched in a balding tree.

Tom turned to the other grave. Someone had moved a huge rock over the dirt they'd disturbed when they dug up the bone. It would have taken two men to move that rock. Ella couldn't have moved it alone. Who else knew about this grave? A bright image of the skull lying on the kitchen table at Eldorado sprang up, with that brutal crack across it. Who are you? What did Ella find out? And when had she come back to the grave and carried the bone and skull to the house? He shivered.

Liam's ute was gone when he pulled up at home. Tom knew where he'd be — at the pub, drinking. That was his go-to for everything, and Ted's. Booze was the answer to all their problems. Silver-bright moon shadow bathed the garden. One yellowed light shone softly through the window of the study. His father would be slouched in his large leather chair, an open bottle of whisky beside him and the small television murmuring. He'd be asleep by now, most likely. Incoherent at any rate.

Tom switched on the barbecue before pulling off his boots and clothes at the back door. He dumped his clothes in the laundry basket and walked naked into the kitchen and straight to the fridge. He opened the bag of sausages and freed five with the large butcher's knife that poked out of a wood block near the stove. With frozen veggies steaming in a small pot and beer in hand, he watched over the sizzling snags, spitting fat as he turned them. Abruptly he set down his beer and rushed into the laundry, dragged out the clothes he had just dumped and rifled through until he held up his jeans. He pushed a hand into one pocket, then the other, and his shoulders relaxed. Holding the gold chain between thumb and forefinger, he held it to the light. It had definitely been snapped. The links weren't delicate; it would have taken a fair bit of force to snap it. He dropped it into his cupped hand and returned to the sausages, turned them again with a long set of tongs.

He sat eating his meal, staring down at the broken gold chain. Penny was slumped nearby, flat-bellied against the floor, head resting on paws. Not a muscle moved, except for her bright eyes watching the fork's arc from plate to mouth. When he'd all but cleaned up the plate, he upended the last mouthful of beer, picked up the remaining sausage and squatted in front of Penny, who stared at him without moving, every muscle tensed, ready. He patted her head and proffered the sausage. She scoffed it back in one gulp.

Once the dishes were cleared, he padded down the hallway and flicked on the light. Bent down to the bottom shelf and tugged out maps. After opening and refolding several he pressed three large neatly folded maps under his arm. Back in the kitchen, he pulled the cordless phone from its cradle, dialled and listened to the dial tone turn to message then a beep. 'Hello, it's Tom MacDonald here. Keeping you in the loop about Ella. Call me when you can…' He hung up. The night was silent except for the faint buzz coming from Ted's office. But beyond that? Yes, the sound of a motor. He knew Liam would be drunk, coming the back roads, drinking a couple of roadies on the way home. He'd come in fisty with jutting chin.

Tom picked the phone back up, walked along the hall to his bedroom and closed the door. He grabbed a sarong off the hook behind the door, tied it around his waist and pulled back the curtains on the glass doors that led out to the veranda. Headlights sliced the night, bouncing and darting on the rutted road.

The phone rang loudly.

'Hello? … Yes, it's Tom. There's been developments.' He sat down on the bed and filled in the gaps since his last conversation with Portia. The back door banged and he heard Liam crashing about in the kitchen.

'Yep, still here. Um. Anyway, this chain … I'm sure it's Ella's. Do you remember her wearing a gold chain?' His eyes fixed on the cobwebs in the corner of the ceiling. 'I thought so. It's definitely been snapped … I don't know what to think, either. I'm worried enough to try to get a search under way, but looks like I'm it … Any luck with that friend of hers? …Yeah, Jaz. Right … No, I don't know why she went to Adelaide. And why Andamooka? None of it makes sense … Bert? No, doesn't ring a bell.'

Portia spoke at length and Tom began to pace the room. 'Okay, yes, Herman was the guy that Biddy left town with… No, I don't know why Ella was obsessed with finding out what happened to Biddy. I didn't know she went to look for Biddy until now. Jaz said that?'

He only half-listened as Portia described her conversation with Jaz in detail. Obsession, yes, that was the right word for it. His mind wandered. He stood in front of the flyscreen and stared out into the night. Why had Ella become obsessed with Biddy? Because of Queenie's relentless mantra to *Find my Biddy*? She'd been saying that since Biddy left twenty years ago.

'Pardon, I missed that?' He shook his head, trying to make sense of what she was saying. 'A pay-off? … Ted's my father. What's he got to do with Biddy leaving? … None of it makes sense. No one's heard from Herman the German since he left … Uh-huh … right. No idea. It's Biddy, not Bitty … Hmm. He didn't know anything about Biddy?'

His eyes scanned the room as Portia talked. His frown deepening.

'I agree. The priority's finding Ella.'

Portia started on her rant again about Ella's mental health. He heard the door slam into Liam's room. Thumping and banging sounds came through the wall. Something crashed.

'My brother. I've got to go … Yes … yes, I will. Bye.'

The house was still. Liam was probably passed out on his bed.

Tom picked up the map sitting on top of the pile he'd left on his bed and unfolded it. He walked to a desk in the corner of the room and picked up a pen. Kneeling, he leant over the map and made a tiny red X close to where Ella's car should be. He ran his hand in a circle around the spot, smoothing the map and imagining the topography out there. Flat, dry spinifex and small tussocky grasses. Occasional mulgas and coolabahs. Snakes and crows. Lizards of all sizes. If Ella had left her vehicle she was in real trouble. Surely, she knew not to leave her car if she broke down? A flash of that night after her accident with the eagle crowded in. He shrugged it off. But why was the vehicle there? So far from the highway if it had broken down? As if someone had tried to hide it. Things happened on that highway with its long, lonely stretches.

He looked more closely at the map. Lifted his hand. Peered even more closely, at an angle to avoid creating a shadow from the overhead light. Small angular symbols clustered where his hand had been. Squinting, he read the place name. 'Yorick.'

He stroked the thick smooth paper. Checked the scale again, calculating. Yorick was less than an hour's drive as the crow flies from Ella's abandoned car. He moved his finger across the space between the small X and Yorick, letting his mind ramble over the map, not looking at anything in particular.

A vivid memory-flash of Lil telling him about her dream made his finger freeze. He shook his head to dislodge the sudden feeling of vertigo. He needed to check the car first but was ninety per cent sure it was Ella's. It was the right colour and the metal was still shiny, so it couldn't have been out there long. They'd seen the tracks from the air, but they'd probably blown over with dust by now. He was alone in this. There was no one to help. He didn't want to risk a re-run of his brother's cruel jokes, or Ted's nodding sneer when it came to women. Plus they wouldn't want him missing another day or two of work. But this time of year was always quieter. And with the years of drought they had lost a lot of stock. His mind drifted that way, and swung back. Law of the bush: he needed someone to know where he was going.

Tom took the phone and walked quietly along the hallway, past the loud snores coming from Liam's room. In the kitchen he pulled out the directory and flicked through the pages until his finger hit its target. He punched in the numbers and walked out through the laundry door and on to the veranda towards his bedroom.

'Is Lil there please? … Tom MacDonald … Okay, thanks.'

'Hi, Lil … No, not ringing to get that kiss. But thanks anyway.' He smiled. 'Well … I'm wondering if you can tell me anything else about your dream? I know it sounds cracked, but I'm going to Yorick to check some of those abandoned mines.' Until he heard himself say it, the plan had been a muddle of instinct and possibility laced with nagging doubt and desperation.

'Glad it doesn't sound crazy to someone … Yep, following the dream. Indeed.' He stepped into his bedroom. 'What do you mean, one of *those* dreams? … so you think it *is* … important? …okay. Good. It's all I've got at the moment, other than an abandoned car and a pushy psychologist.'

He dropped on to the edge of the bed and picked up the gold chain. Felt the tiny weight of it in his free hand, bounced it up and down in a small puddle of gold links as he listened.

'Okay. Thanks. Thought there might've been something I missed. Some clue that might help me find her … Yeah, I know it's a long shot. But I have to do something. Everyone here reckons it's my busted heart. But I think she's in some kind of trouble … First thing in the morning. Before dawn. Need to check the abandoned car first. Might be some clues. Then turn back southwest to Yorick. Probably only an hour or two from town as the crow flies. Depends on the tracks … Me too. Gut feeling about those abandoned mines … Yep, exactly. Got to do something … Okay, thanks Lil. Take it easy … Yep, sure. I'll call in at the pub on the way home. No point camping out there. Reckon if I haven't found anything in a few hours … what time do you finish? …Okay, cool, should be back well and truly by then … yeah, me too, Lil. See ya.'

He turned to the map and drew a straight line with his index finger. Leant in to read the tiny writing. 'Muttagundi Station'. The house was almost silent as he headed back to the kitchen, except for the soft hum from Ted's study and the usual boards creaking in the hall under his bare feet.

Muttagundi Station was in the yellow pages with a large ad for cattle breeding. He dialled. Elbows on the kitchen bench, he surveyed the mess

Liam had left. Minimal. Only a few greasy plates and a blackened frypan stacked in the sink.

'Hello… Barry, hi. Tom MacDonald. Not too late, is it? …Good to hear. No rest for the wicked, eh?' They shared a beefy laugh of camaraderie. 'Just letting you know I'll be on the east side of your property tomorrow. Heading out to Yorick … Nah. Not into opals, mate. You? …Don't reckon there's any opal left out there anyway.' He turned on the kettle as he talked. 'Boulder opal didn't pull the same dollar as the crystal…' Listening, he pulled a mug from the cupboard. 'Looking for a mate's gone missing. Her car is dumped out near there. Northwest of the highway. Looks abandoned. But I'm going to check the car then drive over to Yorick…'

He pulled two teabags from the jar on the bench and dropped them into the mug. 'Hard to say. Probably nothing … No. No cops. No SES. I'm it. One-man search party. Probably a wild goose chase. But a few things don't add up … Probably won't be seeing you then, Barry … Up in the ridge? I thought it was abandoned … Okay, I'll watch out for them. Don't imagine they'd bother me anyway. Whitefella scratching around in rusty tin and holes in the ground.' After a brief conversation about the weather and a possible "drought-breaking storm" predicted, which no one believed, he hung up. He poured hot water into the mug. Jiggled tea bags, pulled a large carton of long-life milk from the fridge and filled it to the brim.

The lopsided fat moon, so close to full, hung bright in the night sky by the time he finished packing up the old troop carrier. She was a beast and older than he could remember, but reliable. All the camping gear was already packed if he did have to camp out the night. On the back step he paused to take in the nightscape. Last full moon he'd been sitting with Ella on the veranda at Eldorado. He jerked away and went inside.

In the kitchen he checked the charge on the sat-phone, cocked his head at the message board, and frowned. He didn't want them to know he was out looking for Ella. He picked up the marker and pulled off the lid. Pen poised, the moment stretched wide as he mapped the route in his head, calculating time and distance. Drive north along the old highway, close to the northern boundary of Melville. Check the abandoned vehicle … Drive to Yorick, across the edge of Muttagundi Station. Two hours at Yorick, three max. If he hadn't found anything in that time he might as well give up. Couple of hours back into town. Drop off to see Lil before she knocks off at six. Home before dark.

He wrote, *Gone to check north fence. Taken the troopie for a run.* Part truth.

Chapter 4

Tom left before dawn. Driving alone in the wide-open space tasted of freedom. He watched the sun soak the indigo sky with slow gold. The landscape bumped past, dry, ancient skin of earth, red dust freckled with spinifex and stumpy grasses. Scrappy trees huddled in patches, sheltering each other like spindly old women waving their arms against the strong breeze. And the space. It opened something in him that he'd never been able to explain. A flash of memory skidded sharp-edged into his imagination; riding the land with Ella. Dadirri. Tree stories. Biddy stories. The memory nested in, close and warm. The sweet pleasure of sharing the land, and now the close sorrow of her absence. His eyes misted and the land grew hazy.

'Ella,' he whispered, like a prayer to the wide sky.

Two hours later, he stood staring down at the closed car boot, crawling with a dark mass of flies. He hesitated before flicking the catch, and his fingers stung by the momentary burn of hot metal. A thick cloud of tiny black flies burst up, buzzing. A wave of relief ran through him. Apart from more flies, the boot was empty. He waved an arm above the swarm, uncovering traces of dried blood and thick lumps of something smeared across the coarse dark carpet, now a wriggling mass of maggots. The flies settled again the moment he stopped waving. He pulled away, gagging, as much from the smell as from the horror of what the flies might be feasting on. He slammed the boot shut, spat out the stench and turned away to suck in a deep breath of hot clean air.

Back at the troopie, he reached for the sat-phone and dialled. It rang through to messages.

'Sarge, it's Tom. I've checked the car. It's been dumped alright, number plates gone. Definitely Ella's. But no sign of her.' His thoughts stumbled for a moment, as he wondered what to say that would mobilise assistance to search for Ella. 'I'm heading over to Yorick to check –' A bright tinny voice cut him off, told him his time was up and his message would be sent as 'a ten-second text'.

Tom shifted his thumb to hover over the number, ready to press again. But there was not much point explaining that Ella's gear was gone, or describing the smears of blood and muck in the boot. The SES was probably still cleaning up after that accident down south. He couldn't expect any help anyway. Unless he found something at Yorick.

The faded sign to Yorick, full of bullet holes, had been twisted to point to the ground and a message painted in black down the post, 'Hell on Earth – this way'. Tom pulled up in the patchy shade of a lone mulga. Around him were abandoned lean-tos and gaping holes dug into the hard earth, burnt out vehicles, broken lounge chairs and wire coiled around poles, rusted drums and machinery. Spinifex grew in the gaps. It was a wild, sad place; difficult to imagine anyone had ever lived out here in this cruel heat. Yorick … Alas, poor Yorick indeed. Behind the shanties reared a ridge of dark, ochre-red rock, rising like a great beast out of the earth.

The afternoon filled slowly with heat and frustration. Red dust covered everything; there were no obvious new tracks. Holes littered the ground, some covered, others exposed and collapsing; it would be impossible to check down each one to see if there were any signs of Ella. He wandered the abandoned camp, lifting corrugated iron, opening rusty-hinged vehicles and peering into dark dwellings, unsettling lean rats. Under one sheet of corrugated iron, he disturbed a king brown. It slithered off into deeper shade.

Tom felt as if he'd been searching for hours. It was futile. His heart felt old, divided, and weary. Not torn, just wrecked, like the land after long drought. Cracks open and split into deep fissures as precious moisture leaks away. He headed back to the troopie and pulled out the esky. Gulped water, letting it spill down his shirt to cool his chest.

At the far side of the ramshackle camp, a murder of crows clustered on the rusted broken iron roof of an old shanty like black pips spilling from an overripe rust-pink melon, squabbling and heckling. He watched for a moment. Nothing else moved. Tom put down the pannikin, slammed the heavy back of the troopie shut, and walked slowly towards the rabble of crows.

As he drew closer, the crows only squabbled louder, cawing complaints at each other. He stood staring up at them. They ignored him. One crow, larger, blacker and more ragged than the others, separated from the black-feathered throng. It waddled with the rocking gait of old men. He'd noticed Ted had begun to walk with that same stiff-legged rocking motion lately. The crow bleated its lament into the hot-thick air, launched off the roof and swooped down and out of sight without a wing beat.

He walked towards the place where the crow had disappeared. The other crows flew off as he came near, landing further off to watch. Amid the chaos of rusted vehicles and unrecognisable junk, he saw the crow pecking at something. Something white or maybe pale blue. It had a corner of the white thing in its beak, trying to dislodge it from a tangle of wire. It was so busy in its task it didn't notice Tom until he was almost on top of it. The crow bolted up into the air, landed on a crooked pole and sat watching from its perch. Tom tugged at the pale scrap of stained fabric, hooked around a tangle of rusted wire, until it twisted free. He opened the soft knot of fabric, examining the stains. Blood.

His mind flew into a blur, thoughts reaching for coherence. He squeezed his eyes shut, blinked hard. The crows were quiet now, watching him. His lower legs prickled with goosebumps. The square of cloth in his hands wasn't faded. No mistaking it was put there recently. He felt a tingle of certainty that it was a message from Ella. His imagination flashed hot and bright: an image of Ella, struggling. Her one desperate reach for salvation, a scrap of torn cloth, poked under a broken log and jumbled wire. He groaned aloud. A crow moaned back. All the other crows were gone except for the one watching him from the top of a pole cross. It opened its beak and moaned again.

Tom scanned the ground, and his eyes landed on a pile of rusted junk. Nothing unusual except that it was only a few strides from where the cloth had been stuffed. He grunted with effort as he dragged, then rolled the heavy rusted metal axle away, and the sturdy log beneath it, revealing two sheets of corrugated iron making a large X on the ground. He hauled the sheets aside to expose a gaping hole, about a metre in diameter.

'Ella,' he called, leaning over the black hole. He lay down, peering into darkness. Called again, his voice flat against the rock sides. Turned his ear to listen. Silence. Black silence. He called again. Listened again. Nothing. Only the cool silence of rock and deep earth.

A ladder on one side of the mine shaft looked old but solid. He strode back to the troop carrier and gathered ropes, a headtorch and a larger torch. What else? There might be tunnels he'd need to check. String. Ariadne's thread, just in case. What else? He grabbed the small daypack and tossed in a full water bottle.

Tom attached the rope to the bottom of a post with a rusted sign on top that read, 'Anybody taking pegs from this claim will be shot dead', with a scrawled illegible signature underneath. He pulled hard against the rope, checking the tension, before dropping it down the hole. A just-in-case rope. Looped another line of rope around his belt. He stood for a moment and looked around. No, that's all he needed. He could climb back up if he found anything. Radio for help. He put his hat on the ground and fitted the torch to his head, then grabbed a heavy rock and rested it on the rim of his hat to stop it blowing away. He looked up at the old crow.

'You leave my hat alone, okay!' he said. One pale, almost white, eye watched him back, unblinking.

Tom lowered himself into blackness. The railing at the top of the metal ladder was too hot to hold, forcing him to grab for the rope, but the metal cooled a few steps down.

When the ladder ended abruptly several metres above the bottom of the shaft, he peered down using the headtorch. Lowering himself with the rope, he dropped on to the cool-dust floor of a narrow cavern. He moved his head and body in a slow circle, sharp white light cutting through the claustrophobic blackness. There was only one tunnel. He took a last look at the rough circle of sky above for a moment before stepping into the narrow tunnel, thin light leading the way through thick black.

After five or six metres the tunnel opened abruptly into a much wider rock cavity. The ballroom. Numerous poles held the rock ceiling up in places. Some looked smooth, others were covered in rough bark. An old miner had once warned him never to touch the pine uprights in mines because the fungi on them could be deadly if the gas was released. The silence of solid rock swelled out from the stone walls, but there was something lovely about the rough red-pink walls and smooth, cool floor. Darkness pressed in close, fast swallowing the thin blade of light from the headtorch. The resinous, citrus scent of cypress gave a frisson of forest and fresh air, befuddling in the dark, closed space. Tom shivered. The fake news smell of the pine uprights confused his senses. Another smell, human excrement, came from one of the tunnels to the right.

He flicked on the large torch attached to his waist and shone it around the small cave. A filthy striped mattress was pushed against one rock wall, an old lump of pillow and crumpled blanket on top. Nearby was a large plastic drum and a blue backpack, clothes spilling out on to the floor. He shone the light into the drum. The puddle of water in the bottom was filthy. A couple of muesli wrappers were strewn nearby.

He bent to the spillage from the backpack, lifted a crumpled T-shirt and held it to his face. The scent of Ella flooded his memory banks, filling his blood with a raw, burning ache. His mind was blank as he bent on to one knee, placing the large torch beside him on cold rock-ground. He used the small sharp light of the headtorch to look through the bag. In one compartment was a large purse. He unzipped it: licence, credit cards and a bit of cash. In secret pockets, lists on folded pieces of paper. He reached into a fat side pocket, and his fingers brushed the hard, smooth surface of cool metal. Her phone. He pressed the on button, waited. Nothing. He slipped it into his shirt pocket and buttoned it closed.

When he'd finished rummaging through the dust and muddle of clothes, he stuffed the purse, a wad of papers in a zip-lock bag, computer and passport inside his daypack and zipped it up. He took a deep draught from the water bottle, then straightened and turned slowly, following the knife of light from the headtorch until it landed on the stained striped mattress, lumpy pillow at one end and an old grey blanket crumpled at the other. A blurry image of Ella lying there shivering in terror swam into his mind's eye. He lifted the stained pillow, so threadbare it was tearing in places, exposing lumps of wadding; the smell of mould and musty unwashed humanity skulked out of the greasy fabric. Underneath the pillow, nestled into the mattress like a small animal huddling in the dark, lay a red book.

The small book felt solid and cool in his hands, smooth against his fingers. He opened it and flicked through the pages, crammed with handwritten notes. The handwriting changed dramatically from small and neat, almost childlike, in the first pages, to jagged and chaotic. It was definitely Ella's handwriting.

He went back to the first page. *Desert writing.* It pulsed with life, possibility. Ella's life. He flicked the pages slowly, snagging on occasional words. *Liam*, repeated. *Liam.* Eyes bouncing, caught, hovered for a moment over his own name. Bright image-memories of Ella sprang from the book. That particular angle of her head, cap askew, those curious green eyes taking everything in. He blinked hard. Turned the pages slowly, his fingers thick and awkward on the paper.

Tom stopped. Cast the light from his headtorch around. Listened. Silence. Deep and dark as death. He shuddered. Shoved the notebook into his daypack alongside her other possessions. Stopped again and lifted his head. Was that a sound? 'Ella!' he called. Silence.

He fished the ball of red twine from his pack and tied one end around an upright that looked sturdy. Then, shining the torch into the opening of the tunnel to the right, he stepped into its depths.

For what seemed like hours, he followed tunnels, bend after bend, unravelling red thread as he went. Calling occasionally, 'Ella, Ella. It's Tom', his voice was a lone, flimsy thing against the solid walls of stone. He peered into rocky crevices, narrow hiding places, bending under low rock ceilings, whispering, 'Ella, Ella, it's Tom.'

At each dead end he turned back and retraced his steps, winding in the thread. Started again where he had left off. His eyes were always on the ground, not wanting to trip over something unexpected. Each time he encountered shapes in the darkness – piles of rubble, a fallen prop – he felt shock, followed by sudden relief. He called her name. Stopped moving to listen. But silence was the only sound beyond his breath.

Although it was cool, he was sweating by the time he'd travelled every tunnel he could find and arrived back in the ballroom where the striped mattress hunkered. It wasn't the physical effort that made him sweat, but the tearing, squeezing tension between wanting to find her and not wanting to find her. He untied the red thread, wound it into a fat ball and stuck it back into his pack. Again, he looked around the small space. Shivered. She's not here. How did she get out? Did someone come back for her?

He walked the few metres back to the shaft out, aware of a sense of relief that he hadn't found her. He came to the ladder, looked up, and the shock of the unexpected prickled his skin. There was no light. For a moment he wondered if he had been down here all day and it was night. He checked his watch. It was only 3.10pm.

His thoughts became slow and ponderous. Someone had covered the mine shaft, as they must have done with Ella. His mind felt thick. Greasy thoughts hung like phantoms unable to land. He looked up again, his eyes following the narrow beam of light from the headtorch. The rope was gone. He shone the torch on to the ground. Light struck his hat, upside down in the dust.

Of course, they must have been watching. Waiting.

Slow questions arrived. Could he climb to the top? Even if he could, there was no way he'd be able to lift off the tin if it was weighted down with axle and logs. Had Ella escaped? How? There must be another way out.

The red notebook? Yes.

Chapter 5

Tom retrieved the notebook from his pack and stared down at it in the bright pool of light from his headtorch. A tight knot in his chest formed around the tension between invading Ella's most private thoughts and needing information to escape this dungeon. He opened it and skimmed through the pages. Words leapt at him, dragging him in. He closed the book, one thumb holding his place, and headed back into the ballroom. Dropping on to the mattress, he opened the red book again.

His eyes speared, snagged by the ragged shape and texture of a word. *Pregnant.* Pregnant? He couldn't look away. *Pregnant.* Did Liam know? A sudden dark shadow loomed in his mind. Liam's fisted rage. No. He shook his head. No. Liam's an idiot, especially on the booze, and worse lately, whatever he's been taking with his idiot mates. More aggressive. But no, he wouldn't hurt Ella … a small seed of doubt pushed through a wilderness of possibilities. Would he?

A tiny, pale spider ran up his hand with a soft tickle. He watched the small traveller cross the vast geography of his wrist. A sharp image of Ella thrashed into view, so close, so real. He gagged. Ella sitting down here alone, writing in this notebook. Writing her last words? The tiny spider disappeared under his khaki shirtsleeve.

He turned the crowded pages rapidly, flipping towards the end for some clue, something that would tell him what happened to Ella. If she had escaped. Was that a sound? Dark angular shadows jumped across the rock wall as the torchlight followed his gaze. The chill of the cave pressed in. Walls of rock infolding. He shivered, turned back to the book. Jagged, fitful writing …

He raped me. Left me here to die.

The words kicked hard into his solar plexus. The page was smudged and stained, covered in heavy cross-hatching. Some words were written so violently that they'd torn through the paper. He leant, torchlight glaring down in a narrow circle, trying to read what was hidden under the thick scratchings. He could only make out a few words.

Vile … ugly … Stinking … hate, maybe.

horror under my skin … cunt stinks … violated …

One word was repeated. Seized his gaze.

Rape. Rape. He raped me.

A sudden image of Ella's bruised face ruptured the silence of rock and cool earth-air. He smelt her fear, the horror inside those words.

Tom closed the book and held it against his chest. He sensed her fear, a bottomless primordial fear. A storm of violence crowded the air. He shut his eyes. Dark shadows shifted closer. Raised voices reverberating through rock, bearing echoes. Figures shifting in shadow.

His body recoiled, trying to get away from the images that filled his head, but he felt compelled to open the book again. Horror in thick-skinned words inhabited him. He swallowed air, ripening with putrid memory. Felt the breath of rock murmuring. Rock shifting, rising into giant waves, tumbling, rolling. Woman running. Running and calling.

running and running. Can't breathe. calling without sound. Panting. It's him. snake eyes watching through dark tunnel.

Everything quakes, shifting. Turning into rolling turbulence. Nothing solid. Nothing to hold on to. Ice burning inside words remembering.

He's on me. inside me. his voice growling, a feral animal. tearing clothes. tearing at skin. skin peeling away. he's pushing and grunting. stabbing inside.

Swimming-and-drowning. Ugly words sucked him in. Wave on wave tumbling him over; down is up and up is down. Nothing familiar to hold to. Dark turbulence breaking open. Tumbling, upside down. Around and around. The dark shape of this thing was around him, closing in, dragging him down, inside him. He couldn't watch. Couldn't look away. Do I see this? Not eyes seeing. Blood searing into bone, seeing, knowing. Rock-into-flesh knowing.

he's grunting, panting, spitting foul words black slut-black cunt-black slut repeating over and over, panting. chanting a devil's prayer.

Words alive. Living memory burning dark air.

skin burning black, earth crumbling into dust and bones. uncovering white bones. so white.

river of blood boiling, running with bodies. so many dead bodies. women and girls and little children. dark skins. uncovering bones. swimming deep into the river inside white bones, ocean of blood and dust. silent skull under dust, waiting. quiet.

Head aching with confusion. Touching words, ink against paper. Head pounding. Heartsick fingers stroking lines, touching anguish. Then sensing the shift.

it's quiet now. I'm flying above. so quiet. I can hear the breath of my bones. these bones are singing. white bones singing the wind. One singing. Rock singing. Bones singing. Dust singing. Wind singing. All singing. Flying above the grunting animal. watching down. red dust the colour of blood. bleeding. a river of blood and dust, of roaring music, drowning brute sound.

Tom's fingers were burning. Words on fire against flesh. Too hot to hold. The red book fell, breaking the spell. In a shock of confusion, Tom was standing.

He stared down at the book splayed open in the dust. He shook his head to shift the curious sensation of swaying inside, as if something had come loose, ungrounded. Taking a long breath in, he exhaled into the silent rock that surrounded him and bent down to pick up the book. He smoothed the page, wiping away fine, red dust.

He slammed the notebook shut. Lifted it to his chest, held it against his heart. His heart was a hard muscle clenched against pain. He blinked. Opened the notebook again. There must be something. He turned towards the back of the book. Ella's neat handwriting. He flicked through the back pages. Lines and lines from poems. Some he recognised; Blake, Hesse, Keats. Olivia Parsons. Underneath some lines she had written a name. Many lines of … he leaned in, Vesaas? Proust. But that wasn't going to help him escape. He flicked to the final entry in the front section of jagged writing. Let his eyes tumble down the page. Words leapt up at him, grabbing his heart into a fist.

I don't want to die.

He blinked away tears.

His gaze trickled down the lines, pooling into her last words. Not just bones and dust, Ella. I will never forget you. I will call your name until there's no breath in my body. Well, that might be sooner than expected if I don't get moving and find a way out. He closed the red book as if the covers were delicate butterfly wings. Pulling his shirt out of his jeans, he pressed the book against his belly and tucked his shirt back in. He needed it close to keep Ella with him, skin to skin.

He shifted his weight and stared at his watch, not seeing the time. He had entered an-other time. He knew he had been changed, as if Ella's words had penetrated some lost thing in his heart. There was no turning back from this knowing. Somewhere in the fundament of him a crack had opened.

He moved aimlessly. Not thinking. Shining the large torch randomly around the tunnels, the flicking wedge of light struck something out of place high on a wall of rubble. He held the torch steady but couldn't make it out from this distance. Some kind of small metal container? He crawled up the rubble wall, sharp stones cutting into his knees and shins. Keeping his torch fixed on the object, he reached for it. It was an old dish. Good for digging or moving rock. He shone the light along the top of the rock wall, revealing a narrow tunnel, just large enough for a small person to climb through.

Cool dust filled his nostrils as he dug. He shifted rock and rubble, using the dish for the smaller rocks. He sneezed. Coughed. It was a relief to focus on a task. He felt the close red skin of words, sticky against his belly as he worked.

After he'd cleared enough stone and rubble for him to fit through, he poked his head inside the narrow opening. It looked not much more than a metre or two through to the other side. He pushed in deeper. As he pulled his body into the narrow dark canal, lying with his belly against cool rough stone, his feet pushed against lose rocks, then empty space. It was hard to breathe through the dust. His nostrils tickled. He held his breath. There was no room to sneeze; his shoulders were tight against the stone. He needed traction to pull himself through. Arms pinned to his side, no room to reach forward. He wriggled to propel his body, the fist of rock squeezing more tightly as he writhed and pushed, grunting loudly. A sharp edge of rock tore through flesh in his right shoulder.

He stopped. Laid still, panting. Made himself give a long breath out, trying to slow the staccato rhythm of his heart. He pushed forward, feet dislodging loose rock. Panic was close, a breath away. Pushing against fear, he expelled his breath, sensing more room to move. He sucked in a deep breath, flesh pressing against the edge of cool rock. He breathed out slowly, emptying his lungs, pushing and worming forward, until his lungs gasped for air. He laid still, allowing his breath to return, slowly. Rock pressed in, tight and close, as his lungs filled. Again, he expelled air, wriggled and squirmed forward until his lungs gasped for air. He laid still, breathing against the hard wall of panic and rock that squeezed his chest. There was no turning back. He counted to ten, waiting for the wave of breathless panic to subside. Expelling air, he wriggled again. Repeating the rhythm, he inched forward.

Finally, one boot touched solid rock. He pushed. Felt a space around his right arm. He wriggled and dragged his arm through, pushing with his feet at the same time. His head was through. He gasped in clean, cool air. Reaching forward to grab on to a ledge of rock, he pulled his body through.

Tom laid still with his head on the jagged rock, panting. A shudder of relief ran through his body. He lifted his head, the torchlight cutting through darkness into nothingness. He clambered down the rocks. On solid, uneven ground he scanned the small cavern with the headtorch. He scanned the floor with a soft-wash of relief; there was nothing but dust and rubble.

'Fuck.' He groaned, realising his pack was on the other side of the opening he'd just come through. There was no way he was going through that again. His water bottle. What else? He couldn't remember. He put a hand to his belly, felt the sweaty warmth of the red notebook against his skin.

Beyond his torchlight was only more blackness. He stepped slowly on the rough rock floor, the light of the headtorch making shadows jump each time he turned his head.

'Ella,' his voice broke the deep stone silence, making thin circles of vibration in the cool air, hitting impenetrable mass. 'Ella.' A puff of word against rock, like hurling complaints at death.

The image of a frightened Ella flashed behind the blackness. He blinked hard, squeezing his eyes against his imagination. He stumbled as his feet caught on something soft. He tripped, grabbed out in the dark, touched a rough-smooth pole, and felt it shift, then give, as he fell hard against it. A creaking, followed by a slow rumble, crowded the silence. Falling into blackness, amid an avalanche of dust and rock, his hand pressed the warmth under his shirt, the notebook hugged against his heart.

***

Head bowed over that red-skin thing. Sipping ink-words to sustain your vanishing life, you turn back a page, taste each line, chew remembering, of that beautiful and stupid world you yearn for, then swallow it slowly into your stuttering heart. Words fly up in urgent invocation and flutter-in-murmuration, only to perish then rise again. Each divide between time and place, yours and mine, I-and-thou, between dreamer and dreamt, poet and listening heart, melt into one breath.

Poet, lend me your words. Conjure verbs like tiny beacons of hope against the dark, to be-hold all the beauty and sorrow of the world in one line. Light the invisible membrane humming between us; as if you know me, see me, hear me. You speak the mystery of unsayable questions, unbearable knowing, and intimate, ancient for-ever things. Your earth-song of homecoming grows deeply rooted through my heart. Borrowed words shape sound in my mouth. Breath-warm words, summoning past into presence; to wake the dust. Land, and tree, rock, and sun on my tongue, sung through bone-white teeth. Calling and listening back. Calling …

Reading with whispered breath, her mind reaching.

Only listen.

Looking up, she turns her ear to the sound-all-round of silence. Then bows her head again.

Listen with the soft-shell of your heart, that speaks back through blackest night.

Poet, hold me in your words. Give me something to tame the dark. Don't let me drown in this loneliness and despair. Don't let this hatred and brutality be my last remembering.

Never forget, none can steal your liberty; your inner freedom of mind to find its own direction. Choose your target, aim your attention true, and let fly your imagination towards that new possibility … Reach through darkness to touch the anima mundi; bright Arcadia and lost Edens of your dreaming.

Questions burn my blood with fierce longing. Answer me, poet. Sing the world awake in me. Show me the way back into that first-tender magic of the world that I lost along the way. When I knew that I was beloved of all the earth, and her creatures; echidna and emu, wallaby and red-bellied snake; were my brothers and sisters. The home I am returning to, soon.

Your true home is within you;
in the bright blood of your heart - let it beat you,
in the sound of your breath - let it sing you…
Each dawn kisses your sweet face, the face you wore before you were born,
calling you home through night's dreaming….
You are star, and red earth, and tree spun with wonder.
Listen for the chorus of night singing you ever home.

Give me back the world. The close-sorry pain of it, the mess of it all; that secret beauty hiding inside everything. Give me the scent of a eucalypt at dusk. The taste of first summer strawberry. Smell of rain on dry earth. Give me back the stars. Give me laughter and grief and the jumble-tumble of loving and hot desire. I want it all back. Even the grief and heartbreak. Yes, even that.

All the world is alive inside your heart,
in corridors between remembering and imagination (let it all in).
Possums and broken dragons (only waiting to be loved),
rock and tree and worm,
and those mysterious sea creatures that glow in the deep-dark.
They are all there, held in the mycelium of your heart,
rooted in wonder;
where all the broken, lost, and forgotten things hide,
mixed up with odd socks and buttons you never found.

Poet, do you speak the language of death? Sing a dirge to lullaby me as I turn to stare into that final mystery, come too soon.

Each moment is a little death, between what was, and what is becoming,
you stand between; a handmaiden of time, be-holding each-to-each.
Day is dying to become tomorrow, as
yesterday perishes into each day's waking.
You were born into the song-line between living and dying
where everything is possible in your heart's imaginings.
Sing back in-to that break between breath; waiting to begin again.'

Not much solace there, Poet. What about this final death?

You are dust and bone, mineral and water. Each returning slowly home to earth from whence it came. Each thing singing its own lullaby in harmony with the wild-ecstatic song, sung through everything. Raise your voice, you who are lonely and bereft, or twisted in pain, raise your voice to the stars. Sing-high into that tree, and shake its

Sweet Orpheus, 'truth's undaunted lover'; sing me home.

Brave Antigone; take my hand.

All you lost, exiled, and forgotten Ones; show me the way through darkling corridors, to bring me home again.

Who will remember me when I am dead? Who will weep for me?

I will. I will remember you. Tom's lips moved without sound, as if dreaming. His eyes fluttered. He lay still, listening. Was that crying? His cheek pressed hard against the rough, cool rock floor. He opened his eyes. Black. Closed them. Black. Blinked. Still black. He sensed throbbing against his belly, where the red-skinned notebook laid, warm against his reaching fingers.

'Ella?' he whispered.

Call my name, Tom.

He listened.

'Ella?'

Find me.

'Yes, Ella. I'll find you.'

Silence.

'I'm here, Ella. I'm here.'

Am I dreaming? He held his breath, clutching for sense. Felt his body solid, alive. Heard the echo of words diminishing.

'Ella?' She felt so close.

His eyes were gritty. He blinked again and again, trying to blink away the blackness. The air tasted of dust. How long had he been out? He reached up and touched the throbbing at his forehead. His fingers came away sticky. Blood. His cheek was pressed hard on to the cool rock floor. Reaching out, he patted the floor around, trying to find the headtorch. Stone and rubble. No torch.

Tom tried to move his legs. Something was pinning them. He twisted on to his side, grunting with the effort. He felt woozy, and laid his head against the floor again until the wave of strangeness passed. Twisting further, he reached down to touch his legs, felt the rough shape of a pole across them, buried in rocks and rubble. He pushed the pole. But something was jamming it. Too many rocks. He shifted several rocks from his sideways position. Rested against the cool floor as his head throbbed violently. Slowly, he moved rock and rubble between rests.

At last, when he shoved hard against the pole with his twisted strength, it shifted. Pushing and grunting, he dislodged it and his legs came free. He ran his hands down each leg, feeling for injury. Except for a few cuts and sore spots, they seemed fine. He put a hand up to the throb in his forehead; it was oozing again, a trickle of blood into his left eye.

With a sudden shudder, he remembered that he had tripped on something soft. He ran his palms over the rough surface, cool and solid. His fingers felt a corner of fabric and he reached along the length of it, tugging until it came free. No body attached.

On hands and knees he moved around, patting the ground for the torch. But there was too much rock and rubble. He sat back, resting his head against folded arms wedged on knees. Hopeless. He licked his lips. So thirsty. He thought of his pack on the other side of the rock wall and swallowed dust.

His body froze, listening. A creaking sound. Nearby? On hands and knees again he crawled unbearably slowly around the pile of rubble. Stopping, he listened. Nothing. Only the harsh sound of his own breath. His head throbbed and he laid it on the ground for a long moment. Raising his head, he dropped his hand to his stomach to cover the notebook, stroked the heat of it through his shirt.

'Ella,' he whispered, 'Where are you? Show me the way out.'

He looked up abruptly, the way you look up instinctively at a window when someone is watching you. Up ahead, yes, soft light. He blinked. And the light remained. Faint. But yes, definitely a light at that end of the tunnel.

'Thanks, Ella,' he said. Blew a dry kiss into empty-black air.

He tried to stand, but his head spun wildly. He dropped to the floor again, on to all fours, and crawled slowly, resting frequently as his palms pressed against sharp rock; they were soon cut and bloodied. But it was better than the swaying nausea when he stood, or the threat of bumping into another pole and risking another cave-in. He stopped occasionally, wiping away the sticky ooze on his face with his sodden hanky.

Again he let his head rest on the cool floor. He had vertigo inside the darkness, as if he were standing at a great height looking down. It was so lovely to rest. He licked his lips and dreamt of cool sweet water.

'Biddy?' He felt a hand on the back of his head, stroking his hair against the grain. 'Biddy?'

Hovering between dark and light, waking and oblivion. Sliding in-between; smooth skating down and down, then sudden slap, shifting, tug of return.

'Biddy.' He whispered into the cool-dark air.

There was hard rock against his cheek. The place on his head where the warm hand had been was cooling now. Biddy's smell, the empty space of her leaving, was a familiar dull ache in his chest.

Tom lifted his head. It felt thick, heavy as a lump of granite, and throbbed wildly. His forehead was tacky and filthy with dust, but at least it had stopped bleeding. He dragged himself to his knees. Peered in the direction he'd been travelling. There was still light, but it was dimmer. He needed to hurry before the sun went down; he'd never find his way out at night.

Again, he tried to stand. The world swayed and wobbled like a child's toy boat on the ocean. He leant his hands on his knees, letting his head hang down, not daring to touch the walls or upright poles for support. Waited until his head cleared.

Biddy's face flashed behind his eyes. Her beautiful dark eyes, watching him back. Then Ella was there — not a clear picture, more a sense of her presence. Her vitality. Like the sound of humming outside a window. He staggered, stumbling against the solid rock wall, following. The wall felt cool and solid, held him steady.

His legs managed no more than a shuffle, even so, he tripped over and let himself fall again to hands and knees on the cool floor. He wanted to lie down. Lie down and die. Knew that's what it meant: to lie down was to die. He'd never get up again if he rested now. His mouth was caked with dust; he tried to swallow but his throat was too dry. Couldn't close his mouth. Lips and tongue numb. Tongue swollen.

He crawled, animal instinct carrying him forward. There was nothing left but the will to survive, stronger than his body's weakness. The fierce animal drive to live, pushing his body on. The pain in his hands and knees was gone. His head hung between his arms. Lift one hand. Down. Lift one knee. Down. Lift other hand, down. Lift other knee down. Again and again.

And then he felt it. A warm breeze overhead.

'Biddy?'

He stopped, kneeling still, all his senses alert. Yes, it was definitely warmer here. Right here. He twisted to raise his head. Tears stung his eyes as he looked up into a deepening blue square of late afternoon sky. He blinked up, opening his eyes wide. Warm air coming down the square shaft caressed his cheek. It was real.

A wave of hopelessness washed through him. Freedom seemed too far. It was such a long way up. His body was trembling from the endless crawling, lack of water and loss of blood.

Ella had done it. She must have been in a terrible state. He touched the notebook, traced the shape of it through his shirt, felt it sticky, burning against his skin. He thought of Ella's fierceness. Reaching for that memory, and Biddy's face too, close and bright, he whispered, 'Help me, Ella. Biddy, help me.'

He closed his eyes and reached up to the first handhold in the rock and pulled his body up. And up. With each step he whispered his silent mantra.

'Ella-Biddy, Biddy-Ella.'

Finally, his head poked out from the square cavity of rock and he sucked in warm, fresh air. With a final push he dragged himself out of the shaft. Laid on his back, staring up at the first winking stars. Tears trickled down the side of his face, stinging cracks and tiny cuts in his skin.

Between gasps, dragging in air, he whispered, 'Ella-Biddy …'

A lone crow called from nearby, its harsh sound breaking the still twilight. He smiled, his eyes misted, and the stars danced and swam in shimmering light. Inwardly he bowed to the crow, the coming night, the stars, to life. To being alive.

When a crumb of strength had finally returned, he rolled over and dragged himself up. The world glowed with light from the enormous round butter moon rising above the horizon. He scanned the terrain. A few hundred metres away he could make out the angular shapes of Yorick. And stumbled towards the troopie.

He yanked open the back door and dragged out the water esky. Filled a pannikin and drank. Sipping at first, lips and mouth stinging, he felt the water arrive in his stomach and retched. Swallowed hard against his body's reaction. Waited. Sipped again. The need to gulp water was urgent. He rested back against the door. Watched the giant moon grinning over the dry earth. Pressed his lips together as they cracked painfully.

Tom sipped slowly until the pannikin was empty. Filled it again. He had to keep moving; knew that if he rested for too long, he might not wake. He needed to get home, or at least somewhere that he could rest where there was someone to wake him. He could get to Muttagundi Station. How far was it? Half an hour maybe. Yes. He'd call as he drove, get directions. Come back and look for Ella again in the morning. He hoisted himself up into the driver's seat and turned the key.

Nothing happened.

Turned it again.

Nothing. Not even a sputter.

The fat moon beamed in through the windscreen, daffodil yellow now, strange territories of shadows and craters playing across his moon-face. Tom reached for the sat-phone, sitting in its pouch. Pressed it on. Nothing. Pressed again. Dead. He rested his aching head on the steering wheel, felt the creeping shiver of being watched, and checked over his shoulders. His mind felt too hazy to reach for meaning.

Maybe he was close enough to get a signal on the radio. He picked it up.

'Hello…?'

Not a crackle.

Again he felt that creeping shiver, and he swivelled to look left, right, and behind. The night was bright and full of shadows from the strange shapes of abandoned dwellings and machinery. If someone was watching, they could be anywhere in this place of wreckage.

Not much to be done tonight. No energy to do anything anyway. Need to eat. He opened the fridge, found the remainder of the lunch he'd made a lifetime ago, and began eating the soggy sandwich between mouthfuls of water. His mouth felt unfamiliar, numb, as if he'd just been to the dentist. He bit his sluggish tongue, winced. Tasted blood. He shoved the sandwich back in its wrapper and stuffed it back into the small fridge.

Too exhausted to pull out the swag, he crawled in through the back door of the troopie and pulled it shut behind him. Shoving things off the seat along the side of the vehicle, he laid with his hand clutching the notebook beneath his shirt, and fell into deep sleep.

Chapter 6

'Tom.'

Someone was calling his name. Dream-close and warm as lover's skin. 'Tom.'

Am I awake or asleep? He put a hand to his throbbing head and opened his eyes. The sharp light of headlights filled the back of the troop carrier. Someone *was* there. He held his breath to listen. Voices? The rifle was inside the box seat he was lying on. Had *he* come back to finish Tom off?

'To-o-o-m.'

A woman's voice. He waited. The bright light from the headlights threw hard shadows on the ceiling. He listened to the hum of an engine close by.

His eyes jolted to the figure looking in at him through the back window. Dark eyes. He didn't move.

'Biddy?' he whispered, staring at the dark face.

The face turned away and said something. Then two faces were looking in at him.

'Thanks for coming, Lil,' he said quietly over the firelight a half-hour later.

'Needed to get out of the house. Them fellas at home giving me the shits. Old man fighting with them boys. All they talk is football. All of 'em fulla shit.' She jerked her head towards Possum, lowered her voice, 'Needed to get that one away fer a bit too. Pissed 'n greedy, his mob, always hanging round them young girls. Sniffing round like a pack a mongrel dogs.' She spat into the fire: a tiny hissing sound above the crackle.

Possum was in shadow with her hoody up, her back to them.

Lil spoke louder, 'She's pissed off with me.'

Possum said nothing.

'Want some tucker, Poss?'

Possum stayed sulking, unmoving.

Tom moved the billy further into the red coals with a short, thick stick and dropped back on to the ground heavily. When the lid began to pop and bubble, he set the billy on the edge of the coals and dropped in a handful of tea.

'Hope you've got plenny-a sugar?'

'Nup. No sugar.'

'I got some in the ute.' She stood with a grunt.

Ten minutes later she was back, puffing hard. 'Little bitch of a hill that one, eh.' She handed him the sugar and settled back in front of the fire. 'Better stop them fags,' she said, pulling out a packet of cigarettes.

Lil held out two stained mugs while he tipped billy tea into each, and then filled his own pannikin, the dark liquid reflecting gold from the firelight. When she'd spooned in the sugar, then squeezed sweetened condensed milk into one mug, she carried it to Possum, returning with a grunt-to-sit.

They drank their tea in silence. Beyond the circle of firelight, the moon threw softer silvery shadows.

When Possum had settled among the canvas and bedding nearby in the shadows, Lil spoke in hushed tones. 'Needed to get that one,' rolling her head in the direction of Possum, 'away from that mob she running with. Need some yarning. Get 'er out on country. Good kid, but too many bad men sniffing round. Don't know how to look after herself.'

'Well, thanks for coming this way. Not sure I would've made it if you hadn't showed up.'

'Yeah, thought I better come and check yer sorry arse when you didn't show up at the pub.'

He raised his pannikin in salute.

She laughed. For a little while she stared into the fire. 'Find anything besides that crack on ya head?'

He told her what he'd found in the shaft. But he didn't explain why he wanted to camp away from the vehicles. Didn't want to alarm her, knowing that *he* might come back.

'And I found this.' He pulled out the notebook, opened it. Even in flickering firelight those words on the page, violent, invasive words, stuck his gaze like a sharp hook.

He raped me. Left me here to die.

The night air filled with the dreadful knowledge of it. No longer contained by rock and blackness of earth, it seeped into the still night. A sheen of moonlight hugged the world bright. But the ugly shadow hung close. He closed the red book.

Lil was poking a stick into the coals.

'Did you know she was pregnant?'

Lil wobbled her head, a shrug of maybe I did or maybe I didn't.

The notebook lay closed in his lap, his hand resting on it. He leant over, holding it out to Lil. She took it in her long fingers, eyebrows raised in question.

'Ella's. There's some ugly stuff in there. About what happened to her.'

Lil opened the red book and began reading. Her hand flew to her mouth. He knew she must have opened it to the page that was scratched and torn with Ella's anguish.

Their eyes met. No words needed.

He leant back against the cooling rock. Lil peered down at the notebook, holding a small torch close to the page. She shook her head, bit her lower lip and made a small noise of animal in pain. Barely audible, but it filled the night air, remembering ancient sorrow, a mother wailing for her daughter lost, taken, a child calling for their mother, afraid in the dark.

Lil grunted loudly and looked up from reading with an odd expression on her face that Tom couldn't read. Like a question and a certainty at the same time.

'What?'

'She didn't think much of yer old man.'

'Nuh-uh. No one thinks much of my old man. Just an old drunk these days. The man's gone out of him. But he's still my father.'

He watched the fire while Lil flicked through the notebook, stopping occasionally, and leaning more closely to the page. Ella felt close between them.

He drifted, on the edge of sleep.

'Did you two ... you know?'

Lil was regarding him with her black eyes that saw everything. How could he begin to explain anything about him and Ella? About Liam. His own regret. Instead, he said, 'We had a fight.'

He stared down at his boots. Lil waited.

'She made all kinds of accusations about my family. About me. Said I was just like my brother.' He drew in a long breath. 'I called her an

ungrateful brat. That was …' his voice stumbled, 'the last time I saw her
…' The breath stuck at the back of his throat on the last word. He closed
his eyes.

'Hmm.' It was a strange sound, Lil's heart-to-throat that said, I get it, I
hear you. It vibrated with understanding, like the plonk of a pebble hitting
still water and rippling out forever. The sound of being seen. Someone
taking the gentle pulse of his soul.

Mist pooled at the outside edges of his closed eyes as the cool night
drank his tears. He drifted.

'Why was she so interested in Biddy?'

Lil was a blur on the other side of the fire. For a moment he thought it
was Biddy. Then the reality of *this* night crashed in and he blinked wide
awake. Sat up.

'What?'

'Why was she so concerned with what happened to Biddy?'

'Dunno.' Tom rubbed his eyes. 'Maybe easier than worrying about her
own problems?' He shrugged and slumped back down again. Who knew
what went on in Ella's mind and heart? He had no idea. Until the past
couple of weeks he'd thought he knew her. But opening that red notebook
was like seeing Ella as a different person. He shook his head. Lil was
reading again.

'Tom?'

His eyes jolted open, meeting her black eyes across fire.

'Something here I don't understand.'

He didn't move. 'Hmm?'

'This bit at the end here.' Her voice sounded raspy, like she'd been
calling and calling into empty space.

'What is it?'

'The part about the serpent eyes and the baby swan.'

'I didn't see that.'

'Eh, you still with me?'

The moon was high in the sky now. He blinked. It was hard to focus.
Maybe that bump on his head had shifted something. His concentration
wavered. He propped himself up on one elbow.

'She's describing the … the thing he did to 'er. Then it's like she's talking
about some serpent and a swan. Don't make any sense.'

'Maybe her way to make it okay was to write about. Some stuff I read in there was like a dream.'

Lil angled the torch to the page and read aloud, '...*those red slit-eyes watching me. Serpent eyes. Dark hair circling iris. Snake tongue licking cygnet. Can't look away. Snake eyes shift and wrinkle each grunt and thrust, jamming inside. Tearing pain. Leave my body. Hovering above, watching down at that grunting beast, that whimpering girl below.*'

Lil stopped. Looked up at him expectantly.

He had nothing to say.

She returned to the page. 'Something scribbled out here. Can't read it.' She sucked in a long breath, read again. *But even now, writing to get this filthy thing out of me, burning under my skin, those eyes are watching. Faded red slits, inside black, fangs raised to strike. When I close my eyes, snake eyes watch back. His ugly words in my ears, 'Black slut, black cunt.'* Lil shrugged. 'Maybe like *she's* the swan? Flying overhead? But why the black cunt?'

He shook his head, frowning, 'Beats me.'

'Hmm.' The night pressed down around them. Lil's loud voice startled the air, 'Hey, weren't one a them swans raped by Zeus?'

'Leda? Leda and the swan? It's a painting I've seen. A metaphor for what happened to her, you reckon?'

'That's right, Zeus turned into a swan. Raped her. That guy was always raping young virgins.' She made a face of disgust. 'No wonder your mob is so fucked up.'

He ducked his head. Opened his hands in surrendered agreement.

'Ya reckon it's some kinda clue?'

'Dunno,' Tom put a hand to his aching head. 'But then what's the serpent?'

She shook her head. 'There's the obvious one, a course.' She made a wanking gesture, eyebrows raised.

'Hard to know ...' He gathered the blanket in around him. 'She would have been disturbed. Upset, of course. Mightn't mean anything. Just a way for her to deal with it. No help in finding her, or who did this to her.'

A scratching sound woke him.

Lil was poking the fire vigorously with a long stick. The notebook lay open in her lap. He watched her from under sleep-heavy eyelids. Sadness was etched into the lines and shadows of her face. She stared into the fire, speaking softly. He felt groggy, confused, couldn't understand her words. Wasn't sure if she was speaking to him or to herself.

Her voice grew louder. 'Plenty-a ugly, bad men, black and white. Men!' The last word she spoke like a bullet of disgust.

Their eyes met across the fire. 'It's men that are the problem with the world, not the colour of skin,' she said, flicking a look over her shoulder towards where Possum slept in the shadow away from the fire.

'Thanks,' he said, his mouth screwed into hopeless assent. He felt the sadness in his own face, knew firsthand the ugliness and brutality of his sex; Ted and Liam could be ugly cruel bastards too, especially the way they treated women. But there was a darker blame-shadow in his guts for all that was ugly in himself. Shadows he had boxed and fought against his whole life. Tears pricked his eyes. A sob stuck at the far back of his throat, and he swallowed hard. As he always swallowed. Gotta always be the man. He wanted to let it out, to sob loudly and uncontrollably, without having to understand why he was sobbing. Let it all burst out of him, that trapped animal-beast inside. That part of him that was so like Liam in its hunger and rage. The difference was that he refused to feed that hateful wolf.

'You're one of the good ones.'

He shrugged. Swallowed. 'Thanks.' His voice scraped raw emotion. 'Not sure that's true.' Maybe I'm just a coward hiding from the world, trapped in regret, he didn't say out loud. Lil poked at the fire so that tiny sparks erupted, crackling up into the night sky. 'Maybe there's something ugly in each of us,' he said. 'But when we hide it, we make the world carry it for us so we don't hate ourselves?'

'Dunno about that. Plenty to hate about the world if you ask me.' Lil kept her eyes on the fire as she spoke.

Easier to hate the world than hate yourself. But his thoughts were for himself, not for her.

Chapter 7

Land wakes, dreaming under fat-bellied moon. Whispering an endless song – come, come. Singing in ten thousand things. Different skins: dark, white, fur, bark and scale, same like me. Grass in my arm, tree in my blood, same like me.

Listen! A call, a step. Rock and dust, land, all talking.

You have wings, hands with claws, earth's wild blood in your veins. That perfect animal inside, watching out through dream-bright eyes, following. The always knowing inside skin-and-blood-bone-of-place-knowing before you were born. When you belonged to everything, and everything was bare-rooted in your soul.

Doors of perception, cleansed, open to glimpse infinity. Entering, arriving into mystery. Give back your heart to everything. You belong to this. Be-held in grandmother-soft arms. Beloved in vast-familiar love. I am yours, come.

Call and step. Leading dark feet, white foot, claw and silver belly, come.

Spirit of old ones all a-round, muttering, singing old songs in that first-tongue of your secret heart. Kangaroo spirit, emu, goanna and python, red-rock spirit singing. Frog and eagle, ant, crow, waking, dust awake.

You are part of this. You belong. Your bones belong. Salt of your bones belongs. Blood and beating heart, remember this belonging. Voice and flesh, and bones of feet, each singing in one wild choir of red-beating heart-of-earth, with every animal, every people, tree and rock and blue-night air.

Come, come.

Chapter 8

'Tom! Tom, wake up!' Lil burst into the small orbit of light around the fire, her face rigid with fear. 'Possum's gone.'

He jumped up, shock ricocheting through his body. Half-formed thoughts and images jammed his brain. He stood frozen, staring back at Lil, haloed in silver light from the moon still high overhead.

'We need to find her.' Her voice was loud, cutting through the slow fog of his mind.

'How long since you've seen her?'

'Thought she was asleep. Just there.' She pointed to the mess of canvas and bedding at the shadowed edge of the rocky enclosure. 'Not long, don't reckon. Didn't hear her go.'

'Okay, let's split up. You circle around the camp, I'll go down and check the vehicles. And get the rifle.'

Eyes wide, Lil held his gaze for a moment, then walked out into the night and began calling in a singsong voice, with an undernote of fear, 'Possum. Hey, Bub. Where are you?'

He turned abruptly. Felt the world sway with the sudden movement. A wave of nausea lurched in his stomach. He swallowed, put a hand to his forehead, drew in a deep breath, and set off down the narrow rocky track towards the vehicles.

He called softly into the shimmering night. For a moment he stood on a rocky outcrop just above the abandoned shanty. The ugly rusted shapes were now painted silver. The two white vehicles shone brightly. Nothing stirred, only the unexpected bump of his heart, loud inside his ears.

He opened the back of the troopie and pulled out the rifle. He only ever used it for shooting sick or injured stock. Had used it frequently in the drought. He grabbed the box of bullets and unbuttoned his shirt pocket to slip the crumpled box inside. His fingers touched the warm metal of Ella's phone. He'd forgotten about it. No time now. He rebuttoned the shirt pocket and shoved the box of bullets into the back pocket of his jeans instead.

'Possum?' He checked Lil's vehicle. But there was no sign of the girl. He turned and strode back towards the path, then stopped, turned back to the vehicle and shone the torch into the equipment in the back until the light fell on to the small package he was searching for. He pulled the flare from the heap and tucked it under his arm.

Back at the campsite, Lil was pacing, words erupting the moment he appeared. 'She's nowhere. Can't find her.' Her face crumpled in a knot of anguish.

'Let's take things slowly. She's only wandered off somewhere. We didn't hear a vehicle. I don't think anyone's taken her. And she was only lying close, so we would've heard something.' He looked around the enclosed rocky space. 'She can't have gone far. That's the only track down from the ridge. She must have headed along the ridge.' He spoke as his thoughts arrived in a rush.

'Okay, yep, yeah right. She does wander in her sleep.' The distress on her face softened.

'I've got a flare here. We can shoot that off. And if she's lost, she'll find us. Anyone can see it for miles.' He didn't add that if someone was watching them, they would see it too.

Once they'd watched the red flare rise high into the clear bright night, he said, 'Let's go back to the start again.'

There was a mess of tracks around the bedding nested in sandy soil. 'Any good at tracking, Lil?' he asked, shining the torch around.

'Nah. Not enough blackfella in me, don't reckon. Messed up any tracks anyways, by the looks of it.'

'Hard to see where she wandered off. And too rocky to tell over there,' he said, turning the torch on to the rocky track. 'But she must've gone that way.'

'Nowhere else to go, eh.'

He stepped on to the path, shining the torch on the ground ahead, the rifle hanging loose in the other hand. Bright moonlight cast deep shadows from the ridge above. After walking slowly for ten minutes, their torches glaring left and right into shadows, the path forked. He turned to Lil, who was following close behind. 'I think we should go back to the campsite and wait. I don't think she would've come this far. There's no point both of us getting lost.' He swayed as he said it and rested against the wall of rock on one side of the path. 'I'm sure she'll turn up. Or we can search in the morning. She probably found a comfy place to sleep.'

'We need to find her. She'll be scared out here on 'er own. I'll go this way.' Lil set off rapidly along the left fork of the path sloping downwards around a bend before he could respond.

He called loudly, 'Don't go too far, Lil. Meet back here in ten.' No reply. He turned and walked along the right fork. In places it was so narrow he had to squeeze through, the rifle bumping against rock. Surely, she wouldn't have come this far?

He stopped. Was that a voice calling? He held his breath to listen. The rock created a tunnel of silence. Yes. Calling his name. He turned and started to run, but his body felt heavy. His head pounded. The stock of the rifle banged against the rock. Back at the fork in the track, Lil's voice was stronger.

'Coming,' he called in response. 'I'm … coming, Lil.' Breathing heavily he ran-walked, stumbling on the rough track. Abruptly, at a twist in the path, two figures came into view, one leaning over the other, huddled on the ground.

Lil pointed between a small stand of she-oaks. 'Ella,' she gasped.

He stared at her, uncomprehending, then looked down at Possum.

'Ella's in there. *Go*!' Lil's voice rose in urgency as she stabbed at the air with her finger.

A shock of understanding jolted him forward. Leaning the rifle against the rock, he turned to the small trees leaning in towards each other, hiding the narrow entrance. Stepping through a curtain of soft-needles he shone the torch down the narrow track.

Tom staggered along the rough path as it wound down between high rock on either side. At last the path levelled out and he stumbled into a wide gorge, lit brightly in silver moonlight. He fell to his knees panting, his palms pressing hard into the prickle of coarse sand. His eyes fixed on a deep pool of water a few steps in front of him and he crawled forward. Bowing low, he scooped cool, so-cool water into his filthy hands and splashed it over his face and neck. Cupping his hands, he drank water that tasted of deep time.

He stared into the reflection of night sky in the pool, shivered by ripples where he had disturbed the mirror. The fat orb of moon waved back. The shadow of his own face leant in. For a lingering moment time dissolved into infinity, and he breathed deeply. Pure air through cool, wet lips. Skin of scalp tingling.

Tom scanned the gorge, gaze alighting on the one thing out of place. A bundle of dark rags wedged against rock on the far side of the gorge. An animal sound erupted from his wet lips, breaking the deep silence. His mind bolted, but his body was slow to follow. He dragged himself to standing and walked towards the bundle. With each step his feet sank deep into the coarse sand; his legs felt leaden: drag, lift, step, drag, lift, step, no way to move faster, never taking his eyes from the bundle. Finally he bent to his knees in front of it. One knee touched the rags, felt the solid weight inside the filthy fabric. A hand protruded from beneath, pale in the moonlight. It was so small, like a child's hand. Pain clawed his chest, squeezing blood from his heart.

Tom leant forward, his fingers outstretched, but his hand froze in its slow arc. He inched his hand forward again, fingers trembling with the tension of wanting to reach and wanting to pull back, torn between wanting to know and not wanting to know what laid under the rags.

Tentatively he pulled back the cloth to reveal a face covered in dried blood, with dark bruising around the left eye. He drew a sharp inbreath. A lone fly wandered drunkenly along the mouth, inside the lips, along the exposed bottom teeth.

He touched Ella's neck; it was warm, cool-warm, clammy. He pressed into the skin, holding his breath, fingers listening for a pulse.

Yes. Yes, there was a pulse. Weak and thready. But it was there. Ella was alive.

'Ella, Ella, can you hear me? Wake up, Ella.' He shook her gently. She didn't stir. Her face looked like the death mask of someone who had died violently.

Urgency pushed him to action. He carefully cradled her into his arms and staggered up, lifting. She was so light it was like holding a bundle of air. He turned and trudged through the sinking sand as fast as he could, his strength returning with one throbbing purpose: to keep Ella alive.

Chapter 9

When he staggered into the warm glow around the fire, he found Lil was there, holding Possum against her chest. The peace of them was out of rhythm with his drumming heart. Lil was instantly alert; she didn't move, but her eyes were wide, watching as he laid the floppy bundle gently on the ground.

When he had settled Ella, head propped against his blanket, he pulled back the veil of filthy rag and pressed two fingers to her pale throat. Checking again for life. So weak. For the briefest breath, he cupped the lower side of her cheek in his palm, felt the clammy coolness of her skin.

Lil raised her eyebrows with the impossible question. He shrugged and gave a slow I-don't-know shake of his head. Strangely unhurried now, he picked up his water bottle, opened it and raised it to his lips. His hand stopped halfway. The moon ensnared him; he remembered the dream taste of deep water in the gorge, quenching. He closed the water bottle without drinking and swallowed the clear taste of memory.

His mind refused to change gears. His head was pounding again. The night was liquid-thick, wide open with nothing to hold on to. Except that one thread, Ella – alive. His eyes fell on the red book, abandoned in the dust. He reached down and picked it up. Brushed it against his jeans and shoved it inside his shirt, warm against his skin.

His words came slowly, 'We need to get help for Ella.'

Lil nodded. Possum didn't stir. Her head was a dark mess of curls resting against Lil's chest, body hidden in a grey blanket.

'Got a radio in your vehicle?'

'Nah. Phone.'

'Sat-phone? Satellite?'

'Nah.'

'No use out here then.' He looked towards the track down to the vehicles. 'Shit.' Turned back to Lil. 'We need to call the flying doctor. Get Ella to a hospital.'

His brain turned slowly. No point driving her back to Broken Ridge. The trip might kill her. There'd be an airstrip on Muttagundi. How far was it to the homestead? What had Barry said about the track from Yorick? He hadn't taken it in. What was it? Hard to find. Rough. He had to do something.

Tom pushed himself to standing, grunting with the effort. He stared out across the moonlit plain. Stared at the distant lights. His attention fixed on the lights, at first without comprehending. Realisation came with a jolt. 'Lights headed this way.' His voice was urgent now, all dream gone.

Lil frowned, 'What? Who?'

'Dunno. But whoever did this to Ella could be coming back to make sure …'

Lil didn't move. Her arms seemed fixed around Possum.

'We'd better hide. Put the fire out. Just in case.'

Her eyes grew wide with understanding. She shook Possum and dragged her to her feet with a moan. Possum allowed herself to be manoeuvred up, the blanket cloaked around her shoulders. 'I'll go back up the path with this one, eh? She still dreaming.'

'I'll leave Ella with you and go and wait down at the vehicles.' With a clunk of remembering, he pictured the rifle resting beside the entrance to the gorge. He stood over the pale face bundled in rags, lifted her up and followed Lil as she steered Possum along the path.

When the three women were settled into a small pouch in the rock, he ran along the track, retrieved the rifle, then headed back along the narrow path to their campsite and threw sand on the fire. The lights out on the plain, less than a kilometre away now, bounced erratically.

Down on the flat, his eyes darted around in the moonlight, glancing over the hulking shapes of humpies and wrecks, searching for a place to hide with a clear view of the vehicles. The sound of motor was close, a low growl filling the still night. A flash of light hit the front vehicle and he ducked. Moving quickly, he stepped behind sheets of rusted corrugated iron nailed to several sagging posts that might have once been someone's home. He pulled the bullets from his back pocket, squatted, loaded the gun and cocked the rifle. A wave of ugly fear prickled up his spine. He knew how hard it was to shoot a sick or injured animal. Could he shoot a man if he had to? He didn't know. Wouldn't know until that moment.

The arc of lights poked and bumped against the night sky as the vehicle bounced over the rough track. Kneeling, one knee raised as an anchor for the rifle, he steadied his elbow, the gun barrel resting over a rusted drum. Body locked into position, he stared down the barrel, eye fixed on the driver's side door of the roaring vehicle as it slowed. His heart drummed; the rifle throbbing with the pulse of his blood-beat.

The Hilux, halted. Lights blazing. He thought of Lil, Ella and Possum in their rocky hiding place, easily found if anyone walked along the path. He steadied his gaze and held the rifle firmly, finger on the trigger, swallowed. Two figures stepped from the vehicle and walked towards the two stationary cars, silhouetted against the sharp headlights. They were talking, but he couldn't hear what they were saying over the engine noise.

'Tom,' The taller man called into the night when they had finished checking the vehicles and stood together, shadows against hard light. 'Tom, you okay?' Then louder, 'Tom!' the man's voice, his own name, filled the night.

It was no one he recognised. But they seemed concerned. He stood, rifle limp in his left hand, and stepped out of hiding. He walked towards the two men. Couldn't see their faces.

'Tom?'

'Yep.' It was no more than a grunt, tight with fear.

'Barry,' the big man said, 'manager of Muttagundi. We spoke on the phone.'

Cold relief ran through him. His body relaxed with chemical waves of aftershock. He reached out his hand and Barry grabbed it firmly and shook.

'Everything okay, mate?' Barry was inspecting him closely. 'Jimmy, the stockman here, was camped over the ridge there. Saw your flare and called it in. I guessed it must've been you. Picked Jimmy up on the way.'

Jimmy nodded at Tom, the whites of his eyes contrasting with his dark skin. They shook hands. Tom leant the rifle against the side of the nearest vehicle.

'Shit mate, who you expecting that you need that?' This time Barry waited for Tom to speak.

'We've had some trouble.'

'I thought it was just you?'

'It was … But … too much to explain. We need to call the flying doctor. Where's the nearest strip?'

'Decent strip this side of the homestead. Need some bog rolls to light the plane in. One of the fella's can grab 'em on his way to meet us. You need the doc?' He peered at Tom.

'No. The friend I came looking for.' Tom waved an arm towards the ridge. 'She's in a bad way. Might be too late, but we need to try.'

'Okay, I'm on it. Jimmy, if you give Tom a hand to bring the girl down, I'll call the doc. What am I telling them?'

'Young woman. Exposure, dehydration. Injuries to head and maybe others. Pale and clammy … Thready pulse … not responding. Unconscious, I guess.'

'Okay, that'll do.' Barry stepped towards his vehicle. 'Big storm coming in from the north. Might be trouble getting through for a small aircraft.'

As Tom started towards the track, Barry called after him, 'Hey mate, is that thing loaded?'

Tom turned. 'Yep.'

'Reckon I'm gonna shove it in yer troopie, mate. Don't like loaded weapons sitting around.' Barry picked up the rifle. 'Still don't know why ya need –' his words were swallowed by the sound of the motor.

The engine was running, headlights blinding when Jimmy and Tom finally returned, breathing hard, with Ella slung between them. As Barry opened the back door, Lil and Possum emerged from the track. 'Blimey, how many more ya got stowed up there, mate?' He grinned.

Resting Ella on the backseat, Tom stepped back, and said, 'This is Lil, and Possum, who found Ella in the gorge. That's when we sent up the flare.' His words were laboured.

'Gotcha.' Barry frowned. 'Still don't get why you needed the rifle.' But he didn't wait for a reply. 'Doc's on 'er way. Heading straight into that storm. Sounded a bit on edge. Might be a bumpy ride out for that girl.'

Lil was standing at the edge of the beam of headlights, and Possum had an arm across her eyes.

'Better come with us, Lil,' Barry said. 'Follow in your vehicle? Too hard to find those tracks on yer own in the dark.'

Lil nodded.

'Strip's not far from the homestead. Plenty of beds there. Get a bit of sleep before you head home in the morning. Better than heading back to town at this hour with that storm coming in.'

Lil nodded, looking down at Possum, who was leaning into her, eyes closed.

'One of the boys'll meet us there with diesel and bog rolls to light the strip.' At this Barry dropped into the driver's seat and slammed the door. Tom climbed into the back seat, lifted Ella's head gently and rested it on his lap. He placed a hand on her, a shape of shoulder, but it felt like a cool lump of clay.

They stopped next to the airstrip. Stars blinked through scudding cloud; the moon was hiding now. The radio crackled. Barry talked loudly, giving instructions. Then Barry and Jimmy exited the Hilux and stood silhouetted talking to someone else in the headlights of another vehicle. Abruptly the three shadowy figures started moving in different directions, a strange ritual unfolding under shifting moonlight. They dragged out unidentifiable objects from the back of the ute and occasionally one or the other gave a hurried instruction. Tom sniffed the air. Diesel. Dark figures moved about on either side of the airstrip. A rumble sounded in the distance. Was that thunder or an engine? Both? Tom looked up to see lights in the sky. And beyond that, a flash of lightning.

Small fires erupted in lines on either side of the airstrip. The nightscape lit up as one fire after another licked the night air. It was strange and beautiful, and for a moment Tom felt as if he were swimming among the stars. He imagined ancient shamans calling down their gods from the skies to heal the sick and dying. Ella would have loved this night scene.

The low hum overhead grew louder and louder until it was roaring; the fierce lights in the sky were descending towards them. When the noise was close, he put his hands over his ears, but it roared inside his head anyway. The lights and roaring hit the ground in a cloud of red dust between the lines of small fire-lights.

'Not long now, Ella,' he whispered, stroking her forehead where it was free of cuts and bruises. Her skin felt cool and clammy. Figures emerged from the aircraft. From this distance they looked like red-and-blue angels, their faces haloed in light. Barry met them and pointed towards the vehicle.

A few moments later, two people emerged from the gaping mouth of the aircraft carrying a stretcher, and approached. Tom opened the door, lifted Ella's head gently and slipped out from under the weight of it.

He stood and watched as they manoeuvred Ella on to the stretcher. Figures moved in and out of darkness. Occasional words broke the silence.

'What's her name?'

'Ella.'

The taller woman spoke loudly, close to the pale lifeless face. 'Ella. Ella?'

Ella didn't respond.

The woman grasped the top of Ella's shoulder and pinched hard. Ella pulled her shoulder away from the pain. Was that a slight moan?

'She's responding to pain.' The woman seemed to be speaking to someone in the shadows. Abruptly, as if the show were over, the stretcher was gone.

He looked towards the aircraft as they huddled under a bright light, three figures hovering around that small bundle clinging to life.

He leant against the warmth of the bonnet as they carried out their ministrations. The wide night seemed alive, watching down on them. Ancient spirits of healing called to witness.

Tom jumped as Barry spoke loudly, appearing beside him with someone in the red-and-blue. 'Thought you might need that head seen to.'

The woman stepped forward and shone a small light on to the wound on his forehead. 'Could you bend down?' She was short. Only came up to his chest.

He bent, pressing his backside into the vehicle, until his head was level with hers.

She didn't speak as she examined the wound on his forehead. Then said, 'What's your name?'

'Tom MacDonald.'

'Do you know what the date is?'

'Hmm, maybe a Thursday? No, could be Friday?' But all the days had blurred together.

'Do you know where you are?'

'Yorick. No, Muttagundi.'

'Any headaches?' she said, shining the light into each eye.

'Yep. Deadly.'

'How would you describe the pain?'

'Um. Bad. Like there's a drum in there and a little man is pounding on it.'

'Any vomiting, dizziness?'

He nodded, 'If I stand up suddenly. Or move too fast. Maybe vomited in the mineshaft. Just waves of nausea now.'

'Do you know if you were unconscious after you struck your head?'

'I was knocked out for a bit.'

'How long?'

'No idea. I was alone in a tunnel.'

'Are you sleepy?'

'Have been.'

'And drifting off?'

'I guess so. A bit dreamy. Unfocused.'

'Think we should take you in. Just to keep an eye on you. Could be concussion,' she said, speaking rapidly. She turned to Barry, 'There's room in the aircraft, but we need to get moving. That storm's coming in fast.'

'Okay, thanks, sister.'

'*Doctor.*' She walked briskly back towards the aircraft.

'Better go, mate,' Barry said. 'Doesn't look like she'll hang around waiting.'

Tom kept one hand on the bonnet as he turned to Lil. 'You okay, Lil?'

She nodded and opened her mouth to speak, but Barry cut in, 'We'll look after things here mate, you go and take care of your girlfriend.'

'Yep. Betta get going. Look after 'er, Tom,' Lil said.

'Thanks, Lil,' he said, and reached over to touch her arm.

It was cramped inside the aircraft. He stooped to look around, head tucked in, body feeling too large. Ella was already strapped into the thin stretcher, her face very pale. He felt hands on his arms guiding him towards the other stretcher. It looked too small and narrow, but his body ached to lie down. He dropped on to his back closed his eyes. He felt someone strapping him in, but his eyes were too heavy to open. He heard a crack of thunder close, a thud of metal as the door closed.

Resting a hand against the smooth contour of red notebook under his shirt, he patted it gently. The imprint of Ella's pale face was close behind his eyes: hold on Ella, hold on … lips too tired to move, he repeated the mantra in his mind.

Tom's eyes sprang open and his body jolted awake as the aircraft dipped suddenly, cavorting like a bucking horse. A loud crack. So loud it ricocheted inside his head. The night outside was alive with colour and sound. Another loud crack ripped through the cabin. He ducked reflexively.

Voices, loud. Hard to hear over the hum of the engine and the vicious storm. 'Lights are down.'

Tom drifted again. Words echoed through the metal cabin, 'Low fuel. Emergency landing.' But he couldn't see any faces to know who was speaking or if he were dreaming.

He woke with a jerk as the aircraft plunged so fast it made his stomach lurch. They were flying inside the storm now, and light exploded through the cabin.

Ella's pale face was the only face in view. His body was too tired for fear, and his thoughts came lumpy and slow. What an irony to end like this, to drop out of the sky in a metal bird. He closed his eyes.

When he opened them again, everything was still. The engine silent. He jumped as another crack echoed close and lightning flashed. In swift efficient movements, the crew began moving.

BOOK 3

Ella and Tom

Come, fly into this final mystery, crazy for the light
you flutter-thrash, then vanish.
Until you know this; to die and so to live,
you are only the restless wanderer upon dark earth.
Rapture of Longing –

Johann Wolfgang von Goethe (trans by Olivia Parsons)

Will you wake? Fly back little bird who has come so far.
Sing her back sweet Orpheus, who sings the world awake with your beautiful song. Let us believe in love again.
And there stands egregious death, squinting in at the window. She has forgotten her glasses again. Whom do you seek old gardener?

' i am light
        hovering over honeysuckle-pale-flesh '

Tom's scalp tingled, tiny hairs stood up, alert, as if stroked by a feather. His gaze tugged from the small hand cradled in his to Ella's puffy eyes.

' singing in those scents of being
        calling and remembering '

Her eyes seemed to twitch for a moment under closed lids, or had he imagined it? He stared at the face, so pale and still, barely recognisable under the dark bruises, ugly scratches and scabs. One eye was so puffy it had disappeared in a dark pudding-swell of flesh. Tiny hoses into her nostrils gave off barely-there white noise. He looked down at the hand lying in his, cut and scratched. So fragile.

' warm hand holding this cold clay
        fluttering hearthold still '

The hugely pregnant nurse walked in, shoes squeaking. She waddle-squeaked on tiptoe towards the bed. Smiled over at him. Still holding Ella's hand, he watched as she changed the drip on the other side of the bed. It was impossible not to stare at the huge pregnant belly, straining navy fabric against dark buttons.

She caught his gaze and smiled. 'Yeah, kinda takes over, doesn't it?' she said softly, rubbing her belly.

He smiled back, felt the warmth of the woman flush out the strain of the longest night.

'I call it the kicky-whale,' she grinned, continuing to stroke her swell-of-belly affectionately. 'Keeps me awake all night.' She began to change the drip. 'Rugby player for sure, the fellas reckon.' She laughed softly. 'It's a girl. Guess she'll keep her big brother in line. He's three, and a bit wild.'

The nurse reached up and unhooked the empty drip bag from its hook. 'Should be home in bed. So short-staffed with this storm. Flash-flooding in the creeks, staff out on properties can't get in.'

They were silent for a long-full moment as he watched her finishing her ministrations.

'Do you think she'll make it?'

'Couldn't say. She's been through a lot. Body can only take so much of that heat out there. Heat exposure is deadly. Could be damage to the organs. Electrolytes out of whack. We don't have equipment here to do those tests. Don't usually have patients here. Only terminal. Terminal old age. Same with a lot of small country hospitals these days.' She looked across the room at the faded, baby-blue curtain pulled around the bed opposite Ella's. Lowered her voice, 'Your neighbour in there,' she nodded towards the closed curtain, 'had a fall at home. Ninety-five next month,' she said, raising her eyebrows.

'Okay … Any word on when we can fly out?'

'The crew are resting up in case they get the call. But it's not looking good. They're calling it an "extreme weather event". "Unprecedented".' She made rabbit ears with her fingers. 'That's what they keep saying. You might have to sit tight till the storm blows over.'

'There's nothing more you can do for her?' He felt the pain behind his eyes and forehead as he focused again on Ella's pale face.

'She's in good hands. RFDS crew's just there,' she flicked her head towards the door, eyebrows raised as pointers along the corridor. 'Best care in the world; be here in a blink if anything changes. She's stable for now. What she needs is rest and rehydration.'

He nodded.

'Why don't you go back to your bed and get some sleep?'

Tom shook his head. 'I can't sleep. I'd rather sit with her in case she wakes.'

'You feeling okay? Looks like you took a nasty crack on the head.'

'Yeah, I'm fine.' He didn't meet her eye. 'There's really nothing more you can do?' His words hung helplessly in the heavy-cool air-conditioned air.

'Not really.' She wrote something on a chart. 'We keep her fluids up, rehydrate and hope her body hasn't had too much damage. She's young and strong. Keep talking to her. Let her know you're here.'

A wave of something like nausea, fermenting in hopelessness, washed through him. 'Do you know what time it is?' he asked, rubbing the bare place on his left wrist.

A frozen sliver of time peeled off into disordered memory. Arriving last night in the chaos of the storm. One of the nurses taking off his watch to take his pulse. His right wrist scratched and crusted with dried blood. A bed with crisp white sheets, covered with a pale blue bedspread that he laid on for a moment. But when he closed his eyes, Ella was there. That pale face. Her voice in his head, as if she were calling to him. He had sat up, ignoring the headache. Wandered barefoot along cool-floored corridors until he found her, following the sounds of voices and movement. All the other rooms and corridors were silent.

The nurse consulted the fob watch pinned to her chest. 'Four-twenty.'

'Thanks.' He wasn't sure why he needed to know the time. As if it might give some containment to this eternal night without edges, and no end in sight.

'Will I bring you a cuppa?'

'Thanks,' he nodded.

'How do you take it?'

'Builder's tea. Strong, thanks.'

'Gotcha.' She left on her squeaky tiptoes.

He turned back to the bed. Squeezed the hand, not sure what to say. Words seemed so small against this gaping space between living and dying where Ella was caught. What was there to say?

Rubbing his wrist again, he remembered Ella's pesky curiosity about why he wore a watch. Memories of her littered his thoughts. He hadn't wanted to explain, not sure that he could. How ticking-time was all he had to hold on to as a kid during long nights at boarding school. Then after Suni. Insistent tick-tock, the passing of time, was the only flimsy lifeline when it felt like loneliness and grief were bleeding him out, each moment like a little death. Two-and-a-half hours until dawn. Tick-tock, tick-tock. Two. Tick-tock. One hour. Tick-tick-tock. He held to that slim pulse of tomorrow inside this blackest night. Tomorrow-tomorrow, tomorrow must be better than this.

'Why don't you go back to bed?'

He opened his eyes, blinking groggily. Felt the hand, warm-kind on his back.

It took a slow, jumbled moment to understand where he was. Ella. Ella was there. But nothing had changed. The hand on his back shifted and he turned his head to see the nurse holding a mug of tea. She spoke, her voice gentle, 'Why don't you go to bed? We'll look after her while you're asleep.'

'I'm okay, thanks.' He sat up and took the mug of steaming tea. 'Thanks,' he said again, and lifted the steaming liquid to his lips.

He sat sipping tea, staring at Ella.

What was that sound? A soft juddering, thumping, agitated noise. Nothing stirred behind the closed-curtained cubicle across the room. The sound came again. It was a moth, hurling itself against the window towards the sharp light of a security spotlight outside. Its soft grey-white wings flapped furiously as it fell back, then hurled itself towards the light again.

Tom put his mug down and walked across towards the window. For a moment the moth was still. Then it shifted, quieter now, and flew a jagged path to the other end of the large window. Laid still. Abruptly, it recommenced its relentless hurling at the light, its wings flapping with frantic effort. Halting occasionally to lie still, exhausted. Then an intermittent flicking of wings, like soft, silent clapping.

He dragged open the stiff window, pushed against the flyscreen, slid the metal clasps open and pushed. The flyscreen clattered against metal as it fell to the ground outside. Carefully, he tried to guide the moth with waving hand movements towards the open window. But the moth kept pushing back into the glass. He persisted for several minutes. It struggled against his saving hands, as if it wanted to die. In one final attempt, with cupped hands he herded it gently towards the open window. In a burst of energy, it flew up, flapping its pale wings close to his face, hovering as it passed within a breath. A single wing kissed his nose and cheek, barely touching. The moth continued rising upward for a moment, then dropped, fell on to the window sill and laid still. He stood staring down at it, knowing its wings were too delicate to touch. If he tried to pick it up to take it outside, it would certainly die.

'Is anyone there?'

The voice was loud, interrupting this small commotion.

'I'm here.' He spoke to the curtain.

'Please open this curtain. It's like a coffin in here. I want to see the rain.'

He crossed the room and pulled back the blue curtain around the bed nearest the window. Sitting propped up in bed was a tiny old woman. The image of her didn't fit the strong commanding voice he'd just heard.

'Oh, there you are,' she said, looking up at him. 'Aren't you a big one.' Her mouth didn't change but her whole face smiled. Her eyes were bright, taking him in. When he finished pulling the curtain back and she saw his filthy clothes, she said, 'Oh, you're not the nurse.'

'No, not the nurse. I'm here for a friend,' he said, lifting back the curtain across the end of the bed to reveal Ella on the other side of the room.

The old woman put a hand to her mouth. 'Oh, dear.' Her face creased in pain. His eyes itched, seeing the woman's reaction. He let the curtain drop back.

She peered towards the window. 'I thought it was morning.' She blinked, as if trying to recalibrate to here and now. 'Do you know what time it is? I thought it was morning,' she said again.

'About four-thirty.'

'It's a bit too bright.'

He closed the curtain, leaving a narrow gap near the end of the bed.

She nodded. 'Could you pass my rosary, dear.' She waved a hand towards the small cabinet beside her bed.

He looked down at the faux-wood cabinet.

'Yes, in there,' she pointed to the drawer. 'Right in front. Red rosary beads.'

He opened the drawer. A rope of red glass beads nestled in a small heap among dirty tissues. They dangled between his fingers, the wooden cross hanging down.

'Thank you, dear,' she said, as he dropped them into her ancient, smooth-wrinkled palm. She had large hands for a tiny woman. 'I'll say a prayer for your girlfriend. What's her name?'

'Ella. And I'm Tom.'

'I'm Sarah. Keep talking to her, dear,' she said in that strong voice, closing her eyes almost before she finished speaking. Her lips began to move silently. He stood there for a moment, but the old woman didn't open her eyes again. He went back to his chair beside Ella, picked up her hand, and whispered, 'Stay, Ella. Please stay.' It felt awkward to speak aloud what was bursting against the rock walls of his heart.

' reaching out
    warm-flesh-of-heartholding '

He let his words form and hover on the inside, the heart-side. His lips didn't move. When I thought you were … even in the privacy of his mind, 'dead' seemed too loud, too final … gone. When I thought you were gone …

But there were no words here. This place that had never been spoken between them. Couldn't be spoken. It was all unkempt feeling. A ramshackle, abandoned place. The Yorick inside him. Beyond words. Except poetry, perhaps. Was there a poem to say? Out the window, a lemon-scented gum tree, silver-sleek with rain, stood close, as if watching over the silent waiting room. Yes, poetry. He squeezed Ella's hand.

'Oh, hell.'

He shifted awake as the words drifted into his consciousness. Blinked and raised his head to look across at the pale blue curtain. He listened. Nothing. Wait … maybe a soft grunting noise?

'Anything I can help with, Sarah?'

'Oh, yes, could you pick up my rosary for me, dear.'

He walked around the curtain and was again surprised at the incongruence between that strong voice and this tiny frame of hunched woman in a mountain of pillows. Her bright blue eyes shone up at him from her smile-wrinkled face, surrounded by a nest of white, bed-messed hair.

'There.' She pointed to where the red beads had spilled on the floor. 'I must have nodded off.'

Tom lifted them by the finger-worn wooden cross and placed them in her palm.

'Granny always said you mustn't let your rosary drop on the floor. Bad luck.' She cast her eyes up at the ceiling. 'But I can't for the life of me remember what sort of bad luck. I think it was something about the devil catching your soul.' She held the beads against her chest. 'Thank you, dear.'

He smiled at her. 'Anything else you need? I can get one of the nurses?'

'No, don't bother them.' She waved a large, unadorned hand towards the door. The knuckles were bulbous, the hand pale and spotted, thick-veined, index finger turned outward at an awkward angle. The red beads were vivid against her translucent skin. Her hands were strangely beautiful, like an ancient gnarled trunk of tree.

'How's your friend doing, dear?'

'Not much change. She seems comfortable enough, but …' His sentence trailed off, an eruption of anguish swallowing his words. He could feel the surprise quiver of near-tears in his throat.

'Pray with me,' she said.

Tom sat down on the chair beside the bed. The white head was already bowed, eyes closed, rosary beads clutched to her chest with both hands, moving them in familiar rhythm. He closed his eyes and bowed his head, spoke his silent prayer.

God let her live, please let her live.

But his words, his prayer, tasted fraudulent on his stone tongue. He didn't know how to pray. Or to whom he should pray. He opened his eyes, watched the bowed head. She rolled one smooth red bead between her fingers, lips moving, soft breath of mantra into cool air.

His old arguments against god lined up as loud as circus ducks. Pop-pop went his armed and loaded hijacker mind. Pop-bang. Stupid white men in positions of power holding up a Bible. As if a holy book gave them some god-given right to truth and power, while holding a loaded gun behind their back to defend that same god-given righteousness in the name of their god.

Pop-bang. God is dead.

Tom's thick-weary mind slumped back into a childhood memory. His mother taking them to church in town on Sundays. Dressed up in little matching twin suits. All the church ladies oohing-and-aahing over them, calling them little angels. Then abruptly and without explanation his mother stopped going to church. He never understood what had happened, was too young to ask or care. For young boys it only meant they were free to play and not have to wear those annoying little suits with the uncomfortable ties. He hadn't thought about it since. It was probably something to do with Ted.

None of those good church ladies ever came to the house again. Not even when his mother was dying. Only old Mrs Myrtle showed up. Rough-and-ready, not the churchy kind. One tooth missing at the front-side of her mouth. He was intrigued by that dark hiding gap and tried to catch a glimpse of it whenever she spoke, which was not often. She never smiled. She drove out each week in a rundown Holden ute to bring casseroles and scones or some other offering. She made the best lamingtons. Then she would sit with his mother.

One afternoon he ran into his mother's bedroom, forgetting that Mrs Myrtle was there. She was sitting on the end of the bed with their mother's feet in her lap, holding one foot close to her belly and rubbing it. The room smelled of eucalyptus, covering the sick smell that usually hung in the room. Before he could speak, the woman put a finger to her lips. From the doorway he looked over at his mother's face. Her eyes were closed and she was smiling, as if for the moment she felt no pain.

Pop-bang. Re-loading, pop-bang. Now Lil's nasty neighbour came to mind. The plant murderer, hiding behind her twitching curtain. That's what these people did – hid behind the curtain called religion. Judged their neighbours from behind the safety of lacy veils, holding their little cue cards of right or wrong, black or white. Pulled out the god card like a Round-Up gun to poison and kill whatever didn't fit their narrow, god-infested view of the world. He didn't want anything to do with their punitive, man-made god.

There was a sound on the other side of the curtain. His whole body froze, straining to listen. It was the soft movement of nurse or doctor checking Ella again. He breathed out, listened to the quiet footsteps; it wasn't the squeaky-toed pregnant nurse.

Tom rested back in the chair alongside Sarah and felt his old despair for the world slow-burning his heart. It was a sickening feeling, like knowing a cancer is growing inside, its dark presence taking hold, growing stronger, eating healthy flesh. Pop-bang. Hijacker mind. People aren't evil, just ignorant. There's no conspiracy; only an epidemic of fear and human fallibility. We are just blind sheep following whoever or whatever offers us reassurance, promises meaning and belonging, or something to feed-and-fuel that constant hunger. Easier than walking alone and asking the hard questions, making up our own minds. Easier to follow the established path, repeat the party line, to avoid our own uncertainties by joining other people's categories and loud convictions. Easier to hide from our obstinate fear, deep-rooted inside not knowing, and laced with quiet desperation. It's hard to wake from fear and uncertainty, to discover and live by our deepest values, which are messy and complicated, and often contradictory. Much easier to follow someone or something that is lactating hope, much easier to reach for blind certainty. Pop-pop.

Beside him, the old woman's white head was nodding.

He knew how hard it was to be kind in the face of hatred and stupidity. He'd given up trying to be 'good' a long time ago. Who knew what 'good' was anyway? He only meant to be kind. That was his way. So simple. And so damned hard. It was love for nature that showed him the way. The wind was the same wind for everyone, and everything. But the wind didn't blow *for* anyone, it blew because that was its nature. The tree didn't discriminate but offered its kind shade for all creatures. It grew not to show how beautiful or useful it was, but because it *was tree*. By being itself, it was beautiful.

How has humanity grown so ugly? Everywhere there is hatred and cruelty, greed and ignorance.

Yes, it takes courage to be kind.

Good implies bad. Us and them. Bang-bang, you're dead. Kindness exists for its own sake. It has no expectations; no price tag. Any deed or word that expects a return isn't kindness, but do-gooding or point-scoring or something else. Kindness is its own truth. *A religion of kindness*. Now, that would be something, if the world embraced kindness as its new religion, and the politics of being kind. Pop. Bang.

Tom blew out a long breath and rubbed the new ache at his temples that had come with contemplating god and humans and trees and wind. His relentless and lonely search for knowing. A way of knowing that was large enough to hold his uncertainties and guide him in darkest night that he never spoke to anyone about. He had seen it in Ella too. But she didn't try to hide it. Couldn't hide it.

His gaze dropped to the serene face of the old woman, who had recommended whispering her prayers, eyes closed. She looked beautiful.

Perhaps we can only see the beauty of another up close? Otherwise all we see is the hard outer shell. Deep down, in those tender places, that's where we are beautiful. But we hide it from the world. How strange we are. Of course we hide it, because that's where we're messy and confused. Wounded, too. The flinch of his own regret twitched close. The things he hadn't dared, regret hiding in deep where the wound rubbed.

As if sensing the tight-balled tangle of his mind, and without opening her eyes, Sarah dropped one hand from the rosary beads to rest on the bed, her palm an open invitation. He placed his hand in hers, aware of how tanned and vital his looked in comparison. Her skin felt surprisingly warm and dry-smooth, like fine paper, the kind you find in an old Bible. She squeezed his fingers and spoke quietly.

'Just think of someone you love; God will do the rest.'

Tom's thoughts catapulted to his long climb out of the mine. Calling to Ella and Biddy, like a mantra to give him strength. Yes, that had been a prayer, when strength and resolve were gone. He'd been praying for his life.

'I talk to my Arthur all the time. He talks to me like he's in the next room.'

Tom squeezed her hand and looked again at the old face, the closed eyes with their fine wrinkles and delicate criss-crossing of grey-blue veins. She was smiling, remembering her beloved.

Sarah opened her eyes suddenly and stared towards the end of the bed. Spoke as if in a dream. 'I've never told anyone this, but when Arthur would call me from the other end of the house, expecting me to drop what I was doing and come running …' Eyes glazed, she looked into some distant field of faded memory, 'usually to find his glasses that were right under his nose, or perched on his head …' She let her eyelids fall and continued so quietly he had to lean in more closely to hear her. 'It annoyed me. Then I'd be cross with him. I could see the hurt in his eyes.' Pause, like a silent hiccough, 'But I never said.'

The milky-blue eyes stared into the past once more. 'When he was gone, I missed it dreadfully. The house was so quiet. At first, I thought I heard him calling me … forgot he was gone … but when I got to the room, it was empty.' A lone tear rolled down the soft, weathered cheek.

She held the red beads tightly to her chest. Strength returning to her voice, she said, 'He's my angel', and paused. 'I'm just waiting to catch that last rattler home. That's what Arthur called it, the last rattler home. I only want to go to him.' She fell silent, smiling, the fine track of a single tear shining.

Pop. Tom's mind dropped unexpectedly into the scene at the gorge, remembering that moment inside infinity, tasting the cool earth-tang of still water. The moon shimmering silver overhead and inside the pool. A sense of deep belonging, being part of this great breathing land. *Dadirri*, yes *Dadirri*. He let his mouth and lips shape the words, the prayer of his heart held in grandmother earth, inside time and place, a forever home inside one boundless moment, full-awake. *Dadirri*.

His gaze shifted to the gap in the curtain on the other side of the bed. Through the window dawn was arriving, slow and heavy with rain. As he watched, a surprise shift in light – not a crack in the clouds, just a brightening of light – lit the world for a quick-blink. The wet-smooth silvered skin of the tall lemon-scented eucalypt came aglow in the near-dawn light. The leaves shone, slow dancing with rain. His focus narrowed to one leaf, bowed down by the weight of droplets arriving, flicking up in abrupt release as the droplets rolled off. Rain and leaf and slow light dancing a soft-wild chorus of life outside the window. Another blink and the shaft of light was gone.

'Trees are my angels.' His voice sounded quiet, reverent.

She followed his gaze.

'And I think god must be a great poet,' he said, smiling down at her. She returned his smile, creasing the delicate skin around her eyes.

Tom let her hand go and stood to pull back the blue curtain and reveal more of the large window framing the rain-drenched eucalypt.

'Yes, it does look like a beautiful angel, dear.'

He dropped back into the chair next to her, and she opened her hand again to receive his.

Together they watched the rain-soft drizzle caress the tree as dawn climbed slowly into day; they stayed a long time quiet. When he finally looked down at Sarah, her eyes were closed, her hand limp in his. She looked asleep. Peaceful, still smiling.

Sarah didn't stir as he gently removed his hand from hers. He stretched and walked slowly across the room to sit in the chair beside Ella, her red hair bright against the pillow. Carefully, he lifted her hand to his lips. 'Come back, Ella, please come back,' he whispered, soft breath against the cool skin of her hand.

' old woman walking out ahead, inside square tunnel of pale stone.
shoes squeak … face hidden and familiar … at a fork in the tunnel, she
    turns left towards light … carrying light, following light …
    this-me
    following-becoming old woman. … i-am-me-and-she. …
    leading and following, dreamer and dreamed … i-we dreaming'

'Ooh, it's dark in here.' A different nurse rushed in, flicking on the light as she came through the doorway, a sense of urgency and impatience in her presence and voice, her movements sharp and angular. Startled out of sleep, Tom lifted his head from the bed, struck by the full glare of fluorescent light.

'Who left the window open? And the flyscreen's fallen out. We'll be inundated with mossies.'

The nurse walked briskly across the room and slammed the window shut. He moved his arm; it was numb. Ella laid beside him, tubes everywhere, eyes closed, unresponsive.

'You're Tom, I take it? Tom MacDonald?' the nurse said, beside him now.

'Yes.' His mind felt confused, still caught in the otherness of dreaming. Called back across the threshold too quickly for his mind to catch up.

'Phone call for you. I transferred it to your allocated room … 10.'

She marched out of the room on silent soles, and he followed her down the corridor to number 10.

'Hi, Lil … No, not much change … How did you track us down? …Yeah, emergency landing. Lights down at Garreth, couldn't land. Low fuel. Now we're stuck here till we can fly, or the creeks go down, I guess … no, haven't seen the news … uh-huh, extreme weather event they reckon. Unpredictable … yeah, rain's great … said there's not much more they can do anyway. Rest and rehydration … hmm.'

Tom laid on his bed, his mind wandering over last night's events, only half-listening to what Lil was saying. The elderly man in the bed opposite was asleep, his head lolling off the pillow. His mouth sagged, a slow line of thick dribble sliding on to his blue-and-white striped pyjama collar.

'I can wait.' He turned towards the window. Stared out into the rain.

'Yep.' He listened, frowning. 'A tattoo? … Slow down, Lil, I'm not following … yeah, I've still got the journal.' He opened the drawer in the small table beside his bed, shifted his watch sitting on top, pulled out the red notebook and laid it on the bed. 'Hold on.' He put the phone down and flicked through the pages until he found the jagged and scratched-out words, then picked up the phone.

'That strange writing about the swan and the serpent eyes?' He rubbed his chin. 'A tattoo?' He stared down at the page, 'I suppose cygnet could be ring, not swan. Misspelled?'

Tom's eyes grew wide as Lil talked.

'Sarge?!' He lifted his hand to his forehead, placing the palm flat over the lump of bandage. 'Holy crap.' He shook his head slowly, 'I know the guy's an arsehole but I can't believe he'd do something like this.' His thoughts raced, trying to catch up with what Lil was saying, mind cavorting wildly through a jerky recalibration of events, propelled by this new possibility.

'But it makes sense.' He sucked in a whistling breath. 'I called Sarge to tell him I was going out to Yorick. He was the only other one who knew … yeah. Shit.'

The man in the blue-and-white striped pyjamas grunted loudly. His eyes twitched open, then closed, unseeing, as he settled back into dreaming.

Lil continued to talk excitedly. It was hard to concentrate. 'Leave it with me, Lil. I need time to think … I'll have a look at the journal again. See if all the pieces fit. But I reckon you could be on to something. Good sleuthing,' he said, rubbing his chin again. 'Yes, definitely deserves a big kiss,' he smiled. His face felt stiff. 'Okay, I'll see if I can find anything. Call you when I know more. See ya.'

Replacing the phone in its cradle on the wall, he eyed the tray on the bedside table. A packet of cornflakes and silver jug of milk. Two slices of thick cold toast, nestled with small plastic containers of various jams and Vegemite, and foil-wrapped butters. A squat, thick-lipped cup of tea with a saucer on top, dark-tan stains on the paper towel under the cup. He lifted the tea and sipped; it was lukewarm. Scraping butter on to toast, then Vegemite, he chewed at the rubbery thing, tearing off hunks that were hard to swallow. He ate a full slice, then buttered and jammed another. After one bite he abandoned it and gulped the last of the cool tea.

He stared out the window at the steady rain, touching a hand to the dull ache in his forehead. Stood and stretched. His body felt stiff and tight from all the sitting. He needed to move. The old man in the bed across had got his head back on to the pillow and was snoring like a hibernating grizzly. It was somehow comforting.

Tom stepped into the corridor and strode towards the exit. He needed to clear his head, try to make sense of Lil's theory about Sarge. It was hard to take it all in. Could Sarge have done this to Ella? But why? It didn't make any sense.

Outside, the rain was clearing. Heavy clouds hung close, holding down the sky. He breathed deeply, drinking in the air, moist with rain, bursting with the stuttering grace of new life. His senses came alive with the smells, sounds and taste of rain at last on country.

Occasional sharp-long fingers of golden light pierced through the grumbling clouds, illuminating the gleaming-after-rain world. A rainbow arrived bright-edged, then faded into a broken halo of coloured arc across the sky. Yellow, pink, indigo. New life pulsed in the red mud, seeds pushing up after waiting for years in dry dust. A tiny miracle of frogs croaked their waking chorus: *I'm alive, I'm alive.* Butterflies rose as waves of colour from glistening leaves. A circus of noisy green parrots screeched among the trees, rushing upwards into dripping scud of sky.

A sudden image of Ella's slack face came to mind, so contrary to the life erupting in this rain-drenched world. He blinked the bright-vivid image away and stared up at the sky.

His chest ached and he pressed his palm over his heart. With a crackle-and-smack of sharp attention he felt the smooth weight of the phone. Ella's phone. He'd forgotten all about it. He unbuttoned the top pocket of his filthy shirt and pulled it out, his veins suddenly pulsing hot with a sense of urgency. He needed to find a charger.

Inside, the speckled beige lino was cool against his bare feet. He stopped at the nurse's station.

'Hello, anyone there?' No sound or movement came from the open door. He looked along each of the corridors; nothing stirred. A television blared from a room on one of the corridors. Following the sound, he stood in the doorway of a large common room. Several grey heads were nodding or talking, but there wasn't a nurse in sight. An enormous television attached to one wall called loudly into the room, though no one seemed to be watching it. Large words ran beneath the image on the screen; clouds on a weather map of Australia. Swirling white cloud covered the whole eastern side of the map. Cyclone Eris, the caption read. A man in a grey suit, talking and pointing to an animated map. Extreme weather event. Unprecedented. Repeating the same words. Extreme weather event. Unprecedented. Unpredictable. There were warnings in red across all the eastern states from north to south.

He returned to the nurse's station.

'Hello?' He called more loudly this time, but there was still no reply. A sign on the desk read, 'If unattended, please ring'. He rang the bell, waited several minutes, then rang it again.

A nurse appeared from a doorway along a corridor and hurried towards him. The grumpy one.

'Yes?' she said, when she was a couple of metres away.

'I was wondering if I could borrow a phone charger, please?'

She walked past him and around behind the high counter. Looked around, then walked through the door into another room behind the station. She came out a moment later shaking her head. 'If you bring the phone up to the desk, I can charge it for you.'

'Thanks.' He handed the phone across the high counter and, after a moment, heard the click into the charger.

When he returned to Ella's room, the door was closed with a large 'Do Not Disturb' sign on it. He waited in a chair in the corridor outside the door, holding the red notebook to his chest, feeling a strange reluctance to open it out here, away from Ella.

The two women from the RFDS crew walked out of the room, stopped speaking when they saw him.

'How are you feeling this morning?' the shorter woman in a red T-shirt said.

He nodded. 'I'm fine.'

'No dizziness or nausea?'

'Nope.'

'You sure look a lot better than when we found you last night,' the younger, taller woman said, smiling.

'Do you think she'll be okay?'

'Signs are good. She's settled and rehydrating well. Seems to be stabilising. Until we get to a tertiary facility we won't know if there are head injuries or other internal injuries that are stopping her waking.'

'Any word on when we can fly out?'

'Daryl's on it. Checking the weather situation constantly. Reckons the weather's misbehaving. Too unpredictable to get through. He's been flying for more than thirty years and never seen anything like this.'

Daryl? Must be the pilot. Dark patches hung over his memory of last night. Yes, maybe they had introduced themselves.

Another nurse came out of the room carrying a bundle of linen. She pushed the door back until it clicked, and removed the 'Do Not Disturb' sign. She nodded to them as she walked away, oofing under the huge bundle.

'Don't fancy flying through another storm like the one last night,' the shorter woman said, raising her eyebrows.

'No, I wouldn't be too keen either,' he agreed, and the taller woman smiled and nodded.

'We'll let you know the minute anything changes. And we're right there,' she pointed to a door along the corridor, 'if anything changes with Ella.'

'Thanks.' His voice sounded thick. He blinked and turned towards the door.

Stepping into the room, he fixed his eyes on Ella. Nothing had changed, but something felt different. He looked across to Sarah's bed. The blue curtains were pulled back and tied. The bed was empty, and all was tidy as if she had never been there. Perhaps she'd been moved to another room. He went to the empty bed and stood looking down for a full-wide-open moment, the hair on the back of his neck alert as if there were a cool draft behind him. He touched the pillow, smelt the slight tang of disinfectant. All trace of Sarah was gone, yet the air was thick with her presence, as if the particles of space still held the shape and texture of her. Her imprint, a tough membrane of memory, tenacious as mallee root.

'I was wondering about Sarah?' he said, standing back at the nurse's station.

'Oh, of course.' He watched as the nurse's posture and demeanour adjusted to the question. 'Yes, she died sometime in the night. She went peacefully. She had a big smile on her face when we found her this morning. Reckon she must have seen Arthur. That was her dead husband. Ran a huge property back in the day. Well-known in the district. She was always talking about her Arthur and couldn't wait to see him again.'

He nodded. But he had no words. They stood together in silence. The presence of Sarah's absence was a delicate-strong invisible thread, taut between them, connecting them in a heart-moment that stretched out beyond time.

The nurse shifted, her face and pace recovering their everyday shape.

The silence grew awkward.

She gave a quick smile, eyebrows raised slightly into a well-if-there's-nothing-else-I gotta-go-smile, and said, 'Better get this lot washed and dressed or we'll be here till tea-time. Sing out if you need anything.' She turned and was gone.

Back in the room, he walked across to Sarah's empty bed. 'Goodbye, Sarah,' he whispered. 'I hope he was there to meet you in your heaven.' He smiled and raised his hand to rub the tickling at the back of his neck. As he stepped away, his eyes snagged on something shadowed on the floor under the bed. He bent down and pulled out the red rosary beads. Breathed out in a half-laugh. 'Did you leave these for me, Sarah? They might help me pray? Thank you, my friend,' he whispered as he pushed the beads into his shirt pocket.

Back on his seat beside Ella's bed, for a long moment he allowed a strange liquid silence to seep in through his skin. It was like drinking clear light. He had felt it before but couldn't remember where. The gorge? Yes, like the gorge, but somewhere else, another time he couldn't remember. He rested into the quenching silence. He felt both tired and fully awake, as if he had just climbed to the top of a mountain where the air was cool and rare.

Opening the notebook, he studied the pages as Lil's words echoed around in his head. His eyes bumped over words pinning pain to paper. Words that were like open wounds, bleeding and suppurating as he read.

He wanted to look away. Couldn't. The way someone watches as a car hurtles irrevocably towards a crash. No, he couldn't look away. He needed to find something to confirm, or otherwise, Lil's theory about Sarge.

    ' tearing inside this-that-was-I-not-me-now

          sharp words stabbing '

Words snagged his eyes and mind. Clusters of hurt huddled on the pages, holding dark secrets. It was so hard to read what Ella had been through.

    ' cool so cold black

          far under dark glass '

He flipped through the notebook rapidly. So many questions. He squeezed her hand, whispered, 'What do you mean here about leaving a message?'

He read silently, about Biddy and what had been done to her.

'What does that mean, about the red eyes and "snake tongue-licking cygnet"? Is there a message in here? A clue?' He spoke softly, staring down at the page. Words and lines pulled him in. His mind was searching for something without knowing what, but he was certain that Ella was trying to tell him something.

He jumped as a loud crash came from somewhere along the corridor, jarring the smooth air.

Again he flicked through pages crammed with writing, then stopped, squinting at numbers written roughly on the top of a page. 'What are these numbers, Ella? Is this the message?'

He closed the red book. His mind felt soggy and jangled, like the morning after a rock concert that's been rained out. Ella had been through so much. He squeezed her hand, it felt small and cool.

    ' so cold. darkening. falling and rising and falling '

'Ella … I …' Tom turned to stare out the window, watching the slow drizzle. He sensed the land sighing out with relief as good, soaking rain seeped into the cracks and crevices that long drought had dried out and opened up. His eyes drank the moisture. Even inside he could see life greening, birds singing their loud gratitude for the rain the way the heart sings for love. He turned back to Ella. Stared at her face. A thicket of emotions seemed to tighten around his throat and tongue. No words could form out of the riffraff of his heart.

' warm heart reaching
    holding empty jug of flesh '

'Ella.' He lifted her small hand in both of his, studying its delicate geography. Words budding inside his head, forming, but too flimsy to be spoken out loud … wish we'd had more time together … didn't know how I felt …
His mind dropped into familiar cool silence in that abandoned cave of his heart, as if saying too much might bring forth some dread thing his mind could not allow. Instead he pressed the cool skin of her hand against his lips.

Time slowed into a relentless blur of shapeless moments that offered no texture of change or movement. Endless cups of lukewarm tea in thick-lip white cups and saucers, with the same plastic-wrapped pack of two sweet biscuits, tasteless plates of sandwiches and custardy desserts in squat bowls. Snatches of conversation with the nurses, the aircraft crew as they appeared and disappeared, or a stray inmate in the corridor or out on the veranda when he went to stretch his legs and get some air.

There was nothing else to do but sit beside the bed and read the red notebook inside this strange, shapeless, time-space warping and wefting through waiting that refused to move or change. Then walk when he couldn't sit still for another second.

Minutes soaked into hours. One moment held a lifetime of possibility. A word, a question quivered with significance, making it hard to speak his thoughts.

He flicked through the pages, scanning for information and yet trying not to invade Ella's private world. At the back of the notebook were pages of handwritten poetry. There was a whole section with lines from Olivia Parsons' poems. She must have copied them from the books he'd lent her. He read silently, while memories as sweet as orange blossom perfumed his mind. Those nights at Eldorado with Ella, in deep conversation and reading poetry together, had been like a surprise shower of happiness. Unexpected. Perhaps that's the best kind. A sharp pang of regret tore through the muscle of his heart. He shifted and blinked. Turned the page.

'What are these?' he said quietly, pulling several sheets of folded paper from the sleeve at the back of the notebook. 'Looks like you were writing your own poetry.' He rifled through the loose pages. 'This looks like the only one that's finished. No date on it though.'

He read,

'My heart grows lonely in this prickling solitude.
Scratched and bleeding it grows ~~too large for itself~~.... grows out of itself,
like a solitary bloom, offering its fragrance to the poem.
People can't quench my loneliness,
even the best of them,
it belongs to something larger than warm skin.
Only the quiet
inbetween spaces
— between blind-night and sunrise,
— between letters on a page and
taste of word on tongue,
feeds some possibility my heart remembers yet.'

' words calling, kiss to tongue taste of sweet words … music
     melting cold jug heart '

He let the book, and loose pages, drop into his lap, watching Ella's face. I didn't know you were lonely like that. We could have talked. A memory dropped in like a shooting pain. He was the one who had shut her out. Ella had wanted to talk. Wanted more intimacy. His thoughts echoed like a loudspeaker in this chasm of silence.

'Can you hear me?' he whispered. Where are you, Ella? Come back.

He blinked and shuffled through the sheets of paper again, until he found a dusty, crumpled page. He opened it and read, *Lines from Wordsworth.*

' music-warm
     reaching returning
calling back '

'You kept this? You never mentioned it.' He spoke softly, eyes glued to that blank face. 'So much you didn't tell me, Ella.'

He stroked out the creases of the dusty, crumpled page. His head ached with waiting and wanting. He lifted Ella's hand to his cheek and closed his eyes. The memory of her body lying close next to his. Her vital body, so full of life. Her hand burning against his skin. His blood thick-hot with desire. Hungry ghosts of his past crowding in, chilling his heart with their howling. I'm sorry I didn't turn to you. I was afraid.

He spoke in a whisper, 'I love you.' He felt the warm rain of relief wash through him as the words fluttered into the air.

   ' clinging closewarm '

Tom rang the bell at the nurse's station.

The nurse walking towards him began speaking before she arrived. 'So busy; short-staffed.'

'I was wondering if that phone's charged yet?'

'Hold on, I'll check.' She walked to the other side of the small space and disappeared through a doorway before he could explain where the phone was. Returned, shaking her head. Eyes scanning beneath the counter, she reached down and held up the phone, 'This it?'

'Thanks.' Tom took the phone and returned to Ella's bedside. Switched it on. The apple insignia lit up. He waited.

Passcode.

He gritted his teeth.

Outside it was raining again, the rumble of thunder close. His mind rested in nature for a moment as he gazed out the window. Flash. The stray numbers Ella had etched in the notebook. He picked up the notebook and flicked through it quickly.

Bingo. He held his finger to the page and pressed in the numbers.

The phone burst into life.

Scrolling across to voice memos, his finger hovered over the last entry. He took a deep breath in and pressed the arrow. The air filled with Ella's ragged voice. Sobbing.

It was uncanny to hear her voice, even as he stared down at her pale, unmoving face. His stomach growled loudly as if protesting the extreme incongruence of that familiar voice and this colourless face and still lips.

The voice spoke slowly, between laboured breaths. 'He raped me. Left me here to die. I'm going to die here alone. But I want someone to know what he did to Biddy. I want her to have justice. For Queenie. I want her to get some peace for her daughter.' Pause. 'Before the battery dies. Before I die.'

He pressed pause. Head spinning, he leant back in the chair, legs stretched out in front, holding the phone against his chest, breathing deeply. Drew in another deep breath, and pressed play.

'I hope someone finds this one day. Not him.'

He pressed pause again. Heart hammering, he took another deep breath in and blew out. Pressed the arrow.

'He …' Long silence and soft crying, ' … Sarge raped Biddy … So many ugly words he spat into air down here … when he did it to me …' Long pause. He could hear Ella gasping for air.

When the voice spoke again it sounded strangled. 'When he raped me.' The voice stopped again, took several tight breaths. Spoke in a stop-start rhythm of words, like a child just learning to read. 'So many ugly words. He said. They stuck. In my head. Repeating. Black slut. That's what he called Biddy. Said she was putting out for Ted. Thought she was too good for him.' Muffled words, sobbing. 'Can't get his ugly laughing out of my head. Ugly, so ugly.'

He pressed pause again. Let his head hang down, a dead weight. It was agonising to hear. Biddy. Biddy.

He stared out the window, letting the rain wash through his mind. Wash away the horror of that man. What he had done. A close crack of lightning made him jump. Something on the phone was flashing. He ignored it and pressed the arrow.

'He murdered her because she scratched and bit him, tried to fight him off, called him names. Like I did when he came for me that last night after I buried poor Harry.' Long silence. She took a deep breath and continued. 'He called Ted "stupid old Mac". Said Ted cried like a baby when he told him Biddy was dead. Sarge laughed, called him a stupid old man, in love with the black slut. That's what he kept calling her. Ted was passed-out drunk.' The words came in a breathless gush. 'Sarge woke Ted. Blamed him. Said Ted must have killed Biddy in one of his drunken rages, then blacked out. He kept laughing when he talked about it. Made Ted sort it. Bury the body and pay off Herman to disappear. All Sarge's idea.'

The words rushed, 'He spread the rumour that Biddy was pregnant and ran off with Herman. Made the whole thing up. Ted went along with it. Thought he'd killed Biddy. Stupid man. All of it… so stupid.' Long pause. Soft crying, ragged breath, 'He spat out all his secrets and lies while he … did that to me.'

Long silence. 'Sarge didn't know where Ted buried her. Not until we found that bone. Must have worked out I knew something. And realised I wasn't going to leave town without telling Queenie.'

Another, longer silence. He listened, studying Ella's face. His heart ached; it was too heavy, numbed with the weight of it all. How could anyone hear all this, go through what Ella went through, and survive? No wonder she couldn't wake up.

He squeezed her hand, letting fat tears roll down his cheeks. 'I knew something wasn't right,' he said aloud. 'I couldn't believe Biddy would leave us. Even though we were at school. But Ted wouldn't talk about it. Flew into a rage if we mentioned Biddy … or Queenie. Liam ran off the rails. There was no one to talk to.'

His eyes burned, and his body shuddered with a deep sorrow that had been buried for half a lifetime. He pinched hard into the bridge of his nose. Took several long, deep breaths until his breathing was smooth.

Again, he pressed Play, leaning close to the phone to listen. When Ella's voice continued, it sounded different, stronger, resolved now that the confession was done.

'Whoever you are listening to this, you need to tell Queenie, Biddy's mother, that Biddy's buried down at the spring on Melville station, next to Tom's mother. I took that skull and the bone we found back to Eldorado. It's in the freezer. You need to find it. Get justice for Biddy. Let Queenie know where her little girl is buried so she can have some peace.'

Another long silence.

'And one more thing, if I don't come back from this … I don't think I will. My phone is flashing, battery's going to die any minute. There are so many things I want to say.' Sound of sobbing. 'I don't want to die. Even after all this. I don't want to die alone. If you find my bones, bury me at the spring. That place was my friend when I needed a friend. Felt more like home than anywhere except the farm.' Long pause.

Her next words came in a rush. Hard to understand. He stopped it when he heard his name. Rewound, and listened again. 'Ask Tom. Tom MacDonald. Ask him to bury me at the spring. He's my good friend.' Weeping … 'Say goodbye when you see him … and Jaz, and Corey … even Portia, say goodbye to her too … and Mum … and –'

The voice cut off mid-sentence.

Tom brushed the back of his forearm across his face. Ella's presence filled the room. The ugliness of what had happened was there, but her presence was larger. There was a beauty too. How strange to alight on that word, beauty in all this pain and violence, in this amoral universe. But there was no other word that seemed to stretch wide enough to hold all of this, the ugliness as well as the courage it had taken for Ella to speak and write it. Ella wanting justice for Biddy and Queenie. Speaking for voices silenced by violence made the ugliness somehow more bearable. The way that a beautiful line of poetry, a hand to hold in the dark, made it possible to endure darkness and terror.

An ache of sob had trapped in his chest. He gagged, like a cat coughing up a furball. He felt a hand on his shoulder. Warm. He didn't open his eyes. The warmth of the hand let the sobbing come. He folded his arms on the bed and buried his face. Keening. The warm hand was barely there, but vivid inside his heart. It infiltrated tough skins, opened the dark centre where his wounds laid fallow. It was as if he'd been waiting for a warm hand of kindness the way the land had waited for rain.

Returning from a walk outside to breathe clear air, he stood in the doorway. The room was full with silence, a hush like an underwater cave. His sweeping glance took in Ella and the empty bed Sarah had occupied. Nothing had changed. The monitors were beeping quietly. Outside the window radiant light streamed between a crack in the clouds, lighting the room. The world was glowing after the rain. The lemon-scented gum's skin was shining, green tendrils of leaves shivering in a barely perceptible breeze.

But something *was* different. His focus snapped back to Ella. Her eyes were flickering in their dark pudding of bruised flesh. Kept flickering.

' call and response,
between
reach and return,
light and dark '

His heart leapt wildly in his chest, watching those eyes trying to open.

'music calling, come '

Trying to arrive back into the material of her body.

' music of earth-sweet breath, calling come '

Trying to live.

' singing come-come, surrender into dust '

Then nothing.
She laid still.
Time stopped for Tom as he watched her face. There was not a sound in this close-wide-abyss of waiting, opening between life and death.
come, come, everything is calling you, beckoning, a wild choir,
singing in a thousand things. that first song of childhood,
whose pulse you had forgotten, wakes in dust;
wing and snout, warm-fur, each keeps-beat in one-blood, humming in your
veins, remembers your belonging. Ever homecoming.
heart-song weaving between beetle and grasshopper, rock and crow, spider,
brother moon and — sister star —
moss and seed, fragrance of orange tree, leaf and fruit and blossom,
fat worm feeding in rain-dark soil,
mushrooms among tangled roots. all singing land's true-dreaming; a belonging song,
to welcome you home.
song of tree, of eucalypt, birch, and wattle, of peppercorn and oak, and ancient yew
tree singing back.

Tom's heart held one pleading beat: please-live : please-live: please-live.

' come dance bright dust '

A sudden high-pitched-scream-of-beeping made him jump. The digital-screech of alarm. It was coming from the small monitor near Ella's bedhead. The beating pulse of life: a flat-line.

An urgent rush of people filled the room. Noise. Disconnected words. 'Code blue.' 'Defib.'

He stepped back against the wall inside the door.

Urgent-gushing voices jangled the cool air.

A trolley squeak-wobbled past.

Equipment appeared, lifted in practised hands.

Loud *zi-i-i-i-ip* of curtain closing around.

'Charged.'

'Stand clear.'

POSTSCRIPT

That bright opal of your heart forms slowly, under a great pressure of courage. So, never give up on love.
Inspired by Hafiz

They drove the rough road in silence; it was too jerking-loud to speak. The landscape bumped slowly past. A tender flush of green showed across the plains where only a week ago, a lifetime ago, it had been nothing but red dust; the way a broken heart can blush open with the gentlest touch of surprise kindness. Delicate white flowers clustered closely against the verge of gravel road. Creeks that had been nothing but dry tracks when he had last driven this road, gurgled with rusty water. New russet growth was visible on the tips of eucalypts.

He let the scene with his father run through his mind like murky water, clearing. On the trip back to Melville he'd rehearsed his recriminations. She was little more than a child. You had no right to … but he couldn't get his words to fit what he wanted to say. Have sex with her? Take her into your bed? Treat her as a sex object? It was impossible to find the words to express his disgust of Ted's treatment of Biddy. She was part of the family. You should have protected her. Slowly his thoughts had taken shape around his intense and complex emotions about his father's stupidity.

But when he confronted Ted, and explained that he had not, in fact, killed Biddy in a drunken rage and then covered it up with lies and bribes, Ted had dropped to his knees and wept uncontrollably, hiccoughing like a small child. When Ted finally raised his head, his face, collapsed in grief, had aged twenty years. As if the sudden memory of that crime he had held down like a drowning child had erupted above its dark hiding place and taken in air. It was all there on his wretched face: the pain and guilt of what he thought he had done.

'I-I-I loved … her,' he stuttered through strangled sobs, lowering his head again.

Tom stared down at his father's bowed head. He wanted to shout that he was a stupid old man. But he had no words for what was in his heart. The grief, the aching loneliness of all those years. The ignorance of men; fabricated by a brutish entitlement of a patriarchy that uses or destroys anything within its grasp. Liam's face crowded in to his thoughts, yes, the violence against women, all the ugliness he saw in men. The pain and shame of it. It was all there in the room as Ted wept softly. He had reached down and put a hand on Ted's shoulder. And let his own tears fall on his father's head.

He felt a warm hand on his elbow and looked over.

'You okay?' she said.

He nodded, 'Just thinking about my stupid father.' There was a catch in his voice like ice-wind through a crack in the door-hinge.

And the hand was gone.

But now the dread of what was coming ruptured the bright morning. He saw a track off to the left and pulled over. 'Just need to catch my breath. Not looking forward to this.'

They sat in silence, gazing out towards the wide horizon of desert-plain in bloom.

She broke the silence with her question. It hung in the air with all the other unfinished, unspoken things. He felt her eyes on him. Waiting.

'Yeah, we got that all the time. Rumours that Biddy was our mother. After Mum died, Biddy *was* our mother. Long before that really. I am Biddy's child. Maybe not by blood or birth but by contact, by love. It was Biddy who spent time with us, taught us about life, played and laughed with us.'

He stared out the window.

'I don't know if she carried me in her womb. It doesn't matter. She carried me in her heart and soul. She is in mine, always.' He dragged the back of his arm across his eyes. He spoke slowly. The feelings that were long held behind the wall of grief that had settled when she left his life were oozing out now, unstoppable. 'I don't know if she gave me breath in my lungs. But it was Biddy who gave me the breath of the land and the song of the trees. That's more important than DNA or whose blood runs in my veins. Country is full of ancestors of this place; Biddy showed me that. The land, its old people … the land doesn't judge the colour of my skin, or my bloodline. It responds to my listening; to care and devotion. I call, and it sings back to me because I'm listening, not because of who I am. It's a bond of love and bones, deeper than blood or skin.'

He sensed her nodding. He shook his head as if he were waking from a long dream. 'Yeah, of course, your mob already know that, Lil. But I've been needing to say it out loud for a long time.'

'Black eyes?'

'You've never seen a photo of my mother, have you?'

Lil shook her head.

'Black Irish eyes.' He shrugged. But he barely remembered his mother. It was Biddy he missed. Biddy whose bright face bumped in on lonely nights at boarding school when he cried silently into his pillow. Then later. Always Biddy.

'But I getcha. It's not about blood. S'bout love and care. Barely knew my own blood mother. Was Gran I was close to. She the one I went to when I'ze in trouble.' Lil ran her fingers through her hair. 'My mob know family's as wide as desert.' She grinned at him, adding with a half-laugh, 'And messy and complicated.'

He smiled back.

Possum opened the door to let them in.

When they were settled in chairs, hugging mugs of tea, Possum broke the silence. 'Ella?'

Tom looked up, opened his mouth to speak, but his voice failed. His words were lost to the howl inside his throat. A thick sob breached. He pressed palms against his eyes.

'She never woke up,' Lil said. 'She broken. In here.' Lil thumped her chest hard with a fist, expelling air, making the hollow-full rhythm of a lone drum. She drummed.

— *thump-thump* —

Ella's presence filled the room like a great tree

— *thump* —

a wild perfume

— *thump-thump* —

a fine wind humming the air

— *thump* —

sound-scent of rain on red dust

– thump-thump –

The room grew still as Lil ceased her heart drum. As if the silence was listening back. Beholding everything. He shivered and blinked.

He felt them watching him. Sensed their waiting. Lil's hand warm on his arm. He nodded and put his hand over Lil's, gathering strength from kind skin. He took a deep breath, turned to Queenie.

'Ella was determined to get to the truth about what happened to Biddy. She wanted justice. And for you to have some peace, Queenie. It cost Ella her …' His voice lost its momentum. He took a deep breath in, blowing out slowly through tight lips, like a runner at the top of a steep climb. He continued in a quiet, resolute voice. 'Ella gave everything to find the truth.' The room was as still as that barely-there-vast-space between breath leaving and breath arriving. 'We know what happened to Biddy.'

The old woman didn't move, apart from a sharp intake of breath. Her eyes were shining beneath half-closed lids.

Tom swallowed hard and brushed the back of his hand across his eyes. 'This is the hardest thing I've ever done,' he said, staring down at the floor. 'We…' his voice shuddered to a halt. How to speak such an awful truth?

Possum leant forward from her seat near Queenie, nodded for Tom to continue. She whispered, 'She want to know. She been waiting to know what happened a long time.'

Tom nodded. 'Sarge, he was the cop back then … he …' his voice broke open, heart tearing against the words. He swallowed. He breathed in tight air and blew out long breath. 'He …ra … he killed Biddy. Blamed Ted. Ted was drunk and believed him. Ted buried her.' The words came in a rush now, pushing hard towards the end. 'He paid off Herman the German to disappear, and started the rumour that Biddy had run off with him.'

Queenie hadn't stirred.

'They're out searching for Sarge now. He's gone underground.' He looked around at the eyes watching him, felt the air listening. Shook his head. Stared at Queenie. Knew she didn't care about whitefella justice. Only about her lost child. Bringing her daughter home.

He took a deep breath in. 'We know where she's buried.'

Queenie let out a strangled animal sound. Possum put her arm around the old woman's heavy shoulders. Queenie bowed her head and wept. Great wracking sobs shook her large body.

Deep sorrow filled the room, pouring out of the breaking heart of the old woman weeping. It was as if the small room contained all the sorry of lost children, a sadness too large for any one person to carry alone. Each heart calling the name of their lost ones, remembering them back. A river of sorrow, singing veins through vast desert.

Finally, Queenie lifted her head, eyes clear and bright, and reached out a hand towards Tom. She looked deeply into his eyes, whispered like the sound of wind, 'You found my baby girl …' A sob caught her words and carried them away on the river of sorry.

He reached out to hold the hand of the old woman, felt the cool-soft skin. Lifting her hand to his lips, he kissed the honey skin that tasted of earth and wind and trees and deep-cool water.

Bibliography and References

The following poets are quoted in various places of the proceeding story, but this is a fiction and so I determined not to pepper the manuscript with footnotes or in-line references. The majority are of course, well-known by most readers, but on occasion you may have found a quote or two you were not familiar with and so I thought I would provide this reference. If you have time, you should treat yourself and have a slow and loving walk through their works.

Rita
Ballarat, 2023

Jeffries, R. (1891) *The Story of My Heart.* London. Longmans, Green, and Co. [Downloaded 2020].

Lawrence, D.H. (1930) *A Propos of Lady Chatterley's Lover.* London. Mandrake Press Ltd. Books.

Hesse, H. (1972) *Wandering.* London. Farrar, Straus and Giroux, Inc. Books.

Neidjie, B. [commentary: Stephen Davies, Allan Fox] (2007) *Gagudja Man.* JB Books Australia. Books.

Proust, M. (1924) *Remembrance of Things Past.* Translation C.K. Scott Moncrieff. London. Chatto & Windus/Alfred A. Knopf. (Revised by author*).*

Parsons, O. (1988) *Olivia Parsons, Lost Letters and Poems.* Edited by Simone Bailey. *To discover more about Olivia, visit https://ritamcinnes.com/*

Tolkien, J.R.R. (2020) *The Lord of the Rings*. London. Harper Collins Publishers Ltd. Books.

Vesaas, T. (2013) *The Ice Palace*. Translation Elizabeth Rokkan. Kindle Edition. London. Peter Owen Publishers. [Downloaded 2016].

Vesaas, T. (2014) *The Boat in the Evening*. Translation Elizabeth Rokkan. Kindle Edition. London. Peter Owen Publishers. [Downloaded 2016].

Wordsworth, W. (1962) *Lines Composed a Few Miles above Tintern Abbey*, in *The Norton Anthology of English Literature. Fifth Edition*. London. W. W. Norton & Company, Ltd.

Also lines or quotes from William Blake, Vincent van Gogh, Fyodor Dostoyevsky, Johann Wolfgang von Goethe, and Hafiz.

Acknowledgments

To the first readers of my awkward drafts, Lizzie Horne, Lou Goggin, and Fran MacDonald, thanks for your honest feedback and encouragement. And other writers and editors along the way who gave me what I needed to continue, especially Nadine Davidoff and Kirsten Cameron.

Thanks to the opal miners of Lightening Ridge who offered suggestion and clarification of the mining process, especially Kelly Tishler. Big thanks to all the rural librarians who assisted me with my research and vague questions and offered suggestions. To all librarians with that shine in their eyes, for the love of books.

And thanks to my colleagues and friends at RFDS (Royal Flying Doctor Service) at Mount Isa base, who offered practical information, especially Shell for helping me keep it (fairly) real. A bow to you all for your dedication to your valuable work in rural and remote Australia.

And finally, to the team at Book Reality for all their efforts in getting this book across the finishing line: Ian for your persistence and patience; great working with you. To Juliette Middleton for your commitment to a high standard of editing that nudged me to the next level. For your great cover design, Brittany Wilson. And the final proofread, thank you Mark Butler.

Gratitude and respect to the Miriam Rose Foundation, and Kathleen Cole, for permission to use the term *Dadirri* in the novel. A word, and presence of deep listening that we all need to hold close to our heart in hard times.

To all the poets and writers who have held my heart with their words, a deep bow of gratitude.

To all my friends and writing companions over the years of writing this novel, who have encouraged and critiqued me, and listened to me bang on about these characters that possessed, and occasionally bullied me into writing them down, thank you all.

About the Author

Rita McInnes is a writer and psychologist living and writing in Ballarat, Victoria. She writes from an indwelling curiosity for the many lost and forgotten, hiding or vanishing things that we seek and yearn for, and a deep abiding love for this vast continent she wanders and lives with-in.

Her first book, *I-brainmap, freeing your brain for happiness,* was published in 2014 (and recorded as a podcast in 2023). This is her first novel.

www.ingramcontent.com/pod-product-compliance
Lightning Source LLC
Chambersburg PA
CBHW061526210726
48287CB00006B/1849